Battlefield Pacif

Book Four of the Red Storm Series

By

James Rosone & Miranda Watson

Copyright Information

©2018, James Rosone and Miranda Watson. Except as provided by the Copyright Act, no part of this publication may be reproduced, stored in a retrieval system or transmitted in any form or by any means without the prior written permission of the publisher.

Disclaimer

This is a fictional story. All characters in this book are imagined, and any opinions that they express are simply that, fictional thoughts of literary characters. Although policies mentioned in the book may be similar to reality, they are by no means a factual representation of the news. Please enjoy this work as it is, a story to escape the part of life that can sometimes weigh us down in mundaneness or busyness.

Table of Contents

New Year's Day 6

The Frozen Chosen 18

The Xi'an Accords - Eastern Alliance 46

Overwhelmed 54

Pacific Strategy 67

Battle of Kaliningrad 86

Pacific Invasion 111

The Indians Are Coming 134

Deceiving Appearances 140

Hunter Becomes the Hunted 152

Long Fork in the Road 160

Ohio Massacre 166

Potential Unrest 186

Professionals Talk Logistics 195

Battle of Britain 206

Asian Rivals 231

Passing the Torch 259

Ambush in the Pacific 280

Pyrrhic Victory	313
Filipino Madness	324
Britain's Out?!	332
Operation Nordic Thunder	341
Russian Resolve	349
Operation Strawman	359
Pacific Prep	366
Battle of Fort Mag	394
Formosa Fortress	445
ANZACs	454
Eastern Alliance Reckoning	490
Cowboys and Indians	500
The Resistance	533
From the Authors	564
For the Veterans	567
Acronym Key	569

New Year's Day

London, England

After spending an hour riding on the Tube and another forty minutes riding three different buses and taking two different taxi cabs, Anthony Chattem was exhausted. Had he not been receiving instructions from his head of security through his Bluetooth headset on what to do next, he never would have been able to figure out how to find the man he was about to meet. Putting all of that aside, Mr. Chattem was no spring chicken, and he felt every bit his sixty-two years of age.

He pulled the collar of his coat up and made sure his hat was situated just right to help hide more of his distinctive features, just as his head of security had told him. As the cab approached the café near the St. James's section of London, Mr. Chattem pulled a twenty-pound note from his wallet and slid it through the hole in the plexiglass wall.

"Keep the change," he said as he opened the door to the cab.

After the cab pulled away, Mr. Chattem surveyed his surroundings, making sure to keep his head down so as not to be caught by one of the hundreds of thousands of CCTV cameras across the city. Strolling casually down the street, he spotted the slight blue chalk mark on the side of a lamppost across the street that indicated he hadn't been followed. Crossing the street, he spotted the next chalk mark, letting him know the man he was to meet had also not been followed, and he was officially in the clear.

He made his way to 71-77 Pall Mall, in the same St. James's section of London. He smiled when he reached the set of stairs that led to the entrance of the extremely exclusive and private Oxford and Cambridge Club. Mr. Chattem quickly climbed the stairs and opened the ornate door. Upon his entering the club, Michelle, his personal assistant, guided him past the check-in desk, where people usually stopped to present their private club cards to gain entry.

Walking into this exclusive club was like walking into a time capsule from the early 1900s British aristocracy. It almost felt as if he had walked onto the set of *Downton Abbey*. Michelle led him up the stairs and down the hall to the Chancellor's Suite to meet with his secretive guest.

"Is he already here?" Mr. Chattem asked, hoping he wouldn't need to wait too long. It was a huge risk meeting this man, and if he were caught, it would be the end of not just his political career, but most likely his freedom.

****

Max Weldon was a managing director for Rothschild Group in London. The firm was incredibly wealthy, with a rich and storied family history. It was the investment firm of choice for not just the wealthiest 1%, but the wealthiest .01% of the world, which meant Max was often in contact with some of the most influential men and women on the planet. This was not his first time sitting in the Oxford and Cambridge Club.

What everyone else at the establishment that night didn't realize was that Max's real name was Maksim Sokolov. He was the senior Russian spy in London, charged with managing a host of both intelligence and sabotage operations across Great Britain. He had been assigned to this post for twenty-six years, which meant he had now spent more of his adult life living in the UK than he had in any other country. He almost felt British, though he knew that everything he did was in the service of his true homeland, Russia.

During his undergraduate studies at the University of Oxford, Max had completed an internship with the Bank of England. There he'd met an investment advisor who had worked for Rothschild Group. The man had been so impressed with his language abilities, he'd offered Max a job on the spot. That advisor had no idea that Max had been recruited by the GRU shortly after the fall of the Soviet Union. As he had neared the end of his schooling in Switzerland, Max had been tasked with infiltrating the global aristocracy through the financial world. Going to work for the Rothschild Group was the surest way to gain access to some of the world's wealthiest people.

  Max was a legitimately gifted young man. His father had been a diplomat abroad and married a wealthy French woman while stationed in France. Max had grown up speaking Russian and French on a daily basis, and while he was in school, his parents had made sure he learned English. When he'd turned fourteen, he had been sent to the Aiglon College, an exclusive boarding school in Switzerland. It was there that Max had honed his language and finance skills and developed his network of highly connected and influential friends.

  When he'd graduated, the GRU had ensured that he was accepted to the University of Oxford to increase his likelihood of gaining the level of access Russian intelligence was after. While at Oxford, Max had used his connections from his time in Switzerland to leverage several coveted internships, which had ultimately led to his securing employment with the Rothschild Group.

As a financial advisor, he had worked hard to grow his book of business and develop a strong reputation within the firm. Being fluent in English, French, and Russian, he was able to handle a wide variety of clients. His position also enabled him to recruit people sympathetic to the Russian cause. In addition, he successfully obtained a lot of financial dirt on some very influential people, which the GRU made sure to use when needed.

In normal times, Max would never have met Mr. Chattem in person, but these weren't normal times, and Mr. Chattem was not a normal man. He could not pass up an opportunity to meet with the leader of the British opposition party. If this meeting went according to plan, Max would have successfully recruited the highest-ranking source of any Russian operative in history. Max was determined to do whatever was necessary to ensure "his man" moved into 10 Downing Street and Britain left the war.

Max was getting impatient. He looked down at his Breitling Cockpit Night Mission watch. "*Wealth does have its privileges*," he thought. Mr. Chattem had a few more minutes before he would be considered late.

A moment later, he heard a light knock on the door, and then it slowly opened. In walked Anthony Chattem, the head of the Labour Party, alone and doing his best to look as inconspicuous as possible. Standing, Max took a step forward and extended his hand to Mr. Chattem, shaking it as they exchanged greetings.

"Max, I'll come straight to the point, since I don't have very long to meet with you," said Chattem. "I understand you have an offer you'd like to make?"

Max saw Chattem eyeing him over, attempting not to scowl. "*He really does loathe anything to do with the elite, doesn't he?*" he mused.

Smiling at Mr. Chattem's bluntness, Max gestured for the two of them to sit down. "I like a man who is direct and to the point. It makes negotiations a lot simpler," he said.

Chattem took his hat off and placed it on the table between them. "So, this is a negotiation? What is it you're offering?" he asked, carefully measuring Max's facial features.

"Mr. Chattem, as you know, I work for a large, wealthy firm that represents a lot of varying financial interests. War can be profitable, but only profitable if it has been planned well in advance of the opening salvos. This is war without warning, and that has cost some interests I represent a lot of money." Max paused for a second to let his words sink in. "There has to be a way to end this war peacefully and return the world back to its normal order."

Anthony Chattem covered his mouth to keep himself from snorting. Max knew Chattem held a deep disgust for the rich, but he figured his target would come around once he really thought about the big picture. An awkward moment passed.

"I agree peace is in our nation's interest," Chattem conceded. "However, to return our nation, if not the rest of the world, back to peace takes more than the musings of one old man. I'm sure you're aware of my many attempts in Parliament to extricate Britain from this American war. Sadly, the Tories have tied our nation to the whims of that bloviating idiot in the White House who started this entire war. I'm not sure that there's much I can do at this point to change that fact."

"My concern is with Britain, Mr. Chattem, not America," Max replied. "I, like many other Londoners, do not want the country to go down with a sinking ship. We want to salvage what we can and position ourselves to rebound when the eventual recovery from the war happens. To that end, if you were to become PM, what would be your stance toward the Russian Federation and the Eastern Alliance?"

Chattem smiled. "If I were prime minister, I would end British involvement in the war. This is a war that we should not be involved in, and I, for one, do not believe we should lose any more of our youth fighting a war that the Americans forced NATO into. As to the Eastern Alliance—again, Korea and Taiwan aren't a concern to the UK. And Asia is a long way from Britain. Does that answer your question?" Chattem asked.

Max nodded. "From a business and policy perspective, this makes sense, and that is what the people I represent also want to see happen. Your stance has always been antiwar, and your policies have been focused on solving the problems of Britain and taking care of those in need domestically. I admire that about you, Mr. Chattem, and I'd like to do my best to help you get to 10 Downing Street one day."

Chattem rubbed his chin, deep in thought.

Sensing some concern, Max pressed in. "What would it take for you to become the next PM? The interests I represent may be able to help, but ultimately, we need to know what will make the difference. And please, do not hesitate to tell me exactly what you need, no matter how crazy it may sound."

Chattem laughed. "Eliminating half a dozen Tory MPs would be a start," he said jokingly, not realizing that Max was very serious about doing "whatever" it took to get him into office, even if it meant offing a few pesky members of Parliament.

Chattem paused, calculating a more useful response. "I need a public relations disaster for the current government," he remarked. "Suffering military defeats is one thing—my party is already using that to our advantage with the antiwar marches and protests—but if London and some of our other major cities were ever attacked, especially after the PM said we were well protected, I think that would go a long way in destroying the moral support of the people for the party in power. If a scandal were thrown in at the same time, it could be enough to cause the current government to collapse, or at least give me the leverage needed to call for a vote of no-confidence," he concluded.

Max took a deep breath and let it out. "That is a big list, Mr. Chattem. I'm not sure that my backers can carry out any or most of that. However, I'll bring it up to them, and we'll try to help where we can. As situations do happen to your advantage, you will need to capitalize on them, Mr.

Chattem. If we're to spend enormous political and financial capital to help advance you into the PM office, you will have to pay us back some favors when we call upon you. Is that understood?" he asked.

This was the moment of truth. Would he get Chattem to agree to a quid pro quo? Once he approved their little arrangement, he would forever be ensnared in the web of the GRU and be their perpetual pawn, unless he wanted to be exposed.

"Mr. Weldon, I won't agree to a blank check of support to the global elites your firm represents," Chattem asserted. His face softened. "I have made my positions on the war and internal policies clear, which I believe coincide with your own interests. If I *am* so fortunate as to become the next prime minister, I won't forget those who helped me get there. I will give your concerns due consideration."

Max nodded, then pressed him a bit further. "If we're able to help you become PM, your position is that you would end British involvement in the war and sue for a separate peace with the Eastern Alliance, correct?" Max asked a bit more directly and forcefully. He needed to know beyond a doubt that Chattem would be sympathetic to their cause if he rose to power.

15

Mr. Chattem looked nervously at his watch. He was probably starting to worry that this meeting was taking too long and thinking about how they might get caught.

"Mr. Weldon, as I said, if I were PM, Britain would end our involvement in the war. If I were PM, I'd pursue a separate peace with the Eastern Alliance and end British involvement in the war…immediately."

Max smiled. *"Got you,"* he thought. *"You now work for me, whether you know it or not, Mr. Chattem."*

Max stood and extended his hand. "Mr. Chattem, it was good to finally meet you in person and work through some of these critical details. The world is at a precipice. We find ourselves standing at the edge, looking down into the abyss. If calmer heads do not prevail and step back from the edge, I fear the world may fall into that black nether, and God only knows what may become of us if that happens…I will speak with my backers, and we will do our utmost to ensure you're the next prime minister of Great Britain. If we need to meet again or convey any information between ourselves, my secretary will reach out to yours."

Chattem nodded. As he began to turn to leave, Max stopped him.

"One more thing—you'll need to transfer your retirement portfolio to the management of my firm immediately. That will be the cover for any future meetings between us."

Chattem nodded again, and the two men left the suite and headed out the building through different exits.

The Frozen Chosen

The wind howled fiercely outside, rocking the amphibious assault vehicles, or "amtracks," with each gust as the 5th Marines raced down the Pyongyang-Kaesong Highway. They were battling against the clock in a desperate attempt to reinforce the US Army's 7th Infantry Division at Taechon, 128 kilometers north of Pyongyang. If they didn't arrive soon, many lives would be lost.

A blizzard had swept down from northern China, devastating the Allies' ability to stop the Chinese Liberation Army's massive counterattack at the Yalu River. The whirling snow had hidden the movement of tens of thousands of Chinese soldiers and prevented the Allies from using the one asset that neutralized the overwhelming infantry numbers—their air power. Without close air support, the units defending the Yalu line were simply overrun by the sheer volume of enemy soldiers being thrown at them. It was now a race against time to prevent an all-out massacre from unfolding.

Five hours into their race north from Busan, South Korea, the twenty-one Marines riding in the amtrack with Master Sergeant Tim Long were getting a bit antsy. Aside from a pit stop to refuel, they had stayed on the road, which meant no one had been able to fully stretch out or even take a proper bio break.

Master Sergeant Long had just rejoined the company three days ago, after recovering from a few broken ribs and a punctured lung suffered six weeks before. He had been eager to get back to his unit and knew some of the hardest fighting was still ahead of them. However, he hadn't anticipated this particular fight.

"*I guess we're paying for sending so many of our troops to Europe,*" he thought.

Eventually, they turned off the main highway and moved up a winding road to get to the top of a ridgeline. The higher-ups had decided that this crest would be the Marines' "line in the sand." As they continued traveling along the twisting road, the constant cutbacks and turns caused a couple of the Marines to get car sick. Then, one of the pee bottles' caps came undone, and urine spilled across the floor of the track, further adding to the stench.

"Are you kidding me? I told you guys to take a leak when we refueled!" Master Sergeant Long yelled, irritated.

"Oh, for crying out loud! How much longer is it going to take us to get there already?" one of the young privates moaned. "My butt is killing me and this track stinks like a port-a-potty at Oktoberfest."

Just as Long was about to respond to the young Marine's grumbling, the vehicle commander yelled back to them. "Heads up, guys! I just received word we should be approaching the Army's positions."

"The track finally seems like it's on level ground," Long realized. *"We must be at the top of the ridge."*

Master Sergeant Long's radio crackled to life in his ear, and he immediately recognized the voice of Captain Chet Culley. "Falcon Three, Falcon Six. When we approach the Army's lines, I'm going to need you to get your platoon filtered into their prepared positions. Remember, these guys have been fighting nearly nonstop with the Chinese for two days. They're going to be exhausted. Take charge of the situation, and I'll check in on you later. How copy?"

"Copy that. Out," Long responded.

When their vehicle got closer to the Army's positions, bullets started to hit the hull of their armored vehicle. The vehicle gunner in the front of the track returned fire at an unseen enemy.

"Get ready to dismount! Enemy troops to our front, 500 meters!" the vehicle commander shouted over the roar of their chattering gun. Shell casings fell to the floor of the vehicle. They came to a halt and the back hatch dropped, allowing the twenty-one Marines to exit the vehicle and rush out into the cold air.

The chattering of machine-gun fire from the heavy and light machine guns on the amtracks continued as the Marines fanned out to take up positions in front of their armored chariots.

"Shift fire to that gun position on the right!" one of the sergeants yelled.

Snap, zip, snap, snap!

Master Sergeant Long heard the distinctive chattering of the nearby gun and immediately agreed with the other sergeant's assessment. It looked like a small cluster of Chinese soldiers were setting up a heavy-caliber weapon a few hundred meters below them.

"*Jeez, where did all of these enemy soldiers come from?*" he thought in bewilderment.

As his Marines set up their lines, small clusters of Army soldiers fell back to his position, gladly accepting the reinforcements.

An Army lieutenant walked up to Long. "Man, am I glad to see you guys," he said. "I'm Lieutenant Nick Davis. Where's the rest of your company, Master Sergeant?"

Looking around as his platoon started to secure some defensive positions, Long realized his men were heavily outnumbered, even with the Army soldiers falling back into his lines. "This is it for now, Sir. The rest of the company is scattered along the line," he explained as he waved to the rest of the ridge.

Lieutenant Davis sighed. He was exhausted but determined to hold this position. "OK, Master Sergeant. We'll make do, then…. Here's what I need from your Marines. I've got maybe 42 soldiers left from my company, and they're steadily falling back into the lines here. I need you to get your heavy weapons set up facing this section of the line. The PLA pushed us off that ridge over there, and now this ridgeline we're on is our last line. We have to hold them here no matter what. I'll get my remaining soldiers organized into the line here, but I need to know that your Marines can help us hold this spot."

Long nodded as he took in the information. Their amtracks had followed a trail up to the top of this ridge, so they could still provide fire support, but they were also bullet magnets. "Copy that, Sir. I'll get our tracks moved back to that location over there, so they can still provide us fire support while hopefully not attracting artillery fire. We've got plenty of ammunition in the tracks, and the rest of the 1st Marine Division is coming up behind us. We've got this,

Sir!" he said with enthusiasm, trying to reassure the young Army lieutenant.

Turning to his men, Master Sergeant Long shouted, "NCOs, get your positions ready!"

Several of his machine gunners were exchanging shots with PLA soldiers a few hundred meters away. The sergeants in Long's platoon yelled at their men. "Get digging!"

Every third soldier or Marine kept his rifle and continued to engage the Chinese soldiers when an opportunity presented itself, while the other two soldiers or Marines pulled their e-tool entrenching shovels out and started to reinforce their positions. The light and heavy machine gunners set up their guns, and extra ammunition was brought over from the tracks.

Pulling a small set of binoculars out of one of his pouches on his vest, Master Sergeant Long surveyed the ridge across from them and the valley that separated them. The swirling snow had stopped, and the sun was starting to break through the cloud cover in beautiful shafts of glowing light.

"*As long as the snowfall doesn't pick back up in intensity, we'll be able to get some air support soon,*" Long realized.

Lieutenant Davis interrupted his contemplation. "What are your thoughts, Master Sergeant?" he asked.

Long lowered his binos. "Well, if they try to bum-rush our positions, they're going to take some horrible losses. The intense snow has finally stopped, and if it truly is done snowing, then we'll have air and artillery support, which will decimate them. I'd place our chances of stopping them at better than 50%, Sir," he responded.

Davis nodded in approval. "I think you're right, Master Sergeant. When we fell back yesterday, they let us take up residence on that ridge, and that gave us a bit of time to organize ourselves. Then they hit us relentlessly. It's like they stacked all their units up and then threw them at us one after the other. At first, we were slaughtering them. Though the first two assaults were brutal, we decimated them. But then the third, fourth and fifth waves came, and they just kept coming. We started running out of ammunition, the barrels on our rifles and machine guns were overheating, and eventually we had to fall back again. We nearly didn't make it out of the valley below, but then you guys showed up, and they turned their attention to you. That allowed us to get away," he said.

Master Sergeant Long placed his hand on the young officer's shoulder. "It sounds like you guys did your best,

Sir. That's all any of us can do. You held them long enough to let us Marines come rescue you guys. Now we're here, and we'll save the Army," he said with a slight laugh, trying to add a bit of humor to an otherwise horrible circumstance.

Lieutenant Davis snorted. "Yeah, I'm never going to hear the end of this from my West Point classmates—the Marines coming to rescue me," he said with a smirk.

****

The next hour was spent trading pop shots with the PLA soldiers and getting their positions set up. The Army soldiers took the opportunity to reload their empty rifle magazines, grab additional hand grenades and chow down on some MREs. Once those essential tasks had been completed, many of them simply fell asleep, desperately trying to catch up on some rest while the Marines remained on watch.

The radio crackled. "Falcon Three, this is Falcon Six," Captain Culley said.

Master Sergeant Long depressed the talk button, responding, "Falcon Six, this is Falcon Three. Send."

"Falcon Three, we just received word that we have an artillery battalion assigned for use by all Falcon units. The unit's call sign is Thunder Five. How copy?"

Long smiled and suddenly felt a lot more confident in their ability to hold their position. "That's a good copy. We are in intermittent contact with the enemy to our front. We'll make use of the artillery support. What is the likelihood of getting some air support? Over," asked Long.

There was a short pause in the dialogue before Captain Culley responded, "Air support is focused in other areas right now. Will be limited, if available at all. Try to make do with the artillery. How copy?"

"That's a good copy. How about additional reinforcements to my position?" he asked, hoping there might be additional Marines headed his way.

"The rest of Falcon elements should be consolidating on your position within the next couple of hours. Please ensure additional fighting positions are ready. Out."

Long nodded in approval and saw that Lieutenant Davis had moved next to him, apparently trying to listen in on the conversation. "We have an artillery battalion assigned to support us. Our CO said the rest of the company should be arriving at our position within the next couple of hours," he explained.

"That's good news, Master Sergeant, because it looks like the PLA is gearing up for another attack," Davis said, pointing across the ridge.

As his eyes followed the direction of the lieutenant's finger, Sergeant Long's skin began to crawl. The top of the ridge was packed with enemy soldiers who were now filtering into the densely forested area that lined the ridges and valleys below them. They were moving down the valley to get in position to attack them.

Master Sergeant Long signaled for his radioman, or RTO, to head over to him. The radioman had a rucksack that contained their SINCGAR radio, which would allow them to make contact with the artillery unit and their battalion and brigade, if they needed to call in for air support.

As the RTO made his way over, Lieutenant Davis yelled to his soldiers, "Wake up and get ready for another attack!"

Lance Corporal Teddy Tipson finished trotting over. "You need me, Sir?"

"I sure do, Lance Corporal. Get on the horn to Thunder Five. Tell them I have a fire mission for them," he directed as he kneeled down and pulled out his map. One of the other sergeants came over to him and pulled out his compass. The two of them identified where they wanted the artillery to land and wrote down the different coordinates according to the map. The RTO then handed the handset to Sergeant Long.

Long quickly picked it up. "Thunder Five, Falcon Three. Fire mission, fire mission, we have an imminent attack. How copy?"

The radio crackled with a bit of static, but a soft voice broke through. "Falcon Three, this is Thunder Five. Good copy, send fire mission."

"I could barely hear them," Lance Corporal Tipson said after he listened in on the conversation.

Master Sergeant Long nodded. "The PLA is trying to jam the spectrum right now. You got those coordinates?" he asked, holding his hand out to the sergeant who had been helping him identify the target grids. The sergeant quickly handed over the sheet of paper. "Thunder Five. Fire mission. Tango One, NK 7423 8724. One round HE. How copy?"

"Falcon Three, this is Thunder Five. That's a good copy. One round HE…shot out!"

"Shot out," replied Long as they waited for the round to impact.

"Splash," the artilleryman said over the radio.

"Splash out."

A few seconds later, they heard the scream of the round flying over their heads and watched as it impacted just shy of where they wanted it to hit.

28

Depressing the talk button on the mic, Long directed, "Thunder Five, adjust fire. Three hundred meters left, drop one hundred meters. Fire for effect, five rounds HE. Second fire mission, Tango Two, NK 7214 8435. One round HE. How copy?" The second set of coordinates would send additional rounds to the enemy soldiers who were gathered on the ridge across from them.

"Falcon Three. Good copy on Tango Two. Standby for a fire mission," the artillery battalion responded as they prepared to fire the first mission. A minute later, they called back, "Shot out on Tango One. Shot out on Tango Two."

As the Marines and Army soldiers on the ridge prepared for the coming onslaught, the outgoing artillery fire assaulted their ears with high-pitched screams overhead. As the rounds hit their targets below, they felt the reverberations in the ground. Twenty rounds bracketed the valley below, destroying trees and decimating the enemy soldiers moving underneath the pine trees. Then a lone round landed squarely on top of the ridge. A handful of enemy soldiers were thrown into the air from the blast, their bodies ripped to shreds.

"Thunder Five, good BDA on Tango One. Tango Two, right on the mark. Fire for effect, three rounds HE. How copy?" he called over the radio.

While Master Sergeant Long was relaying the next fire mission, they heard the sound of rockets flying over their heads, heading in the direction of the artillery battalion that was supporting them. Thunderous explosions roared from the rear area, where presumably their artillery support had been operating.

After not receiving a response from the Thunder unit for a few minutes and not hearing or seeing the second fire mission hitting the target they had just called in, Tim tried to raise them again. "Thunder Five. This is Falcon Three. What's the status of that second fire mission? Over."

The only thing they heard was hissing, popping, and static over the radio. "They may have just been taken out," Lance Corporal Tipson offered. The others slowly nodded.

"Ugh—I was really hoping we'd be able to get a few more fire missions," Sergeant Long thought.

Lieutenant Davis chimed in. "It was good while we had it. Looks like we're back on our own," he said, stating the obvious.

A few minutes later, they heard the distinctive sound of artillery rounds heading toward their own positions. The soldiers and Marines on the ridge ducked down in their hastily built fighting positions as the first artillery rounds arrived. The ground shook. Dirt, snow, and parts of the pine trees that surrounded their positions landed all around them.

The smell of smoke, cordite, burnt flesh and split-open bowels filled the air. Screams from the wounded rang out. "Medic! Corpsman!" they yelled.

The barrage lasted for maybe two or three minutes, but the damage had been done. All around them, their fighting positions had been torn asunder. Several of the amtracks had also been hit and were adding their own thick, oily black smoke to the surreal scene.

Master Sergeant Long poked his head above the foxhole he had jumped into. As he did, he heard the loud shrilling sound of a whistle being blown in the distance. Then the roar of hundreds, maybe even thousands of voices shouting sent a shiver of fear down his spine. The first wave of enemy soldiers that had survived the Americans' first artillery barrage was charging their position.

"Here they come! Everyone up and ready!" Master Sergeant Long yelled to his Marines. His sergeants echoed his orders, as did Lieutenant Davis and some of his own sergeants as they, too, prepared themselves for the onslaught that was charging toward them.

Long moved out of the foxhole and ran toward a shallow slit trench that a couple of his men had dug. They were manning one of the platoon's heavy machine guns, an M240 Golf mounted on a tripod with the spare barrel sitting next to it, ready to go.

"How many extra belts of ammo do you guys have here?" Master Sergeant Long asked the assistant gunner, a private who had been newly assigned to the platoon.

"Five, Sir," he replied. The young private's eyes were filled with fear and there was a tremble in his voice as the crescendo of the charging enemy grew louder as they continued to claw their way up the side of the ridge.

"Private, run back to the track and grab another five belts. We're going to need a lot more ammo than that. You should have grabbed at least ten belts when you guys set up this gun position," Master Sergeant Long said, directing his comments more to the corporal who was looking down the barrel at the charging enemy.

"*The corporal should have known better,*" he thought. "*Once the shooting starts, they won't have a lot of time to keep running back and forth for more ammo.*"

The young Marine grabbed his M4 and ran back to the track to grab more ammo. Looking down the ridge, Sergeant Long could see the enemy soldiers were probably 500 meters away now. The corporal looked at him for permission to start firing. Master Sergeant Long nodded, and the corporal immediately looked down his barrel and squeezed off several controlled three- and five-round bursts. While the M240 could chew through hundreds of rounds a minute, the corporal knew not to burn through ammo too quickly, especially since doing so could overheat the barrel in the first couple minutes of the fight.

With the enemy now less than 300 meters away, the rest of the Marines and Army soldiers opened fire with their M4s and their newly issued M27 infantry automatic rifles. The barrage of hot lead being thrown at the enemy tore into their ranks, decimating the advancing hordes. Thousands of bullets crisscrossed back and forth between the American and Chinese lines, intermixed with red and green tracers. The thunderous noise of war was deafening as the two sides tried their best to kill each other.

"Incoming!" yelled one of the Americans. Suddenly, the whistling noise of mortars screamed out from the enemy lines, moments before half a dozen explosions rocked their positions. More American soldiers cried out for help as the Chinese soldiers continued to mortar their positions. Meanwhile, their ground troops continued to close the gap between their two forces.

Long brought his rifle to his shoulder, placing his cheek firmly against the stock of his M4 with the tip of his nose centimeters away from the charging handle as he gently squeezed off one round after another at the advancing enemy soldiers. He saw, two, three, then four enemy soldiers drop to the ground after each trigger squeeze.

"Stay calm, just keep pulling the trigger," he thought. *"Focus on one target at a time. Kill the guy in front of you and then move to the next one,"* he told himself.

As the Army soldiers and Marines continued to decimate the advancing Chinese, they heard another set of whistles, softer and further away.

"Dear God—that must be the next wave of enemy soldiers. If we don't get more help soon, they're going to overrun us," Master Sergeant Long realized in horror.

He turned and looked for his RTO. "Tipson! See if you can raise Falcon Six! We need fire support now!" he yelled to his radioman. Tipson stopped shooting and tried to get their CO back on the radio.

Long took aim and fired another four more rounds before he heard some static and pops in his ear and the response he was hoping for. "This is Falcon Six. Go ahead, Falcon Three," replied Captain Culley.

"Sir, we're under heavy attack. We've beaten back the first wave, but the second wave is hitting us now. How soon until we get additional reinforcements to our position?"

He yelled to be heard over the continuous gunfire happening all around him.

"We're halfway up the ridge behind you. We should be to your location within the next thirty minutes. Continue to hold the line. Reinforcements are nearly to you guys," Culley said reassuringly.

Master Sergeant Long handed the handset back to Lance Corporal Tipson and picked his rifle back up, ready to resume fire on the oncoming horde. "Keep trying to reach the artillery group, OK? Maybe we get lucky and their signal was just jammed."

Tipson grabbed the handset and depressed the talk button. "Thunder Five, this is Falcon Three. Fire mission. How copy?"

The fire direction officer on the other end replied, "Good copy, Falcon Three. We're back online now. Send fire mission."

"I need one round HE. NK 7413 8774. Danger close!" he yelled, trying to be heard over the constant machine-gun fire.

A minute went by with silence on the radio. Then they heard, "Shot out, advise on adjustments."

Long took aim at the enemy soldiers now constituting the second wave as they continued to close the

35

gap. They were less than 200 meters away when he heard the whistling sound of the incoming artillery round. The high-explosive round landed roughly a hundred meters behind the enemy soldiers, throwing shrapnel in all directions, killing many of them.

"*Spot-on. Now we need to lay it on thick,*" Master Sergeant Long thought.

"Good BDA. Adjust fire, down one hundred meters. Fifty-foot airburst, fire for effect, three rounds HE. Danger close!" he yelled into the handset. He had readjusted the target to give his own troops more of a safe radius. The airburst rounds would also throw significantly more shrapnel at the enemy and cause a lot of the pine trees to splinter, throwing wood chunks at the Chinese soldiers.

While Master Sergeant Long was waiting for the fire support to decimate the advancing enemy, a series of thunderous explosions rocked their position. Long felt himself being lifted into the air. He floated briefly above his soldiers' position, weightless, before gravity took over and he was thrown violently to the ground, knocking the wind out of him.

Long regained consciousness a few seconds later, desperately trying to breathe. As his lungs filled with air, his body ached everywhere. His brain was still trying to register what had just happened to him. For a moment, he wasn't even sure where he was. Then his hearing began to return, and the roar of explosions and machine-gun fire brought him back to the reality of where he was and what was happening.

"*How long was I out?*" he asked himself. He patted down his chest and legs, checking to make sure everything was still there and working properly. Sitting up, he saw the fighting position he had previously occupied with the heavy machine gun was gone. In its place was a smoldering crater, surrounded by the torn body parts of the two Marines who had been operating the heavy weapon.

Long turned to his left and saw his RTO, Lance Corporal Tipson, crying out toward the amtrack, where several of the corpsmen and medics had set up a triage point. Both of Tipson's legs were gone, and his left arm was shredded. Tipson desperately tried to use his right arm to pull his body toward help. A few seconds later, he stopped and went limp.

Turning to look back toward the advancing Chinese, Master Sergeant Long saw that the enemy soldiers were now less than thirty meters from him. He looked around him, desperately trying to find his rifle. Bullets kicked up dirt all around him. He frantically continued searching, but he still couldn't find his rifle. His mind was still a haze. Now desperate for a weapon, his eyes settled on an entrenching shovel less than a few feet from him.

Long reached down, grabbing the entrenching tool. At that moment, he knew he was most likely going to die, and an inner rage welled up within him. His grip on the shovel tightened. He brought it up like a bayonet and yelled a primordial scream, charging fiercely into the rushing enemy soldiers.

In his peripheral vision, he saw both Marines and Army soldiers firing point-blank into the Chinese, and he swung the shovel for all his worth at the enemy soldier nearest to him. The blade of the digging tool sliced cleanly through the man's throat, ripping it open. A stream of arterial spray reached Sergeant Long, hitting him in the chest. The Chinese soldier dropped his weapon, both of his hands reaching for his throat in a desperate attempt to stop the rushing flow of blood.

Long turned to face the next enemy soldier, still filled with an instinctual rage. Like a demonically possessed crazy person, he ran into a throng of enemy soldiers and screamed wildly. He slashed at the enemy soldiers with the entrenching tool, oblivious to his own pain and everything going on around him.

A Chinese soldier, not more than a few feet away from Master Sergeant Long, leveled his rifle at him. Knowing he was seconds away from being killed, Long instinctively grabbed the man whose throat he had just sliced open, and with every ounce of strength he could muster, Long threw him at the man who was about to shoot him.

In that instant, his right hand fell to his side, and his mind registered that he still had a sidearm on him. He grabbed the SIG Sauer and leveled it at the enemy soldiers who were overrunning their position. He fired multiple rounds at them, killing several of the advancing soldiers with headshots and hitting several more in the center mass before his pistol locked to the rear, empty.

Master Sergeant Long reached down to grab another magazine. Just then, he heard the familiar sound of American machine guns firing. Suddenly, the enemy soldiers near him clutched at their chests, hit by multiple rounds. Half a dozen Marines ran past him, killing the remaining Chinese soldiers as they pushed them back down the ridge.

Long spotted an M4 on the ground next to a dead Marine and quickly reached down to grab it. Checking the chamber, he joined the fray, picking off the remaining enemy soldiers, now in full retreat.

Master Sergeant Long looked back behind him and saw dozens of tracked and wheeled vehicles bringing additional reinforcements to their position.

"*'Bout time the cavalry arrived,*" he thought. Suddenly, he involuntarily dropped to his knees and fell forward on the ground. His body ached everywhere, and he felt incredibly tired and thirsty.

"Hang in there, Master Sergeant. I do not give you permission to die yet," Captain Culley said as he knelt down next to him. "This is the second time I've come to your rescue and seen you surrounded by dead enemy soldiers. We're going to have to award you another valor medal, aren't we?" he joked with a smile.

Tim snorted. "Cutting it a little close there, Captain. They nearly had us this time."

"You just hang in there, Tim. You guys did a heck of a job. Now if I could just get you to stop collecting Purple Hearts and actually stick around long enough to do your job…"

A corpsman ran up to them and began to treat Tim's multiple shrapnel wounds.

****

The battle for Hill 597 at Taechon lasted for nearly 24 hours before the Americans managed to stop the Chinese advance. As the weather cleared, the Allies were able to resume tactical air support. Between that and the multiple Arc Light missions by the heavy bombers, they eventually decimated the Chinese assault into North Korea. With the aid of 60,000 Marines, the Army and ROK Forces were able to recapture nearly all the territory lost and pushed the Chinese back across the Yalu River, saving the Allies from a repeat of the disastrous retreat that defined the previous Korean War.

****

Chijiabao, China
Ten Kilometers North of Yalu River

Sergeant First Class Ian Slater stumbled briefly as the older Chinese soldier shoved him with the butt of his rifle and yelled at him, "Move faster!"

Only one of their captors, the crotchety old soldier who kept shoving him, spoke English. He kept insisting that they walk more rapidly and telling them that hot food and shelter would be given to them once they made it to their end destination.

"I'd like to take that rifle and club him with it," thought Slater angrily as he continued to march further north with the two dozen or so American prisoners. While the blizzard-like conditions had largely dissipated over the last few hours, the heavy cloud cover and steady snowfall still meant visibility was shoddy.

"At least the wind has died down," Sergeant Slater thought, trying to be positive for a moment. *"Now if I could just keep my hands from freezing, I'd be in better shape."* When he had been captured, the Chinese soldiers had stripped him of his body armor, but at least they had let him keep his jacket once they had made sure he had no weapons in it.

Slater's mind kept flashing back to that horrific walk out of the shattered bunker when he had been captured. He felt sick to his stomach as he pictured the ground, littered with bodies. He heard the crunch again as he unwittingly stepped on a hand that had been separated from one of the members of his unit—there had hardly been a place to step without walking on body parts that had been torn apart and mangled by high explosives, grenades or heavy machine-gun bullets. A wave of grief washed over him. Many of the dead had been part of his unit, and some of them had been friends.

"*I miss Joe,*" Sergeant Slater thought as he remembered his friend who had died dramatically in his arms. He wished Joe hadn't been lost in the bunker, but as he trudged along, he wondered if maybe his friend had gotten it easy compared to what was about to happen to him and the rest of the prisoners.

Slater wasn't sure what time it was since his watch had been taken from him, but as his column of prisoners neared the city of Chijiabao, they heard a soft whistling noise high above them. That noise steadily grew in intensity as it got closer. Sergeant Slater knew immediately what it was, and he suspected the other American soldiers recognized the sound, but the Chinese soldiers didn't seem to care.

The first explosions rocked the ground, and then thunderous booms followed as bombers delivered a high-altitude bombing run across their old positions to wipe out the Chinese advance. The noises drew hastily closer. Sergeant Slater quickly ran to the ditch next to the side of the road, trying to seek even a semblance of shelter. The other Americans quickly followed suit.

The Chinese soldiers suddenly realized the imminent danger approaching them and scattered in all directions, looking for a place to hide from the incoming bombs. Some of them ran into each other as they scrambled away in a disorganized horde.

Sergeant Slater saw this as his golden opportunity to try and make a break for it. All of the Americans had instinctively followed their training, dropping to the ground; however, they were all still somewhat clustered together. The Chinese had run off to every corner of the field, leaving them alone and unguarded. As the bombs got closer and the explosions louder and more violent, Slater yelled to the others, "Follow my lead!"

Slater ran toward a small cluster of their captors who had taken shelter in a ditch not far from them, several of his American comrades right behind him. Together, they pounced on their terrified captors like lions on their prey. The PLA soldiers were so surprised by their captives' attack, they hardly had time to react. They had been so terrified of the falling bombs heading toward them that they had forgotten about the danger of leaving a group of American prisoners alone.

While dozens of 500-pound bombs landed nearby, the American soldiers attacked their captors in hand-to-hand combat, using their fists, rocks and anything else they could grab to overpower them. As shrapnel flew everywhere, Sergeant Slater and his fellow prisoners grabbed their captors' weapons and ammunition and summarily killed the remaining cadre of PLA soldiers the bombs had missed. Once the dirt, snow, and chaos from the bombing subsided, the newly freed soldiers looked to Sergeant Slater and asked, "What do we do now?"

Slater hadn't thought about that just yet. He'd figured they might just die right there from the bombing run, and if they were going to die, they might as well as try and kill their captors in the process. Now that they had survived, they were suddenly free, but very far behind enemy lines. He took a deep breath and calculated all the options.

"OK, guys, here's what we're going to do. We're going to try and get back to our own fighting line…"

The Xi'an Accords - Eastern Alliance

Xi'an, China
Angsana Hotel

The city of Xi'an had once been known as Chang'an, which translated in English as "eternal peace." It was a fitting name, considering the meeting that was to take place within its city limits. The city was also the endpoint of the famed Silk Road, the meeting of East and West that had introduced Europe to Asia and spurred economic trade that still continued to this day. In addition, the city was also home to the famed Bingmayong (Terra Cotta Army).

Today, the leaders of Asia who weren't included in the new American-led Global Defense Force would meet to discuss joining a similar alliance. It had been incredibly difficult to organize—especially with war spreading to more and more countries across the globe—but the leaders of India, Thailand, Malaysia, Indonesia, Russia and the Stan countries of Kyrgyzstan, Tajikistan, Kazakhstan, Uzbekistan, Iran, Syria, Yemen, and Sudan were set to discuss the future of the world, and a new treaty that Russia and China were spearheading in response to the West's creation of their new Global Defense Force.

****

Looking out the window of the presidential suite, Xi noticed the slight drizzle of rain had now turned into a steady downpour, bringing much-needed rain to the city of Xi'an. The moisture helped to remove the pollutants in the air and lowered the level of smog in the city, at least for a few hours. Despite the rain, the hotel building was bustling with security both inside and out. High above the city, fighters patrolled the skies to help ensure no American bombers tried to attack the facility that was playing host to this crucial meeting, one which in all reality would most likely change the future of the world.

Looking in the mirror, President Xi felt confident about the proposal they would be discussing. While the Americans were negotiating the creation of a new military alliance, Xi was also negotiating a global realignment that he believed would change the course of history—one that would see America and Europe replaced as world powers, with China and Russia as the new global leaders of the 21st century. He made a last-minute adjustment to his tie and then quickly headed toward the door and the elevator that would lead them to the conference room for the negotiation.

As he walked into the ornately decorated conference room, Xi surveyed the other leaders at the table. He smiled when he spotted Petrov sipping a cup of tea, grinning and talking with President Pranab Nath Kovind of India. Sitting next to them was President Jusuf Subianto of Indonesia, who didn't look happy to be in this meeting, and Prime Minister Najib Razak of Malaysia, who was equally unenthused.

"They will come around to our line of thinking, or they will be replaced by leaders who will see the benefit of being a part of this new world order," thought Xi as he forced himself to keep smiling and play host and salesman.

As Xi continued into the room and slid into his spot near President Petrov, the discussions of the various leaders slowly ended, and all eyes turned to him. Petrov smiled and nodded toward Xi, which reminded President Xi of the conversation the two of them had had the night before, strategizing ways to work the room. Xi took the nod as Petrov's signal that he was carrying out the plan they had discussed.

Xi cleared his throat. "Welcome, gentlemen. Prior to the Second World War, France, Great Britain, and the nations of Europe ruled most of the world as colonial powers. They divided the world up, drawing national borders with the intent of pitting us against each other to keep us weak—to keep us focused on fighting each other so that even in relinquishing colonial rule, they could still hold power over us."

He tapped the table for emphasis. "Following the end of the end of World War II, the United States joined their elitist club. And what have *they* accomplished for the good of humanity? They brought us the two world wars, then they instigated the Cold War against the peace-loving people of the Soviet Union and spurred numerous regional wars, using them to gain access and control our national resources for their benefit, stripping us of our wealth."

Xi surveyed the other world leaders. So far, their affect was flat. He continued, "When a government didn't bow down to their authority or corporate interests, they interfered with our internal elections and actively worked to subvert our governments. In many cases, they'd be the driving force behind a coup or popular uprising to install their own puppet regime. Look at what the Americans did in Chile, installing that brutal dictator Pinochet rather than allowing the people to form their own socialist government. Even more recently, we can look at Libya, a nation that functioned and provided for its people. Now it's a complete mess run by warlords and terrorists."

Xi looked directly at each of the leaders from Muslim-dominated countries, making sure he had their full attention before he continued. "In 1949, the West unilaterally took the lands of Palestine and gave it to the Jews to create the nation of Israel. The West, led by the United States and Great Britain, have meddled endlessly in the Middle East, stoking one war after another, all in the name of 'freedom.' In reality, it's just a ploy to enrich their nations at the expense of those who cannot resist them."

Several leaders nodded, and Xi smiled inwardly. "The West looks to divide us and corrupt the minds of our youth. They insist that we accept their moral perversion of homosexuality, and this mental disease they call transgender. They pervert our religious views and insist that we change our culture, religion and belief systems to accept what they deem acceptable to *their* version of freedom. I say enough of this moral depravity and the insistence that we adhere to their forms of government, religion, and morality."

More leaders nodded. The only exceptions were the leaders of Saudi Arabia, Thailand, and Malaysia, who looked on with passive expressions.

"During the past six months, the Russian Federation and my nation, China, have shown you that even the vaunted American military can be defeated on the battlefield. Now is the time to unite and finish the West off," Xi concluded. He nodded to Petrov to take the lead.

President Petrov went over the progress his forces had made in Europe, and how the Allies had essentially fought themselves into a stalemate. He talked about the battle losses the Allies had sustained, and the estimates of what it would take for their economy to replace them. The more he talked about these specific facts, the more interested the leaders at the table seemed to be.

Seeing that the audience was moving more in his favor, Petrov decided to drive the point home. "Now is the time for everyone to unite and stand against the imperialist nations of the West. If we unite and act now, we can secure a better future for our nations. If we sit by and let this opportunity pass us by, then we will never be able to break free from their yoke of bondage they've kept us in," he said, rapping his knuckles against the table. Petrov went on for some time, discussing what needed to happen for them to defeat the Americans and the nations who were allying themselves with the West.

President Reza Pahlavi of Iran interjected, "With all due respect, Mr. President, Russia is being bombed into submission by the Americans. The Americans and NATO countries are amassing hundreds of thousands of soldiers on your border. My own military advisors don't believe your regime will survive another year of this war. Why should Iran join this alliance if it appears that it'll be defeated within the year?"

"That's a fair question," responded Petrov. He leaned forward in his chair. "While the West is building up their forces in Europe, significant challenges still need to be overcome if they are to remove my forces from Ukraine and the Baltic States. Even now, we're starting to see the Americans buckle under the strain of fighting a multifront war. They had to sacrifice the Baltic States because they had to rush forces to Korea. Now they're having to fight a much slower war of attrition in Korea because they cannot commit their entire military to that fight without conceding defeat in Europe. Likewise, they can't commit to defeating my forces in Europe because they're heavily engaged in Korea."

Petrov paused for a second, letting some of that information settle before continuing, "Gentlemen, we have a once-in-a-lifetime opportunity. The Americans and the West are realizing that they've overextended themselves and are unable to respond to everything that is being thrown at them. If there were ever a time to remove the Americans from the world stage, it's now, before they can fully retool their economy and rebuild their military. We must put them down for the count now, or we may never get another chance like this again."

Overwhelmed

Washington, D.C.
White House, Situation Room

A steward brought in a fresh pot of coffee to the President's war council, which had been hard at work in the Situation Room through most of the night. They had been sifting through the latest intelligence summary from the Bangkok Embassy on this secretive meeting that had been held in Xi'an. From what they had gathered, it wasn't looking good for the Allies. Tom McMillan, the National Security Advisor, had spent an hour on the phone with the Bangkok station chief, going over what had transpired during Thai Prime Minister Nopparith's secret meeting in China.

The Thais were very concerned about what had been transpiring in Southeast Asia. One by one, the People's Liberation Army had acquired their neighbors, and they knew it was only a matter of time before the Chinese turned their attention on them. In addition to the enormous tourist value of Thailand, they also had rich, fertile farmland and a strong manufacturing base—all economic motivations for these other nations to try and control the country. When the

Chinese government had requested the PM's presence in Xi'an, Thai officials had reached out to the US embassy and asked for help. The station chief had suggested employing a very sophisticated and highly undetectable listening device, to be placed on the PM during the meeting so the information could be relayed back to the Allies.

As Tom McMillan skimmed through the transcript, he began to feel like a knot was forming in his stomach. Things were much worse than he had anticipated. If the new alliance were to be formed, he wasn't sure how the Allies could ever win the war. "*The boss is going to go through the roof when he learns about this,*" he thought.

Admiral Peter Meyers, the Chairman of the Joint Chiefs, had been trying to wait patiently for McMillan to say something, but he was getting a little impatient. "So, Tom, what are your thoughts on this 'secret' meeting?" he asked. He poured himself another cup of coffee, knowing that it was going to be a late night.

"It's not good," McMillan replied bluntly. "If these plans really do come to fruition, then this war is going to drag on for a lot longer than we initially thought…I mean, we just averted a disaster in Korea, and we finally solidified the front lines in Europe, but there's only so much we can do with the resources we have."

Admiral Meyers took a swig of his coffee to give him a second to calculate his response. "The boss isn't going to like this. We're going to need to go ahead and expand the military a lot more than we already have. Whether we like it or not, the war is spreading. Not only that, but we're also tearing through our war stocks of equipment and our reserve forces faster than we can replace them."

McMillan sighed. "The President isn't going to want to hear that, Peter," he said in frustration. "He's going to tell you that you asked for a five-million-man army and he's given you that. If you try to go back now and ask for more troops, he's going to take a lot of heat in the press and with Congress."

"That may be so, but it doesn't change the reality on the ground," Meyers asserted. He held up the transcript. "If even half of this is true, we're toast. How in the heck are we supposed to defeat China, Indonesia, and India if they mobilize their populations and declare total, all-out war on us? Add the Iranians to the picture, and now we have the Middle East to consider. We haven't even talked about our current forces still operating in Afghanistan—those poor guys have been almost completely neglected since the start of the war. We need to get our forces out of Afghanistan now, before they become trapped there."

Before they could continue their conversation, Jim Castle, the Secretary of Defense, walked into the room with a couple of his aides. Judging by the scowl on his face, he wasn't happy. Jim was probably the most dominant person in the President's cabinet. Since the outbreak of the war, his prominence in the White House and media had only increased, and so had his influence with the President.

Holding his own copy of the transcript, he slapped it down on the table and bellowed, "This better be fiction I'm reading!" He fixed each of them with a steely gaze, waiting for them to explain the transcript.

McMillan held up a hand in protest. "Perhaps you should sit down, Mr. Secretary. This is the unvarnished intelligence we just obtained from the Thailand station chief. We're still sifting through it ourselves, and our staffs are still working through the implications of this."

Secretary Castle looked past McMillan to Jedediah "JP" Perth, the Director of the CIA, who had been sitting against the back wall of the room, talking quietly with one of his analysts. "Is this the big news out of China you mentioned was headed our way a couple of days ago?" Castle demanded.

JP just nodded. "I'd hoped it wouldn't be quite this bad. We're pinging all our sources in the affected countries, trying to determine if this is really happening, or if these nations were just agreeing to this out of fear of military retaliation if they said no. I'm hoping for the latter, because if that's the case, then we may be able to work around this development and turn it to our advantage," he offered.

Sighing deeply as he took his seat, Castle replied, "We need to all get on the same page with this when the President arrives. He's going to want answers, not more questions."

The group sat there silently for a few minutes, thinking about that. This Xi'an accord was not something they had anticipated. The casualties from the war and the loss of equipment were far beyond what the country had experienced for many generations, hitting the country like a punch to the gut. During this last major battle in Korea, nearly sixteen thousand Americans had been killed in only two weeks of combat. The viciousness of the battles was horrific. In this GoPro generation of soldiers, raw combat footage was constantly being uploaded to social media, despite the attempts by the defense department to keep soldiers from doing it. Those videos were having a terrible impact on the psyche of the country.

A couple of minutes later, President Patrick Gates and his Chief of Staff, Retired Army General Liam Greeson, walked into the room. Everyone stood, silently waiting for the President to signal for them to take a seat. Gates stood at the head of the table for a second, surveying the faces of his war council. It was pretty obvious that no one was feeling especially optimistic.

"Take a seat, everyone. It looks like we're going to be here for a while, so let's get this going. What are we looking at, JP?" he asked.

JP put his two index fingers together, forming what looked like a steeple. "We have a new and dangerous development, Mr. President. Roughly a week ago, the Chinese government extended an invitation to the leaders of a number of Asian and other adversarial nations for a secret meeting. The Thai PM and senior military leaders knew something was up, and they reached out to our station chief in Bangkok. The PM agreed to wear a new type of undetectable listening device that we've developed to the meeting. When the PM returned from the meeting, he summoned our station chief and proceeded to tell him exactly what transpired."

The President saw the various transcripts of the conversation in front of everyone. He hadn't had a chance to look at a copy yet. He grabbed one and started thumbing through it.

"OK, so what are we looking at?" he pressed.

"President Xi and Petrov are proposing a new global alliance—an economic and military alliance—with the sole intention of defeating the West and removing the United States and Europe as the leaders of the 'free world.' President Xi has masterfully laid out a case for why the US should be removed from the global stage by any and all means necessary, and they're inviting a host of nations to join them in retooling their economies for total war and the complete destruction of Europe and America," the CIA Director explained.

Chief of Staff Greeson leaned forward and asked the obvious question. "How is this going to affect the current war operations?"

McMillan chimed in, "*If* these nations do move forward with joining Russia and China, then in the short run, it wouldn't affect us much. In the long run, it would be devastating, unless we were able to end the war quickly. Look at it from this perspective, Mr. President. Right now, the Chinese have nearly 1.6 billion people. They're in the process of mobilizing their entire population for war. It'll take time to retool their economy and produce the needed additional aircraft, ship, and tanks—not to mention train their soldiers. In the meantime, they have to fight with what they have, and right now they're losing troops and equipment at an astonishing rate. However, in another year, that equation will shift dramatically in their favor."

He cleared his throat and then continued, "If you add India to that mix, you have a country of 1.3 billion people with an incredibly large manufacturing base. They also have an enormously large army, and when combined with the Chinese and the Russian—"

The President cut him off to interject, "—I understand the numbers are bad. Isn't our technological advantage enough to counter them?"

Admiral Meyers reached out and placed his hand on McMillan's arm to let him know he'd handle this question. "Mr. President, during World War II, the German Tiger and Panther tanks were unrivaled on the battlefield. Even against the Russian T34s and KV tanks, they were far superior in their fire control system, weapon power, and accuracy. They were devastating to the Russian and Allied tanks that faced them. It was said that during the Allied advance toward Germany, the Germans were averaging a ten-to-one kill ratio, and in the east, sometimes as high as twelve-to-one. The problem for the Germans was that there was always an 11th, 12th, or 13th tank that kept coming at them. There would be times where a group of five or six Panther tanks would destroy fifty-plus T34s, but ultimately they would get overwhelmed by the sheer numbers the Russians were able to throw at them."

Meyers paused for a second before continuing. "My point, Mr. President, is that technology does not provide us such a huge advantage as one might think. At some point, the volume being thrown at us will eventually overwhelm and defeat us," he concluded.

The President snorted incredulously. "So, in this scenario, you're saying we're the Germans of 1941 and we're about to be overwhelmed by the Allied and Russian hordes in another year?"

There was an uncomfortable pause after that question. Gates took the silence as confirmation, and his face fell.

"OK, gentlemen," the President began, "if this is the new reality we have to work with, then I need solutions. How are we going to counter this new development, and what is the plan to defeat them before they're able to overwhelm us?"

Jim Castle decided that he had sat on the sidelines of this conversation long enough at this point, and jumped in. "We ramp up production of everything, and we simply out produce them, and outfight them on the battlefield. Let's look at Korea, for example. The Chinese just threw a massive counterattack against us that lasted for nearly four straight weeks. In that time, they sent nearly 300,000 soldiers against us, the Japanese and the ROK, and they ultimately lost that battle. They didn't remove us from North Korea, and they didn't defeat us on the battlefield. They suffered nearly 82,000 casualties and lost over a thousand tanks and hundreds of aircraft in a monthlong battle."

"They hurt us, but they did not defeat us, Mr. President," Castle continued, tapping the table for emphasis. "The equipment and aircraft they lost in this battle is going to take them a long time to replace, and that's going to hurt them in the short run. What we have to do now is keep the pressure on them. We have to keep going after critical functions of their economy with our strategic bombers and continue to deprive them of the natural resources and minerals they need to keep their economy running," Jim said.

Gates thought Admiral Meyers looked like he was holding something back. "What's on your mind, Peter?"

A bit surprised at being called out, Admiral Meyers figured this would be about as good a time as any to make his pitch for the second round of military drafts. "Sir, I think we need to look at another draft. If this intelligence is correct," he said, holding up the report from China, "then we're going to need a lot more soldiers. We also have to keep in mind that we can't just snap our fingers and have a million new soldiers just appear. It takes a lot of time to train a soldier to fight the kinds of wars we're now fighting. If India, Indonesia, and Iran do fully join in this war, then the current size of our military isn't going to be enough. Plus, I'm very concerned with the quality of the soldiers we're currently sending to Europe and Asia. We're rushing them through basic and advanced training and sending them straight to the front."

Holding a hand up so as to not be interrupted, Meyers continued, "I know that we had to do this in order to stabilize the lines. Going forward, though, I would like to return to our standard training program and incorporate the type of fighting our soldiers are most likely to encounter so we can better prepare them. My concern right now is that we're spread so thin in Europe and Asia that we're going to be stalemated because we can't focus on one theater. We're still at least two years away from being able to fight and sustain a two-front war."

The others in the room pondered that statement for a minute before anyone responded.

Gates let out a deep breath, more in frustration than anything else. *"Lord, help guide me and lead our great nation out of these troubled waters we now find ourselves in,"* he silently prayed.

"Peter, you mentioned a second draft. We just completed the last draft of five million men and women. Most of them are still waiting to start basic training. How many additional men and women are you suggesting we draft?"

All eyes turned toward the admiral to see what he'd say next. Jim Castle smirked a little at his friend, knowing he had just walked into a minefield.

Admiral Meyers took a deep breath. "We need additional computer programmers and cyber-warfare experts. Drone operators and other technical fields. We also need more combat arms soldiers. Because of the training length of some of these professions, I believe we need to move forward with drafting an additional six million." A collective gasp was let out.

The President realized that his mouth had been hanging open in shock and quickly snapped his jaw back in place. "Admiral, the press and Congress have been eating me alive over the last draft. Have you seen what they've been saying about the casualties we sustained during this last battle in Korea? They're calling it the 'Gates Massacre' because I hadn't ordered enough soldiers to Korea. If I ask for another draft of six million more young people, they're going to try and impeach me. I'm not even sure I could get Congress to authorize an increase," the President said incredulously.

"If I may, Mr. President," the SecDef said, finally coming to the aid of Admiral Meyers, "it takes time to train and equip an army. There's going to be a bit of a lull in the fighting for a few months. This is a good time to increase the size of the military again and ensure we have the soldiers we need to win this time next year. If you want, I'll convey that to Congress, and I'll be your pit bull in the public eye to get this done."

Gates looked back and forth between Castle and Meyers for a few moments, calculating out what other options he might have. "OK. If you can sell it to Congress, I'll go along," he finally conceded.

Pacific Strategy

Sasebo, Japan

Captain Jeff Richards, the captain of the USS *Carl Vinson* supercarrier, walked into the briefing room. He was surprised to see so many other carrier captains present, including the Secretary of the Navy, George Leahy, and to everyone's complete shock, the President and the Secretary of Defense. There had been no mention of the SecDef or the President being at this meeting when it was hastily put together less than twenty-four hours ago. Richards had thought he was going to attend a strategy session—he had no idea the Commander-in-Chief would be here. It was extremely risky having the President visit Japan, considering the US naval base at Sasebo was well within the range of Chinese ballistic missiles, bombers, and aircraft.

"This must be a heck of a meeting if the President himself is attending with the Secretary of the Navy," Richards thought as he walked over to the placard that had his name on it. He was seated almost directly across from the President, a true honor that was not lost on him.

Gates raised his hand, indicating that he wanted everyone to settle down. The chattering between the senior officers quickly subsided as they turned to look at their Commander-in-Chief.

The President surveyed the room, looking his captains in the eye and making a mental note of their names, faces and the carriers they commanded. His eyes then settled on Jeff. "Captain Richards," he began, "I wanted to personally thank you for your actions during the opening day of the Korean War and the surprise attack by the Chinese. You handled yourself incredibly well, and the country owes you and your men a great debt. I wanted to personally inform you that you and the captain of the *Reagan*—rest his soul—will be awarded the Navy Cross." This announcement drew a short round of applause.

Holding his hand up, the President continued, "Before you say anything else, the men and women of your ship and the *Reagan* are also going to be recognized for your heroic acts as well. America needs heroes right now. They need to know that we're going to win this war, and right now, you guys are those heroes for the Navy."

Richards didn't know what to say. His face turned red. "I appreciate the honor, Mr. President, and I know my men will as well."

Turning to face the rest of the ship captains, the President continued on. "This is a tough time we find ourselves in. But we will rise to the occasion and defeat our enemies. We didn't want or seek out this war, but by God, we're going to win and make sure a war like this never happens again." Gates paused as he looked up at the ceiling for a second before returning his gaze to the military men and women who would be pivotal in defeating the Chinese.

"With the loss of the *Reagan*, the extensive damage the *Vinson* sustained, and the new Chinese plans for continued expansion fully revealed, it's become imperative that we move our Atlantic Fleet carrier strike groups to the Pacific. It took us a month, but as you can see, we have the captains of the *Eisenhower*, *Lincoln*, and *Ford* carriers from the Atlantic with us. These three additional carriers, in addition to the *Stennis*, *Nimitz*, and *Roosevelt*, give us a total of six carriers in the Pacific for the first time. While I would like to have moved our remaining two carriers from the Atlantic, the SecDef and the Secretary here," he said, nodding toward his colleagues, "convinced me that it would be best to leave them there to support our European operations."

"Most of you aren't aware of what I'm about to reveal to you, so this stays within this room," the President asserted. "The CIA was able to snatch a high-value Chinese government official who, through interrogation, revealed to us the Chinese end state. Their goal is to secure large swaths of the Pacific islands and arm them with anti-ship and surface-to-air missiles, making them nearly impossible to recapture without sustaining heavy losses. This will allow their ground forces to capture and hold the Philippines and Malaysia. This cannot be allowed to happen. With that said, I'm going to turn this meeting over to Secretary of Defense Jim Castle and let him explain to you our strategy for the Pacific." He gestured for Castle to stand and begin his presentation.

The SecDef looked over the captains and admirals in the room with his stern gaze, seemingly piercing into their very souls. "Our first objective is to finish securing the Russian Far East. We need to neutralize that threat to our forces and Japan immediately. We cannot allow the Russians to carry out any sort of spoiler operations against our supply convoys or our oil infrastructure in Alaska. We also need to get our forces ready for the coming offensive against the Chinese mainland. However, we also cannot allow the Chinese to capture the Philippines or Malaysia. It's bad enough that they conquered Taiwan; we cannot allow them to capture and fortify the rest of the South China Sea," he said in his gruff and gravelly voice. When Castle spoke, he spoke with authority, conviction, and a sense of determination, and everyone knew that when he said something, the President fully backed him.

"In addition to the Atlantic carriers, I've spoken with Secretary of the Navy Joseph Leahy, and we're going to move forward with the reactivation of the carriers *Kitty Hawk* and *Enterprise* from the reserve fleet. It's going to be closer to summer before they'll be operationally ready, but I'm confident the army of contractors and naval support personnel will do their best. We'll keep them in the Atlantic for the time being and transfer our other two carriers there now to the Pacific, bringing the number of carriers we'll have to work with to eight—more than enough to do the job when we add in the Japanese flattops," Gates said to the surprised looks of those in the meeting.

Secretary Leahy chimed at this point, "In addition to the *Kitty Hawk* and *Enterprise*, we will now have all three of the *Zumwalt* DDGs in the Pacific. I've also spoken with the folks at Newport News, and the *John F. Kennedy* will be ready to sail by the end of summer, two years ahead of schedule," he said, eliciting more smiles from the captains.

"Now that everyone has been brought up to speed, here's what I want to happen," said President Gates, leaning forward. "The Russian Far East must be secured within the next 90 days. I don't care how, and I don't care what ships you have to use to accomplish that goal, but I want it done ASAP. While that is happening, I want our submarine forces to begin attacking the PLA Navy in the South China Sea. I do not want the Philippines, Guam, or any other islands captured. Is that understood, gentlemen?"

Feeling like a fish out of water, Captain Richards meekly raised his hand to ask the obvious question on his mind. The President nodded for him to speak. "Sir, I'm just curious why I was invited to this meeting. My ship, the *Vinson*, is going to be in the shipyard for at least twelve months, if not longer, and that's with a double work crew working around the clock," Richards said, feeling a bit awkward.

Laughing, the President turned to the Secretary of the Navy. "You didn't tell him yet?"

Secretary Leahy smiled as he replied, "We thought we'd leave him in the dark a bit longer before we broke the news."

At this point, the other officers in the room were all grinning. Clearly, they were in on whatever had been discussed prior to Richards' arrival at the meeting. Castle finally broke the pause. "You're here, Captain Richards, because you're taking over as the new Seventh Fleet Commander."

The President and the SecDef had been known for promoting people well ahead of their peers since the start of the war. The SecDef had told the President that it was important for them to find and promote aggressive, out-of-the-box leaders, and they had consistently promoted those who fit the needs of the military. Even still, Richards was a bit shocked by the sudden announcement.

Castle continued, "Captain Richards, a couple of days ago, you officially made vice admiral. However, with Admiral Kinkaid dead and Admiral Lomas still recovering, we opted to go ahead and promote you two additional grades to take over as the Seventh Fleet Commander. You have the most experience in theater, and we're going to need that experience if we're to defeat the Chinese. When this meeting is over, I'll leave you to confer with your ship captains here, and we'll hold an official pinning ceremony later today before the President leaves for some other pressing matters." Castle slid a set of vice admiral stars to him. The other captains in the room broke out in applause; they were glad to have someone in charge who had already fought the Chinese Navy and succeeded in defeating them.

The official meeting broke up a few minutes later once the SecDef had issued a few other orders and let everyone know the timeline for when he and the President wanted certain objectives to be completed. As the VIPs left the briefing room, all eyes turned to Vice Admiral Jeff Richards.

He cleared his throat. "Well, this promotion is a complete surprise to me," Richards said candidly. "I had no idea they were going to place me in command of the fleet. I hope you'll bear with me as I get up to speed on the disposition of our forces. What I can tell you from my own strike group's experience is that the Chinese anti-ship missiles are exceptionally good—far better than our intelligence had thought at the beginning of the war. To our horror, they seem to have perfected the art of 'the missile swarm' by hitting us with land-based, sea-launch, *and* air-launched anti-ship missiles, all at the same time. Had our DDGs not swapped out their Tomahawk missiles for additional SM-2 and SM-3 missiles, I would probably not be standing here with you right now."

He paused for a second, collecting his thoughts as he looked at the ship captains and three other admirals that would form the backbone of his strike group command. "This is going to be a missile war, which means we need to change our traditional tactics and approach to fleet defense. Looking at the timeline the SecDef and the President have given us, we do not have a lot of time to get ourselves ready.

Effective at once, I want all DDGs and cruisers to swap out their Tomahawk cruise missiles for additional SM-2s and SM-3 antiair missiles."

Richards turned to look at Admiral Shelley Cord, one of the strike group commanders from the Atlantic Fleet. "Admiral Cord, your strike group has two of the *Zumwalt*-class destroyers with you, correct?"

Rear Admiral Shelley Cord was the strike group commander for the USS *Gerald Ford*. The *Ford* was the newest class of supercarriers and was truly an amazing ship. As the flagship for the Navy, it was also heavily protected. When the *Ford* made its transit to the Pacific through Panama, it was met by both *Zumwalt* destroyers, which had been recently upgraded with the Navy's newest weapon, the BAE systems railgun.

Admiral Cord smiled and nodded. "Yes, they're both with us and fully updated. I'd caution you, though, against placing a lot of hope in this new weapon system. While it's gone through extensive tests, it has never been used in combat like our other systems have," she replied.

Noting the uncertainty in her voice, Richards responded, "That's a good point, Admiral. We'll have to take that into consideration in our ship deployment plan. That said, I do want to make sure this weapon system is used in the coming fight."

Admiral Richards paused for a second, looking over the two admirals and the other captains in the room before he continued. He was a new admiral, and by all accounts, had been promoted over some of the very admirals he was now in charge of. This made for a few awkward moments in the briefing.

Richards knew he needed to bring them up to speed and show why he had been chosen to command the revitalized Seventh Fleet. He cleared his throat. "When the Chinese launched their missile swarm attack on us, most of our escort ships burned through their entire stock of SM-2s intercepting the first two waves of missiles. Shoot, my own ship, the *Vinson*, nearly ran out of Rolling Airframe and Sea Sparrow missiles by the time the battle was over. If these new rail guns can help cut down on the volume of missiles we'll be facing, it may give our fleet the edge we need to survive the next battle. Mark my words, they're going to throw a missile swarm at us like we've never seen once they catch a glimpse of our fleet—the possibility of crushing the US Navy once and for all will be too big of an opportunity for them to pass up. They will hit us with everything they have," he concluded.

The other carrier commanders nodded in agreement with his assessment. The captains and admirals wanted payback, but they were also very concerned about losing a few more carriers. Having already lost two in this war, with a third heavily damaged, had caused a lot of the naval leadership and admirals to become very gun-shy in using these weapons of war. Richards hadn't been jaded by the losses thus far; he wasn't afraid to lose a few carriers in a battle if it meant destroying the Chinese Navy in the process.

The meeting continued for a little while longer as Admiral Richards took a bit of time to get to know each of the strike group commanders and ship captains before dismissing them for the day. While he had served with many of them in the past, he needed to gauge how aggressive they would be in the coming battle. He wanted to make sure they wouldn't place the safety of the ship or strike group above accomplishing the mission. Whether or not they wanted to accept it, they were going to lose more ships and aircraft in the coming battle. They might even lose their carrier, and while he would do his best to make sure that didn't happen, he needed to know that they were committed to winning, no matter the cost.

As he walked away from the meeting, he was feeling optimistic. He prepared talking points for the next day's discussion, which would focus on how to accomplish the President's charge to secure the Russian Far East while also keeping the PLA Navy from capturing the Philippines and keeping them away from Guam.

****

Kyoto, Japan
Four Seasons Hotel
Exiled Taiwanese Government Headquarters

President Hung was both surprised and excited to meet President Gates. She'd had no idea he was traveling to Japan to meet with his Pacific allies, but she was glad he was taking some time out of his busy schedule to meet specifically with her to discuss the future of Taiwan and China. Remembering what her minister of defense had said a few months back about the Americans looking at replacing the People's Republic of China with Taiwan's democratically elected government still sent shivers up her spine—a united China, after nearly 70 years of division, would be incredible.

One of her aides poked his head into the room. "President Gates' security just arrived. He should be here momentarily," he said. Several of the presidential Secret

Service agents advanced toward her office. They walked in and quickly fanned out, looking over the room for any obvious signs of danger. One of the agents lifted his hands toward his mouth and spoke softly into the mic on his sleeve, presumably giving the all clear.

A minute later, President Gates arrived with his Secretary of Defense and two other aides. Gates walked up to President Hung and extended his hand. "It's so good to see you, Madam President. I wish we'd had the chance to meet prior to this terrible war, and I truly wish there were more my nation could have done to help you," he said with a deep look of sadness.

He gestured for them to move toward the two couches arranged on the side of her office. They both took seats on the same couch, at opposite ends. Gates paused for a moment before speaking. "I wanted to meet with you in person, Madam President, because I want to discuss the war and postwar plan for Taiwan and China."

President Hung smiled, hoping what her minister of defense had said in the past was true. "Mr. President, thank you for meeting with me. I know you're a busy man and your nation has suffered great loss. Please extend my deepest sympathies to the people of California. We were aghast when we heard a nuclear weapon had destroyed such an iconic American city."

"*Is that a tear I see?*" she wondered as the President raised a finger to his right eye. She saw him take a deep breath and then slowly let it out, steeling himself.

"Thank you, President Hung, that means a lot," he responded. "It was a terrible day in American history. Nearly a million people were killed or injured on that fateful day, and many millions more have been displaced from their homes, living in refugee camps. It's going to take years to clean up the damage, but mark my words, we'll rebuild. That city will be better than ever." As he spoke, the conviction in his voice grew stronger and the determination showed in his eyes.

Shifting topics, the American president said, "I want to talk with you about the end state of this war. It has become clear that the current Chinese regime cannot be allowed to stay in place. This new version of techno-communism that is now blanketing social media and the internet isn't just a threat to America, but to Western civilization. We cannot allow autocratic regimes like this to rule the world using twisted technology against its own citizens and those it hopes to subjugate. This horrible Big Brother lifestyle deprives people of free will and self-determination, monitoring every action through the use of network-connected devices. Their predictive artificial intelligence is used indiscriminately to determine who may pose a danger to the regime, and it is a threat to the very freedoms that are a part of our national identities. We cannot sit idly by and let this take root and spread across the globe. It needs to be nipped in the bud now."

President Hung nodded in agreement. "The new Russian and Chinese propaganda campaign on social media is troubling, to say the least," she replied.

The premise that the Chinese form of techno-communism would bring world peace and harmony was appealing to a lot of people, particularly the idealistic youth. The Chinese insisted that using these technological monitoring systems could end world hunger, provide universal education, and end wars by preventing them from even starting. The theory was beginning to take root in many countries around the world. Russian and Chinese propagandists were masterfully portraying the West as not just capitalism run amok, but a warmongering government ideology that preyed on the poor and underdeveloped nations of the world. Their ability to play the social and economic classes of the West against themselves was having the desired effect of splintering many of the Western nations' populations against their government.

Leaning in, President Hung asked, "May I call you Patrick?"

"Yes, of course," Gates replied. "So long as I can call you Hui-ju," he said with a smile.

"I could not agree with you more about the dangers of this new propaganda campaign. It is a great danger that the world must unite and stand against. If the world falls to the Russian-Chinese alliance, it may never recover. People need to be free to choose what they want to believe and think. If a government takes that away from them, then we become nothing more than mindless bots living a life of little value and creativity. So, what is America's plan to make sure this does not happen?" she asked. She was definitely trying to angle the conversation to bring the topic around to the unification of China.

Pat smiled. He saw what Hui-ju was trying to do. "Right to the point with you. I like that—a leader who knows what they want and moves decisively for it. Our goal in Asia isn't just to defeat the People's Republic of China, but to remove the communist regime altogether. We're going to rebalance Asia and turn it back toward democracy. We want to ensure that communist China doesn't have the ability to threaten world security again. Our goal is to replace President Xi with you, Madam President. We want to unify China under your leadership."

She smiled. Now it wasn't just a rumor.

He continued, "Now, that isn't going to be an easy or quick goal to attain, and it's going to cost the lives of many of my countrymen. When the PRC is defeated, we, the Allies, are going to divide China into governing sectors, just as the Allies did with Germany at the end of World War II. Your government will administer Beijing for several years while you get a government in place and prepare to take control of the country. The Allies will keep an occupation force that will work in conjunction with your government to ensure stability and security while your government begins to take root. Our goal is for you to hold elections sometime within the first five years of Chinese unification."

"Our forces will continue to stay in place following that election to help ensure a peaceful transition and make sure any potential communist agitators aren't able to interfere with the transition or attempt to seize power. My goal is to return full control of China to the duly elected government by the end of ten years. We'll keep a much smaller advisory group and peacekeepers for additional ten years as needed to support the government, much like the

Allies did in West Germany and Japan. Are these terms acceptable, Hui-ju?" asked Gates.

President Hung sat back on the couch, trying to temper her response so as not to appear overly joyful. While she didn't like the idea of China being broken down into administrative zones by the Allies, she also recognized the need for it. Getting to the point that her government had the full support and backing of the people would take time.

"I can work with those terms, Patrick," she responded. "I believe this is going to be the beginning of a great new friendship and relationship between our countries."

"Excellent. What I'm going to need your help with is to work with members of my embassy staff from Beijing to begin crafting social media posts, policy positions and papers advocating for unification of China, but under your leadership. Our diplomats will work with you to help foster support among the Allied nations and garner acceptance for you as the rightful ruler of China," Gates said. He signaled with his hands for the minister and secretary of defense to join the conversation.

Many additional details and coordination needed to be worked out, and they were very limited on time. Gates would be flying back to the US once he finished his next meeting with the leaders of Japan and South Korea. Both nations had been taking a terrible beating since the start of the war; however, they had also successfully mobilized their populations to support the war effort to defeat China.

Battle of Kaliningrad

Mons, Belgium
SHAPE Headquarters

Spring had nearly arrived in Belgium as the winter snows finally disappeared, revealing brown grass that patiently awaited the new season's rain and sunshine. Looking at up at the midday sun, General James Cotton, the Global Defense Force Commander Europe, enjoyed the warmth of its rays after spending the last week deep underground in one planning meeting after another.

"*I need to get outside more often. I can't stay cooped up in that bunker all the time,*" General Cotton thought as he walked around the command center perimeter. He managed to ignore his private security detail, who was never far away.

While the war in Asia had been raging for nearly four months, the war in Europe was ongoing, albeit at a slower pace than in Asia. The Russians had largely pushed the Allies out of Estonia and Latvia but had been unable to remove them from Lithuania and relieve their beleaguered garrison in Kaliningrad. Cotton's subordinate commanders had urged him to capture the Russian enclave in Kaliningrad, but he had resisted the urge up to this point since the small territory held very little strategic value or relevancy once it had been neutralized.

With the Baltic Sea now cleared of Russian naval forces, including the submarines they had positioned there, the Allies were now making heavier use of the Allied Baltic ports. This greatly reduced the distance needed to travel to supply the front lines. In less than four months, the Allies would launch a massive invasion of Russia, and the shorter they could make their supply lines, the easier it would be to keep the grand army on the move. Hence, Cotton was now planning to invade Kaliningrad.

General Cotton turned away from the warmth of the midday sun and began his trek back down into the bowels of the underground complex that made up his command center, toward the high-tech wizardry that felt more like a dungeon with each passing month. As he walked toward the elevator, a guard placed his hand in front of the door sensor to hold it open for him. He stepped into the elevator with one of his aides, closing his eyes for a moment and bracing himself for the controlled chaos he was about to walk into.

"General Cotton!" a British colonel shouted at him the moment the elevator door opened. It was almost as if he had perched nearby, waiting for Cotton to return so he could be the first to bombard him with a question or update.

Cotton took a deep breath, then patiently responded, "What have you got for me?"

"Sir, we just received a report from the port in Hamburg. One of the newly arrived freighters from the Atlantic convoys had just docked at the pier to offload munitions when a mine or some other explosive detonated. That explosion set off a chain of secondary explosions, which destroyed the heavy cranes at the pier in addition to the ship. The shell of the ship's charred remains has settled next to the pier, which is going to prevent any further ships from docking," he explained frantically.

The general sighed deeply. This was just the latest act of sabotage that the Russians had been able to carry out since the start of the war. "How long until they can remove the ship and get the pier operational again?" he asked.

The colonel's face turned red. "I'll have to get back to you with that information, Sir," he responded, rushing off to find out the answer.

General Cotton walked over to the big board and looked at the positions of the various units scattered across the front lines. The Russians had moved nearly 300,000 soldiers to the front. Most of these were reservists and newly conscripted soldiers, who were largely making do with antiquated T-72s and T-62 tanks.

Cotton grunted. *"Even an old tank can be dangerous,"* he thought.

"What's the status of General Ripton's Fifth Corps? Are his units set in their positions and ready to start the attack after the preparatory artillery strike is completed?" he asked, speaking broadly to anyone who might overhear him.

A French colonel, part of the operations staff, turned to respond to the question. "Yes, Sir. The orders were received by them earlier, and now they are waiting on the execution order. The offensive should be starting momentarily."

Cotton turned his attention to several of the wall monitors at the front of the room to observe the battle. Kaliningrad was completely surrounded, which meant that the dozen Global Hawk surveillance drones loitering around the enclave would be able to provide real time images of the entire scene.

As he watched the screens, the battle officially began. A massive artillery barrage lit up most of the known enemy positions. As each round impacted on its target, General Cotton heard the fire support officers calling for adjustments. While the artillery was going to work, a few dozen Reaper drones had moved into the battlespace; they used their precision-guided missiles to hit some of the trickier targets inside the high-density residential areas, minimizing the likelihood of civilian casualties. Fortunately, most of the civilians had left the city once the Allies had encircled them and cut off any source of supplies.

An hour into the aerial and artillery bombardment, Cotton signaled for them to send the ground forces in. It was still amazing to him that he could watch a skirmish take place in real-time while sitting in a bunker several hundred kilometers away.

A second after issuing the order for the ground forces to start their attack, the drone feeds suddenly cut out, leaving everyone to stare blankly at the now-black screens. While they were all still in a state of shock, the rest of the computer screens in the command center cut out, displaying the proverbial "blue screen of death." Text began to scroll across the screens, displaying the message, "Death is coming for you! Surrender while you can!"

Cotton yelled to his communications and cyber-warfare groups, "Find out what just happened to our systems, and get them back online *now*!"

****

Polish-Russian Border

Command Sergeant Major Luke Childers had been released from the Army hospital at Landstuhl just prior to New Year's. After taking a couple of weeks of leave to travel home and see friends and family, he was ready to get back to the job of training soldiers to defeat the Russians and bring this war to a close.

While at home, Luke had toured the damage to Air Force Plant 4, which was located just east of downtown Fort Worth, Texas. The Lockheed, Pratt and Whitney Engine facility there had been heavily damaged by a Russian Spetsnaz team, two weeks prior to him coming home. It was all everyone was talking about, and it was really no surprise. A massive gunfight had taken place there when Russian Special Forces had encountered a ragtag group of Texans. A small group had been celebrating the retirement of a colleague when the attack had started. Within a minute of hearing the first explosions off in the distance, a couple of the men, who had previously served in Iraq, recognized the noise as mortars landing nearby. Many of those at the retirement party and BBQ also had rifles on the gun racks in their trucks and proceeded to organize a small group to go put a stop to the attack. While many of the civilians in the spoiling attack had been killed, their heroics had prevented the Spetsnaz from continuing to bomb the facility. Three

Russians had been killed in the attack, two more had been captured, and six had escaped to live and fight another day.

When Childers had seen the damage to the plant that was so close to his family's home, it had angered him immensely. He had joined the military to protect his country, to avenge those who had been killed on September 11, 2001. Now, fellow countrymen from his own hometown had been killed by foreign invaders. After an exceptionally sobering day, he'd met up with a few of his friends at their favorite watering hole and proceeded to get very drunk and do his best to forget about the horrors he had seen and done in the name of defending his country.

A few days after the attack, when Childers had reported to duty, he had been assigned to the squadron headquarters as the new command sergeant major. In peacetime, his primary duties would have been to advise the senior command officers about personnel issues and facilitate communication with the troop first sergeants. As it was, his new job was to get the squadron trained and ready for combat. Following their escape from Kiev, the entire regiment had been sent to Germany to regroup and reorganize, which turned out to be very necessary as their group doubled in size, mostly with raw recruits fresh from basic training, and they needed all hands on deck to get them ready.

The next two months were spent drilling the young soldiers in how to fight in an urban environment and in a static defense. One strategy Childers implemented within each of the troops was two half-day lectures that went over after-action reviews of previous battles the squadron had taken part in up to that point. He wanted the younger soldiers to listen to what had happened during the battles with the Russians and to ask questions, to learn what had gone right, what had gone wrong, and where they had just gotten lucky. If they could save the lives of his new soldiers, then passing that knowledge on to them was worth taking the training time to do so.

After months of waiting, Childers finally received the news he had been waiting to hear. Lieutenant Colonel Alex Schoolman walked up to him as he was scanning the perimeter with his binoculars and got his attention. "Sergeant Major, we just received word from headquarters. The attack is a go," he announced. He signaled for one of his staff officers to pass the information on to the rest of the squadron.

"'*Bout time we get this war back on again*," Luke thought. He nodded in acknowledgment to his boss, but then quickly resumed his task of looking across the border with his binoculars.

As the artillery bombardment lifted, the Allied forces moved across the border toward their various objectives. Dozens of the squadron's armored vehicles sprinted forward, following the UK's 7th Armoured Brigade and their Challenger 2 tanks. The Stryker command vehicle from which Childers was observing the battle suddenly lurched forward, and they joined the column of advancing British vehicles. Only ten minutes after crossing the border, the British tanks had already encountered the remnants of the Russian units who had been left to defend the small territory.

Boom! Bang! Ratatat! The chattering of machine guns and explosions grew increasingly louder as Childer's vehicle drove toward the action. Suddenly, a loud explosion shoved their Stryker violently to one side, jostling everyone inside. "What the hell was that?" shouted Childers.

The gunner manning the automated 20mm autocannon replied, "That lead British tank just blew up. It looked like a missile strike from the sky."

Everyone craned their heads back and looked up at the sky above them. "*Could a Russian fighter or helicopter have gotten through our air cover?*" Childers wondered.

A moment later, the air was pierced with another loud explosion. The colonel yelled to his driver, "Stop the vehicle!"

Colonel Schoolman quickly grabbed his radio and yelled to the rest of the squadron, "All stop!"

He turned to Childers and barked, "We have to figure out what's going on!"

Childers stood up and scanned the skies for the threat. At that moment, another missile streaked down and hit a third British tank, blowing the turret clean off.

"There! I see it. What the—? It's one of *our* Reaper drones that's firing on us!" Childers shouted, now angry that whoever was controlling that drone had just blown up multiple Allied tanks.

A moment later, the lieutenant who was in charge of the squadron's communications platoon spoke up. "Colonel, I just received a report from regiment. They said they were informed the Russians have apparently taken control of some of our Reaper drones and are using them against us."

The colonel's nose and eyebrows wrinkled up in disgust. "What do they want us to do about it?" he yelled.

A second later, the lieutenant replied, "They said to keep the attack going. The Air Force is working on the problem."

In the few seconds that it took the frazzled lieutenant to relay that information, one of the Reaper drones exploded in spectacular fashion as one of their fighters swooped in and blew it out of the sky.

"It does look like the Air Force is on top of it, Sir," Childers said, pointing to the small smoke cloud in the sky where the drone had just been.

"Order all units to continue the attack. Those blasted hackers—they just cost us several tanks!" The colonel was clearly fired up. His face was red with anger, and a vein on the side of his forehead was visibly pulsating.

"*I'm glad he's on my side,*" thought Childers.

When they got closer to the burned-out wrecks of the Challenger tanks, they suddenly came into contact with some sporadic small-arms fire. The soldier manning the automated turret swiveled the gun in the direction of the incoming bullets and spotted several Russian soldiers manning a heavy machine gun in a burned-out building, shooting at a group of British soldiers who were advancing toward their structure.

Childers leaned down to the soldier. "See if you can't give those guys some help and take that gun position out," he gently suggested.

The young soldier looked up at the sergeant major and just nodded. This was the first time the kid was going to use the gun in battle, and he looked nervous. Allowing his training to take over, the soldier sighted in on the enemy position and depressed the firing button. A short burst from his 20mm cannon slammed into the building. The first burst was a bit high and off target. The young soldier recentered and tried again, this time scoring a direct hit, silencing the gun position.

"Good job, soldier," said Childers. "Do it just like that every time. Make sure your fields of fire are clear and engage the enemy. You may have just saved a few soldiers' lives by taking that gun position out, so it's important that you don't hesitate in the future when you see a threat like that. OK?" He wanted to make sure the young soldier knew he wasn't in training any more—he couldn't second-guess things.

Smiling and obviously feeling a lot more confident, the young soldier answered, "Yes, Sergeant Major. I understand. I'll do better next time."

Forty minutes after crossing the border, the squadron had now moved to the outskirts of Chernyakhovsk. There were two airfields in the vicinity that they had been charged with securing. One of them had been a Russian strategic nuclear base prior to the war, and there was still some question as to whether or not the Russians still had nuclear weapons at the facility.

While they maneuvered toward the air base, they started to hear the distinctive popping of a shoot-out in a nearby neighborhood. Schoolman pointed to the area and asked, "What unit is over there?"

The young communications lieutenant consulted his map and then responded, "That's 1st BN, Royal Irish Regiment, Sir."

"They're kicking the tar out of those Russians over there," the colonel said with a wry grin on his face.

As they continued approaching the air base, a series of heavy machine guns opened fire on the troop nearest the perimeter. Putting his binoculars to his face, the colonel could see several of his Stryker vehicles engaging the enemy positions. The back hatches had dropped, and the infantry was now disgorging from their armored chariots as they advanced on foot toward the enemy.

The infantrymen steadily advanced with fire support from the Strykers, silencing one gun position after another. Suddenly, a missile streaked out of the tree line from just inside the perimeter. At first, it was just the one missile, but seconds later, six more joined the fray. Three of the missiles were destroyed by the vehicles' antimissile systems, causing them to swerve or veer off course at the last minute. Unfortunately for the Americans, the other missiles hit their marks, destroying four of the Strykers.

"Damn Kornets. See if we can get some mortar fire to suppress those missile teams in the tree line," barked the colonel, angry that a dozen of his troopers had just been killed.

The fight for the airport lasted nearly three hours. The squadron had to clear each building and the area around the airfield without the use of air strikes or heavy artillery. Because the Allies didn't know if there were still nuclear weapons stored at the facility, they were barred from destroying any buildings or munition bunkers, no matter how stout a defense the enemy was putting up in those places.

"Colonel, Nemesis Troop is requesting your presence at one of the bunkers they just secured," one of the staff officers said, his voice barely audible over the sound of rifle and machine-gun fire that was still raging around other parts of the city.

"Let's go, Sergeant Major," Schoolman responded. He grabbed his own rifle and trudged off in the direction of his troop commander. Childers followed close behind.

Several additional soldiers headed out with the colonel and the sergeant major to see what they had stumbled upon. As they approached the bunker, they spotted a number of dead enemy soldiers, along with the remains of a few of their own troops. Not far from the bunker, a small cluster of wounded soldiers was being treated by a couple of the medics while they waited on a medevac helicopter to come in and take them back to a higher-level trauma center.

They walked up to the gaggle of soldiers. "Captain Taylor, what do you have for us?" asked Colonel Schoolman.

"Colonel, Sergeant Major, I think we may have found some nuclear weapons," he said, to the shock and concern of the soldiers who had just walked up to the bunker.

Sergeant Major Childers immediately barked at the soldiers standing around. "Set up a wider perimeter around the bunker!" he yelled. "You, over there, start clearing some of the overgrowth around the entrance."

They rushed off to follow his orders. Sure enough, as they cleared brush along the outer wall of the bunker, they found a yellow metal placard with the universal pinwheel symbol that indicated nuclear material.

"Send a message back to regiment," Schoolman directed. "Tell them what we found, and ask them to send an explosive ordnance specialist over here to inspect them. I want to make sure these infernal things are secured and not going to go off on us."

Every moment that passed felt like eternity as they waited for EOD to arrive. Childers started daydreaming, thinking about what Jack Bauer would do in an episode of *24*, and how he would grab his flashlight from his vest and boldly announce, "Sir, I'm going to take a peek at them and make sure none of them are rigged to detonate."

In his thoughts, all of the younger soldiers stepped aside for him, and before the colonel could object, he'd storm his way in there. He'd probably have some eager young gun follow him, and he'd ask him to hold his flashlight. He imagined searching for visible wires, LED timers, or anything that might indicate these warheads had been rigged to detonate. Of course, he'd have to open them up in some glorious show of heroism, just to be sure.

In reality, they just continued waiting until it felt like he would fall asleep. In a very anti-climactic ending, the EOD specialist finally emerged from the warehouse and announced, "Your families won't be cashing in those life insurance policies just yet."

Suddenly, his friend, Captain Jack Taylor, walked up and greeted him. "How's it going, Sergeant Major?"

Childers smiled. "It looks like we've just been given a new lease on life," he answered.

Taylor came over, and then, before anyone could object, he poked his head into the warehouse. He must have known he was breaking all kinds of protocol, because he snapped himself back outside before there was a chance to complain. "I just had to see them," he mumbled. "They really do look like in the movies…it's hard to believe that such a small device can wipe out an entire city."

Schoolman must have overheard Taylor talking. He walked over. "It was a device a little larger than this that wiped out San Francisco. My wife, my daughter, and my twin boys were visiting my parents in Alameda, near Oakland," he said quietly, wiping a tear away.

The colonel had been carrying a heavy burden of guilt for some time now. When the war in Europe had started, he had sent his wife and kids to stay with his parents in California; he'd figured they'd be safe there, far away from the fighting. As things heated up in North Korea, he decided it might be better for them to go stay with his brother in Montana, but he was unable to make a call back home, and less than 24 hours later, his wife, children and parents were all dead, part of the hundreds of thousands who had been vaporized when the bomb had gone off over the port of Oakland.

Taylor didn't know what to say. The awkward silence hung in the air. Finally, Schoolman cleared his throat and addressed Childers. "I want the squadron to bivouac here for the night while we wait for new orders," he said.

"Yes, Sir," Childers answered.

They went around the corner to start issuing the new orders and saw that a small group of Russian prisoners had been collected and were being questioned by a couple of the intelligence members of Schoolman's staff. Lieutenant Colonel Schoolman walked over. "Have you gotten anything useful from them?" he asked.

Chief Warrant Officer 3 Fillips just shook his head. "Nothing yet, Sir. From what I can gather, none of them were even aware that there were nuclear weapons still being stored here. Then again, my Russian is a bit rusty. Regiment said they're sending a couple of Russian translators and an interrogation team over here ASAP."

"I speak Russian pretty well. Let me give it a try," Schoolman responded. He walked toward the prisoners, with the warrant officer quickly following him.

Childers sensed something wrong in the way his boss said he wanted to "try" and talk to the Russians, so he followed him to the group of prisoners. He didn't know Schoolman very well, but he could tell that he was obviously emotionally distraught over the loss of his family.

When the colonel approached the group of prisoners, he identified the two officers among the gaggle of prisoners and proceeded to single them out. He grabbed what appeared to be a young private to join the group and lined the three of them up.

Luke didn't like the look of this and moved toward Schoolman, whispering softly, "Don't do anything you'll regret, Sir. It isn't worth it."

Colonel Schoolman looked angrily at him. "Enough, Sergeant Major!" he yelled. Then he turned back to face the prisoners.

"Are there other bunkers with nuclear weapons?" he asked them in Russian. His hand was fiddling with the SIG Sauer in his leg holster as he grilled them.

The prisoners shook their heads, acting surprised.

He pointed to the bunker with the warheads, where several of his soldiers were standing guard. "Are any of the nuclear weapons in that bunker boobytrapped or rigged to explode?" he shouted.

Now the prisoners looked concerned, but again they said they had been unaware that nuclear weapons were still being stored here. One of the officers, the oldest looking of the two, said in rapid-fire Russian that they had been told all the nuclear warheads had been moved back to the Motherland prior to the war.

Schoolman, now confident that he had gotten a straight answer from the two Russian officers, turned and headed back toward the tactical command center his staff had now set up. As he walked, his signaled for Childers to come closer.

"What did you mean, 'it isn't worth it'? Did you believe I was going to shoot those prisoners?" he asked, surprised that his sergeant major would think that lowly of him.

Childers stopped walking for a minute, forcing the colonel to stop as well. He wanted to have this conversation out of earshot of any of the other soldiers. "Sir, when we were in the bunker, and you told us about your family, I honestly didn't know they had died in Oakland. You had never spoken of them before. When you said you wanted to talk to the prisoners, I wasn't totally sure where your head was in that moment."

Childers paused for a second. "When I was a young Ranger on my second combat deployment, we suffered a terrible loss in the Korengal Valley of Afghanistan. Our captain and platoon sergeant were killed, and we captured a couple of prisoners following an extended battled with the Taliban. One of the Taliban prisoners had been wounded, and our lieutenant at the time was determined to get some useful information out of him before we provided him treatment or brought him back to headquarters. They dragged the prisoner away from the rest of us to question him away from prying eyes. We heard a lot of screaming going on and a lot of yelling. Eventually, we heard a single gunshot, and our lieutenant, and two other soldiers appeared from where they had been questioning the prisoner. They said the prisoner gave up the location of where other fighters were hiding, so we moved out to engage them. The next thing I knew, we were in another gun battle; eventually, we killed a few dozen more Taliban fighters later that day."

The colonel could see his sergeant major was getting emotional about the story and placed his hand on his shoulder. "It's OK, Luke. You can tell me what happened next. I need to know."

Looking up, he nodded. "When we got back to base, one of the sergeants lodged a complaint against the lieutenant. The next day, our entire company was taken off rotation, and we were all interviewed about the situation. I was the youngest and newest sergeant in the company, so I wasn't held responsible for not trying to stop it. But several of the sergeants first class were. The lieutenant was charged with conduct unbecoming an officer and kicked out of the Army. The two other sergeants and one other soldier that was with him were drummed out too. Sometimes, when I sleep or just have a moment to myself…I can still hear that man screaming. I couldn't understand anything he was saying, but I could tell he was in terrible pain."

Childers then looked at Schoolman. "When I heard you tell us about your family, I could see that same rage in your eyes I saw in that lieutenant, and when you said you wanted to talk to the prisoners and had your hand on your sidearm…I just wanted to make sure you didn't do something you would regret. You're a good commander, and we need more like you," Childers finished.

"That could have been me. It probably was going to me…" Colonel Schoolman realized.

"Thank you, Sergeant Major, for sharing that. I can't imagine how hard that has been for you to carry that burden. I wish your lieutenant hadn't failed you guys like that and had been a better leader. We're all humans, and we make mistakes. You saw me losing control, and you interceded in a way that prevented me from doing something I'd regret, and you did it in a manner that no one else saw or noticed. I owe you for that. You're going to make a great sergeant major," Schoolman said. He extended his hand, and the two of them shook hands.

They continued on toward the command center. When they arrived, they found the regiment commander had arrived, along with a few weapons experts. They talked for a few minutes and showed them the nuclear weapons. Everyone breathed a sigh of relief when they learned that none of the weapons had been rigged to detonate and were, in fact, in safe storage and could be transported without fear of something going wrong.

One of the staff officers got the attention of his regimental commander. "What in the world happened with our drones attacking us, Sir?" he asked.

Colonel Hastings answered the question on everyone's minds. "What a cluster mess that was. I was told a Russian hacker group, probably their intelligence directorate, had gained access to our C4ISR network and essentially turned everything off. The Division CG said they lost contact with GDF HQ, and then the Reaper drones in the area that were supposed to help provide us air support were taken over by the hackers who turned the weapons on us. Luckily, the Air Force had some fighters in the area that were able to locate and destroy the drones before they could fire any more of their missiles."

Lieutenant Colonel Schoolman asked, "Are comms back up and running with headquarters, or is our division essentially operating on our own?"

"From what I've been told, the problem was largely isolated to GDF HQ and US Army Europe headquarters staff. We lost our surveillance and digital links, but it hasn't interrupted our HF or UHF radios, so we've switched over to our backup systems," Major Montanya, the regiment's communications officer, replied loud enough for everyone to hear. "Don't ask me when they'll have everything sorted out—I have no idea, but I'll make sure to pass along any additional information we learn," he added.

The Russians had been wreaking havoc on the Allies' communication and computer systems with their army of hackers. While the US forces had largely closed off a lot of the vulnerabilities discovered during the outbreak of the war, several of the Allied nations were still struggling to keep up.

One of the captains piped up. "Well, if this was a dress rehearsal for the summer offensive, I'd have to give us a C. Our surveillance and communications were all sorts of screwed up," he said.

Colonel Hastings looked at his officers and senior NCOs, then added, "Kaliningrad was an easy objective to take, but it still cost us nearly three dozen soldiers killed and four times that number wounded. That's unacceptable. We have a couple of more months before the summer offensive starts. I want to figure out what went right, what we screwed up, and what we should have been better at forecasting. Make sure those lessons are gone over with everyone. Be sure your junior officers and NCOs correct those issues, and let's hope we're able to incur fewer casualties when the big show finally does begin," he concluded.

Pacific Invasion

Angeles, Philippines
Clark International Airport

It was nearly dawn. There were only a few clouds in the sky as the first wave of Xian Y-20 transport aircraft steadily moved closer to the drop zone. The predawn light was slowly increasing, revealing the image of twenty transport planes approaching Clark International Airport, formerly Clark US Air Force Base. The sky was about to be flooded with thousands of paratroopers; the next step in the Chinese plan to expand their sphere of control in the Pacific was now fully underway. Once they had captured this critical airport, they would have Chinese soldiers positioned less than one hundred kilometers from the Philippine capital of Manila.

As Captain Ma Qiliang sat in the dimly lit bay of the plane, he could feel the pitch in the aircraft's engines change as they made one final turn, lining themselves up for the big drop.

The jumpmaster called out, "Everyone stand up! It's almost time to jump."

The paratroopers dutifully listened and went through their prejump checks of each other's equipment. A few minutes later, the doors on the side of the aircraft opened. Cool air quickly swirled around the cargo bay, adding to the excitement and thrill of yet another combat jump for this battle-hardened battalion.

Less than a minute after that, the jump light turned from red to green, and the men shuffled out the door for what was now their fourth combat jump since the start of the war. Ma surged forward with the men around him. After hours and hours of being cooped up in the plane with all their equipment tightly packed on their bodies, he was eager to jump and get back on the ground.

As Captain Ma Qiliang leaped from the aircraft, he marveled at the beauty of the morning sun, which had finally crept above the horizon. The air buffeted his face as he flew steadily toward the ground. Seconds later, he felt the sudden jerk as his chute fully opened, and he began a much more leisurely descent to the earth below. Looking around him, Ma could see that all the men in his transport had exited safely and were likewise dangling below their parachutes, traveling toward the airport below.

Captain Ma smiled. Everything was going according to plan. An hour before his paratroopers had entered

Philippine airspace, the PLA Air Force and Navy launched a surprise attack, hitting many of the country's air and naval bases in preparation for the invasion. While those assaults were underway, the three Chinese carriers operating in the South China Sea had launched their own fighters, to clear the skies of potential threats to the airborne forces. Ma's crew had anxiously listened for updates while waiting to jump, and so far, everything had gone off without a hitch. Once his men had secured the airports, hundreds of Chinese civilian airliners would ferry tens of thousands of PLA soldiers to the Philippines. Captain Ma felt a surge of pride in being a part of this mission.

As the runway got closer, Ma could see five commercial airliners docked at the terminal. Otherwise, the airport appeared quiet. Either there were no flights this early in the day, or they had been grounded once the airport had been made aware of the Chinese invasion. Once Captain Ma reached the ground, he rushed to retrieve his drop bag. He and his fellow soldiers moved to assemble their equipment, and then they were ready to capture their assigned targets.

Ma's unit had been charged with securing the runways and establishing a one-kilometer perimeter on the east side of the airport. He had been told in no uncertain terms that his group had to complete their mission within three hours, because then the civilian airliners would start arriving with all of the PLA troops. They needed to get as many soldiers in place in the Philippines as possible, before the Allies found a way to intervene and interrupt their plans.

Two hours went by uneventfully. Captain Ma's company hadn't met any real resistance. There had been some initial shooting near the terminal, but that had ended just as quickly as it started. Touring his unit's positions had been a challenge on foot, since his soldiers were spread across a very long perimeter. However, from what he had seen up to that point, he was impressed with how quickly they had set up the fighting positions.

"Good, they're preparing for the worst," he thought. He felt that they were prepared to repel any potential attack against the airport.

As Ma was halfway finished with his tour, he heard a truck heading toward him. As it approached, he saw one of his sergeants behind the steering wheel.

"Captain Ma!" the soldier shouted out to him. "I saw this truck had the keys still in it, so I grabbed it. I figured you could use it to check the perimeter more easily."

Ma grinned. *"Now that's a sergeant who is going to go far,"* he thought.

"Excellent idea," Captain Ma answered. "Good thinking, sergeant. Why don't you drive us to the next position in our new vehicle?" He climbed in, and the two of them drove on down the perimeter.

****

A few hours later, Major General Hu, the commander of the PLA's 43rd Airborne Corps, scanned the horizon above Clark International Airport with his binoculars. A smile spread across his face as he spotted a long line of Shaanxi Y-9 heavy-lift transports on final approach.

"Excellent. My light-armored vehicles and tanks are finally arriving," he thought.

He turned to his deputy, Colonel Lei. "When our armored vehicles get offloaded, I want them moved to the perimeter at once," he ordered. "Once those scout jeeps are ready, send them out to the various positions we'd discussed earlier. I want some eyes and ears out on the roads as far out a possible. No surprises, gentlemen. Get it done!"

Colonel Lei and the others within earshot responded, "Yes, Sir!" and rushed off to fulfill their orders.

Steadily, the line of transports landed and then quickly taxied to the parking apron, where they offloaded their vehicles and added supplies. As the transports were emptied of their cargo and refueled, they lined back up on the taxiway and got back into the air, just as quickly as they could. Now that the airport had been captured, the gravy train of supply planes was on its way.

Major General Hu was pleased with the overall progress of this mission so far. Once he had been read on to Operation Red Storm last year, he had felt an intense burden transferred onto his shoulders—he had to lead and train his corps to be on par with the vaunted American XVIII Airborne Corps. So far, the 43rd had been a successful branch of his legacy as they fulfilled their role as the lead element in the annexation of Mongolia, and the invasions of Taiwan, Vietnam, and now the Philippines.

In preparing for these operations, Hu knew a critical ingredient to their success would be increasing their heavy-lift capability. The introduction of the Y-20 was a huge step in the right direction. It pained him that he had only had twenty-four of them at the start of the war. Fortunately, they hadn't lost any in combat up to this point. To his amazement, the manufacturers were now producing an astounding twenty new planes a month, which had already bolstered his starting force to sixty of the planned four hundred aircraft.

Prior to this mission, General Hu had positioned a multitude of aircraft and supplies on Hainan Island, which was a four-hour-and-ten-minute flight away for his cargo aircraft. He calculated that this air-supply bridge would allow roughly two full loads of cargo and troops a day. In addition to the troops the aircraft would be bringing in, they would bring in a vital haul of munitions, food, jeeps, antitank weapons, light-armored tanks and infantry fighting vehicles.

Two hours went by, and General Hu happily watched as aircraft after aircraft brought in reinforcements. Eventually, one of Hu's aides walked up to him. "General, Colonel Tian reports his unit is ready to move. Shall I tell him to proceed?" he asked, holding the radio handset to his chest.

General Hu turned to the young officer. "Have we heard from the aviation squadron yet?" he asked. "Are the helicopters ready to support them?"

The aide shook his head. "Not yet, General. They said it would take another hour to get the helicopters up and running."

Hu grunted. "Then tell Colonel Tian he may proceed to Manila in an hour, when we have the helicopters ready to support him," he replied. "In the meantime, I want those helicopters ready to fly at once. No more delays!" he demanded.

He moved to look at a map in the center of the room, which was being constantly updated by his staff as they had updates on the movements of the Philippine forces.

Seeing that a key piece of data was missing, Hu asked, "How many drones do we have operational over our area of responsibility?"

A major, who was in the middle of making the updates on the map, responded, "Five right now. We have two more that will get airborne in the next hour."

General Hu nodded. "What is the status of Fort Magsaysay airfield?"

"We still don't have eyes on the base yet," replied one of the majors nearby. "We've dispatched some scout units, so it'll be a few more hours before we know something." As soon as he answered the question, the major immediately went back to getting their maps updated with friendly and enemy units.

Fort Magsaysay, also called Fort Mag, was home to the Philippine 7th Infantry Division, along with their military training center, and they were the one immediate threat that could shut down General Hu's airport operations. While the PLA Air Force and Navy made sure a few cruise missiles paid the base a visit, General Hu was still concerned that if left alone, they'd rally their forces and threaten to shut down his operations before he could get them fully up and running.

Hu flagged down his deputy. "Colonel Lei, I want Colonel Luan's brigade to head for Fort Mag once they're ready," he ordered. "Have them bring a battalion from the 129th Artillery Regiment to provide them with fire support."

Colonel Lei looked at a clipboard, which had the arrival times of the various units and transports that were being ferried in from the mainland. He wanted to see if the units his boss had requested had already arrived. "It'll be at least three more hours before that element will be ready, Sir," he explained. "Several of the transports carrying the artillery regiments guns are just now landing."

"That's fine," General Hu responded. "Just make sure Colonel Luan knows he's to head to Fort Mag when his artillery support is ready."

The waves of transports and civilian airliners continued to land in a dizzying frenzy. *"This is going to be a long day,"* thought the general.

****

Natuna Island, Indonesia
Natuna Airport

Major Achmad Basry was leery about the Chinese intentions with his country. While he had no say in what his government agreed to, the prospect of joining the Chinese in their war against the Americans was not sitting well with him. When he had been told his engineering battalion was moving to the Island of Natuna, Basry became even more concerned. He really had no idea what was going on.

The Island of Natuna was a large island that sat in the South China Sea, and it essentially shielded the entrance to the Malacca Straits and the critical port of Singapore from the rest of the South China Sea. If the Americans or Australians were going to travel into the South China Sea, then they were going to have to get past this island to do it. After Major Basry's battalion finished building up the island with surface-to-air missile sites and anti-ship missile launchers, it would be nearly impossible for the Americans to attack Kalimantan or Sumantra without first capturing this island.

It took nearly a week for most of their heavy equipment to arrive. Once it did, they were ordered to get the island's runway expanded and ready to receive fighter planes. Then they were supposed to build launch points for anti-ship missiles throughout the island. Basry's unit began the process of building aircraft revetments along the taxi strip, along with several new bunkers, which would be used for storing munitions.

Then one morning, just four days after starting construction, a Chinese cargo plane had landed at the airport. Seeing that he had been given no heads-up about their arrival, only Major Basry and a couple of his soldiers met them when the plane landed. Nearly two dozen Chinese military soldiers exited the aircraft. As soon as they had deplaned, the aircraft turned around and sped off down the runway, heading back to wherever it had come from.

A Chinese colonel came up to Basry. With barely any introduction at all, he said, "I'm now in command of the island. Other aircraft will arrive within the hour."

They talked less formally for a few moments; Basry learned that his new compatriot was named Colonel Chen. All of a sudden, Chen insisted that Major Basry show him what they had done up to that point. As the Chinese soldiers inspected the various positions they had constructed, Chen became visibly angry at the lack of progress they had made.

"When the rest of my troops arrive, we'll make use of your equipment and get this base operational at once. I'll need your forces to help my men identify various defensive positions on the island that will need to be fortified. We don't have a lot of time to turn this island into an impregnable fortress. Do you understand?" Colonel Chen barked.

Major Basry simply nodded, accepting his new position as a servant to the new Chinese overlords.

****

Hainan Island, China

President Xi observed the controlled chaos below him in the operations room. The planners and operations officers and sergeants scurried about, updating map displays on their computers, which in turn projected those changes on a master map that was being projected on a nine-foot-by-nine-foot monitor. They were twelve hours into the invasion of the Philippines, and frankly, he could not have been happier with how things were playing out. The heavy financial investments they had made into the PLA Airborne Forces were, once again, paying exceptional dividends.

The 43rd Corps had not only captured the old American Clark International Airport—they had decisively crushed the surrounding Philippine Army units that had tried to repel them. Looking at the map, he could see a steady stream of transports strung out from Hainan Island to Clark Airport, bringing more troops and equipment. Likewise, the seaborne invasion by the PLA naval infantry was going extraordinarily well. They had secured several large ports that were critical to the offloading of more tanks and other heavy equipment.

It was now going to be a race against time. Xi knew they had a limited window to capture and secure as much of the Philippines as possible before the American Navy was able to wreak havoc on their ability to supply their forces by sea.

Foreign Minister Wang Yi approached President Xi with a smile on his face. "Mr. President, I have good news to report," he said, moving closer to Xi so only he would hear him speak.

"I take it you've heard from our Asian brothers in Malaysia and Thailand?" asked the president.

"Yes. The Malaysian prime minister has reluctantly agreed to join the Eastern Alliance. I spoke with the PM, and he has said their military will be at our disposal. Although, he did emphasize their limited ability to operate outside of their national border," he replied.

During the Xi'an meeting, the group of world leaders who had now aligned themselves against the West had collectively agreed to call themselves the "Eastern Alliance." The People's Republic of China was still a communist nation, albeit with capitalist tentacles, but still communist at its core. The Russian and Chinese promulgation of techno-communism across social media was proving to be incredibly effective, and the name of their new alliance was getting around on social media. It was all really resonating.

Xi nodded and smiled at the good news. "And the Thais? Have they come around, or are we going to need to send troops across the border to hasten their decision-making process?"

"Troops will not be needed. The Thais have also reluctantly agreed to join the alliance. However, I have a serious problem that perhaps Chairman Zhang would be better suited to handle. While the Thais have agreed to join us, I fear their only reason for doing so is so that they can pass intelligence on to the Americans. As you are aware, the CIA has an extensive presence in Thailand."

Chairman Zhang, who had joined the conversation, nodded in agreement of the foreign minister's assessment of Thailand. "I concur. The Thai government is going to be a problem. With your permission, I'd like to move to replace the Thai leaders with people we can trust. I also believe we're going to need to conduct a purge of their senior military leaders. They've trained with the Americans for decades, and they're going to have loyalties to them. We need to make sure that bringing Thailand into the fold isn't going to create a security nightmare for us."

Thinking about what his two senior advisors had said, Xi wanted to caution them against going too hard on the Thais. "Gentlemen, I appreciate the concerns you've brought up, but please keep in mind that we want Thailand to be not just a military member in our alliance, but also an economic asset. Thailand has a burgeoning manufacturing base, and we need to leverage that as we expand our military production. If we turn the Thai people against us through heavy-handed tactics, we risk a public uprising. I want to remind you that we'll get more cooperation and support with honey than we will with vinegar. Try the soft approach first. If it fails, then we'll adjust. Is that understood?" Xi ordered, staring down Chairman Zhang to make sure his Head of State Security understood his role and position.

With the rapid-growing success of Operation Red Storm and the recent formation of the Eastern Alliance, Xi didn't want Chairman Zhang to think he was more important than he was. Everyone was replaceable, and since Zhang's protégé Wu had been captured and summarily killed by Islamic terrorists, he hadn't been himself. He was losing his edge, and that could cause a person to make mistakes.

Zhang bowed in deference. "Yes, Mr. President," he responded. "We'll go with the soft approach as you suggested."

Xi nodded, although he knew that underneath, Zhang was probably not happy with his suggestion being overruled.

The next couple of months would prove challenging as the members of the alliance worked on unifying their economies and military forces to defeat the West. The Americans had been hard at work building a global alliance to challenge them, and they were also mobilizing their entire economy for war. Once they were fully retooled, they would be hard to beat.

****

Dili, East Timor

Brigadier General Alan Morrison of the 1st Brigade in the Australian Army was not pleased with the progress of his forces in building up the island's defenses. The engineers had done a superb job in preparing the airport to receive the Royal Australian fighters that were now on the island, but they were falling behind in getting the other critical areas of the island fortified. With the formation of the Eastern

Alliance, it was now becoming imperative that Australia prime themselves for a possible invasion.

Sighing briefly, Brigadier General Morrison placed the thick sheaf of reports he had been reviewing on his desk. He looked up at Lieutenant Colonel Kilroy Newman from the 5th Battalion, Royal Australian Regiment or 5 RAR. The 5 RAR would handle the defense of Dili and the airport there, critical to maintaining control of East Timor.

"Colonel Newman," he began, "how are the defenses for the city coming along?"

Newman shifted in his chair as he swatted at a fly that had been buzzing around him. "They're forming up nicely, Sir," he replied. "We've identified the likely avenues of attack against the city, and the engineers have devised a series of fortifications to defeat them. My only concern is our ability to keep the Chinese Navy and Air Force from pummeling us from the air."

Morrison grunted. "I have the same concerns," he responded. "A large portion of our air-defense systems was deployed to support the Americans on the Korean Peninsula. I have been assured, however, that the twelve F/A-18s and the Navy should be sufficient to defend the island. They're even sending us a squadron of F-35s, which should be arriving today."

Newman just shook his head in disgust. "We should be preparing these defenses at home, not on East Timor. The PLA could just as easily leave us alone here and invade Darwin, and we'd be powerless to stop them."

Morrison yawned briefly as he reached for his coffee cup before looking his infantry commander in the eye. "1st Brigade isn't on East Timor to prevent the PLA from capturing the island. We're here to protect the Air Force, so they can keep the enemy away from Darwin." His tone implied that Newman should already have known this.

"I suppose you're right, Sir," Colonel Newman acknowledged. "However, I do wish we had more surface-to-air missile systems to protect the island."

"Ah…you're just mad because you thought our brigade would miss out on the war in Korea, and now that we're deployed to Timor, you think we'll be marginalized again. We will get our chance to get into this war, Colonel—just make sure your battalion is ready when it happens," Morrison replied with a bit of heat to his voice.

Lieutenant Colonel Newman was a newly promoted commander who wanted to prove himself. The outbreak of World War III was certainly one way for him to prove his mettle as a military commander. Morrison liked his industriousness; he just needed to make sure his young commander stayed focused and on task.

"*Our time will come*," Morrison thought. "*Of that I have no doubt.*"

****

East Timor

The sky was beautiful with not a cloud around, perfect for flying. Lieutenant Daniel Lacey, call sign "Raptor," guided his F-35 Lightning through the sky at 25,000 feet above the Flores Sea, east of Bali, Indonesia. Below them was the deep blue open, rippled by small whitecaps from the waves. Sitting in the cockpit of this multihundred-million-dollar warplane, Lieutenant Lacey couldn't help but be in awe of his surroundings. His new helmet incorporated technology that allowed him to see all around him as if he were seated on the front of the plane, whipping through the air with nothing around him; it gave him an unparalleled situational awareness.

When the 3rd Squadron of the Royal Australian Air Force, or RAAF, had arrived on East Timor the day before, their command had told them they would be going up daily to go hunting for the enemy. When the Indonesian government decided it wanted to join the Eastern Alliance, the Australian government made the decision that they would leverage their F-35 stealth fighters to go after their new enemy's air force. They would work to neuter the Indonesian military in hopes of making them a nonfactor in the Asian war.

When the order came down, Captain David Blake, call sign "Tiger," had volunteered to lead the first "hunting expedition." The next morning, Captain Blake and his wingman, Lieutenant Lacey, were given the honor of flying the RAAF's first official combat mission with the new F-35 Lightning. Now they were headed toward the Indonesian island of Bali and see what they could find.

Suddenly, they received incoming communications from the radar control operator on the RAAF E-7A Wedgetail airborne radar control aircraft. "Tiger Flight, this is Eagle Eye. We're tracking two Indonesian Hawk 200 aircraft, approximately 140 kilometers from your position. They are loitering over the Bali Airport. How copy?"

"Finally, we're going to get to see some action," thought Lacey. Other than the beautiful scenery, they had had forty minutes of nothing but boredom on their maiden combat flight.

"This is Tiger Flight. That's a good copy," responded Captain Blake. "We'll head in that direction. Vector us in as we get closer and send us the targeting data. We'll engage them from range." Tiger grinned; he was eager to enter the fight.

Twenty minutes went by as their fighters continued to cruise ever closer to the unsuspecting enemy fighters. Steadily, they came into range of their AIM-120 AMRAAM missiles. The airborne radar aircraft that had been vectoring them toward the enemy Hawks sent the final targeting data they needed.

"Raptor, I'm going to fire off my first missile at target 003," announced Tiger. "I want you to fire at target 004, five seconds after I fire mine. We'll loiter in the area and make sure the missiles find their marks. *If* they miss, then we'll engage them with another set of missiles. Is that understood?" Since the Indonesians had no idea they were in the area, and they weren't actively trying to evade enemy radar or SAMs, he wanted to take this first engagement a bit slower and by the numbers.

"Copy that, Tiger. Standing by for your order," replied Raptor, trying to contain his excitement and nervousness.

"We're birds of prey...about to score our first victory," Raptor thought privately.

A minute later, the silence was broken. "Fox Three, missile away," Tiger announced, initiating the countdown to when he'd fire his own missile.

The first missile ignited as soon as it had dropped free of the internal weapons bay and shot out quickly after the enemy aircraft. Lacey then depressed the firing button on his flight stick. He felt his fighter lift a bit in altitude as his own missile dropped from the weapons bay and raced toward the enemy.

The two of them watched for a couple of minutes as the missiles streaked toward the Indonesian planes, getting closer to their prey with each passing second. Then, the Hawks detected the incoming threats and took evasive maneuvers. They accelerated and dove for the ground, hoping they could lose the missiles in the ground clutter. Unfortunately for them, the missiles had gotten too close to them before they had detected the threats. The missiles quickly entered their terminal speed and slammed into both warplanes.

"Score! We got them, Tiger!" yelled Raptor excitedly over the radio. They had officially achieved the first air-to-air kills for the Royal Australian Air Force of World War III.

"Settle down, Raptor," Captain Blake chided. "Maintain radio discipline. We'll celebrate tonight with the rest of the squadron. Right now, we need to focus on getting back to base without getting shot down. You can bet the enemy is going to know we're operating in the area and look to find us with their SAMs." He did his best to hide his own level of excitement so that they could make it back to base safely.

The Indians Are Coming

Russian Far East
Komsomolsk-on-Amur

Lieutenant General Adhar Chatterji of the Second Indian Expeditionary Army watched the tired and battered Russian soldiers stand in line, waiting to board the train that would take them West, toward the next defensive line. Should his Indian forces not be able to stop the Americans from steamrolling across their positions, they would hopefully be rested and ready to fight. While the Russian soldiers stood silently waiting for the train to empty, Chatterji felt pride swell within his chest as nearly a battalion's worth of his Indian Army soldiers exited the train. These new arrivals were led to a long line of trucks that would transport them to one of the many military camps that had sprung up around the city of Komsomolsk.

A month ago, the Americans had landed a sizeable force of Marines among the coastal cities along the Sea of Okhotsk and the Kamchatka Peninsula. Once on the ground, the Americans had advanced stealthily throughout the Russian Far East, severing the oil and natural gas fields of eastern Russia and disrupting a host of other mining operations. The Marines were quickly gobbling up the Far East, which was why General Chatterji and his corps now found themselves here, as opposed to Eastern Europe.

While General Chatterji was not thrilled with being allied with the Chinese, he understood the reasons why his government had gone along. The one concession the Indians had made the Chinese agree to was that neither country would station soldiers on each other's territories, at least not until both sides felt more comfortable with the arrangement. If it hadn't been for President Petrov's intervention in the negotiations, Chatterji highly doubted India would have joined the new Eastern Alliance.

In the dark recesses of his mind, General Chatterji felt bad about going to war with the Americans. His younger brother had emigrated to America twenty-six years ago and loved being an American. Becoming a US citizen had been one of his proudest moments. He'd brag about it nearly every time he came home to visit.

"*I hope Krishna is still doing OK in America*," Chatterji thought. He hadn't been able to talk to his brother in a while, and he worried that some of his nieces and nephews might have been drafted.

After greeting and welcoming his soldiers to Russia following their nearly eight-day train ride from India, he turned to leave the trainyard and was pleasantly surprised when his soldiers spontaneously started to sing an old military hymn.

"They're excited about going to war..." he reveled to himself.

An hour later, he walked into his headquarters building and made his way over to the room he had set up as his new office. When he walked in, he was pleasantly surprised to see his new boss, a Russian major general, and one of his colonels. Smiling, he extended his hand. "Major General Oleg Chirkin, it's good to see you. I thought we were meeting for dinner in a couple of hours?"

Major General Chirkin smiled briefly at the question. "Yes, I have a reservation made for us. However, I wanted to speak with you now—it's a matter of great urgency," he replied, still standing near the wall of the office.

Chatterji signaled for the two Russian officers to take a seat as he walked around to his desk. Chirkin remained standing. "General, I understand you arrived yesterday and have set this building up as your new headquarters. As my new deputy, I must insist that you pick a new location for your headquarters," urged Chirkin. "I also recommend that you find a way to trim your staff down by at least half and find a more discreet way to run operations."

Lifting his head up a bit, Chatterji clarified, "You're concerned with this location being quickly identified by the Americans and then destroyed?"

Chirkin nodded. "Yes. My predecessor didn't relocate his headquarters when the war started, and the Americans blew him up with a cruise missile. By all accounts, you're a very competent general. I don't want the US to score a quick victory and destroy your HQ the first week you're in Russia," he replied, hoping the new general wouldn't take offense to him saying this.

Chatterji smiled broadly. "We've already thought about this, General. We made a lot of noise about this new location and are setting up enough communications transmissions emanating from this building to be convincing as well. I even have a body double who will come here daily. We *want* the Americans to destroy this building. We want to show our people at home how vicious the US is, and how they will even kill civilians and then blame us for setting up our headquarters near a heavily populated area."

Chatterji wagged his finger with a smile. "I already have a secured headquarters set up. After today, I'll never set foot in this building again. This is all a ruse," he concluded.

Laughing at what they had been told, both of the Russians had to take a minute to regain their composure. "Very clever, General. You're just as crafty and devious as I have heard. Now, can you put that craftiness to use in slowing down the Americans?"

Turning serious, General Chertterji responded, "I have a plan to deal with them. My engineering brigade has finally arrived. We're starting construction of twelve new airfields. When they're completed, the Air Force will be sending 150 fighter aircraft, and we'll also receive a few squadrons of Jaguar ground-attack planes. When our air operations are up and running, we'll stop the Americans from advancing any further, and then as additional brigades arrive from home, we'll work on removing them altogether. Under your leadership, this joint Russian-Indian task force is sure to prevail. By the end of summer, we'll have 90,000 Indian soldiers here, and double that number next spring."

Leaning forward, he looked the Russians in the eyes. "I'm going to rely on you for your help and expertise. You have hard-fought experience fighting the Americans. With your help, we're going to defeat the enemy and end this bloody war," he concluded.

General Chatterji noted the smiles spreading across his Russian compatriots' faces. He wanted to make sure they knew they were going to be equal partners in this campaign; if they believed that, then their forces would fight harder, and the likelihood of them winning would increase significantly.

Deceiving Appearances

Washington State
Joint Base Lewis-McChord

It had been nearly six weeks since Sergeant First Class Ian Slater and a small ragtag group of soldiers had successfully escaped capture from behind enemy lines. It had taken them another seventeen days to make it back to friendly forces. During that time, the small group of "freed soldiers" had done their best to stay hidden when they could and fight when no other choice presented itself. Slater didn't really view himself as the leader of this motley crew, but they had latched onto him like a little brother does to his big brother on the first day of school.

During their seventeen-day ordeal, they had seen the Chinese soldiers getting pummeled from the air. The ROK and US forces were counterattacking hard. It was not unusual for them to run into a cluster of dead bodies as they traveled. Given their situation, they always searched the remains for any useful weapons or supplies that might not have been destroyed.

Then one day, a group of PLA soldiers got closer to Sergeant Slater's motley crew. Searching for a place to hide, his men located a cluster of destroyed armored vehicles. They hid amongst the wreckage, forced to lie down near bodies until the enemy passed by. For twelve hours, they lay next to the fallen American, Korean, and Chinese soldiers, doing their best to hide in plain sight.

Finally, an American unit approached their hiding place, and they presented themselves to their fellow US comrades. Once their identities had been verified, they were brought behind the Allied lines, cleaned up, and sent back to Seoul to see what would become of them. Nearly all the prisoners had some minor injuries that needed treating. However, it was the injuries to their minds that would need more attention.

Slater, along with the other prisoners, was debriefed on what had happened at the Yalu line. Eventually, they had all been sent back to Japan, where they could have a more thorough medical and mental evaluation. Because they'd been prisoners, they weren't going to be sent back to a line unit right away.

Two days after arriving in Japan, and only five days after they were repatriated, a colonel who was also a psychologist decided that Slater and his fellow prisoners hadn't been deserters but rather were legitimate prisoners who had escaped capture, removing any doubt or suspicion. With this prognosis, their treatment changed for the better.

They were all assessed to determine their level of mental stability and to decide if they were fit to serve in a line unit at that time or if they would have to be cycled back to a support function for a time. Many of the prisoners were torn by these options. Some of them wanted to get payback for their comrades that had been killed, while others felt the need to serve in a support unit, or better yet, separate from the military entirely.

They went from having a cloud of suspicion over them to suddenly learning that they were being hailed as champions who had outsmarted the People's Liberation Army. Slater overheard some of the other soldiers labeling his group the "Heroes of the Yalu Line."

Everyone in that group of soldiers was eventually awarded the Prisoner of War medal, the Purple Heart, and a Bronze Star with Valor for overpowering and killing their captors and escaping back to the Allied lines. As a consolation prize, the Army determined that they should not have to return to combat but would all be assigned as drill instructors or other support jobs back in the States. They had done their part for their country, and now it was time for their country to take care of them.

****

A day after arriving in Tacoma, Washington, Sergeant Slater reported to the garrison commander's office at Fort Lewis-McCord for his new assignment. He showed up at 0750 hours, just as he had been instructed. However, he was out of uniform. He showed up wearing a polo shirt, khaki pants, and a pair of Oakley sunglasses on the top of his closely cropped head, an ensemble he had purchased the night before at a Wal-Mart in Olympia.

When his plane arrived from Japan, the first thing he did was check himself into a Marriott in downtown Olympia. He bought some clothes, ate a steak dinner, then found a bar, where he proceeded to get as drunk as possible and try to pick up a local girl for the night. He had succeeded in nearly every goal except finding someone to spend the evening with. Frustrated, he went to the restroom, where he gave himself an honest look in the mirror.

"I'm a bit gaunt right now," he realized. *"I can't blame a woman for running away from me—I'm all skin and bones."*

Since the start of the war, Slater had lost 32 pounds from stress, lack of food, and overactivity. Of course, dodging enemy soldiers behind the Allied lines for seventeen days hadn't helped either. Besides that, the medication the doctors had prescribed to him to help control some of his PTSD-related anxiety had also killed his appetite. Defeated, he had left the bar to crash in his hotel room for the few hours that remained before he had to get up and report to duty.

The next morning hit him like a truck. He barely managed to pick himself up out of his bed. As he walked toward the headquarters building, the sun hurt his head, but at the same time, he wanted to soak up the warmth of the sun's rays. He knew that sunny days were going to be a lot rarer here than in his home state of Florida.

Seeing the entrance to his new company coming up, he briskly walked along the outside of the headquarters buildings. He pulled the door open and walked in, and a young buck sergeant greeted him with a smile.

"Good Morning. How may I help you?" he asked, a bit too chipper for Slater's liking.

"*God, I have one gnarly hangover,*" he thought. "*I hope I don't smell like alcohol…*"

Slater pulled his personnel file out of a small daypack he had been carrying and gave the file to the young sergeant. "I'm Sergeant First Class Ian Slater. I was told to report for duty here this morning."

The sergeant took the folder from him, opening it quickly to review the information. He asked for Slater's ID card and verified the information with what had been written in the personnel file. "If you would please place your right index finger and right thumb on this scanner, I'll make sure you are who you say you are," he said with a smile. It seemed like he had done this a million times before.

"This is new. Never had to do this before," Slater thought.

Looking at the sergeant's uniform, he could see the man hadn't deployed overseas. No combat action patch. Some very unflattering words came to mind as he thought about this green inexperienced soldier lording over him.

The soldier nodded when he received the confirmation that Slater's identity had been verified. "Sorry for the delay, Sergeant. There have been a few sabotage incidents on base, so security has increased. You're now registered as a member of the base and this command. If you take a seat over there, I'll let Captain Wilkes know you're here and he'll let you know what your duties will be."

A few minutes went by, and then a captain walked into the room and spoke briefly with the orderly, who pointed at Slater. The captain walked toward him. "Sergeant

Slater, correct?" he asked, a bit of heat in his voice. As the captain looked him over, his lip snarled in disdain.

Standing as the captain approached, Ian replied, "Yes, Sir. I'm Sergeant Slater."

Seeing the officer's ribbon rack, Slater thought, *"Great, another green newbie who's never seen combat— this time an officer."* He hadn't deployed overseas to Afghanistan, Europe or Asia, and here he was, already busting his chops.

"You're out of uniform, Sergeant," Captain Wilkes barked. "When you report to a unit, you do so in uniform. In this unit, everyone reports to duty in their service uniforms unless you're assigned to be a drill sergeant. Is that understood?" He scowled.

"Yes, Sir. I'll make sure I have the proper uniforms," Slater said as he now stood properly at attention.

"Nothing in my orders said anything about being a drill sergeant—they'd better not make me a drill sergeant," he thought in horror.

"Where did you transfer in from?" Wilkes asked in a more congenial manner as he continued to size him up.

"I just arrived yesterday from Japan," Slater replied.

Captain Wilkes looked over the orders the orderly had just handed him. "Hmm...it says you were just promoted to E-7 four months ago, but you haven't been to any of the Senior Leader Courses yet. It says I'm supposed to run you through several of the professional development courses before you're given a more active assignment." Pausing for a second, Wilkes seemed to change his demeanor a bit when he saw the list of decorations Slater had accumulated up to this point.

"Let's see here…two Purple Hearts, two Bronze Stars with V device, one Silver Star with V device, and the Prisoner of War medal. OK, Sergeant, clearly you've been around the block and seen a lot of action, so I'll cut the crap and just give you the skinny. Follow me back to my office, and we'll talk," he said, and he motioned for Slater to follow him.

As Sergeant Slater walked into Captain Wilkes' office, he nearly chuckled at all of the motivational pictures and posters plastered on the man's wall. On his desk, he saw a handful of challenge coins and other memorabilia. He also saw a picture of a woman and two little children in a frame, most likely his family.

Captain Wilkes sat down in his leather chair. "Look, we're a basic combat training battalion for the 2nd ID," he explained. "Our job is to churn out soldiers ready for combat. The 189th Infantry Brigade, which you now find yourself a part of, is a training brigade. Our battalion, the 2/357 infantry, is tasked with graduating 320 new soldiers a week. The other three battalions in the brigade are doing the same, which means we churn out a new battalion of soldiers every week for the war."

Slater saw his moment to ask a question when Wilkes paused to take a sip of his coffee. "Have they doubled the size of the battalions? That's a lot of new recruits to graduate each week."

Wilkes smiled as he placed his coffee mug down. "Yes, they doubled the size of each of the new battalions. You've been at the front, you know better than I do. They're short on officers and sergeants, so they're doubling the strength of the units while they expand the officer and noncommissioned officer corps."

Sensing that there was a question Wilkes hadn't asked, Slater responded, "When the war started, I was an E-5 sergeant. Within ten days, half the officers and sergeants had been killed in combat. I was promoted directly to E-7 and given command of a platoon, until my unit was eventually wiped out at the Yalu line. I can attest to the casualties among the sergeants and officers. It's as bad as you've heard, Sir."

148

Wilkes looked almost appalled at what Ian had just said. Not a lot of combat soldiers had returned from Korea yet, so the opportunities to hear firsthand what was going on over there were very limited.

"All right," Captain Wilkes said, "here's what I'm going to do with you. I'm going to give you ten days permissive TDY to get yourself sorted, find an apartment, and get outfitted with new uniforms. For the time being, I'm going to have you work with the drill sergeants on identifying potential NCOs among the recruits. As you can imagine, in addition to graduating hundreds of recruits, we also have to identify eight soldiers from each company who have the leadership skills needed to be an effective sergeant. If we find a recruit who has more than two years of college, we're supposed to assess them and determine if they could potentially be an officer or NCO and add them to the list as well. When these recruits graduate training, they're going to be pulled aside and given three weeks of training as an NCO and then promoted to E-5. That is where you come into the picture."

"Sir?" Slater asked.

"While you do not have a lot of time in grade and experience as a sergeant, you've been one for eight months, and more importantly, you've survived multiple battles.

You'll be tasked with helping the drill sergeants identify these individuals, and then you'll work with two other senior NCOs to train and groom these recruits to become sergeants."

Holding a hand up to object, Slater protested, "Sir, with all due respect, I'm not qualified to do this job. I barely even know how to be a sergeant, Sir. I've spent nearly all of my time as a sergeant in combat, not learning the ropes of what makes a good NCO."

Wilkes nodded as he listened to Ian's objections. "I understand, Slater, but here's the deal. You've seen the elephant. You've been to battle and survived—shoot, you've got the medals to prove it. You don't need to teach these guys the ins and outs of being an NCO. You need to teach these guys how to keep their soldiers alive—how to fight as a team and to listen to their officers and senior NCOs. For that, I think you're eminently qualified."

Wilkes sighed. "Look, I have a company to run. I need you to step up and lead. You aren't being placed back into a line unit, so you need to impart your knowledge and experience to those who are going to the front. Understood?" It was more of a rhetorical question. Slater had been given his orders and, like them or hate them, he'd have to execute them.

"Yes, I understand, Sir," Slater responded. "I'll see you again in two weeks, this time in the proper uniform."

"*Now, to go find a bar and a girl who's up for some fun. Then I'll work on getting myself situated...priorities,*" he thought as the meeting concluded.

Hunter Becomes the Hunted

South China Sea

Captain Michael Mohl smiled as he looked at the sonar display. His ship, the USS *North Dakota*, had been stalking the *Haikou*, a *Lanzhou*-class Chinese destroyer, for the past two days. They had seen the destroyer escorting a convoy of roughly twenty-six cargo ships, and they had also spotted four other *Jiangkai*-class antisubmarine warfare frigates in the pack.

"Do you think we can take the destroyer before those frigates would be all over us?" asked Lieutenant Commander Paul Delta, the newly assigned executive officer. Commander Mohl's previous XO had had to be emergency-lifted off the ship when he'd had a medical emergency arise. Lieutenant Commander Delta had assumed the role, at least until the ship returned to port and Captain Mohl's XO could officially be replaced.

"The question you *should* ask is how many of those frigates do you think we can send to the bottom before they figure out we're here?" Mohl said in response to the young officer. Delta was a good officer, if a bit young for his rank. With the loss of so many naval officers and NCOs since the start of the war, everyone was getting promoted ahead of the normal schedule.

"Weps, what are your thoughts?" asked Captain Mohl as he looked at his weapons officer.

"It's risky, Sir. We can easily get a shot off at that destroyer and be well away from the area by the time they figure out they're in danger. My concern isn't so much with the frigates finding us as it is with their helicopters. If they're able to catch a beat on us, they could get a torpedo or two off on us," the weapons officer replied.

Captain Mohl thought about the problem for a moment, looking at the display of where the enemy ships were in relationship to their weapons capabilities. He calculated a plan.

"Let's move to this position here," the captain said, pointing to a spot on the map. "When we're ready, I want one torpedo fired at the *Haikou* and one fired at the *Sanya*, that frigate over here. Then we'll run deep. We'll go down to 1,200 feet and maneuver toward these two frigates here. Thoughts?"

The small group of officers stood there digesting what the captain had just said, going over the pros and cons of the strategy. The more they looked at the plan, the better they all felt about it. The officers agreed with the captain's assessment—not that they had much choice in the matter, but they felt they had a better-than-average chance of sinking more than one ship this way. Maybe they'd even be able to take a couple of freighters down.

Forty minutes went by as the *North Dakota* continued to stealthily move into its attack position. The crew in the sonar room was doing their best to make sure they hadn't missed any other potential threats. Everyone knew they would be firing their torpedoes soon.

A few minutes later, the *Haikou* crossed into the attack envelope they had agreed upon, and the captain gave the order. "Fire torpedoes one, three, and four!" Mohl announced.

Within seconds, they heard the whooshing sound as, one after another, three torpedoes were fired from the sub.

"All ahead full speed. Take us down to 1,200 feet, bearing 273," the captain ordered.

Two minutes into their sprint away from the firing point, the sonar operator's face suddenly went white. "Con, Sonar. New contact. Sierra One. Confirmed, Yuan-class submarine."

Lieutenant Gillan had been observing the sonar operators. He grabbed the mic. "Con, Sonar. Torpedo in the water. 4,500 yards and closing quickly."

The active pinging could be heard now as the torpedo raced toward them.

The captain immediately ordered, "Fire off the noisemakers! Turn sharply to port! And get me a firing solution on that enemy submarine now!"

The tension in the Con was building as they anxiously waited to see if the enemy torpedo was going to go for the noisemaker. As the sub finished making a tight turn and another depth adjustment, the weapons officer shouted, "We have a solution on the enemy sub!"

Captain Mohl turned to the officer and shouted, "Fire!"

Once they had launched the torpedo, the captain put out another set of orders. "Helm, come to starboard twenty degrees. Bring us down another 200 feet."

While everyone in the submarine listened to the enemy submarine's torpedo close in on them, they felt and heard an explosion. The enemy torpedo had gone for the noisemaker. The immediate threat was over, unless they came across another submarine.

Breathing a sigh of relief, Captain Mohl looked at the sonar screen, watching their own torpedo home in on the Chinese submarine. All of a sudden, they all saw a new contact emerge from out of nowhere. A new, strange sound, unlike that of any submarine or torpedo they had ever heard, abruptly blanketed the water, sounding almost like a rocket being fired underwater. The speed at which the new contact was traveling was incredible; it clearly did not have the characteristics of a standard torpedo. This did not bode well for their continued survival.

"Fire another set of noisemakers, ahead flank speed!" yelled the captain. New beads of sweat formed on his forehead. It was clear to him that they weren't going to outrun this new threat. If it didn't go for their noisemaker, they were doomed.

Two minutes went by. The unknown threat barreled through the noisemaker, closing in on them. The noise grew ever louder, until a violent explosion rocked the ship. Water flooded into the ship from the multiple holes that had been punched through the hull.

****

South China Sea

Captain Liu Huaqing was honored to have been chosen as the commander of the new and secretive Type 095 or *Wuhan*-class submarine. It was the only submarine of its design and capability in the world. The *Wuhan* was built on the strengths and weaknesses of the American *Virginia*-class attack submarine. With specially placed moles within the US Navy and the defense companies responsible for building the American submarines, they had stolen many of the classified technical details that gave the American designs an edge against their peers.

After nearly a decade in development and two years of construction, the *Wuhan* was finally operational and ready to go hunting, and it was equipped with the brand-new super high-speed torpedoes. These new projectiles could reach speeds of 150 knots with a range of ten kilometers.

Two days ago, when the surface warships had met the convoy of ships they would escort to the Philippines, Captain Liu's sonar room had picked up a faint signature of a possible submerged contact.

"Move closer in that general direction," Liu had ordered. "Let's see if we can get a better feel of what we may be dealing with."

As the hours and then days had dragged on, they continued to observe the contact coming in and out of focus on their sonar, all the while ensuring they kept themselves positioned near the center of the convoy. Suddenly, their sonar detected the launch of three torpedoes originating from the general area they had been tracking.

"Ahead full speed!" directed the captain. He was moving them toward the action.

They were at the absolute edge of their weapons range, and they needed to close the distance if they were going to have any chance at taking the enemy submarine out. While their sub sped in the direction of the Americans, a *Yuan*-class advanced diesel submarine fired a torpedo at the American vessel.

The Yankee sub quickly went to flank speed and took evasive maneuvers. As the Americans moved to evade the new threat, their sonar room was able to firm up a firing solution on them. Once the weapons officer confirmed with Captain Liu that they were ready to fire the new weapon, he gave the order. "Fire torpedo one!"

A rushing of air and water could be heard as the newly designed torpedo was ejected from its tube into the dark water of the South China Sea. The engine started, and the torpedo got up to speed. At first, it ran up to 45 knots; then its super cavitator took over and the torpedo accelerated to 150 knots.

The Americans quickly reacted to the new threat posed to them. However, the *Wuhan's* new torpedo closed the distance too quickly for them to have a chance at shaking it. As the minutes slowly ran down, the distance between the

American submarine and China's new underwater superweapon slowly merged to become one…ending with a thunderous explosion and the death of over a hundred American sailors.

Long Fork in the Road

Oceanside, California

The cool air intermixed with salt water felt good as it buffeted Master Sergeant Tim Long's face. It felt good to finally get out of the hospital and back to duty. As Long turned onto Vandegrift Boulevard, he saw the familiar sign welcoming him to Camp Pendleton.

"I wish I were returning to my old unit," he thought as he pulled out his CAC card for the gate guard.

After navigating his way around the new construction and other activities happening on or near the road, he eventually pulled up to the headquarters building he was now assigned to. While he'd been out of action for a couple of months to convalesce, his slot in his old unit had been filled, and he was assigned a new one back in the States.

As Long pulled his rental car into an empty parking spot, he turned the ignition off and grabbed his paperwork and cover. He was eager to see what kind of new unit he was going to be a part of. What he saw when he entered the headquarters was a line of other senior NCOs. He walked in a little further, and then a corporal was manning the front entrance got his attention.

"Please sign in here and then wait over there to be called," the young woman said, holding a pen out for him to use. After writing down his name and having his CAC verified again, he proceeded to take a seat in a waiting room with half a dozen other senior NCOs.

"Anyone know what all of this is about?" asked one of the gunnery sergeants.

They all shook their heads, not sure why they all had been called there. Long thought he knew what was going on, but he couldn't be certain. One by one, the senior NCOs were called back. Then it came time for Long.

He picked up his paperwork and proceeded down a long hallway until he came to a room with a door placard that read, "Colonel Micah Tilman, Commander."

When Long walked into the room, he saw the colonel sitting in a chair behind his desk. Another captain and a major were in the room as well.

"*Crap, what do these guys think I did?*" he thought, feeling like he had just gotten called to the principal's office. "*I just got in from Japan, and I know I didn't get into trouble at the hospital.*"

He stood at the doorway and announced, "Master Sergeant Long reporting as ordered, Sir!" and then he took his seat.

Long sat there, ramrod straight, waiting to see what wrath might be about to befall him. The colonel, for his part, was reading through Long's personnel file. He grunted a few times but was very hard to read.

"The Navy Cross, two Silver Stars, and two Purple Hearts in the span of six months. You're either one unlucky son of a gun or one hell of a Marine. In either case, I'm glad to have you as a part of this new command," Tilman said. He smiled and then stuck his hand out to shake Long's.

"Let's get you up to speed. As you're aware, the Corps is increasing to one million strong. I'm sure you saw all the new construction on your way into post," he commented, making a circling motion with his hand.

"Yes, Sir. It looks like they're doubling the size of the base."

The other two officers in the room nodded.

"Correct. With this massive increase in the size of the Corps, we have to create a host of new brigades and battalions as several new divisions have been reactivated from the World War II days. Those new units need leaders. They need senior NCOs and officers to lead them—the very two things I'm short on." He paused as he looked at the other two officers, then turned his attention back to Tim.

"Look, I've read over your file. You're an exceptional Marine, and your combat awards and record only bear that out. You've seen more action in the last six months than nearly any officer presently at Pendleton, to include me. I need men like you to form the nucleus of my leadership structure. I want to know if I can rely on you for your expertise in turning this new brigade into a fighting force that will defeat the Chinese," Colonel Tilman explained. He leaned forward in his chair, looking Tim in the eyes, searching his facial expressions for any sense of doubt.

"Sir, I'll gladly share what knowledge and experience I have gained," Long answered. "I took part in the beach invasion of North Korea's eastern shore, a big battle near the Chinese border, and the US-ROK counterattack in January. What specifically would you like my help with?" he asked, still not exactly sure what the colonel wanted from him.

Relieved that Tim was going to be a team player, Tilman let out a sigh, then presented him with his offer. "I need company-grade officers. My brigade is just now forming, and I'm short five company commanders. Will you accept a commission to captain?" he asked.

Sergeant Long was a bit surprised by the question. He'd thought he might take over as a first sergeant or something along those lines, but not as a company commander. "I'd love to accept the offer, but I'm not sure I meet the qualifications," he replied a bit glumly. In World War II, his great-grandfather had been a mustang officer in the Marines when they expanded the Corps to fight the Japanese. He had been given a battlefield promotion prior to the battle for Iwo Jima. He'd entered the war as a sergeant and finished the war as a captain. Long wasn't sure he was quite the man his grandfather had been.

Waving his hand dismissively, Tilman responded, "Actually you do. You've completed sixty college credits, which means I can promote you to second lieutenant. Because I'm a brigade commander, I can give you a step promotion to first lieutenant, and the division command saw your Navy Cross and has given you a battlefield promotion to captain, pending, of course, that you accept the rank and do not want to stay an NCO," he explained.

Letting his breath out, Tim smiled broadly as he gave his answer. "I accept, Sir. What do you need me to do next?"

The other officers in the room smiled and welcomed him to their club, the officer club. "First we need you to sign some papers, which Major Lykes from S-1 here will provide to you. Then we're going to have you go through a couple of weeks of officer basic training to get you up to speed on what's required of a Marine officer. By the time you complete the training, your new company of recruits should be ready. You'll join Kilo Company as they start training. Our brigade should finish training by the end of June, and then we'll deploy to Asia," Tilman said.

They had a lot of work to do between now and when they deployed, and Long was going to play a big role in making sure everyone understood what they would be dealing with when they got to Asia. As the newly minted Captain Long signed his required paperwork, Colonel Tilman smiled. He felt a little bit like he had just won the lottery.

Ohio Massacre

Lima, Ohio

Spring had arrived in Ohio. The winter snows had finally melted away. With the start of April came the precipitation that lived up to the nursery rhyme of "April showers bring May flowers." The rain drizzled down on the five-bedroom farmhouse Major Sasha Popov had rented for his team four days ago through Airbnb. Using a false identity, credit cards, and smartphone left for them at their last safe house by their GRU handlers, Sasha had found a great little homestead in the countryside, not far from their next target. The team needed a place to organize for their next mission and still have some privacy from the general American populace.

Once the team had arrived at the farmhouse, they reviewed the surveillance package provided to them by the GRU, the Russian version of the American Defense Intelligence Agency. Their primary target was the General Dynamics land systems factory in Lima, where the Americans were mass producing their main battle tanks. Major Popov had been proud to accept this mission.

Destroying or severely damaging the factory would go a long way toward helping the war effort.

Adjacent to their primary target was the Husky Lima Refinery, which produced a large portion of the gasoline for the Midwest. In addition to destroying the tank manufacturing, Popov's team intended to obliterate the refinery as well. The large fuel storage tanks there would make for a spectacular explosion once they caught fire, which would lead to additional damage to the tank factory across the street. It was going to be a campaign of shock and awe.

Deep in thought, Sasha heard the front door to the farmhouse open, letting some of the cool air enter the hallway that led to the kitchen. A second later, the door closed, and two men walked into the kitchen, looking for an empty coffee cup.

"*I do love American coffee,*" Major Popov thought as he poured himself a full mug of the black liquid brain juice.

"Are the weapons there?" asked Popov. He was anxious to get the mission going. While his team was not actively fighting in Europe, the work they were doing here in the US was just as important. What they had seen on the American news, albeit with a Yankee bias, did not look good. The US was massing a massive army in Europe, and it wouldn't be long until they unleashed that destructive force on their beloved homeland.

Lieutenant Egor Vasiliev took two large gulps of the hot liquid before placing his coffee mug on the kitchen counter to answer Major Popov's question. "Yes. They were in the storage locker, just as the handler said they would be," he responded. He held up his hand to prevent Popov from asking further questions before he continued.

"We did a quick inventory of the weapons to make sure everything was there. All three of the 120mm mortar tubes were present, and while they are old, they appear to be in good working condition. We checked the other crates as well. There are 36 rounds for the mortars, exactly twelve mortars per tube, exactly as we had been instructed."

Lieutenant Egor Vasiliev, like many of the other Spetsnaz members, had entered the US nearly four months ahead of the hostilities between Russia and the West. The group of twelve members had entered the US through the H-1B visa program. Their applications had listed them as computer and engineering experts for an Armenian-owned and operated computer software company, LAD Solutions.

Vasiliev, like the other members of this elite Spetsnaz team, was part of the secretive Special Operations Command or KSO within the Ministry of Defense. Prior to being designated as a direct-action sabotage team in the Americas, they'd had to rotate to America and serve a three-month stint with LAD Solutions, where they'd learned more about the specific geographic region of America their unit had been assigned to. They were instructed on the top military targets in their region and the locations of safe houses they could fall back to if discovered. Most importantly, they'd spent a great deal of time driving around their assigned location, so they could better understand the layout of the roads, the surrounding cities, and the people who lived in the region they would be operating in. This familiarization of the battlespace had aided some of their earlier teams in being able to elude capture.

Sergeant Vlad Volkov had been smiling as he thought about the damage they would be able to do with thirty-six 120mm mortars. The mortar system was American, which meant it was reliable. How the GRU had acquired the weapons was not his concern. The fact that they had was all he cared about. "I checked the weapons myself, Sir," he added, backing Vasiliev up. "They're in good working order and should not cause us any problems."

Popov nodded as a slight smile spread across his face. "What about the launch site? Have we found a point that is secluded enough to set up the mortars and still allow us to get away?"

This was the trickiest part of the operation. Granted, each of them would be more than willing to die in the service of their country; however, they wanted to make their efforts matter in the larger scheme of things, which meant they needed to carry out more than just one or two missions. They needed to be able to do their damage and then escape to fight another day.

Vasiliev chimed in. "On our way back from the storage facility, we checked a couple of the locations our surveillance package had identified. Two of them are a bust. A new housing development is where one of them used to be, and the other had a school on it. The third position they identified is still viable and is probably the best position to use. It's still somewhat remote, but it's close enough to the highway for us to be able to put as much distance as possible between ourselves and the attack."

"Excellent," Popov responded. "Tonight, I'll be purchasing the three Suburban SUVs. The vehicles should be ready in a couple of days, once we've the added brush guards. When I have the vehicles, I want you to take your team to the storage facility and move the weapons back here. Things need to be ready to go when the time comes."

****

Lima, Ohio
Allen County Sheriff Department

Deputy Eric Clark had just celebrated his tenth year on Patrol 6-Delta with the Sheriff's Department on Sunday. He had several friends and family over for a BBQ, which turned out to be a great time of reflecting on the major milestone he had just hit in his new career. It was hard to believe it had already been ten years since he had gotten out of the Marines.

Eric and his partner, Cindy Morrison, had patrolled together for three years out in Allen County. At first, Eric was not thrilled with the prospect of having a green young woman for a partner—Cindy had only been twenty-two and fresh out of college when she'd joined the Allen County Sheriff Department. Like most idealistic young people, she wanted to change the world, and she was hell-bent on changing the way police interacted with the people they served. Despite a lot of antipolice sentiment on college campuses, Cindy had pressed forward in becoming a police officer, but she clearly wanted to change the organization from within.

After her six-month probationary period ended, she had changed her tune a bit. She realized the vast majority of calls they were responding to involved having to deal with the bottom of the barrel of society, like the backwoods hicks who thought it was cool to smack their women around, or the young gangbangers who felt the world owed them something, or her least favorite, human traffickers who routinely sold women and children into the sex trade. Cindy marveled at how Eric was able to wade through all the crap and still keep a happy demeanor. She respected his willingness to give each person the benefit of the doubt, even if he was a bit old-fashioned when it came to gender roles.

Eric and Cindy worked the night shift together, patrolling from eight at night until four in the morning, a time that most people tended to be asleep. The ones who were out and about tended to be the riffraff who had nothing better to do than to cause trouble. One night, during their shift briefing, an FBI agent took a couple of minutes to speak with them.

"I'm Special Agent Rich Demarco with the FBI, and I'm here to ask for your help," he began. "We received a report that a Russian Special Forces unit may be operating in the area with the intention of carrying out some sort of sabotage mission against the General Dynamics land systems factory in Lima. While we don't have any further details or leads at this time, we want to make the Sheriff's Department aware of the possibility of an attack. If you see something suspicious, please investigate it. Radio it in and verify that nothing nefarious is going on."

One of the officers raised a hand to ask a question, and Agent Demarco nodded to him. "If we do encounter a Russian Special Forces unit while on patrol, how are we supposed to deal with that? The most firepower we pack in our cruisers is a twelve-gauge shotgun." He knew he wasn't the only one to think of that angle.

"That is a fair question, Deputy," Demarco answered. "If you encounter an armed group of Russians, radio it in and wait for backup. Don't try to be a hero. These guys are highly trained and will probably be well armed. Since we've received this tip, security has been increased at the factory. We also have a joint FBI-Sheriff Department SWAT team on 24-hour standby. The SWAT team can be deployed quickly, so please wait for them to arrive if you believe that you have encountered this Russian group."

With that said, the briefing broke up, and the officers went about their normal patrols, hoping that today would be like any other day.

Four hours later, Eric paid the cashier at the 24-hour Denny's and proceeded to head back to their patrol car.

"I love the Eggs Over my Hammy sandwich," Cindy said to her partner. She held the door open for him as they exited the building.

Eric laughed at his partner's addiction to the fat-laden, calorie-inundated meal Denny's called a sandwich. "Enjoy it while you can, Cindy," he said with a smirk. "When you get to be as old as me, your metabolism will change, and suddenly you'll get fat just drinking water." He patted his stomach. It felt like he had just gained a few extra pounds, even though he'd just had a salad.

Walking over to the passenger side of the patrol car, Cindy opened the door and climbed on in. "Come on, Eric, it can't be that bad, and you're not *that* old," she said, snickering a bit. She knew her partner was self-conscious about his weight. He really wasn't advanced in age, having just turned thirty-six, but he was packing on a little bit of a beer belly.

As they got themselves settled in for another couple more hours of patrolling, the radio came to life. "Any units in the vicinity of Amherst Road and McClain Road, please respond. There are reports of suspicious activity in the area," came the call from dispatch.

"Wow, could they be any more vague with that description?" Cindy remarked.

"It's probably nothing, but we should check on it. We're only a few miles away," Eric replied.

He picked up the radio handset. "Dispatch, this is Six Delta. We'll check it out," he answered, hoping it was just a wild animal or something benign.

****

Lima, Ohio
Outskirts of General Dynamics Land Systems Factory

It was nearly 0100 hours as the Russian soldiers pulled the mortar tubes out of the back of their black Suburban SUVs and got them set up. A soldier used a mallet to pound in a rod used to hold the baseplate in place, making sure it was nice and snug in the ground before they set the tube up and began to use it. Once they fired the mortars, the blast from the propellant had a way of shifting the baseplate, which would affect its aim. Seeing that they were firing these mortars from near their maximum range, they didn't want to spend a lot of rounds having to rezero the mortars if the baseplate moved.

Lifting a small encrypted radio to his lips, Major Popov whispered, "Viper Two, are you prepared for fire mission?" he asked.

Sergeant Boris Stepanov had positioned himself in a forest preserve that was directly across from both their primary and secondary targets. During his recon of the area, he had spotted a tree that he could climb, which would provide him with an excellent view of the targets. He had marked the tree with a chalk mark a couple of days before and had found his way back to it easily enough. He had waited up in his perch there for several hours before his radio had finally crackled to life.

Stepanov smiled. "This is Viper Two. Send one round, grid OH 4561 6823. Stand by for adjustments," he directed. Depending on where it landed, he would fine-tune to make sure the next set of rounds would land amongst the factory they needed to destroy.

"Fire one round. Stand by for adjustments," Popov responded.

Sergeant Vlad Volkov lifted the 31-pound HE round above his shoulder and dropped it down the tube. The second the round hit the base of the tube, the charge wrapped around the stem of the round ignited, ejecting the projectile high into the air at a heavy angle. The round whizzed through the air for what felt like an eternity before it traveled the nearly five kilometers to land in the parking lot of the tank plant with a thunderous explosion.

As the initial flash dissipated and the fireball swelled into the night sky, Sergeant Stepanov called in an adjustment to the next fire mission. The Spetsnaz team fired another single round, hoping this next one would hit the mark so they could drop their ordnance as quickly as possible and get out of the area before they were discovered.

A minute and a half later, a second round hit the roof of the tank manufacturing facility, causing another bright flash and a fireball.

Sergeant Stepanov smiled broadly. He lifted his radio to his lips. "Start dropping the rounds in," he directed.

Major Popov yelled at the mortar team. "Fire right away!"

As the rounds continued to sail through the air, Popov made sure they reserved the last four rounds for the secondary target, the fuel refinery. With each *thump* of the mortars, he could hear the echo as the noise bounced around the forests and the few houses near them. He looked down the dirt road they had traveled down and saw Lieutenant Egor Vasiliev with three other soldiers, guarding the entrance to the field they had set up in.

****

Looking at his watch, Vasiliev could see that nearly five minutes had gone by since they first started firing the mortars. *"We need to hurry this up,"* he thought. *"We're going to have police on us anytime."* He knew that the American police, unlike those in Russia, had a pretty good response time if they were called to investigate something.

Just then, he saw a set of headlights turn down the county road toward their position. As the horizon lit up with yet another mortar round, Vasiliev realized that whoever was traveling toward them would definitely have seen the mortars launching out of the forest.

"Stand by and remain ready," he said to the three other soldiers with him. "That could be a police car coming our way. If it is, we need to destroy it quickly before they can radio in for help," he ordered, making sure everyone knew what was at stake.

****

Driving down National Road, Eric saw a red-hot projectile launch into the sky from a farm field not that far away from them. Cindy saw it too. "What the heck was that?" she asked, pointing at yet another projectile that flew into the sky in the direction of the city of Lima.

"That's a mortar round," he said, matter-of-factly. He grabbed his radio mic. "Dispatch, this is Six Delta," he began. "We have confirmation on the Russian Special Forces unit near the intersection of National Road and McClain. Requesting SWAT to our location immediately!"

"Six Delta, this is Seven Delta. Did you say you found those Russians?" another patrol car asked almost as quickly as they had called it in.

"That's affirmative," Eric responded. "We're less than a quarter mile away, and we're observing them launch mortars in the direction of Lima. I'm not sure what they're hitting, but my money says they're going after the tank plant."

Cindy looked terrified. "How do you know those are mortars?" she asked. "Maybe they're fireworks or something," she said sheepishly. She had never seen a mortar—she wasn't sure if Eric had, either.

Eric looked at Cindy. "I spent six years in the Marines—a tour in Afghanistan and two in Iraq. Trust me, those are mortars those guys are firing," he insisted. He picked up speed as they headed closer to their firing point.

"What are you doing, Eric? We're just supposed to find them and call it in, not go all Dwayne Johnson on them."

"*Dwayne Johnson—God, she makes me feel old,*" he thought.

"I'm getting us to the intersection, and then we'll stop and wait," he explained. "This way if they try to run, we'll see what direction they head in." He could hear the fear in her voice but knew he had to get there.

As their vehicle approached the intersection, Eric spotted a brief flicker of light, which he immediately recognized as a muzzle flash. In the fraction of a second it took his eyes to see it, he veered the car hard to the left and slammed on the brakes, causing Cindy to instinctively grab for anything she could to steady herself.

In seconds, the front windshield exploded in tiny plexiglass chunks. Then Cindy's passenger-side window shattered, peppering her with the same tiny chunks of glass. When the car came to a halt, Eric jumped out of the driver's side door and then pulled his partner across his seat, out the door. As they hid behind the car, dozens of high-velocity rounds tore through their vehicle.

He hastily grabbed his radio. "This is Six Delta—we're taking heavy fire! Requesting backup at once. They have the intersection of National and McClain bracketed.

Approach with caution. I say again, Six Delta is under heavy fire. Requesting help!" He yelled into his mic to be heard over the increasing volume of gunfire.

Cindy lay on the ground with her hands pulled up around her head as she just screamed in fear. Their vehicle was being torn apart by the barrage of gunfire. "Cindy! I need your help!" Eric yelled. "Shoot back at them, so we can get them to stop firing and take cover!"

He reached down and shook her, trying to get her attention. When she looked up at him, he repeated his instructions. She nodded as she tried to regain her composure and unstrap her sidearm. Eric popped up from behind the hood of his car and fired several rounds in the direction of the gunfire. He saw a couple of figures stop shooting as they took cover. Then a slew of rounds tore into the hood of the car, right where his head had just been before he ducked down.

Cindy popped up near the rear of the vehicle and fired four or five rounds at the Russians before ducking back down. Eric fired a second barrage of bullets at the attackers before reloading his firearm. He heard several of them calling out to each other in Russian, and he had no idea what they were going to do next. The sound of the mortars continued to whistle in the background, but the gunfire from the enemy soldiers had stopped. Eric popped up to take a quick look and see if he could spot one of the attackers long enough to shoot him.

Seeing movement to his right, Eric turned his pistol and fired off one shot before he felt something slam into his left arm and his chest, knocking him to the ground. As Eric's body hit the ground, he wasn't sure how bad his injuries were. His arm felt like it had been shattered, and it was hard to breathe, but he knew he had his vest on with the plates, so chances were, the bullet hadn't gone through. He turned to look for Cindy and saw her firing at an unseen attacker. She got off three rounds before he saw the top part of her head explode. Her body collapsed to the ground just a few feet away from him.

Lying on the ground, unable to really move, Eric knew the Russians must be moving in on them to finish them off. As he lay there waiting for the inevitable, his mind wandered to a couple of days earlier, when he was enjoying the BBQ with his wife and their two little girls.

"*I wish I could be there for them,*" he thought to himself as a dark figure rounded the police cruiser.

The figure lifted his rifle and fired a couple of rounds into Cindy to make sure she was dead.

"*No playing possum with these guys,*" Eric realized.

Summoning the last bit of strength he had, he raised his pistol and fired as many times as he could at the soldier that had just shot at Cindy.

Eric saw the soldier grab at his neck just before he felt half a dozen sledgehammers hit his body. Everything quickly went black, just like the night sky his eyes were now blankly staring at.

****

Major Sasha Popov yelled at his men. "Hurry up and get in the SUVs!" They needed to get out of there.

Although Vasiliev's men had managed to kill the two police officers who had discovered them, they had lost one of their teammates in the gunfight. They would have to leave his body. As much as it pained Popov to leave a fallen comrade, they had to head out to the safe house before the authorities sent more vehicles to their location.

They were in such a hurry that they left the mortar tubes behind, along with everything else that wasn't absolutely vital to take with them. When they arrived at the safe house, they would get their next set of orders, and there would be another way for them to obtain further weapons. The only thing that really concerned Major Popov as they rushed away from the scene was the possibility of the police recovering potential forensic evidence. The thermite grenades they'd left to destroy the equipment would do a pretty good job, but there was no way to guarantee they had destroyed everything.

As they sped down the county road, Major Popov spotted a police cruiser with his flashing lights on. The car sailed right past them at high speed, probably heading toward his comrade. In minutes, they approached Interstate 75 and headed south. The three SUVs picked up speed, but the drivers limited themselves to roughly eight miles over the speed limit so as not to draw too much scrutiny to their little convoy. They would need to drive roughly twenty miles down the road before they would get off and change vehicles. There was a small utility van that had been pre-positioned for a situation like this; it could hold the entire team in one vehicle. Driving in a three-vehicle convoy would attract attention if they did it for too long.

Thirty minutes went by before they found the black utility van they had hidden the day before. Climbing into the back of the van and piling their remaining weapons and equipment inside, they placed camouflaged netting over the three SUVs, hoping to hide them for a few more days.

"*I wish we could just burn the vehicles,*" Major Popov lamented. However, he knew that would create too much fire and smoke, drawing the attention of the authorities.

Once everyone was in the van, they drove another three hours until they came to the next Airbnb house Popov had rented for the group. They would hole up at this location for three days before moving on to the next safe house. Then they'd repeat the process over again.

Potential Unrest

Providence, Rhode Island
Brown University
Grad Center Bar

George Philips could not believe what was going on in his country. President Gates' ascendency to the White House had been nothing short of disastrous. He firmly believed that Gates' disregard for the law, the judicial system, and his fascist tendencies were a threat to the core principles and beliefs enshrined in the Constitution. Even his doctoral professor had said the President was a disgrace to the office and should be resisted at every possible opportunity. Like most progressives, George had a very difficult time accepting the results of the 2016 election. There was just no way someone so crass, unprepared, and lacking in political understanding could possibly win the election. Yet here he was, sitting in the White House, irritating the country like sandpaper on a festering wound.

"Well, he's not my president!" George thought.

It was now 7:30 in the evening, and a slight drizzle began as George headed to the Grad Center Bar to meet up with some friends who helped him run the local Antifa chapter at Brown. They were planning a large-scale protest to take place during the Memorial Day holiday a little over a month away. He felt that it was an appropriate day for a protest, since the President would be honoring baby killers and war criminals.

George was a third-year PhD student at Brown University, where he studied political science. When he'd first started college as an undergrad, he had wanted to get a job and work as a staffer in Congress to get some experience in the political world. Once he had completed his bachelor's degree at Georgetown University, that was exactly what he had done. Hailing from Vermont, he easily obtained a staffer position with the independent senator from his home state and got to see how the sausage was made in Washington. After a couple of years working as a staffer, George decided that the best way he could influence future generations wasn't working in Congress. Instead, he decided that he wanted to influence future young people by becoming a professor.

The Vermont senator had given him a book written by Saul Alinsky, *Rules for Radicals: A Practical Primer for Realistic Radicals*, which had changed his life and the way he viewed politics. George had already espoused many of the more liberal political positions, but the wry old senator from Vermont had regaled him with stories of just how great America could become if the country would move more rapidly in the direction of socialism, and he found the narrative compelling.

He came to believe that if the government would just take the $700 billion or more it spent annually on defense and spend it on free education and universal healthcare, the country could really improve the lives of everyday people. In his mind, the government squandered *so* much money on maintaining nuclear weapons and a huge military—for what? Unless they planned on using that military to wage war, it was a waste.

That was four years ago. Now, as a PhD student, he was nearing his goal of finally becoming a professor. Then Gates had won the presidency, and George felt a new calling on his life, to become an activist and lead a new generation of young people to resist the evils of the Gates administration.

As George walked up to the outside of the bar, he saw Jillian pull up in an Uber. Through the window, he could see her putting her phone back in her purse and unfastening her seat belt. As she opened the door, she cheerfully called out, "Thanks for the ride!"

"There you are, Jillian," George said as he greeted her with an awkward side hug. He couldn't dare to be accused of sexual harassment.

She smiled. "How are the studies going?" she inquired. She had been a PhD student like him not that long ago. They shared that same academic bond.

George pulled open the door for her. "Eh, you know how it goes. Research, write a bunch of stuff, and then your advisor shreds it and you have to start over," he replied. They both laughed.

They spotted Daniel Talley, their contact for a British multimedia company, sitting in the corner, and walked over to join him.

Daniel stood. "Thanks for the invitation," he said as he extended his hand to shake theirs. "I love this place."

"It *is* a pretty great hangout," Jillian agreed. "The drinks are cheap, but I will warn you that they make 'em strong here."

"Did you have a hard time finding it?" asked George.

"I would have, but your directions really helped," Daniel responded with a chuckle. "I can definitely see why this is more of a university haunt—most tourists would probably get lost on the way here." He smirked.

"Glad you aren't the average tourist, Daniel," said George. The Grad Center Bar was more than just a cool dive bar; it was also the unofficial meeting place for a lot of the Antifa members. George was very careful who he invited there.

"I think we've been standing here long enough," Daniel joked. "Why don't you take a seat, and I'll order us some food and drinks?"

"Thanks, Daniel," Jillian answered. She and George sat down. "I'm always up for free food."

"So, what's going on with our brothers across the Pond?" asked George. He was eager to hear what the Antifa groups in Europe were doing. Sometimes their approaches to demonstrating and protesting would also play well in the United States.

The waiter came, and they paused long enough to place orders for appetizers and drinks. Once he left, Daniel cleared his throat.

"Things in the UK are going well," he began. "Same with France. As you know, we're organizing a large EU-wide protest to take place during the May Day celebration. What with the war going on, it seems appropriate that we'd have a demonstration to remind people of what these fascist regimes are doing to our countries…" He paused, looking as if he were about to require a tissue. "The loss of life is just horrific. So many young people being killed, and for what? Corporate greed? Nothing is worth the loss of our generation of young people." He looked genuinely depressed.

"It really is terrible," Jillian agreed. "Two of my cousins were just drafted when that tyrant in the White House announced the second draft. George's little brother is currently serving in the Marines. Has he been sent overseas yet?" she asked.

George sighed. He felt terrible that his little brother had been caught up in the war machine. His brother had just graduated from a trade school and had been hired for his first job as an electrician when he'd received his draft card. George had told him to tear it up and move to Canada until the war ended, but their father had ultimately convinced him that his legal troubles would only continue to follow him after the war, and that he should instead try to find a clerical job and do his best to ride out the war that way.

"Not yet," George answered. His drink had arrived, and he took a big swig of it. "He was lucky and got selected to be an electrical technician on fighter airplanes. He'll be in training for the job for a few months before he deploys. Right now, it's looking like he might be eligible to deploy toward the fall."

Jillian nodded and put her hand briefly on George's shoulder to comfort him. "I'm so sorry, George," she said. "We have to fight this with everything we have. This next protest on Memorial Day has to be huge. People have to know how President Gates engineered a war in Europe and Asia at the request of the military-industrial complex and their Wall Street masters."

George nodded and smacked the tabletop with his fist. "This war is destroying our country! Almost 170,000 soldiers have been killed, not to mention the horrific devastation that has befallen the San Francisco Bay Area after that nuclear attack. What are we going to do to make this one count?" he asked.

"Short of someone assassinating Gates, I don't see anything truly slowing the US war machine," Daniel responded glumly. Then he seemed to have a sudden inspiration. "However, what we *can* do is cause a work stoppage to protest what is going on. It's nonviolent, and it will make headline news. Who knows—it might even spread to other countries if we can get it to take root here."

Jillian beamed. "A work stoppage—just like the Occupy Wall Street days," she said, seemingly drifting back to fond memories. "People can bring their tents and camp out."

"Exactly," Daniel replied, "but in this case, everyone camps out in the parking lots of these companies that are manufacturing war materials and tries to stop people from doing their jobs. The country needs to know that these weapons they're creating are responsible for tens of thousands of deaths."

George took another large sip of his drink. "Someone should kill that fascist criminal in the White House," he responded angrily. "My brother could end up dying in this stupid war." He downed the rest of his drink.

The meeting went on for some time as they planned the work stoppage. Their time was productive, but at the end of the meeting, George needed a little help to make it back to graduate housing.

****

Daniel Talley observed his surroundings one last time before entering the flat he had rented for the month—he was sure that no one had followed him. He dropped his bag on the table near the entry way and completed the usual security check of his place. No bugs or signs of disturbance.

"*Paranoid habits die hard*," he chuckled to himself.

He changed out the sim card on his cell phone and made a call.

"Vasily," said the voice on the other end, cheerfully. Vasily smiled at the sound of his real name. "It's good to hear from you, comrade. How was your meeting?"

"Things are going well," he responded. "The Antifa movement will be organizing a work stoppage on Memorial Day. They think it is their idea."

His Russian intelligence handler laughed. "You do have a talent that way," he responded. "What about the other objective?"

Vasily answered, "Things are progressing better than I expected. I do believe we may have a candidate to attempt an assassination of the President, given enough time and grooming. George is becoming mentally unstable, and he jumped at the suggestion I placed in the conversation."

"Excellent, Vasily. Call me after your next meeting." The phone clicked.

Vasily Smirnov smiled. There was still a lot of work to do, but so far, things were going even better than planned.

Professionals Talk Logistics

Arlington, Virginia
Pentagon Basement
National Command Center Briefing Room

Jim Castle was doing his best not to lose his temper as he listened to the briefer tell them about the latest domestic attacks by Russian and Chinese Special Forces teams.

The General Dynamics project manager was present. "Our land systems factory in Lima sustained severe damage. While most of the facility was destroyed, the portion of the plant that maintained the molds for the tanks and other parts was not damaged. The mortars primarily landed on the production side of the factory. Had the rounds landed in the design portion of the factory, this would be an entirely different briefing."

Placing his hands on his face for a second, Jim asked the million-dollar question. "How long is this going to take to repair? And how has this affected the country's production of tanks?"

President Gates leaned forward, waiting anxiously for the response.

"Unfortunately, Mr. Secretary, it'll take us several months to get the factory back up to full production," the project manager answered. "With a 24-hour repair crew, we might be able to start limited production of tanks again in two weeks, but it'll be at least four to six weeks before we're back up to speed again."

The President jumped in. "Ok, how many tanks were we producing prior to this incident, and how many are we able to produce now?"

"Prior to the attack, we'd gotten this factory up to producing forty-eight tanks a month, Mr. President," the project manager explained. "We were still in the process of restarting the other production lines when the attack happened. Right now, the factory can probably produce roughly ten tanks a month until we get the other lines repaired."

"What about the other factories?" the President asked.

The contractors looked nervously at each other. One finally dared to speak. "Sir, the Ford Motor Company stopped production of civilian vehicles roughly three months ago and turned the production lines to military production. They are just now turning out their first batch of forty tanks. In two months, that number should swell to around 160 a month. Prior to this attack, the Lima plant would have been producing 220 tanks a month as well, but obviously that number has now been reduced."

Doing some math in his head, the President realized that with the rate of losses on the battlefield, compared to their ability to replace the lost tanks, they were coming up short, by a lot. "Jim, how short does this make us on military production?"

Castle turned to a piece of paper he had in front of him. He had been scratching some figures on it while everyone had been talking. "Mr. President, with current fighting, we've been losing roughly 62 tanks a month. During the height of the fighting in Europe and Korea, that number swelled to nearly 800 a month—far in excess of what our manufacturers can produce for us. Right now, we've been replacing those losses from our strategic reserve forces. However, we have no further reserves of equipment to draw from. The tanks our factories have been producing have been leaving the production line and arriving on the battlefield within seven days. That is how tight we are on equipment, Mr. President."

Gates hung his head.

Castle cleared his throat. "Sir, it's the same with ammunition, missiles, and aircraft. A bullet coming off the production line in Pennsylvania on Tuesday is being airlifted to Europe or Korea and fired by a soldier on Saturday or Sunday."

"*Dear God—are we really this close to losing the war?*" the President thought in disbelief.

"Surely the Russians and Chinese are hurting in terms of equipment losses as well," Gates said, summoning a morsel of hope.

Castle nodded. "They are, Mr. President. The difference is, their equipment is a lot easier and faster to produce because it's less complicated to make. They *are* hurting, and our strategic bombing campaign is wreaking havoc on them, but it just comes down to time. Our factories have retooled for war, but they need more time to produce the equipment we need."

Shaking his head in frustration, the President stood. "Everyone out, except senior staff. I need a private conversation," he said. Three-quarters of the room exited, along with the representatives from a handful of critical defense contractors. Seeing that the room was now cleared and only his senior advisors remained, the President sat back down and stared at them intensely.

"I want a straight-up assessment. Are we on the verge of losing this war, or are we about to turn the corner?"

Some of the military and intelligence leaders exchanged nervous glances before Admiral Meyers, the Chairman of the Joint Chiefs, spoke up. "It's close, Mr. President. I wouldn't say we're about to lose, but we certainly aren't on the verge of victory either. The recent attacks by Russian and Chinese Special Forces have significantly hurt our military production capability. They knew our Achilles heel, and they hit it hard. However, we *are* grinding their economy to a halt with our strategic bombing."

The admiral paused for a second, searching for the words to say next. "The fallacy of war, Mr. President, is that it can be fought quickly and from afar. That isn't always the case. Russia and China are not scrappy terror states that can be easily subdued. They are first-world nations with military power that rivals ours. The war we find ourselves in now *is* winnable, but it will take time, and a level of commitment our nation has never had to give before."

Gates thought about that for a moment, then nodded. "I understand and agree, Admiral. I think the American people grasp that." He shuffled some papers around, signaling a change in focus. "Now, how are the plans coming along with this new global alliance to stand up to—what are they calling themselves?" he asked.

"The Eastern Alliance," answered JP, the Director of the CIA. "Its signatories now include Russia, China, India, Iran, the 'Stan countries' of Kazakhstan, Uzbekistan, Tajikistan and Kyrgyzstan, Malaysia, Indonesia, Nicaragua, Angola, Mozambique, Madagascar, Zimbabwe, Botswana, Sudan, Chad, the Central African Republic, and the Democratic Republic of the Congo. Please keep in mind that a lot of these countries have had heavy Chinese, Russian, or Indian influences for many decades. Vast swaths of their economy are tied to India and China, who have invested heavily throughout the last thirty years in building roads, bridges, power plants, mining operations and other goodwill gestures. I also want to assure you, Mr. President, that by and large, these nations do not pose a real threat to the US or to the majority of our Allies." He laid down the piece of paper he had been reading from on the table.

JP then added, "I wouldn't be too concerned by these nations joining the East. The only countries that really pose a potential problem are India and Iran. We're not sure what the Iranians may try to do with regard to Israel. I have been in talks with my counterparts in the Saudi Kingdom along with the State Department, and it does appear that they're working closely with the Jordanians, Israelis, and the other Gulf States to hold Iran to the line and make sure they don't try anything stupid. We're hoping this budding Arab-Israeli alliance will help to keep Iran out of any major military activity in the Middle East."

The President nodded, glad to hear some good news.

JP cleared his throat. "The Indians, however, are going to be a problem. Their economy is enormous, and they already have a large military. Although their army isn't uniformly well-equipped, their front line units are very combat ready. Since they don't have any threats to their border, they've been transporting several of their army groups to Russia," he concluded.

Liam Greeson, the Chief of Staff, leaned forward. "And how goes our own coalition, the Global Defense Force?"

The GDF quickly became the United States' new plan to replace the North Atlantic Treaty Alliance after multiple members had reneged on their support to the alliance and had ultimately been forced out. It had been slow going at first getting the idea approved by Congress, but now it was a race by State and Defense to get nations to sign on to defeat the Russians and Chinese and their new cohort of nations.

Jim Castle reached into his jacket and pulled out his reading glasses, which meant he was gearing up to answer this question. He opened a folder. "The formation of the GDF has been a bit chaotic at times, with some signatories expressing some concern over the direction of the war. I've managed to assuage their apprehensions for the time being, and we've secured the final main signatories. Even though they're facing significant popular resistance at home, the United Kingdom has come around and will be a founding signatory of the new alliance. France has also signed, and to my continued surprise, has probably been the most proactive member of the alliance since the start of the war. They were a bit slow in recognizing the threat the Russians and Chinese pose, but now that it has been made clear, they're all in."

"Chancellor Hilde Schneider from Germany has also rallied her nation to the cause as well. It was almost a shoving match between them and France to see who would get to sign their name first to the agreement. All three of the countries on the Scandinavian Peninsula—Sweden, Finland and Norway—signed the agreement, as well as Denmark, Poland, the Czech Republic, Slovakia, Romania, Croatia, Serbia, Bulgaria, Macedonia, Albania, Italy, and, to our surprise, Spain and Portugal. Both of those nations had been kicked out of NATO, but after a lot of public anger by the populations in those countries and seeing the rest of Europe come together to meet this new threat, Spain and Portugal changed their tune and now they've joined the alliance."

"Really?" the President interjected. He was a bit surprised at this change of course.

"Yes, Sir," Castle answered. "Unfortunately, Greece and Turkey are still facing off against each other. It's unclear if they'll come to blows, but if they do, it'll happen soon, so they're both out."

Jim paused from reading his list to look at the others around the table before continuing. "That covers Europe. The other nations that have signed on to the alliance are Japan, South Korea, Taiwan, the Philippines, Australia, South Africa, Israel, Brazil, Colombia, and of course, our brothers to the north, Canada. Privately, the Saudis, Jordan, Egypt and the rest of the Gulf States are with us but won't formally sign on since Israel is a member. I'm confident that situation will change, though, as the Israeli-Arab alliance looks to control Iran. War has a strange way of creating blood brothers, and I suspect a fight with Iran will be a turning point for the better in the Arab-Israeli relations."

"This is encouraging, Jim," remarked the President.

"I agree, Sir, but I will caution you. While all of these nations joining our alliance sounds great, even powerful, please keep in mind most of these nations' militaries are in even worse shape than our own. They've all been given a list of what types of units their military needs to form and troop numbers they need to reach along with timelines, but outside of the partners that are already actively engaged, it'll be nearly a year before most of these countries will be able to contribute to the war."

"Hmm…" said Gates, mulling that over.

Castle pushed forward. "I hate to harp on this point, Mr. President, but it's just going to take time until all of the pieces are moved into place and ready. Until we reach that point, we need to focus on keeping the enemy off balance and reacting to us until we're ready to finish this war." If anyone was going to mobilize the country and alliance to war, it was going to be Jim Castle, the Warrior Monk, as he'd often been called.

The President's expression turned from a smirk into a smile. "General Omar Bradley famously said, 'Amateurs talk strategy. Professionals talk logistics.' I think that expression really applies to our current situation. As you all have said, this war is going to take time to win—time to retool and build the necessary tools for war. It'll take time to acquire the resources, train the workforce, and create the tools needed to win this war. With that said, I want every avenue pursued to aid us in that endeavor."

He made a motion to indicate that his Chief of Staff should write down what he was about to say. "If we haven't already done so, someone please get in touch with the logistics departments of Wal-Mart and Amazon—they have the world's largest logistical networks. Let's see if they can help us in both acquiring and producing the tools needed to win. Talk with Elon Musk about how we can increase our production capability and find the areas of space and cyber that we haven't thought about utilizing yet and get his thoughts on it. If he'll partner with us to help defeat the Eastern Alliance, then I want his help. The same goes with the CEOs of Google, Facebook, and Apple. We need our tech giants to help us in this struggle. They suffered during the nuclear attack in the Bay Area, and they have a vested interest in helping us win. Let's reach out to our titans of industry and get creative on how we're going to win this war. We have to put our differences aside as a country and people and rally around the flag. It's time we focus on our true enemy, the Eastern Alliance."

Gates spoke with passion and conviction. They left the meeting filled with a renewed fire.

Battle of Britain

Harrogate, United Kingdom
RAF Menwith Hill

Major Artem Ivanov looked at the equipment in the back of the van.

"This should do the trick," he thought. *"It's about time we get this show on the road."*

Ivanov's Spetsnaz unit had spent three long months holed up in their safe house, anxiously watching the war play out in the news. It had been too long since their last attack order; his elite team of soldiers was itching to get back into the fight.

It wasn't that they had been completely silent. When the war started, Major Ivanov's team had carried out a complex attack against the critically important RAF base at Croughton—a major communications facility between the US and UK, responsible for coordinating the defense of Europe. On the opening day of the war, Ivanov's unit had launched sixty-eight 82mm mortar rounds at the base, severely damaging its capabilities at a critical moment in the war.

That first mission had put a huge bullseye on their backs. They'd stayed in their position too long and nearly gotten caught. After a brief shoot-out with the police, they'd barely managed to get away and escape to a safe house. They'd spent the next few weeks constantly changing safe house locations, and at one point, they had hidden out in the back of a lorry being driven around Scotland for two weeks. Once things had cooled down a bit, Ivanov's team had eventually settled into a safe house in the North Yorkshire area and waited for the next call to come.

In February, they were given six targeted assassinations to complete—members of Parliament from the Tory Party. Ivanov had correctly surmised that this might have something to do with all of the antiwar rallies he had been seeing promoted on the news by the head of the Labour Party, Anthony Chattem. The reason didn't really matter, though, as long as it was in service to Russia.

Major Ivanov broke his unit into two-man teams and assigned each of them a Tory MP to kill and a timeline to accomplish their task. Each team had two weeks to figure out how and when they would take out their target. Once their task was completed, they would head to a new safe house and stand by to make sure they had not been found out. If it was safe for them to reconsolidate back to the

Yorkshire area, they would wait there for further instructions.

Unfortunately for Ivanov, one of his teams was compromised when one of the team members accidentally left a fingerprint on the scene. His biometrics matched to an MI6 database on potential Spetsnaz members, and the British authorities followed him back to his team's hideout. After two days of surveilling the two-man team, British authorities raided the house they were operating out of. Major Ivanov's team fully utilized their combat training, taking several police officers to their graves. However, they'd ultimately died in a hail of gunfire, which had made for a very splashy headline across the country.

The other teams had succeeded in their missions, with one of the teams scoring a three-for-one when a group of three Tory MPs were killed during lunch. Several months had passed now though, and they were all becoming increasingly anxious for their next kill. The one consolation that they took was the story they saw unfolding on the news; their actions had clearly hurt the ruling party's control of the government. Between the domestic turmoil and the high casualties in the war, Prime Minister Katherine Edwards was steadily losing her hold on the government.

Finally, the day they had been waiting for arrived. Their GRU handler left them a message. They would carry out a mortar attack against RAF Menwith Hill, a critical facility in the British early-warning system. Shutting it down would increase the potential success of an air or missile attack against the British Isles.

Their instructions had been specific; they were to be in position to bomb the base at precisely 2100 hours—not a minute before and not a minute later. Major Ivanov's eight Spetsnaz piled into the two vans and headed out to the Darley Supersonic Bike Park, an off-road bike park. The location was relatively removed from any local population and within range for the mortars to hit the RAF base. This spot gave them the best possible chance of pulling off the attack and still being able to escape. His experienced team would be able to fire off all thirty-six mortar rounds in less than three minutes.

It took them nearly two hours to reach the bike park. When they arrived, it was already dark, so of course, the park was closed. One of the sergeants popped out of the lead van, whipped out his lock pick set, and made quick work of the padlock on the gate. After the vans drove through, the sergeant closed the entrance again, placing the lock on one side without snapping it shut. This way, hopefully no one would spot anything out of the ordinary while they prepared for their attack.

As they pulled up to their launch site, Major Ivanov began issuing orders in rapid fire. "Sergeant Morozov, I want you to work on getting the mortar tubes ready. Alexin, position the mortar rounds near the tubes, so they'll be ready when the firing starts. Lieutenant Nikolaev, get in position to start calling in the rounds. Make sure they're on target, and if they're off, call in the adjustment so we can keep the rounds coming. We need to take those radar domes out—that is our primary mission."

"Yes, Sir," they replied in unison.

Lieutenant Nikolaev grabbed his small pack and his AK-104 and headed off to his observation point. As the other soldiers got the mortar tubes setup and ready, Ivanov ordered one of the sergeants to head back down the dirt road to the entrance of the park. The sergeant dutifully sought out a few bushes where he could hide and observe the road approaching their position. With a high-explosive round in his grenade gun, if someone did manage to find them, he'd be ready to take them out.

Major Artem Ivanov looked at his wristwatch—one minute until showtime. He keyed in his mic. "Viper Two, are you in position?" he asked Lieutenant Nikolaev.

"Viper Six, Viper Two is in position. I'm ready when you guys are," he responded.

Ivanov pulled a notebook out of his pocket. He had been given a set of exact coordinates for their targets from their GRU handlers, so they had a pretty good idea where the rounds needed to land.

"Drop the first round," he ordered.

Sergeant Morozov lifted the mortar above his shoulder and held it over the tube for just a second before he dropped the round down the tube. He instinctively moved to the side just as the propellant for the round ignited and launched the mortar into the air. The round flew high and true, over the protective perimeter fence of the RAF base, and landed just short and to the right of the central cluster of radar domes that they needed to take out.

"Viper Six. Adjust fire. Up 100 meters, right 50 meters. Fire for effect," called Lieutenant Nikolaev.

Morozov made a quick adjustment to the mortar tubes, and the team of Special Forces quickly dropped rounds as fast as they could. In less than three minutes, they had fired all thirty-six rounds. Explosions and sirens both blared off in the distance, a sure sign of their handiwork.

Major Ivanov spoke loudly to the men. "Leave the tubes, and let's get in the vans and get out of here."

As the others quickly climbed into the two delivery vans they were using as cover, Sergeant Morozov pulled a pin on each of the three thermite grenades, making sure each of the three tubes was spiked and would destroy any physical or forensic evidence left behind.

While they were making their way down the trail to the park exit, Major Ivanov heard an unwanted sound—the telltale whoomphing of helicopter blades. *Thump, thump, thump* came the reverberating noise. It was clearly getting closer to their position.

He let out a stream of exceptionally crude Russian vulgarities. *"They must have had a direction finder radar set up at the base. How did we not know about that?"* thought Ivanov.

He ran through their various options, which were very limited. They didn't have a MANPAD with them, so shooting the helicopter down with a missile was out of the question. Trying to run away in the van was also not going to work; it was 2100 hours and this far out in the county, there wouldn't be a lot of traffic. They would be easily found.

Ivanov looked around at the faces in the van, and then he made the only sensible decision he could in this situation. "Listen up," he said. "There's a helicopter coming our way. If that chopper discovers us, it's going to attack us. We do not have a lot of options. If we have to return fire, I want you guys to focus your firepower on the cockpit of the helicopter or its engine. We need to disable it quickly and then do our best to get away and blend back into the population. If we make it out of this and get separated, go to Alternate Plan Charlie and stand by for further instructions. Is that understood?"

"Yes, Sir," they replied.

Ivanov's radio crackled to life. "Viper Six, this is Viper Two," said Lieutenant Nikolaev, who sounded out of breath from running toward the entrance of the park to meet up with the team. "We have a Lynx helicopter inbound to our position…he just flew over me. He's headed right for you guys!"

Ivanov yelled, "Everyone out! Shoot it down as soon as you see it!" Their vehicle ground to a halt on the dirt trail. Seconds later the doors opened, and everyone spilled out of the van just as the roar of a heavy machine gun pierced the air and bullets ripped through the vehicle.

****

Royal Air Force Menwith Hill

Captain Ian Pendleton was aggravated. He took a long pull on his cigarette and slowly released the smoke through his nostrils, trying to let out all of his frustrations with it.

"How am I going to get back into the action that's happening on the Continent?" he wondered.

He had been sidelined for a while. During one of the failed offensives in Ukraine, Pendleton had been on a flying mission when his Lynx had taken heavy enemy fire and had been shot down. While he'd survived with just a bullet wound to the leg, his copilot and two crew members had all perished when the helicopter had caught fire. Ian had barely had enough time to get himself out of the chopper before it had blown up, let alone try and drag all three of the unconscious crew members out of the wreckage.

Pendleton had been plagued since then with the constant cycle of memories from that day. He felt terrible about not having tried harder to see if any of his crew members were alive before he'd fled from the wreckage. All that had run through his mind was that the helicopter was on fire, his leg was bleeding badly, and he knew he needed to get away before he passed out from blood loss.

Following his recovery, Captain Pendleton had been assigned a new helicopter and crew and sent to Menwith Hill to give support to the local RAF bases in case they came under ground attack. It tore him up not being sent back to a frontline combat unit, but even though he wished he were on the front lines, he was slowly trying to accept his new role.

Once a night, Pendleton and his crew would fly around the bases where they were assigned and use their infrared and thermal sights to see if they spotted anything out of the ordinary. Due to a mechanical problem on the earlier shift, they were now two hours behind schedule.

Captain Pendleton finished his cigarette break just before the crew chief, Staff Sergeant Linda Faux, gave him the signal that she had just finished her systems check of his new Lynx.

Suddenly, there was an odd *thump* in the distance. Then the noise disappeared.

"Did you hear that, Chief?" asked Pendleton as he quickly jumped to his feet.

A second later, they heard the unmistakable whistling sound of the mortar flying in. *Bam!* The round exploded next to one of the radar domes.

"Everyone in the helicopter now!" yelled Captain Pendleton. "We need to get airborne and find where that's coming from!" He quickly ran to his own helicopter and jumped in. Before the next round could land, Ian skipped

99% of his preflight checks as he immediately turned the engine over and got the blades going. His copilot jumped into his seat and grabbed for his helmet. The other two crew members hastily did the same.

"Sergeant Faux, make sure the machine gun is ready. When we find out who's firing those mortars at the base, you need to light them up! Understood?" He shouted to be heard over the now rapidly spinning blades.

Before she could respond, explosions suddenly rocked the base. Multiple mortar rounds landed among the radar domes that dominated the southern half of the base. It was clear by looking at where the explosions were cropping up that the attackers were targeting the early-warning radar systems and not the actual members who manned them.

After a few tense moments, Pendleton took the Lynx off the ground. At first, they skidded and slid along the grassy field, and then they rose a little. Finally, they gained more altitude as their power ramped up. Once in the air, everyone scanned the nearby area, trying to see where the mortars were coming from.

"Over there, three o'clock!" shouted Sergeant Faux as she spotted three more mortars lifting off from behind a cluster of trees.

Ian scanned that area, and while he could not see the exact launch point, he did catch a glimpse of the mortar rounds as they reached their zenith point and fell back to earth. He turned the helicopter in that direction and applied some speed.

Lieutenant Samantha Corbyn, his copilot, turned the infrared on and scanned the area. Not seeing anything pop up, she switched over to thermals. Immediately, she and Pendleton saw a cluster of people doing something in the trees and then piling into two vehicles. One person appeared to have lit off some sort of thermite grenade, because whatever he dropped in the glowing hot mortar tubes flared up with almost instant heat.

"That's them. Call it in, Corbyn!" Pendleton directed. He angled the Lynx to come in for a better attack run. With two machine guns fitted next to the side doors, he was going to angle the helicopter to come in with a slight bank to the left so Sergeant Faux would have a good angle to attack them from.

"I see them. Engaging now!" shouted Faux as she depressed the butterfly trigger on her machine gun. Her weapon chattered, spitting out rounds at a high rate in the direction of the lead vehicle. She saw the red tracers hitting just in front of the vehicle, with one or two slamming directly into it. Adjusting her fire, she depressed the trigger again and let out another burst of machine-gun fire. Then she walked the fire back to the second vehicle as Captain Pendleton veered the helicopter to the left and slowed them down.

As she was adjusting her weapon to open fire again, she saw half a dozen muzzle flashes. One of the weapons was using green tracers, which quickly whipped through the air in their direction. The helicopter jolted, and Linda felt bullets hitting the side of it. She fired back at the attackers, desperately trying to silence them before they got lucky and shot them down. One of the vehicles caught fire and summarily exploded, engulfing at least two of the attackers.

"We're taking fire!" Corbyn yelled to Pendleton as he jinked the helicopter hard to one side, giving the chopper additional throttle as he tried to gain altitude. *Thwap, thwap, crunch.* The helicopter continued taking hits.

Alarm bells blared in Pendleton's helmet. He and Corbyn continued to try and pull them up higher to get them out of range of the ground fire. "Is everyone OK?" he shouted over the intercom, hoping no one had been hit.

Sergeant Faux turned to look at her partner-in-crime, who gave her a thumbs-up sign that she was fine. "We're OK back here," Faux replied. "How about you guys in front?"

"We're good," answered Pendleton. "I'm pulling us up and out of their range. I'll come around again from higher altitude. See if you can keep them pinned down while we wait for additional help to arrive."

The Lynx banked hard to the right as they settled into a high-altitude circle racetrack that would allow them to loiter over the area and continue to shoot at them with their machine guns until reinforcements could arrive. Corbyn had already called in the quick reaction force, who was currently en route to their position. They just needed to keep the soldiers on the ground pinned down while they waited for help.

****

Major Ivanov cursed as the helicopter continued to loiter above them, firing at them. *"We need to find a way to get out of here before their reinforcements arrive or we're through,"* he realized.

Reading the major's mind, Sergeant Morozov unzipped the rifle case he had grabbed from the van during their hasty retreat. He quickly pulled the OSV-96 sniper rifle out of the case and unfolded it. Locking the rifle in place, he slapped the five-round magazine of 12.7×108mm AP rounds into place. Lifting the rifle to his shoulder, he took aim at the helicopter that was circling around them, looking to kill more of his comrades.

Sighting in the engine compartment of the helicopter, he took aim at it and squeezed the trigger. The rifle barked loudly as the armor-piercing round flew out of the barrel at 920 meters per second. As soon as the next round cycled into his rifle, he saw a small spark on the engine compartment of the helicopter, followed by a small flame. The helicopter listed a bit to one side.

Morozov took aim at the cockpit of the helicopter as it continued to struggle to stay airborne and fired another round. This time, the helicopter veered hard. The pilot was clearly trying to put some more distance between them as their chopper fell from the sky. A few minutes later, they heard the helicopter crash, though they didn't see an explosion.

"Everyone, get in the van. We need to get out of here!" yelled Major Ivanov as the remaining members piled into the only working vehicle. He was angry that they had lost another three members of their team during this last skirmish.

As soon as everyone was inside, the driver immediately gave the van gas, accelerating quickly down the dirt road. In no time at all, they had reached the country road, which they all hoped will lead them to safety. They raced down the back road toward the A61. From there, it should be easier to put some distance between themselves and the scene of the attack.

Five minutes went by as continued racing toward the highway. Then they spotted the first signs of trouble. A small cluster of police cars blocked the road that led to the A61. Ivanov saw the driver look in his side mirrors.

"Sir, we have a police car chasing us and a road block in front of us," he reported nervously. "I have nowhere to turn off right now. We're going to have to engage the roadblock and hope the vehicle survives or steal another ride."

"OK, everyone, here's what we're going to do," declared Major Ivanov. "When the van comes to a stop, I need everyone to focus your fire on the police at the roadblock—use suppressive fire and charge them. We need to take them out and then split up. Try to steal one of their squad cars or another car in the village if you can on the way out. Take separate routes to the alternate location, and I'll see you there." Ivanov readied his weapon for what was certain to be a brief and violent shoot-out with the police.

Approaching the roadblock at high speed, the driver suddenly slammed on the brakes as the police officers began to shoot at them with their pistols. In less than a second, the Spetsnaz soldiers jumped out of the vehicle and immediately emptied their magazines at the two police cars and the four officers manning the roadblock.

While Ivanov's men were attacking the police in front of them, he went around the other side of the van to face the police car giving them chase. He leveled the 40mm grenade gun at them and pulled the trigger. He watched the round fly toward the vehicle and impact on the front hood, sending shrapnel into the front of the vehicle and either killing or severely wounding the officer driving the vehicle. The car veered off the road and hit a tree; flames burst out from the hood.

Ivanov carefully moved around to look at the carnage at the roadblock. He saw two of his soldiers laying down suppressive fire while two more of his men charged the police. In seconds, all four of the police officers lay dead on the ground from multiple gunshots. As quickly as the engagement had happened, it ended. All five of the Spetsnaz soldiers survived.

They were all in the process of moving to find getaway vehicles when they heard the thumping of another helicopter coming toward them. Turning to look over his shoulder, Ivanov spotted the nose gun of the Apache attack helicopter blink a couple of times before his brain registered that his body was being torn apart by the 30mm chain gun. In seconds, all five remaining members of the Spetsnaz team were wiped out in spectacular fashion.

****

Norwegian Sea
40 Meters Above the Water

Skimming just above the water, the Russian Tu-160 Blackjack bomber was closing in on their firing point. Colonel Petr Orlov was perspiring profusely as he fought to keep his plane just above the sea. This was probably the most nervous he had been on a combat mission since the surprise attack on the first day of the war, and it was also his longest mission. To avoid detection, Colonel Orlov had his flight of four bombers top off their fuel tanks over the Barents Sea before dropping in altitude to just above the wavetops for the remainder of their flight.

At precisely 2110 hours local time, they would rise up to 500 meters, fire off their twelve Kh-101 long-range cruise missiles and then drop back down to the wave tops. If all went well, they would successfully strike several key industrial and government buildings in Aberdeen, Birmingham, Liverpool, and London.

"I wonder how many of our cruise missiles will hit their targets?" Orlov pondered.

The British had an exceptional antimissile picket system along their coast. To date, they had succeeded in intercepting every cruise missile attack the Russians had tried. During their preflight briefing, they had been informed that a Spetsnaz team was going to handle the early-warning system at RAF Menwith Hill. If that came to fruition, then chances were a lot of their cruise missiles might just hit their targets this time.

As Orlov's bomber neared the launch time, he moved his left hand to wipe the beads of sweat that were now running down his face as the aircraft sped above the water at 960 kilometers per hour.

His radio crackled. "We're two minutes away from launch," announced his bombardier.

"Copy that. Rising. Stand by for weapons release," Orlov replied. He pulled back on the controls, keeping an eye on the altimeter until he saw he was at the launch height and leveled out. If there were an enemy ship or aircraft operating in the area, he would suddenly appear on their radar. He was exposed now.

Listening in on the radio net, he could hear his fellow bombers releasing their cruise missiles. Then his bombardier came over the intercom. "Weapons release," came the order.

"Releasing weapons," Orlov answered. One after another of his twelve cruise missiles dropped from his internal weapons bay, igniting and speeding off to their preprogrammed targets.

Just as the last missile dropped free of the weapons bay and sped off, the defensive systems officer jumped on the intercom. "We have a search radar painting us. I'm working on jamming it now. It appears to be from a ship in the area," he explained.

Colonel Orlov's radar warning alarm blared in his ear. Someone was trying to get a lock on them, and he had to do his best to throw them off.

As soon as the light from his bay door turned from green to red, he banked the aircraft hard to head toward home. Then he dropped back down to 40 meters above the water and increased speed to nearly Mach 2. His heart pumped wildly.

A painful minute went by. Suddenly, the radar warbling in his ear stopped. Orlov sighed in relief—they were in the clear again.

When he had placed a hundred kilometers between them and the spot where they had been detected by an enemy radar, he slowed the bomber down to its cruise speed to conserve fuel. Thankfully, a refueling tanker would be waiting for them once they entered the Barents Sea area and the safety of Russian airspace.

****

St. James, London
Oxford and Cambridge Club

The following morning was relatively cool as the sun finally rose and burned away the remnant of the morning twilight. Anthony Chattem depressed the call button on the outdoor table of the Oxford and Cambridge Club. Despite being a senior member of the British government, he hadn't been whisked away when the capital had been attacked, and for that, he was supremely irate. Seeing that he was considered not important enough to protect by the Tories, he opted to go have breakfast at one of his favorite private locations.

Mr. Chattem liked to eat breakfast at the exclusive club at least once a month. He particularly liked drinking his tea on the outside terrace. The cool morning air was always invigorating before a busy day.

His Chief of Staff greeted him somberly. "It's a shame what happened last night, isn't it, Mr. Chattem?" he remarked.

Chattem nodded, doing his best to conceal any hint of happiness at the misfortunes of others.

"*The thing is—this is going to play well in the press and with my supporters*," he mused. He imagined a headline splashed across the front page of the paper. *Tories Secretly Hope Labour Leader Gets Killed in Russian Raid.*

Looking out into the city, Mr. Chattem could see the pillars of smoke still hanging in the air from the multiple cruise missiles that hit a series of defense and government buildings across the city. The maître-d' opened the door to the terrace, and a colonel from the Ministry of Defence walked out to join them, along with a couple members of Chattem's security detail.

The MOD colonel cleared his throat to gain Chattem's attention. "Sir, it is highly recommended that we move you to a more secure facility," he announced. "We're not sure if the attack on London is over."

Mr. Chattem stared him down with daggers. "Interesting how the government only deems it necessary for me to be moved to a protected bunker several hours *after* the attack, as opposed to before the missiles landed," he replied angrily.

The colonel's expression did not change, which further annoyed Chattem. "I think if the Russians were going to launch another surprise attack like they did last night, they would have done it already," he replied.

The colonel remained stoic and unchanged. Chattem was boiling now. "Answer me this, Colonel—how was it the Russians were able to get close enough to hit us with cruise missiles and not be detected? How is it our defensive systems were unable to intercept these missiles, as they had in the past?"

The colonel stood there for a moment, looking as if he wanted to say something course, but he managed to hold his tongue. Instead, he let out a soft sigh and replied, "A Spetsnaz team disabled our early-warning system just as the enemy bombers fired their cruise missiles. By the time we were able to get other radar systems operational to fill in the gaps in coverage, the enemy missiles were raining down on our cities."

Chattem grunted. "What targets were hit here in London, and what were the casualty figures?" he asked. He planned on using the information in his upcoming press conference he would call later in the day.

The colonel pulled a notepad out of his breast pocket and flipped it open. "The Ministry of Defence building, Her Majesty's Treasury, Scotland Yard, Houses of Parliament, Waterloo Station, Kings Cross Station, and the Lloyd's Building were all severely damaged, along with several other buildings in the insurance district. The remaining five missiles hit Heathrow Airport, causing significant damage to Terminal 5 and Terminal 3."

The colonel paused for a second before continuing. "It appears the intent of the Russian attack was twofold: first to damage our transportation system, which is why they targeted Waterloo, Kings Cross, and Heathrow, and second to go after our government centers to prove the MOD could not protect them and the population. As to casualties, fortunately, the attacks happened late in the evening, so it could have been worse. So far, there have been roughly two thousand people killed, and almost the same number injured. Most of those who perished died at Heathrow and the two train stations."

"*This is a disaster for the Tories*," thought Mr. Chattem. He had to work to keep his face calm as he realized that he might really have a legitimate chance of unseating

PM Edwards. Then a sick feeling hit him in the pit of his stomach. *"Could Max's backers have caused this?"* he wondered. He didn't think it was possible that they were really that powerful and influential.

"Very well, Colonel. We'll come with you to the bunker," he conceded. "Please lead the way." He got up and followed the colonel to a waiting vehicle.

Asian Rivals

Washington, D.C.

General John Bennet grabbed his backpack from the overhead bin and headed toward the baggage claim. He was feeling a bit disoriented after his long flight from South Korea. Even though he had mastered the skill of sleeping anywhere, anytime—a necessity in the military—the time change was throwing him off. He wasn't sure if it was day or nighttime anymore. It didn't help that he still didn't know why he had been called to meet with the President. He wasn't sure if he should be happy or frightened about losing his job.

When he arrived at Carousel 3, he heard a familiar voice call to him, "John!"

He turned around. His wife, Stacy, and three youngest sons were standing there, waving to get his attention.

A flood of emotions washed over him. Bennet hadn't seen his family for months, and he hadn't been expecting to see them during this trip. Despite the tough guy persona, he shed a few tears as they all hugged each other.

General Bennet relaxed a bit as they all rode together in the black Chevy Suburban that had been sent to pick them up.

"They sent my family—this has to bode well for my meeting with Gates," he thought.

Bennet allowed himself to chat with his sons about school, girls, and their sports teams. He held his wife's hand and shot her a few smiles in between his sons' chattiness; she never got a word in edgewise when they got together after a long break.

Meanwhile, he kept mulling over what he would possibly be discussing with the President. He secretly hoped that maybe this meeting might result in him finally getting what he really wanted, which was to get General Cutter's Marines assigned to him for the invasion of China. They had already succeeded in securing the Russian Far East, pushing the Russian forces all the way back to Khabarovsk; he was certain that if he had been able to keep them in the fight for a few more months, they would have been able to reinvade China and push through to Shenyang. Maybe they could have even threatened Beijing…but his multiple requests to the SecDef had not gone in his favor. So far, General Cutter's forces were being consolidated in the Northern Mariana Islands and Guam to retake the

Philippines and Taiwan before the Chinese could turn them into island fortresses.

The Suburban pulled through the security check point in front of the White House, and he was startled out of his sea of swirling thoughts.

"Dad, this is so cool!" exclaimed Tyrone, his youngest son.

General Bennet remembered the first time he had seen 1600 Pennsylvania Ave.—it was pretty awe-inspiring.

"I'm excited to share your first White House trip with you, son," he said with a smile.

Once they made it through the security checks to the inside of the building, Bennet's family was brought around the facility with a very comprehensive tour. Finally, they ended up in the Oval Office. At that point, even his sixteen-year-old son, Elijah, who was rarely impressed by anything, was basically awestruck.

"Dad, you just earned me some serious points with the girls at school," he commented.

"Glad I could help," Bennet answered with a smirk.

"Dad, Dad, can I sit in the President's chair and get Mom to take a picture?" he asked.

Just then, President Gates walked in.

"Sure," Gates answered, smiling.

"Mr. President, it's an honor to meet you, Sir," said Tyrone in awe.

"It's an honor to meet you, too, Tyrone," he responded cheerfully. He greeted the whole family with handshakes and kissed Stacy Bennet on the cheek. Then he posed with Tyrone at the desk, pretending to hand him an important document, as if Bennet's son were the President and not the other way around.

"It's just so surreal watching the President interact so naturally with my family," thought General Bennet. Gates happily did selfies with Elijah and his thirteen-year-old, Isaac, as well.

The SecDef walked over to Bennet. He leaned in. "I'll bet you're wondering what in the heck is going on, aren't you?" he asked with a crooked smile.

"Um, yeah, I think you could say that," he responded, not sure what else to say.

"We are shifting to your theater," Secretary Castle explained. "You've been in charge of operations in Korea—and by the way, the President has been impressed with your work there—but we need a new commander to take over as overall commander of Asia. The President asked me to nominate you."

General Bennet didn't respond. He was a bit stunned.

"You're going to be given your fifth star," said the SecDef, half punching him in the shoulder. "You're going to be only the seventh person in American military history to be a five-star general, and the first of African-American decent. If I weren't the Secretary of Defense and your boss, I'd be really jealous of you right now."

A White House photographer came in and took some official photographs of Bennet's family with the President before his wife and sons were escorted to an anteroom and asked to wait while Gates spoke with Bennet privately.

The room was suddenly quiet with just the four of them there: the President, his Chief of Staff, the Secretary of Defense, and General Bennet. They all took a seat.

"General Bennet, I'm sure the SecDef here gave you a little heads-up as to why you are here," said Gates.

Bennet nodded.

"I've been supremely impressed with your ability to handle what's been thrown at you," the President continued. "You've had to liaise and coordinate with the Japanese and South Korean governments, something that I know has not been easy, considering the two countries' past histories. With your assistance, these two nations are fighting side-by-side to defeat the Russians and the Chinese. You helped orchestrate the defeat of the North Korean regime, and you held things together against all odds while our focus had been on Europe."

Bennet held up his hand, ready to protest and say something about it being a "team effort," but the President spoke before he could object.

"I don't know that many other people who could have handled that the way you did, General Bennet. Therefore, I am going to promote you to be America's seventh five-star general, and you will become the Pacific theater supreme commander. All US and Allied forces will now be under your command." The President paused for effect before he continued. "I'm hereby ordering you to defeat the People's Republic of China and the Eastern Alliance. You're charged with liberating the Philippines and Taiwan in addition to your objectives in the Russian Far East and the Koreas. Do you accept this promotion and position?" he asked.

Bennet didn't skip a beat. "Absolutely, I accept, Mr. President. It's been an honor to serve under you as our Commander-in-Chief. I won't let you or the country down, Sir. Of that you can be assured."

"Excellent," responded the President. "Be warned, though, Bennet, I hold my commanders to a high standard, and I never hesitate to replace commanders that are not up to the task. I expect you to hold that same stance with your own command. I want you to think about who you need to promote or move to a different position and utilize your people to the best of their abilities."

"Yes, Sir," said Bennet, already mulling over how he would form up his new command.

"As you know, I'm not a military man," conceded Gates. "That's why I have Castle, and now you, to implement the execution of this war. Remember, we need to apply maximum pressure on the Chinese at all times. I know you wanted to keep General Cutter's Marines in the Russian Far East, but right now, we need his Marines in the South Pacific. I need you to do whatever is necessary to make sure he's successful in liberating the Philippines and Taiwan."

The President paused for a moment, clearly giving some thought as to what to say next. "Cutter's success is your success, and his failure is your failure as well. You two need to work together on this. He's a good commander—use him and his skill set to meet your goals.

Understood?" he asked, in a tone that was more of a warning.

General Bennet smiled. "I understand, Mr. President. I see you've heard of the rivalry between me and General Cutter. We have had a bit of a competition between us, to be sure, but we are also good friends." He thought about his eldest son, Isaiah, who had joined the Marines against his advice. Cutter had moved him to be his aide as a personal favor; it wouldn't keep him entirely out of danger, but he wouldn't be an infantry platoon commander on the front lines, either. Bennet definitely owed him one. "The two of us will win Asia for you, Mr. President. You can count on that," he asserted.

"Excellent," replied Gates, clearly relieved by the response he had received. "Then I believe we have a press announcement to make, and my wife has arranged for a special dinner for all of us—well, Jim and his wife, Liam Greeson and his better half, and our families." He smiled and stood up. The other men followed suit.

When General Bennet entered the room to reunite with his family, he found his sons chatting excitedly with the President's son, Connor Gates. They were all comparing notes about their favorite computer games.

He walked over to his wife and chuckled. "I guess we can catch up now," he joked.

******

South Korea
Camp Humphreys

General Bennet had enjoyed his whirlwind trip to D.C. and the time with his family, but the task at hand had quickly called him back to the reality of war. It was time to get down to the brass tacks of destroying the Eastern Alliance.

He spent most of the long flight on his way back thinking of how he was going to form up his army and who he was going to promote. Bennet contemplated for some time and then came to the obvious conclusion that he needed to promote his three corps commanders: Lieutenant General Tony Wilde, Lieutenant General Jacob LaFine, and Major General Amy Cooper.

Amy Cooper was probably the most obvious choice for a promotion, and not just because she was the first woman to command a combat arms corps during the war. It was no accident that she had become a general to begin with. She had served valiantly as an attack helicopter pilot during the first year of Operation Enduring Freedom in Afghanistan, and then during the invasion of Iraq, she had become a battalion commander of an attack helicopter unit. Her unit had single-handedly destroyed an Iraqi Republican Guard tank unit that was on its way to attack her US brothers-in-arms. She had gone on to serve two more tours in Iraq. In 2006, she'd gained a bit of notoriety when one of her wingmen had been shot down and she'd landed her helicopter, somehow managing to strap the pilot and copilot of the downed chopper onto the wings of her helicopter, saving them from certain death. It wasn't long after that that she'd received her first general's star and completed her obligatory tour at the Pentagon.

Prior to the start of this current war, she had served as the operations commander at US Army Europe. When the Russians had launched their surprise attack, she had been wounded, along with most of her staff. After spending four months recovering from the wounds incurred during those missile attacks, she had been given command of a newly formed infantry division in the States. Her division had fought well during the Chinese counterattack, and she had landed on General Bennet's radar. He had promoted her to be one of his three corps commanders, and she had only continued to impress.

Lieutenant General Tony Wilde had also been serving as one of Bennet's corps commanders, out in the Russian Far East. He had earned a PhD at Harvard, although he had been highly intelligent way before that. As a battalion commander during the invasion of Iraq in 2003, and a brigade commander during the infamous Iraq Troop Surge in 2007, he had distinguished himself above his peers and managed to earn a Silver Star.

Rounding out the group was Lieutenant General Jacob LaFine, an Army Ranger who had also earned a Silver Star when he'd led a rescue effort to recover a downed helicopter. He had worked as General Petreaus' aide during the troop surge, and later worked as an aide to the Secretary of Defense. After a lot of high-level training, he had become the deputy commander of ISAF forces in Afghanistan. General Bennet was grateful to have him on his team.

It wasn't long before Bennet was sitting in a room with all three of them and their staff officers. As Bennet's aide brought in a fresh pot of coffee for everyone, they all took turns congratulating him on his new promotion to Supreme Allied Commander of Asia. The aide returned with some sandwiches—this was going to be a working lunch. General Bennet allowed some chitchat to continue until everyone had their food and drink situated, then he tapped his knuckles on the table as if calling a meeting to order.

"All right, it's time to get down to business," he declared. "The President and the SecDef have directed our theater to become the new priority theater. That means we will be going to the front of the line when it comes to new troops and equipment coming straight from the factory. The President has tasked us with getting our forces ready to defeat the Chinese and the Eastern Alliance—it's a tall order, but we command the greatest fighting force the world has ever seen. We will rise to the occasion and defeat our nation's enemies."

Everyone in the room nodded in approval.

Bennet went on. "Things are going to move fast over the next couple of months. We're going to promote a lot of people as we fill our ranks and units. Effective immediately, I'm forming up new Army groups. Each Army will be assigned a specific set of goals that will coincide with our theater objectives."

He turned to Lieutenant General Tony Wilde first. "Tony, you're being given your fourth star and will form Army Group One," he announced matter-of-factly. "Since your current corps is already in the Russian Far East, your new group will be charged with defeating the Indian Army that has set up camp in Irkutsk. Once you have accomplished that mission, I want you to set up your new headquarters there. Then you are to tear into the Chinese rear areas and look to liberate Mongolia. That will place a large force in the Chinese backyard."

"Yes, Sir," General Wilde responded.

General Bennet looked down at his notes. "I'm going to swell your ranks to 240,000 soldiers, Tony. I can't guarantee you that you'll get all of those troops immediately, but we'll reinforce you as our offensive progresses. I'm giving you three weeks to prepare and organize your forces to attack, so that means your offensive needs to be underway by June 21st. Is that understood?" he asked.

General Wilde nodded. "You can count on Army Group One to accomplish our mission, Sir," he answered confidently. "We'll make that Indian Army wish they had stayed neutral. They'll regret the day they took up arms against the US of A."

The other generals were smiling broadly. They liked his style; he liked to get into the weeds and did a lot of the briefings himself or would interrupt his briefers. There was never a dull moment.

General Bennet turned next to Lieutenant General Jacob LaFine. "I'm also promoting you, General LaFine. You're going to take command of the newly formed Army Group Two. Honestly, you will probably have the hardest task of all—your group will be invading the People's Republic of China."

LaFine pursed his lips. Invading China was not going to be an easy challenge. He also was not one to shy away from adversity.

Bennet checked his notes again. "You've got, what—90,000 soldiers right now?" he asked.

"That sounds about right, General. I have a few divisions arriving this week, so that will add another 25,000 to my ranks," LaFine answered.

"OK," said Bennet. "I'm going to direct most of our new reinforcements to your Army group. Eventually, your forces will number around 350,000 soldiers." He scratched out a few calculations before he continued. "Because it's going to take a little longer to get your Army group the numbers, you're going to need to break out of Korea. I'm going to delay your offensive until July 30th. This will give General Wilde time to get his offensive well underway and time for your ranks and equipment to swell."

At this point, all of the staff officers in the room were furiously taking notes.

Bennet continued, "I want your Army group to drive the Chinese back to the ruins of Shenyang. This will place a lot of pressure on the Chinese Army to stop you from advancing, which will in turn keep the PLA distracted from our efforts to liberate the Philippines and Taiwan."

"Yes, Sir. We will get this done," said General LaFine emphatically.

Bennet turned to General Amy Cooper. "Saved the best for last?" she asked, trying to lighten the mood of the room a little.

General Bennet smiled. "Major General Amy Cooper, I'm promoting you two grades to a four-star general, and you're going to take over Army Group Three. Right now, your forces have formed up in Vladivostok, Russia; I want your Army group to push into northern China and capture Harbin and Changchun. These two provinces are a major part of the Chinese manufacturing base, and a large portion of their steel factories and other critical war production factories are located in these provinces. Their capture will go a long way toward defeating the Chinese."

General Cooper beamed with pride. She was excited about this opportunity to lead an army group in combat.

"Your group is probably going to be the slowest to form right now," said Bennet. "Not because it's not a priority, but because of the timeline for Army Group One to meet their goals before the winter months and because of the pressure Army Group Two will need to apply in order for your command to succeed in capturing the manufacturing northern half of China."

"No problem, Sir. When do you want my group to move?" she asked.

"I want your command ready to execute your offensive on August 30th," he responded.

General Bennet turned to look each of his three new army group commanders in the eye. "The key to our success, Generals, is going to be speed," he advised. "We need to be agile in our movements, adjusting where we need to and hitting the enemy fast and hard when the opportunity presents itself. I need your groups to inflict maximum force on the enemy. Be aggressive, and do not let up. Is that understood?"

Seeing no objections, Bennet dismissed the group to get back to their commands and implement their new orders.

****

Guam
Anderson Air Force Base
US Marine Corps HQ

General Roy Cutter picked up speed as he made the final turn on his morning run. He was now sprinting at full speed as he raced down the parking ramp of the airfield for the last mile of his five-mile run. Cutter felt the flood of endorphins rushing through him and the stress melting away; he really enjoyed this daily ritual. As the wind whipped past his face, he formulated his plans for the coming day.

Parked on the ramp where he was running was the newest squadron of F-35Bs, which had arrived the night before.

"*These are really going to add to our Marine capability*," he thought with a smile on his face.

Cutter completed his run and grabbed a towel to wipe the sweat off his face. It was time to make the rounds.

As his Marines extricated themselves from the Russian Far East, they were all making the time-consuming transition to Guam and the Northern Mariana Islands in preparation for the eventual invasion of Taiwan and the

Philippines. He had his troops getting ready for the dramatic change in battlefields by engaging in extensive jungle and amphibious assault training. Cutter made his way to one of the observation points to watch that day's mock amphibious assault.

One of General Cutter's lieutenant generals, Al Pinkett, joined him.

"Good morning, Sir," Pinkett said, a little too chipper for that hour of the morning. He had a cup of coffee in his hand, and it might not have been his first.

"Good morning, Pinkett," Cutter responded. "How do you think today's practice run is going to go?"

"I expect it to be successful, Sir. My only real concern is the integration of all of the new graduates that they are sending us from boot camp. So far, we have been able to successfully absorb those Marines into our current forces without any significant issues, but as we continue to grow, it may lead to some disorganization."

General Cutter grunted. "Well, if it does, you need to work that out quickly," he asserted. "We don't have a lot of time to get everyone ready for our operation in Taiwan. Right now, I want two amphibious assault practice runs a week, but if you start to have issues, maybe we go to three."

"Understood, Sir," answered Pinkett. "I know this tempo of training has been intense for our Marines, but I personally would like to make it to the Republic of China before their military units that have been fighting in the mountains and the jungles are wiped out."

"Well, for that, we have to hope that the US Seventh Fleet hurries up its operations. They need to secure the waters around Taiwan and the Philippines. Until they do, we can't set a date for landing our forces."

"Hmm…" said Pinkett. "I can't help you with that one, Sir."

Just then, a flurry of activity began, and they shifted their focus to observing the men and women below them, practicing their drill like a well-choreographed dance.

****

Sumay, Guam
US Naval Base
7th Fleet Headquarters

Vice Admiral Jeff Richards was still getting used to his new command. The past several months had gone by in a blur of activity. His carrier air wings had been beyond busy, providing support to the Marines as they captured the

Russian Far East and providing round-the-clock air cover over the Korean Peninsula.

Fortunately, his carrier air wings had scored over 230 kills, and he had only lost 48 of his own aircraft. Most of those losses had happened while supporting the Marines on the ground. While the Russian air defense was not nearly as dense or well organized as what they had faced in Europe, they were still wreaking havoc on his planes. To help counter the Russian and Chinese air-defense systems, the Navy had transferred nearly all the EA-Growler aircraft from the Atlantic fleets to Asia. The added electronic countermeasure planes had significantly reduced his losses.

The next challenge Admiral Richards had to deal with was clearing the waters around Taiwan and the Philippines. For that, he was going to need some help.

Richards walked into the briefing room of his newly established South Pacific headquarters, where he saw his three strike group commanders waiting for him, along with the carrier commanders, the Pacific submarine commander and a couple of destroyer squadron commanders.

"*Good, everyone was able to make it in for this meeting,*" he thought with relief.

Admiral Richards took his seat quickly, wanting to get the ball rolling. "Gentlemen, we have four weeks to clear

250

the waters around Taiwan and the Philippines, so the Marines can begin their ground operations. We've danced around when we want to go after the PLA South China Sea fleet, but time has run out. We need to make a move on them now."

Richards looked at the rear admiral in charge of the Pacific Fleet's submarine force with a look that was less than friendly. "I need to know what the holdup is with the PLA submarine force," he asserted. "Why are we still losing subs to the Chinese and not getting them cleared out? What's the problem?"

Rear Admiral Toby Dag had known this question was going to come. "Sir, several months ago, the Chinese fielded a new high-speed torpedo. The technology surrounding the torpedo has been discussed and researched for decades by DARPA, the Russians, and China, but in a nutshell, they appear to have cracked the code on it and are now inflicting some heavy losses on us as a consequence."

Toby saw a few puzzled looks and realized he needed to say more. "The new torpedo is able to travel at speeds of up to 150 knots, with a range of ten kilometers. That obviously creates a very big problem for us. With these kinds of speeds, it's impossible for us to defend against it. Fortunately, it appears that only one of their submarines is currently equipped with this new torpedo. Their Type 095 or *Wuhan*-class submarine is currently the only submarine in their fleet that presently uses this torpedo."

He continued. "I've made it a top priority to sink the *Wuhan*. In the last several months, we've lost eight submarines to the *Wuhan*, as well as three destroyers. That said, I did receive word a couple of hours ago that three of our destroyers believe they may have the *Wuhan* in their sights. We're vectoring in additional P-8 Poseidon to help prosecute the attack. My concern, Admiral—and I'm not sure if naval intelligence can confirm this—is what if they're able to equip this torpedo to their naval bombers or antisubmarine warfare planes? That could prove to be disastrous for us."

Admiral Richards hadn't thought about that before. He'd read reports about this new "super torpedo" and had known it was a problem, but he hadn't considered the torpedoes' use by aircraft. A sinking feeling hit him in the stomach.

"I want every available asset we have hunting the *Wuhan* down and sinking it," Richards ordered. "I want a plan put together on how we're going to engage the South China Sea fleet and sink it. We have to figure out how we're going to support the Marines' liberation of Taiwan and the Philippines, to be executed in the next thirty days."

The meeting went on for another hour as the senior officers strategized how the US was going to engage and destroy the Chinese fleet while not losing more carriers in the process. The Navy was already down three carriers and could ill afford to lose any more. Some creative strategizing was required.

****

Philippine Sea

The past several weeks had been absolutely exhilarating for Captain Liu Huaqing. The *Wuhan* had sunk eight American submarines and three destroyers. It had been a truly marvelous feat and had proved beyond a doubt that this new torpedo was not only going to change the future of naval warfare, it could shift the balance of power in the Pacific.

Looking at the map, Captain Liu contemplated whether his sub should try and go after the American aircraft carriers now or keep nipping at the edges, sinking the ships the US kept sending after them. The *Wuhan* only had twelve more of the experimental torpedoes left, and once they ran out, they'd have to return back to base and hope the factories had built a more for them.

Sensing that someone had walked up to him, Liu looked up and saw that his XO had joined him at the maps table.

"Trying to figure out where we should go next?" inquired his executive officer, Commander Wei Gang.

Liu nodded. "Part of me wants to sail north and go after the Japanese Navy, or perhaps the supply convoys providing men and material to the Korean Peninsula. But I also know the real battle is going to be right here, in the Philippine Sea."

Commander Wei let out a short breath before responding, "It would be inspiring to our people back home and the men if we could sail to the West Coast of America and begin sinking ships off the coast of California."

Captain Liu let out a snort of laughter. "That would be great, but there is no way the admirals would allow us to venture that far away from the main American fleet. I tried to argue that, if allowed to patrol the West Coast of America, we would divert resources away from the American carriers, but they insisted that our new super weapon would be the deciding factor between winning and losing this next battle."

"Should we head toward Guam, then, and seek out the carriers directly?" offered Commander Wei.

Captain Liu traced his hand across the map, running his finger across Guam, then moved his finger to the north. "Let's move in the direction of Saipan. Intelligence said the US Marines are doing a lot of training on Saipan and Tinian Island. Perhaps we can find their amphibious assault ships and sink a few of them."

His XO nodded and smiled at the idea. The two of them began to plot the best avenue of approach and how long it would take them to reach their destination.
****

Unbeknownst to Captain Liu and Commander Wei, several thousand feet above them, a Boeing P-8 Poseidon had been sniffing around them for the past several hours. When the *Wuhan* changed course and began to head toward the Island of Saipan, it increased speed from its stalking speed of seven knots an hour to twenty—this change in speed gave the Poseidon just enough added noise for its incredibly sophisticated sensors to collect enough data to start narrowing down the submarine's exact coordinates. The pilot used that data to call in additional antisubmarine warfare ships and aircraft to help them prosecute an attack on the elusive *Wuhan*.

****

An hour into their new course, Commander Wei received a call from the sonar room. "Commander Wei, we are detecting a series of sonar buoys. Probable enemy aircraft trying to guide additional enemy assets toward us," informed his sonar chief.

A shiver of fear ran down Wei's spine as he realized they might have been discovered. "Have you detected any possible American submarines or other surface warfare ships in the area?" he asked.

"We thought we had a possible underwater contact maybe ten minutes ago, but it's gone. If we could slow down, we might be able to see if we can get a better bead on what we are facing."

Wei looked for the captain and found him talking to another sailor nearby. He quickly got his attention, letting him know he needed to talk with him.

"What's going on, XO?" Captain Lei asked.

"Sir, sonar reported a possible underwater contact and detected sonar buoys being dropped on the surface.

They are recommending we slow down and try to listen for a bit to see what we're potentially facing," explained Wei.

Captain Lei nodded in agreement. "Do it, XO. Slow us down and let's see what's out there."

In minutes, the *Wuhan* had slowed to a mere crawl as they listened with their towed sonar array, hoping and praying they had not been found, or worse, triangulated by the Americans. Over the past several weeks, they'd lived through this type of situation multiple times. In each case, they had been able to identify the hunters and successfully take them out. They hoped their luck would hold in this situation.

As minutes turned into hours, the tension on the *Wuhan* only increased. Their sonar array had detected at least one underwater contact and multiple surface contacts, in addition to a lot of sonar buoy activity on the surface. Clearly the Americans had caught their scent—now it was a matter of whether or not they could slip away. They might get lucky and sink one or more of the contacts, but in doing so, they would most certainly be fired upon.

****

The USS *Indiana*, the newest *Virginia*-class attack submarine, had managed to get within 2,000 meters of the

Wuhan. With their outer torpedo doors opened and lined up for the attack, they proceeded to fire off two of the newest MK 48 Mod 7 torpedoes. The updated torpedoes had a significantly improved sonar and targeting capability, enabled them to effectively navigate past the current antitorpedo defensive systems and decoys.

The *Wuhan* would have had virtually no time to react to the sudden appearance of two American torpedoes, but it suddenly raced forward at maximum speed, attempting to escape through evasive maneuvers. With no time to obtain a proper firing solution on the Americans, and lacking the proper equipment to listen for *Indiana* above the noise they were generating, the Chinese never had a chance to return fire.

In less than a couple of minutes, the two American torpedoes impacted the hull of the *Wuhan*, sinking the vaunted terror of the seas and ending any hope the PLA Navy had of using the *Wuhan* in the final battle of the Pacific.

Passing the Torch

California
SOI West, Camp Pendleton

Captain Tim Long stood at attention with his company of Marines as they graduated from their final course at the School of Infantry. With nearly 50,000 new trainees graduating a month, this ceremony was certainly not unique, but Long was feeling nostalgic.

"*I remember standing here five years ago myself before I became an officer,*" he thought as he looked out on all the young Marines arrayed in their dress uniforms, their families looking on from the bleachers.

Up at the podium, the colonel in charge of recruit training tapped the microphone to gain everyone's full attention. "I'm not going to sugarcoat it and give you some pep talk to make you feel good," he began. "You Marines are going to face adversity. There's a hostile nation bent on fundamentally changing the world and our country. It's incumbent upon you Marines to listen to your NCOs and officers and defeat this dastardly enemy. Remember, these are the same people that enabled the North Koreans to launch nuclear missiles at our cities. This is the same nation that had a hand in the destruction of Oakland and San Francisco just a few hundred miles north of here. Never forget what these enemies have done to our nation."

Surveying the newly-minted Marines, the colonel continued, "Like the Marines after the surprise attack at Pearl Harbor, and the terrorist attacks on September 11th, 2001, we too shall overcome our grief and sorrow, rising up to answer the call of our nation and defend our country, family, and friends from this vicious enemy. I couldn't be prouder to be a Marine than I am right now. To see your young faces and know that you will be the avenging angels protecting our nation and bringing the fight to the enemy gives me great joy. I'm proud to call you fellow jarheads and leathernecks. Dismissed!" said the colonel. With that, the official celebration and R&R began.

Captain Long's troops were being given a four-day pass to be with their loved ones and family before the entire division was shipped out to the Northern Mariana Islands and the eventual invasion of Taiwan or the Philippines. No one knew exactly which country they would be liberating first, but secretly Long believed his regiment was most likely slated for Taiwan.

As Long made his way through the crowds of well-wishers and family members, one of the young Marines happened to grab his attention. "Dad, this is our company commander, Captain Long," he said excitedly. "He's already fought the Chinese *and* the North Koreans." He was clearly proud of his commander.

Long blushed a little as he tried to play it off. "I just happened to be in the Corps when the war started, that's all. We had a duty to do, and we did it, just as these fine young men will do theirs," he replied, trying to be as reassuring as possible to the parents.

Just then, Captain Long noticed a Marine tattoo on the father's forearm. "I served with the Marines in Afghanistan," said the Marine's dad in a gravelly voice. "My son may still be a bit naïve in his view of combat, but I know better. Judging by the two Purple Hearts on your chest, you do as well. Just do your best to keep these young boys alive and win this thing, OK?" the father said sternly. He shook Long's hand, and the group turned to walk away and enjoy the next few days together as a family.

Long watched with a certain sense of longing as the family walked away. He wasn't married himself, not really having found the time to look for a girlfriend. He had put most of his time into learning what it took to be a good Marine and getting as much of his college done as he could while the military was still willing to pay for it. His ultimate goal was to get out and use the GI Bill to finish paying for the rest of his degree and do what everyone else does—find a job, get married, and start a family. Of course, those plans had been interrupted by the war, but his personal philosophy was that when life throws you lemons, you make lemonade. Besides, being an officer for the next few years would certainly help him polish up his resume.

With no family living nearby to spend time with, Long did what most Marines would do—he spent time at the beach or doing something fun outdoors and having a good time hitting a few bars and restaurants in the evening with a few of the other single officers he had become friends with. Many of these other newly-minted officers hadn't seen combat yet, so they had latched onto Long to learn from him and gain as much insight as possible before they eventually shipped out. Captain Long, for his part, tried to spend as much time as possible with his young lieutenants. Most of them had the same amount of time in the Corps as the young Marines they would be leading into battle.

A few days after the ceremony, Long and a couple of his young lieutenants went over to Miss B's Coconut Club on Mission Boulevard in San Diego for some strong drinks, and possibly also to gawk at the pretty college girls at the beach nearby. Knowing this would be one of the last times he and his officers would be able to have some fun and relax, he wanted to take them somewhere fun and give them a chance to create a few pleasant memories to help them get through what would undoubtedly be a challenging time ahead.

Snagging one of the outdoor tables, Long waved down the waitress and placed an order for a round of shots and some appetizers to get them going. They started out with a seafood ceviche, crispy calamari that the Yelp reviews said were to die for, and finally, some jerk-rubbed chicken wings, followed by their world-famous Chester Copperpot drink, which was essentially a large chest that took up a good portion of the table. The sharable drink was filled with enough alcohol to subdue a rifle team of Marines.

As the officers chowed down on some good old-fashioned food and started to become undeniably drunk, Long sat back and surveyed the scene. He knew this would be a memory he'd hold on to for some time to come. Captain Tim Long was a country boy from Iowa, so being this close to the ocean was a real treat—and the good-looking women walking by didn't hurt anything either. After all the horrors he had seen in Korea, he just wanted to focus on having a good time while he could.

He did have to remind himself that he wasn't an NCO anymore—he was a Marine officer and a company commander, so he had to remember to not get too carried away. A lot more was expected of him now, and he had to be the adult in the room, especially as the commander to these young lieutenants. They followed his lead; if he acted crazy, they would act crazy. It was incumbent upon him to be aware that he needed to be the kind of leader and example they needed and deserved.

Long allowed himself to cut loose a little bit, anyway. He was starting to get just slightly tipsy and was enjoying a bit of flirtation with a couple of the young women at a table nearby when one of his young lieutenants put his hand on his shoulder and asked, "So, what was it like over there, Captain Long? What should we expect?"

The question caught Long off guard. He was just inebriated enough to have lost his inhibitions though, so he responded honestly. "Chaos, death, and fear," he began. "During the invasion of Hamhung, guys in my squad were getting hit left and right as we desperately tried to get off the beach. Once the amtracks got to the shore, they started taking heavy fire. When the back hatch dropped, we had to run out as fast as we could. As soon as we were out, the amtrack left to go pick up the next load of Marines. It was bad.

Explosions were happening all around us, and bullets flew everywhere. Before we made it to the seawall, I had already lost three guys in my squad—mind you, at that time I was an E-5 sergeant in charge of a squad."

The happy chatter of the other young lieutenants had died away. They were listening to him very intently. It was the first time he had actually shared his experiences in the war in anything more than broad strokes to them.

"What happened next, Captain?" asked the young lieutenant tenuously. He didn't seem completely sure that he wanted the answer.

"When we made it to the seawall, I saw where most of the enemy fire was coming from. There was a two-story house made of cement, maybe three hundred meters in front of us. We eventually hit the house with a couple of AT-4 rockets and then charged the enemy position. Two more guys in my squad got hit, but we pressed on. It took us an hour to fight our way off the beach, and that was just the beginning. We spent four days fighting in and around that city, even after the North Koreans surrendered. Then it was a rush to secure as much of the country as we could before the Chinese came in."

One of the lieutenants let out a low whistle.

"Maybe a week later, my platoon leader, a guy by the name of Second Lieutenant Chet Culley, was promoted to captain and took over command of our company—"

The young lieutenant who had started the conversation interrupted. "—What happened to the other officers?" He was clearly curious how a guy the same rank as him had suddenly become the company commander.

Long paused for a second. The young lieutenants weren't even drinking at this point; they were simply hanging on to his every word. "The CO and the XO were both killed, and two of the other platoon leaders had been injured. At this point, Lieutenant Culley was the last officer alive in the company, so they promoted him up. I suppose that's why I push you guys so hard to know each other's jobs and be ready to step into new and unfamiliar roles. You never know when you may suddenly find yourself in charge. It was at that point that I was promoted from E-5 to E-7 and given command of the entire platoon until a new officer showed up. There just wasn't anyone else to lead the platoon, so I had to step up."

"Wow," said one of the young men. The mood was now very somber.

After a long pause, another lieutenant asked, "What happened next, Captain?"

"Well, we kept fighting the People's Liberation Army, and let me tell you, they were fierce. They fought significantly better than I'd thought they would've, or anyone else had led me to believe they would. That's why I yell at anyone who says the Chinese don't know how to fight—they *do*, and they're good at it. They fight like men possessed, and they won't surrender. They fight to the death. Anyway, we were attacking a heavily fortified ridgeline, and as I was charging an enemy machine-gun position, my rifle ran out of ammo. I had no time to reload it. I charged forward and jumped right on top of the men, tackling them to the ground. It was hand-to-hand combat at that point. One of the guys shot me three times in the chest, but fortunately, I was wearing body armor."

Captain Long rubbed his chest as if talking about the memory had sparked some phantom pain there.

"At first, I thought I was fine," he explained, "but then I vomited up blood. My CO told me I had to be medevacked out. Apparently, the trauma of the gunshots from such close range had broken several of my ribs and punctured my right lung. I spent the next six weeks recovering at a hospital in Japan before I was sent back to my unit, which was now down in Busan, getting ready for our next assault in the Russian Far East."

"Is that where you were awarded the Navy Cross?" asked one of the lieutenants as he looked on with a new sense of awe.

"Sadly, no. I was given a Silver Star and Purple Heart for that action. It was during the Chinese counterattack that I was awarded the Navy Cross and my second Purple Heart. That story, however, is for another day, because I think I'm in love with that beauty over there," said Captain Long. He nodded toward a gorgeous woman in shorts and a bikini top who had long flowing brown hair and big beautiful brown eyes. Long got up to approach the young lady and her friends; she spotted him staggering a bit as he walked toward her but smiled warmly at him nonetheless.

Forty-eight hours later, Long's company boarded a 737 that would ferry them to Saipan International Airport, where the rest of the 6th Marine Division was forming up for the next operation.

Coming Storm

Guangzhou, China
Southern Theater of Operations

General Yang Yin sat in his office sipping on a cup of tea as he reviewed the latest casualty report from the Philippines. Following his success in the Vietnam campaign, General Yang had been given command of all PLA forces responsible for capturing the Philippines and Formosa. It was a daunting challenge, but one he thrived on.

Still, things hadn't exactly been going his way lately. What Yang hadn't predicted was the level of casualties the northern army group was taking. The "trap" they had laid for the American and ROK forces by allowing them to cross the Yalu River had been nothing short of disastrous. While the counteroffensive appeared to have worked when they'd lured the Americans across the border, the Americans' ability to make use of their heavy bombers and the quick reassignment of the US Marine Force from Busan had ultimately doomed the offensive. The northern army group had sustained nearly 112,000 casualties over four weeks and at the end of the day, had been pushed out of Korea for the second time in four months.

As he read the papers in front of him, General Yang was happy to see that the 43rd Airborne had done a superb job in capturing key targets within the Philippines. However, the rest of Lieutenant General Sheng's Army Group B, which consisted of the 20th Army and the 27th Army, hadn't secured all their objectives yet. It was frustrating for Yang having to use General Sheng's army group rather than his own. Yang's Army Group A had been given the tasks of reuniting the renegade province of Formosa, which frankly had been consuming most of his time.

Looking up from his papers, Yang eyed General Sheng's deputy, a brigadier general. "Why hasn't General Sheng captured the remaining objectives yet? We're under a strict timeline to secure the Philippines and begin fortifying them against the Americans. They're going to invade soon, and your boss is failing to get the country secured," Yang grilled.

Squirming in his seat a bit, the general did his best to respond. "As you can see, General, our forces are sustaining heavy casualties. The Filipinos are fighting more fiercely than we had anticipated. I know that the objectives we haven't secured will be captured in the next couple of weeks. We ask for more time and reinforcements."

Yang took a deep breath to stop himself from having a loud outburst over Sheng's inability to complete his objectives. If he had his way, he would have replaced him. Unfortunately, General Sheng was politically well-connected, so removing him without sufficient cause would be difficult. "General, do you know how many casualties we sustained unifying Formosa?" Yang asked through gritted teeth.

The deputy's face remained stoic and emotionless as he shook his head.

"During the first day of the invasion, we suffered 31,000 casualties. On the second day, we sustained another 18,000 casualties. To date, a total of 72,000 soldiers have been taken out of commission during this effort. During that same time, General Sheng has also lost nine thousand."

General Sheng's deputy now looked nervous as he realized their request for more reinforcements in light of the number of casualties being sustained on Formosa seemed trivial. Even during the Vietnam campaign, they hadn't sustained that level of casualties.

Knowing he needed to try and save face for his commander, the deputy inquired, "Sir, is it possible for us to get some added ground-attack planes and additional landing crafts? Part of the problem we're having is getting our various units to the many islands. Presently, we're bypassing the smaller islands until we've secured the larger, more populated ones. We've prioritized the capture of the islands where the engineers have said they need the anti-ship missile batteries to be placed."

General Yang grunted. "Tell General Sheng that I'll order an additional squadron of ground-attack aircraft and additional troop landing ships to your command. I won't give you more troops. The reinforcements we have available are being sent to reinforce Formosa and our forces in the north battling the Americans. I'm also giving you a hard deadline to complete your objectives. You have four weeks to finish securing the Philippines. No more delays, or there will be problems," Yang said with a bit of heat in his voice. He didn't have time to deal with incompetence, and his reputation was also on the line. The Americans were coming, and he was still not ready for them.

After dismissing Sheng's deputy, he returned to the task at hand, getting Formosa ready to repel an American invasion. While his forces now controlled the eastern beachheads that would most likely be used, the challenge was building them up sufficiently to withstand the brutal assault the Americans would launch.

He signaled for his own deputy, Brigadier General Yi, to come join him. As soon as Yi entered the room, General Yang bluntly asked, "What is the status of the Yilan County beachheads? Are they ready to repel an invasion yet?"

Yilan County was a province with a large area of relatively flat lowlands and beaches on the eastern side of Taiwan. It was by far the most likely area the Americans would invade from. Aside from the low-lying area, which would make it easier to offload their heavy equipment and armored forces, it had a number of major road junctions the Americans would want to use as they looked to expand off the beaches.

Pulling some data up from his tablet, General Yi answered, "Yilan County is prepared to meet the Americans at the beaches, Sir. The engineers have built hundreds of small machine-gun bunkers, covering nearly every approach off the beaches. They have also completed dozens of hidden anti-ship bunkers several miles inland. Per your instruction, we have placed most of our antiaircraft guns and missile systems intermixed with the civilian population. If the Americans decide to attack them, then they will hit a lot of civilian structures."

General Yang nodded and smiled. The Chinese all knew that the Americans were incredibly risk-averse when it came to collateral damage. They would sooner lose hundreds of soldiers taking an objective than accidentally kill a few dozen civilians—a trait the Chinese Army did not share.

"What about the Japanese Islands? Are they going to pose a threat to us?" asked Yang.

General Yang was still a bit angry that his senior leadership had ordered him to capture the Philippines before he had had a chance to secure the Yaeyama district, which was so close to Formosa. By the time they had finished their operation in the Philippines, the Japanese Defense Force had moved a large number of soldiers to those five islands. Invading them at this point would have been very costly, so the higher-ups had decided they would have to be invaded at a later date.

General Yi shook his head. "We've been hitting the islands with multiple short-range cruise and ballistic missiles for the past month. None of the airfields are currently operational, and we've hit the known military installations multiple times. It's my assessment that the islands do not pose a significant threat to our occupation now, although that may change once the American Pacific Fleet moves into range of our forces."

Yang nodded. "Excellent. Please continue to get the island ready to repel the Americans. It won't be long until they arrive, and once they do, they'll unleash everything they have on us."

****

South China Sea

Vice Admiral Shen was getting anxious for the final battle of the Pacific to start. The loss of the *Wuhan* a couple of days ago had been a real blow to his plan. Unfortunately, he had too many moving parts going now to stop the attack. They had lured the American fleet into the Philippine Sea, and it was nearly time for him to spring his trap.

Despite this setback, Shen was not feeling completely hopeless. To gain entry into the Chinese bastion that was the South China Sea, the Americans really only had two viable options: they could maneuver south and slide between the southern Philippine Islands in the Celebes Sea, or they could move toward the northern side of the Philippines, which would also bring them close to Formosa, or Taiwan, as the Americans called it. Going south through the Celebes Sea would mean traveling through dozens upon dozens of small Indonesian islands where the PLA Navy had installed hundreds of anti-ship cruise missile batteries. Traveling north would bring them closer to the Filipino landmass of Luzon and the now-occupied province of Formosa, where, again, the PLA Navy had placed hundreds of anti-ship missile batteries.

Shen smiled as he remembered his secret weapon. Unbeknownst to the Americans, a small group of five Malaysian cargo ships had taken up position between the Island of Palau and Colonia, which was several hundred miles southwest of Guam.

During World War II, the German Kriegsmarine had operated a series of merchant raider vessels in the Pacific, which were essentially commercial ships that had been converted to operate as clandestine raiders. The commercial ships were often outfitted with a series of torpedo launchers and cannons, which were hidden by collapsible panels or other disguises, allowing the ships to sneak up on Allied freighters or convoys. Once the raider vessels were close enough to their prey, they would unveil their weapons and engage the convoys. In one case, the German raider *Orion* had sunk fourteen Allied ships before it was hunted down and sunk by the Royal Navy in 1945.

Pulling a page from history, Admiral Shen had had a series of cargo vessels converted to merchant raiders prior to the war, so they could be used in this elaborate trap he had set to destroy the American Pacific Fleet. The ships chosen for this special mission had originally been used for transporting grain or other dry goods in their cargo holds. Unlike the large container freighters, the upper decks of these cargo ship holds weren't covered by shipping containers. This allowed the Chinese engineers to fill the cargo holds with vertical launch systems, or VLS. The newest PLA Navy destroyer, the Type 055 *Renhai*, packed 112 VLS missiles. The cargo ships were able to hold an astounding 600 VLS missiles.

The merchant raiders were equipped with 300 YJ-18A anti-ship cruise missiles with an operational range of 220 to 540 kilometers, and a 140- to 300-kilogram warhead that could reach speeds of Mach 0.8 when cruising and Mach 2.5-3.0 when in terminal attack mode. This gave the ships an incredible offensive reach. The raiders were also equipped with 200 YJ-100 long-range anti-ship cruise missiles. These missiles were particularly nasty, as they had an operating range of 1,500 kilometers and packed a 500-kilogram warhead. Between these raiders and the cruise missile batteries that awaited them, the Americans would not be able to approach them without some major losses.

For the past four hours, Shen and his staff had been monitoring the progress of the American fleet as it sailed toward the Philippines. They were eagerly waiting to see which direction the fleet would travel. If they headed south, then they would sail right into the merchant raider trap he had waiting for them near Palau. If they headed north, then the raiders would have to turn north and move at maximum speed to stay within range of the American fleet. That way, when the time came, they would be in range to add their missiles to the mix.

What Admiral Shen and the Chinese Navy had learned during the opening days of the Second Korean War was that the American fleet was vulnerable to a missile swarm attack. While the American Aegis system was still far superior to their own system, it lacked enough ships with sufficient missiles to shoot down the incoming threats. Had the PLA Navy leadership listened to Shen's original request and converted ten merchant raiders, they would have had enough anti-ship missiles to completely wipe out the American Seventh Fleet. Instead, they had only converted five ships to fit this role, and he had to keep those five ships situated with him, since his naval counterpart in the north didn't share his same vision of how these ships could change the outcome of the war.

Finally, there was some perceptible movement in the blinking lights on the map display. "*Ugh, they are turning north*," thought Shen.

Admiral Shen turned to one of his communications officers. "Send a flash message to the merchant fleet for them to execute Operation Lightning Wind." With that simple coded message, the merchant fleet would move quickly to their preplanned attack position. They would hold off on launching their missiles until they received their final targeting data from the Pacific radar ocean reconnaissance satellites.

The officer nodded, typed out the message and hit Send. While the message made its way through the ether, the entirety of the South China Sea's fleet moved at flank speed toward the Americans for what would arguably be the largest naval battle since World War II.

Ambush in the Pacific

Philippine Sea

After nearly a month of consolidating the Allied fleet around the US territory of Guam, Vice Admiral Jeff Richards was ready to launch his offensive to once and for all crush the People's Liberation Army Navy and begin the liberation of Taiwan and the Philippines. Richards had spent the better part of a month wargaming the plan they were now going to implement and felt fairly confident in their ability to respond to the different types of threats the PLA Navy was going to throw at them.

His biggest relief was that the Chinese submarine *Wuhan*, which had been equipped with the new Chinese supertorpedo, had finally been hunted down and sunk. Sadly, two additional destroyers and another *Los Angeles*-class submarine were lost in the process. Fortunately, naval intelligence had no indications that the Chinese had figured out how to equip the specialized torpedoes to their aircraft, and apparently, the torpedoes required special modifications to the torpedo tubes, which meant that for the time being, the *Wuhan* was the only sub equipped to use them.

"*If only we knew exactly how many anti-ship missiles the Chinese have to throw at us,*" he thought.

However, there was no turning back now. The battle plans had been set, and now it was time to once again place his sailors in harm's way. As the Allied fleet headed toward the Philippine Sea, the four Japanese light carriers fell in line with the six American supercarriers, adding their own capability to the mix. Those ships had been quickly modified at the beginning of the Korean conflict, adding arrestor wires to the rear deck of the ship and magnetic catapults along the front deck. With the equipment needed to launch and retrieve aircraft, they were now functional as carriers in their own right, capable of collectively carrying 96 combat aircraft.

Admiral Richards smiled as he saw these ships move with his forces. "*The Japanese finished those modifications rather quickly. This should be a nasty surprise to the Chinese,*" he thought.

The fleet had already been at sea for nearly two days as they sailed ever closer to the inevitable battle that might ultimately decide the outcome of the war. Sitting in the wardroom on the USS *Gerald Ford*, Admiral Richards again reviewed the plans for how they were going to incorporate the Japanese aircraft into the fleet's defense. Although half of the pilots flying off the Japanese light carriers were actually US naval pilots, it was still important to make sure they fully understood the plan and their role in the coming fight.

Richards had nearly every EA-18 Growler in the Navy assigned to his fleet for this coming battle. Eight of them were operating on the Japanese ships while the rest of the aircraft composition comprised F/A-18 Super Hornets. Admiral Richards knew that the Chinese were going to hit them with one or more missile swarm attacks, and he had the fleet prepared accordingly. To increase the likelihood of their survival, the Hornets were equipped with AIM-9X Block II Sidewinder missiles, which had the ability to also go after the cruise missiles that would be swarmed at them. It wasn't a sure bet they could hit the enemy missiles, but if they could help thin them out, then it was worth using them. When Richards had been in command of the *Carl Vinson* at the outset of the Korean War, this had been a tactic he employed with his airwing. It was probably the one thing that had saved his ship and the rest of his strike group from certain doom. He hoped it would save them again in this coming battle.

In addition to the Japanese light carriers, the Allied fleet had the two *Zumwalt*-class destroyers, which had recently been upgraded with the Navy's new railguns. The

USS *Michael Monsoor* and the USS *Zumwalt* were about to make their combat debut, and they fielded a new and revolutionary combat system, the magnetic railgun. The penetrator rounds the railgun fired weighed ten kilograms and could travel 160 kilometers, hitting their targets traveling at speeds of Mach 7. The *Zumwalts* could fire a sustained six rounds a minute for three minutes before dropping to one round a minute to allow for their capacitors to recharge. Admiral Richards hoped these two ships would be his ace in the hole.

For the time being, Vice Admiral Richards planned on making the *Gerald Ford* not only his floating forward command but the centerpiece of the Allied fleet and the nerve center for the coming battle. To that end, he made sure to place a *Ticonderoga* cruiser on either side of the carrier for added antimissile defense.

****

Thirty thousand feet above the largest naval fleet since World War II, the Northrop Grumman MQ-4C Triton surveillance drone observed everything happening below. The continuous data it provided was feeding a steady stream of intelligence to the ships below, as well as the 7th Fleet's forward headquarters in Guam, Hawaii, and the Pentagon.

While the Triton kept its high orbit above the fleet, it intercepted a short burst message to a group of five cargo vessels near the Island of Colonia and Palau, 530 kilometers to the southwest of the Allied fleet. Within minutes of the transmission, the five ships changed course and headed in the same direction as the fleet.

****

Rear Admiral Shelley Cord was both excited and nervous as her strike group continued to near the enemy and the coming battle. While she reviewed their current plans, she became lost in a sea of reminiscent thoughts.

When Shelley had been given command of the *Ford* strike group, she'd figured that would be her last command, and then she'd would retire. As a two-star admiral and woman, she felt she had helped to pave the way for other women to achieve the same rank and hold the same commands a man could. She was the first commander of what was arguably the most powerful warship in the world, and that said a lot for how far women had come in being considered equal to their male counterparts in the Navy.

While the *Ford* was going to be the most powerful warship in the world, it was still technically not supposed to be ready for combat for another year. Her job was to oversee its sea trials and the myriad of certifications needed to make the strike group ready for combat operations.

Once the war in Europe had started and the *George H.W. Bush* had been sunk, the *Ford* had suddenly become inundated with contractors and support personnel, rushing to get the supercarrier ready for combat operations. Instead of being in charge of the final stages of the carrier's readiness for the fleet, Admiral Cord found herself in charge of an entirely new strike group that would center around the *Ford* and be the anchor for the Seventh Fleet. The Secretary of the Navy and SecDef had waived hundreds of certifications and tests to get the ship ready for combat—the only thing that mattered was getting the *Ford* ready and staffed up with fighters and personnel.

When the Second Korean War had started, the loss of the *Reagan* and the *Vinson* had placed renewed urgency and strain on Cord to get her strike group ready for battle. They were desperately needed in the Pacific.

When she'd heard that the captain of the *Vinson* would be taking over command of the entire 7th Fleet, she'd felt a bit miffed that a captain who had essentially lost his own ship was going to be taking over command of the entire fleet instead of one of the more seasoned rear admirals. However, within twenty minutes of listening to Richards speak about his experience in fighting the People's Liberation Army Navy and how his strike group had survived the missile swarm that ultimately overwhelmed the *Reagan*, she felt guilty for her earlier feelings. Richards had gained something that none of them had, combat experience fighting the Chinese—and neither she nor the senior admirals in the Navy currently had that knowledge.

That first battle with the Chinese had cost the Navy two rear admirals and a vice admiral, along with the lives of nearly 8,000 sailors. It had been the single greatest loss of life in the Navy since World War II. Senior leadership who had experience fighting the Chinese were in short supply, and as her strike group neared the enemy, she was glad they were being led by an officer who understood what they would be facing.

The combat information center or CIC commander pulled her out of her thought bubble and back to the real world. "Ma'am," he said. "We've spotted something unusual that I think you should take a look at."

"What do you have, George?" She stood up and walked toward him.

"I'm not sure. The Triton just intercepted a burst transmission to what appears to be a small cluster of cargo ships near the Micronesia Island chains. We've looked at the area, and there are no PLA Navy ships in the area. There don't appear to be any hostile planes in the area either," he explained, a bit puzzled by the information.

"Hmm. Well, let's take a closer look, shall we?" she commented. They walked over to the console, where a couple of the intelligence folks were looking at the drone's feed.

"Petty Officer, are you able to zoom in any closer to those ships so we can see what flag they're flying?" inquired the admiral.

The petty officer nodded and zoomed in as far as the camera would allow. She wrinkled her face as she realized the image wasn't going to get any clearer. "I'm going to need a better image," she said.

"Those ships are roughly 500 kilometers away from us right now," replied the petty officer. "My camera is good, but it's not a telescope." With that, she nudged the lieutenant next to her, who was flying the UAV.

"I can turn and head in that direction, but the best I can do is get us maybe 80 kilometers closer," said the lieutenant. "I have to stay in a certain orbit over the fleet to keep providing us the coverage requirements. If you want a better image, I'd recommend we send a fast mover. They can get over there a lot quicker than I can."

Admiral Cord nodded. "You're right, Lieutenant. Good call," she said, patting him on the shoulder.

She turned to the commander, air group, or CAG, who had walked over to see what they were discussing. "CAG, get me a fast mover to head over to that cluster of ships. I have a feeling there's more than meets the eye with them, and I want a little more information before I let Admiral Richards know something might be amiss."

"Yes, Ma'am," replied the CAG. He rushed off to complete his new mission.

Cord grabbed the attention of a couple of the other petty officers nearby. "Also, someone send a message to the captain to come to CIC and join us," she ordered.

"Yes, Ma'am," one of them replied.

Three minutes later, the alert fighters on the flight deck were given the task of investigating the suspicious ships. Seeing how far away the ships were from the fleet, they would need to top off their fuel tanks before they began their journey.

Once the planes left the deck, Captain Patricia Fleece, who had only just found out about their mission, walked into the CIC. "I just saw the alert fighters take off—anything important I should know about?" she asked, directing her question to the CAG.

Admiral Cord knew she should have told Captain Fleece before they'd launched the alert fighters, but she'd felt she needed to get them in the air ASAP. Something just didn't feel right. "It's my fault, Captain Fleece. I ordered the CAG to launch them ASAP and get them heading out to investigate something. Let me show you what we've found and get your take on this, too."

The small group now walked over to the monitor that was piping in the video feed of the vessels. Cord explained what they had found, and the odd behavior of the cargo vessels once they received the burst transmission. "Has anyone told Admiral Richards about this? He may know something we don't," Fleece said.

"I was going to inform him once we had a better idea of whose vessels those are," Admiral Cord answered. "The Triton doesn't show any PLA Navy ships in the area, and we don't see any air activity."

Fleece bit her lower lip. Admiral Cord knew by now that this meant Fleece was uncomfortable with the decision to wait. However, she didn't voice any objections.

"*Let's just hope I know what I'm doing,*" Admiral Cord thought, second-guessing herself. It would take some time for the Hornets to check the situation out, and if there was truly something amiss, they might have lost too much valuable time.

Suddenly, the lieutenant handling the UAV loudly announced, "Captain, you need to see this!"

Sensing something important, Admiral Cord also walked over to see what was going on. Then, one of the communications officers vied for their attention as he waved a yellow paper in the air.

"Admiral, we're receiving a FLASH message from Guam. You need to read this, Ma'am," the commander said in an urgent voice.

Cord turned toward her comms officer and moved quickly in his direction. As she approached his station, he handed her the message traffic:

///////////TOP SECRET//////////

FLASH TRAFFIC – URGENT WARNING – IMMINENT BALLISTIC MISSILE ATTACK

FROM: NORTH AMERICAN AEROSPACE DEFENSE

TO: SEVENTH FLEET

1) IMINT INTELLIGENCE IDENTIFIED MULTIPLE TRANSPORTER ERECTOR LAUNCHERS BEING MADE READY TO LAUNCH ON THE ISLAND

OF TAIWAN. POSSIBLE DONGFENG 21-D ANTI-SHIP BALLISTIC MISSILES.

2) HUMINT INTELLIGENCE IDENTIFIED TWENTY-FOUR TRANSPORTER ERECTOR LAUNCHERS BEING MADE READY TO LAUNCH ON THE ISLAND OF LUZON. POSSIBLE DONGFENG 21-D ANTI-SHIP BALLISTIC MISSILES.

END OF TRANSMISSION.

//////////TOP SECRET//////////

The blood in Admiral Cord's face seemed to drain out of her head, and she almost felt weak at the knees. This was the very thing she was terrified of.

"*Are we cruising into a trap?*" she wondered in horror.

"Someone, get Admiral Richards in here ASAP! Set Condition One. Sound general quarters and send a FLASH message to the rest of the fleet of a possible ASBM attack," Admiral Cord ordered.

In seconds, the general quarters alarm blared throughout the ship, alerting everyone of a possible attack.

The men and women on the ship moved as quickly as possible to their battle stations and prepared for the worst.

Captain Fleece turned to the CAG. "Get on the radio to the Raptor flight and order them to get us real-time video of those cargo ships at once!" she ordered. "They may be part of the PLA Navy attack, and we just don't know it yet."

The CAG nodded and grabbed the handset.

****

Lieutenant Josh McDaniel's Super Hornet had been cruising toward the mysterious cargo vessels now for nearly an hour. "*Oh my God, this is boring,*" he thought. "*We're still roughly twenty minutes away from even being close enough to use our cameras.*"

His radio crackled, startling him. "Raptor Two Two, this is Henhouse. Fleet has gone to Condition One. Initiate afterburners and get a visual of the cargo ships. Approach with caution, possible PLA Navy trap. How copy?"

"That's a good copy, Henhouse," Lieutenant McDaniel responded. "Will initiate afterburners. Please be advised that we'll need to top our tanks off again at the halfway point."

"*Crap, what the heck are we flying into?*" he thought.

The two Hornets hit their afterburners and, in seconds, were zooming toward their maximum speed as they quickly closed the distance to the cargo vessels. In a matter of minutes, they came within range of their cameras and beamed the video back to the *Ford*, where they would analyze the ships for potential threats.

Lieutenant Commander Mary Teller, his back seater, was looking at the video display when she suddenly blurted out, "Those aren't cargo holds, Josh. Those are vertical launch systems…hundreds of them!"

"Are you sure, Mary?" McDaniel asked in shock. "I've never heard of a VLS system on anything outside of a warship."

"I'm telling you, those are VLSs. The entire ship is covered in them," she replied. "I'm going to radio back to the carrier to see if they see it as well."

"Hang on, Mary," he said. "I'm going to make a low pass over the ships, so we can get a better look at them."

He slowed them down and began a descent. Just as McDaniel flew over the first cargo ship, his missile warning alarm sounded in his headset, letting him know an enemy missile had just locked on to him. Before he even had a chance to react, his aircraft was hit by a Chinese FN-6 man-portable air-defense system, or MANPAD, erupting in flames before either he or his back seater was able to eject. His wingman, who had been flying at a slightly higher altitude, suddenly found himself being chased down by three FN-6 missiles as well. The missiles were so quick, they left very little time to react or get away. In mere seconds, both Hornets were downed.

****

Vice Admiral Jeff Richards sat in the wardroom, compiling some notes for a report he planned on writing following the end of the battle with the PLA Navy. He wanted to make sure he captured some ideas and feelings he had prior to the battle starting.

Lifting his cup of coffee to his lips, he took a long drink from the now-lukewarm java.

Suddenly, the general quarters alarm sounded. Instinctively, he got up and quickly made his way to the CIC to find out what was going on.

It took him nearly five minutes to move through the maze of corridors and ladder wells, wading through all the sailors running to and from one location to another. When he entered the CIC, he saw controlled chaos as the men and women running the CIC expertly managed the situation unfolding around them.

"Talk to me, people," he said. "What the heck is going on?"

One of the battle managers, who had been watching the video images being relayed by the two Hornets, yelled out, "Raptor Flight is down! Raptor Flight is down!"

The CAG quickly jumped on that. "What do you mean, they're down? Did they just disappear?"

"Sir, they were transmitting video and then all of a sudden it stopped. One second, they were there, and then everything went black. I think they may have been shot down," he replied.

"Bring up the video they were broadcasting just before it went blank," said Captain Fleece. She began biting her fingernails nervously.

The video began. To their collective horror, they saw what the pilots must have seen just before they died. The forward sections of the cargo vessels were covered in vertical launch systems. These merchant raiders had been converted into cruise missile platforms. They were less than 460 kilometers from the fleet, well within their operational range. Couple that with the flash message they'd just received, and it was suddenly clear—the fleet was moving right into a cleverly laid Chinese trap.

As Admiral Richards realized what was happening, anger billowed up inside him and he lashed out at his strike group commander and captain. "Why were these vessels not checked sooner? How could we have let them get so close to the fleet?" he yelled.

Admiral Cord and Captain Fleece were silent and stonefaced.

"Never mind," said Richards, softening his tone. "We have to deal with them. I want those ships sunk *now* before they can launch their missiles, if we're not already too late."

Captain Fleece turned to the CAG. "Scramble your airwing," she ordered. "Have them focus on disabling the enemy missiles that will be headed our way soon."

Admiral Cord went to work getting the rest of the strike group ready and organized to deal with the newly identified threat. She ordered two more destroyers to move in the direction of the cargo vessels, since this would be the direction the largest quantity of enemy missiles would be traveling from. She also handed Admiral Richards the flash message from NORAD about the imminent attack. He only shook his head, as if he had known this was going to happen.

"This is Korea all over again…" thought Richards.

He turned and walked over to a small cluster of workstations he had taken over, separate from where Admiral Cord would be coordinating her strike group. He needed to make sure the fleet was adjusting their ship formation and placing their defenses in the area most likely to receive the largest volume of enemy missiles. He also wanted to get on the radio to Guam and see if the Air Force would be able to get some tankers headed out in his direction so he could keep his aircraft in the air longer over the fleet while they dealt with this new threat.

****

Twenty-six thousand feet above the Allied fleet below, the myriad of surveillance cameras on the MQ-4C Triton UAV captured ballistic missile launches from the islands of Taiwan and Luzon. Within seconds, a short burst message was detected between the Chinese fleet and the cargo vessels. Shortly after, one of the now-classified merchant raiders fired off its missiles at the American fleet. While the first vessel disgorged its missiles, the Chinese destroyers with the main fleet also fired off their first volley of anti-ship missiles.

When the first merchant raider finished firing off its first set of two hundred missiles, the next two raiders fired off their own barrage. A couple of minutes went by, and then all five raiders fired off another barrage of missiles, holding their final barrage in reserve. As the missiles leveled out and headed toward the American fleet, it became clear the Chinese had timed the launches and elevation of the missiles so they would converge on the American fleet from multiple height levels and directions. This would make it significantly harder for the fleet's close-in defense systems to move from one target to the next.

While the data was being transmitted to Guam and the fleet below, the outer skin of the drone suddenly became superheated. The paint started to peel, and in a fraction of a second, the inside guts of the drone overheated. Then the UAV suddenly crumpled under its own weight and airspeed as it disintegrated from the heat of a high-energy beam.

****

"Admiral Cord, we just lost the Triton feed," announced a very nervous lieutenant. "One minute it was fine, sending us targeting data of the incoming missiles—then it just cut out. It's no longer transmitting any data. Its transponder is also out."

Cord grumbled. "Send a message out to the other strike groups about what just happened. Launch more drones and tell everyone to switch to the alternate plan. Unless the Chinese shoot our satellites down again, we'll switch back to them," she said, hoping the satellites would be able to pick up the slack.

The military satellite system was still recovering from the first Russian attack, when they'd carried out a complex "internet of things" attack that overheated many of the internal systems on the satellites, burning them out. SpaceX had been incredibly busy launching replacement satellites into orbit as fast as the factories could produce them. However, despite the valiant efforts by SpaceX and the satellite producers, not all of them had been replaced yet, so the ones they *did* have operating could only handle so much data.

It was controlled chaos in the nerve center of the carrier as they worked feverishly to integrate and analyze all the data streaming into the command center, and Admiral Cord nervously watched every detail as it unfolded. The sophisticated computer system that ran the fleet's defensive system was now tracking 1,900 inbound threats. The twenty-six EA-18 Growlers went to work with their jamming pods as they tried to confuse the anti-ship missiles defensive systems, while the Super Hornets dove in to attack them with their own weapons.

The fighters were going to have one chance to hit as many of the incoming threats as possible; once the missiles flew past them, they would have no hope of catching up to them again. All 420 fighter planes from the carriers descended on the incoming threats, firing their weapons into the swarm that was heading toward their floating homes.

In an almost miraculous effort, the fighters managed to destroy 509 of the incoming enemy missiles. If it weren't so deadly, it would have made for a beautiful fireworks show. Having dispensed their missiles, the fighters loitered at a high orbit above the fleet to allow the destroyers and cruisers to initiate the next layer of defense.

In seconds, the destroyers *Michael Monsoor* and *Zumwalt* made history as their railguns engaged the missile threats at a rate of ten rounds a minute, scoring a consistent one hundred percent hit ratio. While the missile count was steadily dropping from the railguns, the rest of the destroyers joined the fray with their own SM-2, SM-3, and SM-6 missiles at the carrier killer ballistic missiles and the remaining cruise missiles still bearing down on them. The sky and water around and in between the ships was filling with smoke trails and exhaust plumes of friendly missiles streaking in all directions. It was almost reminiscent of a 17th- or 18th-century naval battle between wooden sail ships, firing gunpowder cannon—except these weapon systems were far more lethal and devastating in their use.

While the battle was well underway above the water, deep beneath the waves, a dozen *Virginia*-class attack submarines moved into position to attack the Chinese fleet while a handful of the older *Los Angeles* attack subs kept the fleet safe from any underwater threats.

It was now up to the CIWS and the remaining RIM-7 Sea Sparrow and RIM-116 Rolling Airframe Missile or RAM system to take over. However, those missiles were going to be extremely difficult to hit as they reached their terminal velocity. The stone-cold truth was that some of the missiles were going to get through.

Admiral Cord stood, not knowing what more to do at this point. She watched as the training the Navy had put its officers and enlisted men and women through took over. What might have appeared to a civilian as dozens upon dozens of individuals shouting and motioning from one item to the next was actually being played out in a well-organized and exceptionally choreographed dance of decisions and reactions to those decisions.

The ship's highly complex targeting system was managing the entire fleet's point defense systems, identifying what CIWS or RAM system was closest to each threat and vectoring them in to deal with it. The system was handling these hundreds of decisions a second far faster and efficiently then the men and women who managed the system could ever hope to achieve.

****

Moments later, the wind blew more of the exhaust and smoke from the missiles away from the ships, and Admiral Richards watched in horror as many of the enemy missiles struck his beloved fleet. Two of the DF-21 anti-ship ballistic missiles slammed into the forward and rear flight deck of the *USS Eisenhower*, scoring direct hits. The flight deck burst into flames.

Richards winced as he saw the billowing clouds of flame and smoke rise, knowing that hundreds of sailors had just perished. It brought back horrible memories of when his own carrier had been hit by one of those missiles at the start of the war. Just as he thought that might have been the only ship to get hit by the ASBMs, another one streaked down from the sky and rammed into the center of the USS *Nimitz*. Seconds later, the *Nimitz* was hit by three more missiles, which nearly ripped the ship apart. The entire flight deck and superstructure of the carrier was now engulfed in flames and was being rocked by secondary explosions. The ship was clearly in trouble as it listed quickly to one side.

"Switch to a view of the *Roosevelt*, and then the *Lincoln* and *Stennis*. I need to see if any of the other carriers were hit," Richards directed the chief petty officer manning one of the video feeds at the terminal near him.

The video zoomed into focus on the *Roosevelt*, which had a bit of smoke from a couple of hits it took to its hull, but no raging fires across her flight decks. The other two carriers appeared to be in good shape as well. Turning his attention to the Japanese ships, he saw that one of them had settled pretty deep into the water and was clearly going to sink; another one had taken several hits and was on fire. The other two appeared to have minimal to light damage, with their flight decks also in good shape.

"Sir, the bulk of Chinese cruise missiles are about to arrive," one of the battle manager officers said.

Richards just nodded. There was really nothing more he could do at this point but wait to see how many of them made it through their defenses. He motioned for the chief manning the video feed to zoom out, so they could see more of the fleet as the missiles closed in. Many of the missiles were being destroyed at the last minute by the *Zumwalt's* railguns, but many more were leaking through to slam into the hulls and superstructures of the Allied warships.

The USS *Port Royal*, a *Ticonderoga*-class guided-missile cruiser, took three direct hits by CJ-100 anti-ship missiles, each packing a 300-kilogram warhead. The ship burned wildly at first as the fires from the explosion quickly spread before the crew reacted and doused them with water and regained control of the flames.

As the rest of the missiles found their marks, Admiral Richards saw a large portion of his fleet had somehow survived the largest anti-ship missile swarm in history.

"*Now it's time for payback,*" he thought.

The Chinese and American fleets had closed the distance gap to get within strike range of their fighters, but that also meant they had just moved within range of his new Harpoon Block II+ extended-range missiles.

He turned to Rear Admiral Cord. "Order the fleet to begin engaging the PLA Navy with our Harpoons. It's time to get some revenge. Also, get our fighters back on the decks of the carriers that are still operational. We need them rearmed and ready to repel the next attack," he directed.

In minutes, the American and Japanese ships fired off their own anti-ship missiles while the remaining aircraft landed on the carriers that still had operational flight decks.

As quickly as the fighters landed, they were being brought below decks and placed into an assembly line system of being rearmed, refueled, and then placed back on the forward elevator to return to the flight deck and get airborne.

Having trained to do this type of operation only once, the flight crews were proving that the heavy emphasis on training by the Navy was paying off. Aircraft were landing and being turned right around for the next flight in record time, which also allowed room for the additional aircraft to land. With several of the carriers having been sunk or heavily damaged, there wasn't a lot of flight deck real estate to go around.

While the American aircraft were being readied to go after the Chinese fleet and naval aircraft, a series of Tomahawk cruise missiles, which had been fired by two of the *Ticonderoga* guided-missile cruisers, hit the five Chinese merchant raiders, just as they were beginning to launch a series of missiles aimed at the US Air Force base on Guam. The five converted cargo ships quickly sank, preventing them from being able to further hit the critical air base or launch any other missiles at the fleet.

****

Hainan Island, China

South China Sea Fleet Headquarters

Vice Admiral Shen was beside himself when he learned his merchant raiders had been sunk. They had managed to successfully fire off several volleys of anti-ship missiles, which had proved his theory that merchant raiders could still play a pivotal role in modern naval warfare. Unfortunately, they had only been able to launch sixteen cruise missiles at the American air base on Guam before they were sunk.

"I should have known the Americans would have had a submarine or some other ship in the area that would be able to sink them," he thought in regret. He wished that he had had them launch all their missiles at the Americans at once instead.

Turning to one of his officers, he asked the question on all of their minds. "How were the Americans able to shoot down so many of our missiles?" he barked. "A significantly larger percentage of them should have gotten through, and we should have caused far more damage to the fleet than we did."

"Sir, while the Americans did intercept a larger percentage of missiles than we'd predicted, we still scored a great victory. We sank one more of the American carriers, and two more suffered heavy damage. One of the Japanese carriers was sunk, and the other two sustained heavy damage. We also damaged or sunk another thirty-eight American warships," the officer responded, not accepting this as a defeat on any level.

"I want our aircraft to attack *now*. Order the carriers and land-based aircraft to launch their attack immediately. We need to finish off their fleet!" Shen ordered. He hoped his remaining naval assets would be more than enough to finish the Americans off. Somehow, he just couldn't shake the feeling that the Americans were about to hit back, hard.

****

"Fast Eagle Six. This is November Six. Engage hostile ships. Get some payback for us, will you?" ordered Captain Grisham, the captain of the USS *John C. Stennis*.

"November Six, that's a good copy. We're moving to engage now," Commander Greg Carlson replied, to the excitement of his fellow pilots. "You heard the captain. It's time to go get some payback. Stay alert, guys, and let's go sink some enemy ships."

The Super Hornets in Commander Carlson's squadron were armed with two long-range anti-ship missiles, or LRASM, which DARPA had helped to pioneer several years ago. The Navy only had a limited quantity of these missiles, so they were being used sparingly. The LRASM was a stealthy anti-ship cruise missile that had a range of 560 kilometers and packed a 450-kilogram warhead. Lockheed Martin had been running round-the-clock production of the missiles to get them in service for this specific battle, and if things worked out, it might just prove to be the decisive weapon needed to destroy the Chinese fleet.

Breathing heavily, Commander Carlson looked around to make sure his pilots were all where they were supposed to be while his backseater, Lieutenant Molly Balmer, made sure they had the proper target punched into the computer. His aircraft had been given the honor of targeting his two missiles at one of the three PLA Navy carriers.

Lieutenant Balmer cleared her throat. "Boss, we're coming up on 320 kilometers from the enemy fleet. Weapons free in sixty seconds. You ready?" she asked.

"Copy that," he responded. He switched over to the squadron net. "Sixty seconds to weapons free. Let's get ready, folks."

The minute went by in the blink of an eye. Carlson lifted the arming button for his missiles. "Weapons ready," he called.

"Targets locked, ready to fire," Balmer replied.

Commander Carlson hit the fire button once and felt the weight of the first anti-ship missile fall from underneath his wings. Then he depressed the button again. In seconds, the aircraft was 5,000 pounds lighter. The small wings of the cruise missiles opened up and the engines started. Commander Carlson watched the missiles for the briefest of seconds to make sure they had ignition and then turned his attention back to making sure they weren't being tracked by any of the numerous enemy aircraft heading toward them.

"I show both weapons have acquired their targets and are moving to engage," Balmer informed him.

"Good copy. Time to go home," he replied. He turned the aircraft to head for the *Stennis*. They would land, refuel and, if need be, rearm with more Harpoon missiles and finish off whatever enemy ships remained.

****

Commodore Zhou Dongyou sweated profusely as he listened to the radar operators frantically call out the nearly one hundred American cruise missiles heading toward their fleet.

"Commander, when you identify a missile headed toward our ship, you make sure you target it first before we target any of the missiles headed to the *Mao*, is that understood?" barked Zhou, not at all happy that their illustrious strike group commander had demanded that all the fleet's defenses focus on protecting the *Mao* at the expense of themselves and the other carriers.

"What about our orders?" the commander asked in an irritated tone. The conversation suddenly drew in the gaze of several men around them.

Zhou knew he could be in a lot of trouble for countermanding the admiral's order, but he also knew the chances of any of them surviving if they focused all their weapons on protecting the *Mao* were slim to none.

"*I have a duty to protect my crew, and my ship,*" he thought.

Commodore Zhou squared back his shoulders and stood a little taller before replying. "I am responsible for the safety of this ship and its crew. I cannot fulfill that duty if I am not allowed to defend my ship. You will target the enemy missiles headed toward us first, and then assist the

Mao when feasible. Is that understood, Commander?" he directed, a bit of heat in his voice.

"The missiles are closing to within twenty kilometers!" shouted one of the radar operators.

At this distance, the carrier's close-in point defense systems readied themselves to engage the incoming threats. While the bulk of the American missiles were nearing the carrier's defenses, the *Liaoning* was suddenly struck on the port side by four missiles. The explosions sent shockwaves throughout the ship, throwing crew members to the ground and temporarily knocking out power to the ship.

"What just hit us?" shouted Commodore Zhou as he looked for answers.

"Point defenses are engaging enemy missiles now!" yelled one of the young officers as the carrier's HQ-10 antimissile system and the Type 1130 CIWS did their best to shoot down the remaining American missiles.

In seconds, another eight missiles impacted against the side of the ship. The fires that had been burning aboard now quickly spread as damage to key structures caused secondary explosions. Before Commodore Zhou could say anything further, the bridge section he was standing on took direct hit from a third wave of cruise missiles to hit his ship, killing him instantly.

****

In less than twenty minutes, the American fleet had successfully sunk the three Chinese carriers and the majority of their defending ships. With the enemy fleet essentially destroyed, the Americans began to pursue the remnants of the PLA Navy to officially finish off any naval threat to the landing force that would soon move to liberate the Philippines.

Pyrrhic Victory

Washington, D.C.
White House

"This is great news, Jim. We defeated the Chinese Navy and sank their fleet!" the President exclaimed jovially.

Castle was a bit more subdued. "Yes, Mr. President. As of three hours ago, our Allied fleet sank the last of the Chinese warships in the South China Sea. We've officially cleared the waterways around the Philippines, Taiwan, and most of the South China Sea for the next phase of our operations. However, it was a pyrrhic victory, Mr. President."

The President went from elated to a bit more somber. While the Allies had defeated the Chinese naval forces in the Pacific, it had come at a terrible cost in lives, treasure, and ships.

McMillian, the National Security Advisor, chimed in, "What was the finally tally on our losses, Jim?"

The SecDef sighed as he walked around the couch in the Oval Office and took a seat opposite McMillian. He then opened his folder and placed his reading glasses on the bridge of his nose as he began to look over the numbers.

"We lost the *Nimitz*, and the *Eisenhower* was also taken out of commission. The *Stennis* took a number of missile hits but is still operational; however, she'll need a lot of repairs once she returns to port. The Japanese lost two of their light carriers, and a third was heavily damaged. Those are just the carrier losses."

He paused for a second to let that sink in. "We also lost seven *Ticonderoga* guided-missile cruisers, twenty-three *Arleigh Burke* destroyers, two *Virginia*-class attack submarines and four *Los Angeles* attack submarines…All told, 13,000 sailors lost their lives, and roughly 14,000 were injured. We won the battle, Mr. President, but it has largely devastated our Navy. It'll take us decades to replace the number of ships lost, let alone reach our original goal of a 600-ship Navy. The loss of the *Nimitz* makes three carriers that have been completely destroyed and three more that will need to be taken out of action due to battle damage."

Gates sat back on the couch as the gravity of what the SecDef said began to set in. In less than a year, the Navy had lost nearly one-third of their vessels, with very little chance of replacing them before this war would be over. However, what really tore at the President was the loss of life. This was a horrific loss for the Navy and their country.

"What do we do next?" asked Gates.

"We continue to prosecute the war, Mr. President," Castle answered. "We will work to isolate the enemy and systematically destroy his will to fight. As terrible as our losses are, the Chinese suffered worse, and those losses aren't going to be hidden from their public. In the Philippines and Taiwan, we'll move to interdict their supply ships and systematically destroy their capability to defend the islands until our Marines are ready to move forward with their invasion."

Pausing for a second, the SecDef took his reading glasses off and placed them on the table. "This is going to be a long war, Mr. President. Nothing has changed. We continue with the current plan we have, and we defeat the enemy."

****

The following morning, as the President prepared his remarks, he tried to keep in mind that the country had been reeling from one crisis to another. The nation still wasn't over the vicious attack in Ohio by the Russian Spetsnaz, and now they were learning about the horrific loss of life in the greatest naval battle in the Pacific since World War II. There was only so much the people could handle before they just became numb to it.

"Are you ready, Mr. President?" asked Press Secretary Linda Wagner.

"I'm as ready as I'll ever be. Let's go talk to the American people. I'll try to do my best not to take too many questions from the wolves and to stay on message," he replied, knowing his press team hated it when he went off script.

A couple of minutes went by with Linda briefly talking with the press before she motioned for one of the aides to open the side door for the President, letting him know that it was time.

Gates instantly heard the electronic shuttering of dozens of cameras as they took pictures of him entering the press briefing room. The President stopped as he walked through the entrance and just paused for a second, as Linda looked at him, willing him to come to the podium. Knowing he needed to speak to the country, he drew up some inner courage and walked up to take Linda's place in front of the reporters and the cameras that had all zoomed in, ready to capture what he would say next.

He pulled a few notecards out of his front jacket pocket and placed them on the podium before turning his attention back to the cameras, doing his best not to look at the individual reporters for the time being. He wanted his focus to be on the cameras, which would be beaming his image to the country, and the families who had lost loved ones in yesterday's battles.

"My fellow Americans, I come to you today with a heavy heart, and news to report to you of the war. Yesterday, our gallant sailors and airmen went into battle against the Chinese People's Liberation Army Navy and were victorious." Before the President could say another word, several of the reporters applauded, and then a few more joined in until everyone was clapping. He raised his hand to get them to stop so he could resume speaking.

"There's a bit more that I need to say, and not all of it is good news. Our forces fought side-by-side with the brave sailors of Japan as we jointly fought against the expansion of the Eastern Alliance being led by the Russians and Chinese. While this battle was ultimately a victory, it came at a high cost to our nation. During the grueling battle that stretched on for many hours, the supercarrier USS *Nimitz* was sunk."

Audible gasps filled the room. Reporters frantically scribbled down notes and began sending texts and tweets of what the President had just said.

"The supercarriers USS *Eisenhower* and USS *John Stennis* also suffered major damage and loss of life. During the conflict, thirty other US naval warships and six submarines were also lost. Our Japanese allies lost two of their own carriers with a third heavily damaged, along with eight destroyers. Loss in lives and ships from this battle was high, and each soul that was lost was a brave hero for our nation—but make no mistake, the Allies defeated the Chinese Navy, and they have been removed as a threat to the world. Yesterday's battle was the first step in the eventual liberation of the Philippines and the restoration of the democratically elected government of the Republic of China."

The President paused again, looking down at a few bullet points on the three-by-five card he had in front of him. When he looked back up again, he saw the faces of the reporters. A few of the women had cried, and they were trying to hide the fact that their mascara was smearing as they tried to dab away the tears. A male reporter also wiped away a tear and was trying to look stoic as he waited for the President to continue.

"As a nation, we the people of the United States of America long for peace. For more than two centuries, our nation has been a beacon of hope and a bastion of freedom that has welcomed with open arms those looking to flee oppression and persecution. Since the end of the Second

World War, America has stood as the standard-bearer of freedom. We stood up to the Soviet Union during the Cold War, and we stood up to the savage terrorists who sought to destroy our way of life during the War on Terror. In all of these struggles, America has never sought conquests, nor have we sought to subjugate the nations of the world, but rather, we've come to the aid of those in need and given shelter to those being persecuted."

"This war was thrust upon us—started as a surprise attack by the Russian Federation on US and NATO Forces in Europe. They came at us like thieves in the night and attacked us without a declaration of war. Within months of the war in Europe starting, the People's Republic of China encouraged the North Korean regime to attack South Korea and US forces. When we found out about the timeline for the war, we were left with no options other than to launch a preemptive attack in hopes that we could destroy the Lee regime's nuclear weapons before they could be used. While our gallant forces were successful in destroying a vast quantity of the regime's nuclear weapons, Lee Pak was still able to launch a series of ICBMs at our country, ultimately leading to the destruction of Oakland and most of the San Francisco Bay Area."

Gates paused and looked down as he mentioned California. It tore at him that he wasn't able to do more to protect the country from such a devastating weapon. He often wondered if ordering the preemptive attack had ultimately led to the city's destruction.

"With the resumption of the Second Korean War, the Chinese launched a brutal surprise attack on our naval and ground forces in Asia. They then went on to invade the Island of Taiwan and the Philippines. Even now, they threaten our other allies, Australia and New Zealand. The Russians and the Chinese have openly stated that they won't end this war until America and the West have either surrendered or are defeated. They've gone so far as to create the Eastern Alliance and convinced the nations of India, Iran and many others to join them in their global conquest for world domination."

Anger burned in his eyes. "I, like many of you, wish it hadn't come to this. I long for peace with our enemies, but I won't accept defeat and the subjugation of the American people at the hands of the Eastern Alliance. Our nation has suffered, and we've sacrificed too much to give up now. I ask that you continue to unite together. We cannot give up. We must not give into their demands, and we must continue to fight on until victory has been achieved."

He took a deep breath. "With that, I will take some of your questions," he concluded.

"Mr. President! How many service members died yesterday in the naval battle? When will the official numbers be released, along with a more detailed description of the battle?" shouted a reporter from one of the major networks.

"I won't give out the exact number yet as many of the loved ones are still being notified as we speak. What I can say is that more than thirteen thousand sailors were killed in action, and close to fourteen thousand more were wounded during the battle," the President answered. Many in the room gasped or looked bewildered by the numbers of those lost. "The details of the battle will be released by the Pentagon, but suffice it to say, it lasted for more than twelve hours and involved over a thousand warships and aircraft on both sides. Next question."

"Has the Chinese fleet been officially defeated? Do they still have a fleet that can pose a threat to our forces in the Pacific?" asked another journalist from the *Washington Post*.

"The Navy successfully sank all three Chinese aircraft carriers and their supporting ships. We also sank an additional eight Chinese submarines. More specifics can be obtained from the Pentagon, but yes, we've officially destroyed the Chinese Navy as a fighting force, and they're no longer able to project naval power beyond their shore," Gates responded.

"Mr. President, do you feel at all responsible for the North Korean regime launching nuclear weapons at American cities in retaliation for you ordering a preemptive attack on their country? Don't you feel that if you hadn't done that, that the people of Oakland and the Bay Area would probably still be alive? Don't you think you should be held accountable for that action?"

Gates tried very hard to control the innate reaction to roll his eyes whenever that particular reporter started speaking—he was the prima donna of the press room and was always trying to bait the President with incendiary questions. Anger billowed up inside Gates, and he had to take a deep breath and calm himself before he said something he and his staff would regret.

"Jim, our preemptive attack saved the city of Seoul and millions of other people in South Korea and Japan. The only ones responsible for the destruction in Northern California are the Chinese government, who provided the Lee regime with the missiles capable of hitting our cities, and the Lee regime, who launched them. Next question," the President said, trying to move past the bloviating idiot who often seemed to be advocating for the enemy above the interests of his own nation.

"Mr. President, more than one hundred thousand military members have died in this war in less than one year. More than a million civilians have died since the start of this war. How much longer will this war last, and how many more people will have to die?" asked another reporter from one of the more progressive news outlets.

Gates retorted, "Are you asking when will America surrender?"

"That's not what I said. Our readers want to know how many more people need to die before this war ends," she replied.

"I suppose it could all end tomorrow, if America were willing to surrender and submit to being ruled by the Eastern Alliance, and while I'm sure many of your readers would welcome that, the rest of the country wants to remain an independent nation. This war is about the survival of our nation. We need to keep that in mind and realize that if we don't fight for our country now, we may not have a country to fight for later. With that, I'll turn the remainder of the questions back over to Linda," the President replied. He turned and left the podium.

Filipino Madness

Philippines
Laur, Luzon Island

The humid heat was starting to become oppressive as sweat ran down Captain Ma Qiliang's back, soaking his shirt. Standing up straight to stretch his back, he let out a slow groan as he twisted from side to side to loosen things up. Looking to his left, he saw his men had made good progress on camouflaging their positions.

"I hope the Americans don't land near us. We're not nearly ready enough to fight them yet," he reflected.

Fang, a fellow captain, walked up to Ma, interrupting his thoughts. "You know, you could round up some people from the city nearby and have them dig these positions for you and your men," he said. He made a sour face at how sweaty Ma had gotten while digging the foxhole he was standing in. Extending his hand, his friend offered to help pull him out.

"I suppose you're right, but I'd prefer the locals not know the exact location where my men are dug in—less chance of them telling the Americans and us becoming target practice for their artillery," he replied.

The snarky grin was wiped off of Fang's face. "Do you think the Americans will land near us or further south?" he asked. It was all anyone had talked about since word had spread of the defeat of their fleet.

Ma rubbed his back briefly and then took a couple of long gulps of water from his canteen before he responded, "My spine is killing me." He pulled himself out of the hole and lowered his voice. "Come over here, Fang. Let's talk a little further away from the prying ears of my men."

He and his childhood friend walked to a pile of sandbags and took a seat. Ma took another swig from his canteen. His face was frighteningly serious.

"Fang, we've known each other since we were little kids, so I'm going to be honest with you. I don't believe any of us are going to make it out of this alive. The best we can do right now is try to take as many Americans with us as we can," Ma said.

His friend was clearly shocked, but he did his best to try and hide his emotions.

Leaning in closer and lowering his voice, Fang said, "Ma, you must be careful with statements like that. If someone else were to hear you say that, they could report you as being disloyal." There was genuine concern in his voice.

325

The two of them had grown up together, and both of their families were good friends. When they completed university, they had both applied to become officers in the elite paratrooper unit, where loyalty and obedience had been pounded into them. His comment about them dying on this island came as a bit of a shock.

"Fang, it's just us. With no fleet, we're not going to be able to keep getting supplies brought to us from home. Look at what we're doing now," he said, waving his hand at the defensive works they were building.

"The airport was pounded last week by the American Navy, which is why we're out here digging ditches and fighting positions. It's only a matter of time until the Americans land their troops here. They could do what they did to the Japanese during the last war and just leave us here and go around us. We're trapped in the Philippines, and everyone knows it," Ma said in a hushed tone, making sure no one around them could hear their conversation.

"I know, and I'm sure the men know as well," conceded Fang. "We have to be strong for them, though. Just because the Navy lost a battle doesn't mean the war is over. You know as well as I do, we have 70,000 soldiers in the Philippines. As long as we hold our ground and fight, we'll bleed the Americans dry." He placed his hand on his friend's shoulder. "If we're fighting the Americans here, then they're not fighting in China. The Americans are weak. They'll grow tired of this war and give up soon enough. Look at what happened to them in Iraq. They won the peace, only to lose the war when a new president was elected. It's summer of 2018; the Americans have a new election in two years, and they'll elect someone new, you wait and see."

Ma smiled at his friend. "You're right, Fang, as always. The Americans will elect someone else who will be more malleable to our way of thinking, and this war will end. If we still have control of the Philippines when that happens, then I suppose all of this will still have been worth it."

****

Major General Hu Wei was getting frustrated with his superiors. The 43rd Airborne Corps was supposed to have transferred back to the Philippines following the capture of Manila. Instead, they had gotten drawn into a battle at the military base at Fort Mag, only finally crushing the local military force *after* the Navy was defeated in their grand battle. With no navy, and Allied warplanes now engaging the PLA Air Force over the Philippines, his paratroopers were stuck.

"*How did it come to this?*" he thought in anger. Then he became lost in a world of memory.

Two days after the PLA Navy was defeated in the greatest naval battle in history, the Americans had hit Luzon with a series of Tomahawk cruise missile strikes. Unfortunately for Major General Hu, several of the missiles that got through their defenses hit the headquarters of the 41st Army Group, killing Lieutenant General Lee Chen. General Lee had been the garrison commander of the Philippines and had been charged with fortifying the islands and integrating them into the Eastern Alliance. When he had been killed, Major General Hu had suddenly become the most senior PLA general in the Philippines and was summarily promoted to take his place.

The first thing General Hu had done when he'd taken control of the country was assess the air-defense and aircraft assets he had available to defend the country. Fortunately, General Lee had been given a large array of air-defense assets, but he had them scattered across Luzon in a vain belief that they would be more effective if the entire country was covered under their umbrella. Sadly, no one had explained to him that this tactic would also make it far easier for the Americans to isolate and destroy them individually.

Hu immediately ordered the surface-to-air missile systems consolidated into five concentrated points around Manila, Clark International Airport, Subic Bay, and the two other airfields the PLA Air Force had based their aircraft on.

Had he not built a heavy concentration of HQ-9 Red Banner-9 surface-to-air missile sites around Manila, Subic Bay and the Clark International Airport, the American fighter planes might have wiped out his remaining fighter planes. He quickly discovered that the vaunted Shenyang J-11 did not fare well against the American F/A-18 Super Hornets. Nearly half of their J-11s had been destroyed in the past three weeks as the American pressure continued to grow. The only bright spot he had seen in the air war was the Chengdu J-20 stealth fighters. Given he only had twenty of them, they had successfully shot down eighteen Super Hornets with zero losses. Had the Americans not lost so many of their F-35s during the naval battle, the air war might have gone decidedly against China, but so far it was even.

His aide handed him the latest reports on the American air raids, pulling him back to the here and now. Upon reading it, he smiled and looked up at Brigadier General Li Qiang, his senior PLA Air Force commander. "Are you sure this will protect our aircraft from further cruise missile attacks?" Hu asked. He wasn't sure if he should reprimand him for this idea or give him a medal.

"General, the Americans are soft. They would never carry out an attack that would kill so many civilians in the process just to destroy a fighter plane on the ground. This plan will work, and it will keep our planes secured. I just need your permission to implement it," Li said, smiling at the genius of his own plan and chiding himself for not having thought about it sooner.

Sitting back in his chair, Hu asked, "How many civilians will you need, and where will you place them so they don't pose a threat to the aircraft?"

"I'll have my people set up a series of tents near the hangars where we're storing the J-20s for the civilians to stay in during the day. We'll also set up some canopies on the roofs of the hangars and place civilians in them as well. Essentially, we'll have all of our hangars, fuel dumps, and other important facilities surrounded by civilians, day and night. If the Americans hit the hangars with a smart bomb or cruise missile, they'll kill hundreds of them." He smirked. "I'd also like to employ this same tactic with our surface-to-air missile sites, to further deter the Americans from attacking them."

"*This man truly is devious,*" thought General Hu with a certain sense of awe. His plan might just be the very action to save their air forces and delay the Americans from capturing the island.

"This certainly won't help our cause of winning hearts and minds," Hu said jokingly, "but I agree with you that it will deter the Americans from attacking your planes. It's critically important that your aircraft work in concert with our air-defense systems to keep the Americans from completely controlling the skies above us. I'm not sure if headquarters will approve this, but I believe there may have been some sort of communications problem when I called to inform them. Until I hear otherwise, you're approved to move forward with this idea, General."

The air force general nodded and grinned at the unspoken word that they would not seek further approval for this plan beyond themselves.

Britain's Out?!

Mons, Belgium
Global Defense Force Headquarters

It was nearly 2000 hours local time when General James Cotton, the commander of all Global Defense Force troops in Europe, received an urgent phone call. Judging by what was unfolding in the British election, he suspected his call had something to with the results. It was looking like Anthony Chattem, the Labour MP, would become the next Prime Minister of England.

Cotton's military aide held the smartphone out for him. "It's the Secretary of Defense," he said in a hushed tone.

Nodding, Cotton took the phone and held it to his ear. "This is Cotton. I assume you have new orders for me?" he inquired.

A grunt could be heard on the other end. "This is a complete mess, James," said Castle. "We just spoke with the outgoing British National Security Adviser, Sir Mark Ricketts. He told us the new government would be announcing a new policy with regard to the war and our alliance. He didn't come right out and say it, but we all know

PM Chattem is going to issue a ceasefire and separate peace with the Eastern Alliance."

"*Is he really going to do it?*" General Cotton wondered. He didn't understand how Chattem could be completely oblivious to how badly that would end for Great Britain. He had worked for years with the British Army and served in Britain with many of the finest soldiers, and it pained him to think of all those people being told that everyone who had died up that point was all for nothing.

"I suppose you're calling to tell me my offensive I was going to start in a few days is now on hold?" Cotton asked.

"Sadly, yes," Castle responded. "I don't want to risk losing many thousands of British soldiers on an offensive they won't be able to fully take part in. It would be cruel and wrong to order them into battle, only to tell them they have to leave because their government has signed a separate peace deal. I won't be responsible for that…and neither will you. Is that understood, General?"

James took a deep breath and slowly let it out before he responded, "I disagree with your assessment, Sir, but I will follow your orders and hold off on starting our summer offensive. If you wish, I'll order the British forces back from the lines as well," he offered, though it greatly angered him to do so.

"We have a lot of details that need to be worked out in Europe with this whole situation in London. Right now, I need you to make sure the French, Germans, and Polish hold together. If we lose more of the alliance members, then I am frankly not sure what will happen," the SecDef replied, not at all pleased with the situation.

"Mr. Secretary, I can postpone my main offensive for a couple of months, but I'd like to still move forward with Operation Nordic Thunder," insisted General Cotton. "It's imperative that we threaten the Kola Peninsula and St. Petersburg. I also don't want to let the Russians gobble up any further land in Norway or Finland. I've transferred a large German contingent to shore up the Helsinki line, and I'd like to move forward with that operation."

There was silence on the other end for a second while the SecDef thought about the options for a moment. "OK, General. You can continue with Nordic Thunder. But Baltic Fury has to be delayed until the end of September. No exceptions on this one, James. The President wants the Philippines and Taiwan captured before the typhoon season starts in November. That means Asia's going to get the bulk of reinforcements and equipment. I think you should plan to start Baltic Fury toward the end of September, or October if you want to be safe."

"OK, I can make that work," Cotton responded. "Just don't turn the supply spigot off entirely, and allow me to keep building up what I can." He knew that was the best he was going to get.

"Look, I need to get ready to brief the President," said the SecDef. "I'll talk with you once we've sorted a few more things out." The phone clicked.

"Why didn't I retire last year like I told my wife I would?" thought Cotton. He had regretted that decision many times over the last few months. He hadn't planned on becoming the commander of all European forces right in the middle of World War III.

"Shall I get you another refill of coffee, General?" asked his military aide.

Cotton grunted. *"Well, I'm not going to sleep anytime soon, so why not?"* he thought.

He nodded, then stood up and walked over to the large wall map he had set up of Finland. The map showed the Allied unit positions in relation to the Russian units opposing them.

Out of the corner of his eye, he saw his J3, Major General Millet, walk into the room. "Is Fifth Corps fully fielded and ready for combat?" asked General Cotton.

Millet walked up and stood next to Cotton at the map. "Yes, Sir," he answered. "They deployed to the field two days ago and are currently making their way to the front lines. The German 23rd Panzer Division is also on the road to the front as well. We'll be ready to commence Operation Nordic Thunder on time. What did the SecDef say about Baltic Fury? Are we still a go for that operation?" he inquired, clearly hoping that they could still proceed.

Shaking his head in disgust, Cotton said, "Nordic Thunder is a go, but Baltic Fury has been placed on hold until the fall. The SecDef said that with the British pulling out of the alliance, we're going to have to wait until they can fully support our operations here in Europe, as well as the ongoing conflict in Asia. The President wants to liberate the Philippines and Taiwan before the next typhoon season rolls in, which starts in November and runs through March. For the time being, we're going to have to try and contain the Russians in Europe while we press them hard in the Scandinavian countries." General Cotton turned to look back at the map, analyzing the various units represented on it.

A devilish grin slowly spread across the general's face. "Millet, I want you to convey to Ernie that I'd really like his forces to capture Kotka and Kouvola, if at all possible. Tell him if he's able to capture both of those cities from the Russians and he still feels froggy, then I would greatly enjoy buying him a beer at a local pub in Vyborg."

Millet snickered. He obviously realized that the general wanted to go way outside of the parameters of Operation Nordic Thunder and invade Russia proper. "OK, Sir. I think I know what you mean, and I'll make sure to craft the orders in such a manner as to indicate your desires while still staying with the general parameters of the original operation," he replied.

General Cotton nodded and took a sip of the hot coffee that had just arrived.

****

London, England
10 Downing Street

Two days after the election, Anthony Chattem was seated and going over a tentative proposal with his new National Security Adviser, the current Minister of Defense, and the Chief of the Army. "I campaigned on the message that Great Britain would pursue a separate peace with the Eastern Alliance, withdraw our military forces from the Continent, and end our membership in the Global Defense Force alliance, and I intend to honor the will of the people who voted for me to enact those policies," he began.

Chattem turned to face the Minister of Defense first. "Sir Craig, I understand the Americans were about to start a new military offensive any day. What is the current status of that?" he inquired, hoping the Americans weren't going to make it any more difficult for him to implement his strategy.

"The American president ordered the offensive to be paused for the time-being, until our situation can be sorted," Minister Martin reassured him. "I have spoken personally with General Cotton, the Allied commander for Europe, and he has ordered all British forces to be pulled from the front lines in anticipation of our withdrawal."

Minister of Defense Craig Martin paused a moment, apparently bracing himself for what he would say next. "I would personally like to commend him in doing that, because it wasn't a popular decision…I'll be honest with you, Mr. Prime Minister, the military is adamantly against this decision and does not support it. If the Eastern Alliance prevails, Great Britain will not have any allies to call upon for help," he replied bluntly. He probably spoke a bit more freely since he knew he was on his way out.

"Duly noted, Sir James. If the generals have a problem with our new stance, they're free to resign, and I'll replace them with ones that are willing to comply," Chattem said with a grin on his face.

He was relishing the angst he was causing within the military. His goal was to keep Britain out of the war, and secretly, he didn't think switching sides to the Eastern Alliance was all that bad of an idea. He was already sold on elements of the Russian-Chinese model of techno-communism.

Clearing his throat briefly, the National Security Adviser spoke up. "The country is still in the midst of a large military buildup, Mr. Prime Minister. We have tens of thousands of soldiers currently in training and nearly a hundred thousand soldiers on the Continent that will be returning. What is going to be our plan with them moving forward?"

"Our country cannot afford to sustain and build this large of a military, especially in light of our withdrawal from the war. This conflict has been the Americans' doing from the beginning, and we never should have been involved. When our forces return from combat, I want an immediate halt to the expansion of the military, and I want a demobilization to start. We will return the military to its prewar size. Once we do, we will look for ways to trim the budget where we can, to give more monies to the reconstruction of our nation from the damage sustained during this disastrous war."

Chattem turned to the Chief of the Army. "General, I'd like your resignation on my desk by tomorrow morning. You are relieved of your duties. Please assign your deputy to take over until I can appoint my own man. Sir Craig Martin, you are also relieved of your duties, and I expect your resignation on my desk by tomorrow as well. I ask that you both leave now so I can work with my own staff. Thank you both for your service," Chattem said, concluding the meeting with the two senior members managing the war during the transition period.

The two got up and left without saying another word, though the scowls on their faces said everything that needed to be said. As they left the room, Mr. Chattem smiled when he overheard the General of the Army muttering something about needing a stiff drink.

Operation Nordic Thunder

Pyhtaa, Finland

Command Sergeant Major Luke Childers walked up to Lieutenant Colonel Alex Schoolman, who was squinting as he looked off in the distance with his field glasses, trying to see if he could spot any enemy tanks or other armored vehicles. His squadron was screening for a much larger tank force that was a couple of kilometers behind him, waiting for the word to advance forward and smash into the Russian lines once Schoolman's unit found the enemy.

"What are your thoughts, Sergeant Major? You see anything?" he asked, hoping that Childers' trained eyes might see something he was missing.

Childers scanned to the right with his own field glasses and then zoomed in on something that caught his eye. "There you are," he said under his breath. A smile crept across his face.

"Yes, Sir. To my three o'clock, near the edge of those trees," Childers responded. "If you look close enough, you'll see the barrel from what's probably a T-90." He pointed in the direction of where the enemy tank was lurking.

"Good eye, Sergeant Major," Schoolman said. He turned to some of the soldiers standing behind him. "Someone plot the grid to that location and send it back to brigade. Let's see if we can get some artillery fire in that tree line and smoke these guys out of their position," he ordered.

A flurry of activity happened around them as one of the soldiers guided one of the Stryker vehicles forward so they could use the laser range finder on the 105mm cannon. In a few minutes, they had the exact grid of the enemy tank. They relayed that to the artillery battalion for a fire mission to hit the tree line and see what else they could stir up. Five minutes later, they heard the whistling sounds of artillery rounds flying overhead toward the enemy lines.

Boom! Boom! Boom! Boom!

Geysers of dirt and tree parts billowed upward. Several large secondary explosions flashed in the woods. Then the counterbattery fire kicked in. The distinct whistles of enemy artillery raced over their heads in the direction of their own artillery battalion.

A loud *whoosh* rushed in the opposite direction. A pair of A-10 Warthogs flew in and strafed the forest, hitting several other tanks. Their attack was swiftly followed by multiple streams of antiaircraft fire as the Russian gunners tried to swat the tank busters from the sky. The 25mm and

30mm rounds crisscrossed the sky, intermixed with a few MANPADS that flew after the aircraft.

As the artillery duel continued and Allied warplanes took turns softening up the Russian lines, the mechanical sound of tanks—dozens upon dozens of tanks—and the low rumbling that shook the ground got closer and louder as the Allied tanks moved forward to their attack positions. Finnish and German tanks moved forward first; they would lead the assault, supported by American Apache gunships and the 2nd Cavalry Regiment. A battalion of American Abrams tanks were being held in reserve while the rest of the 1st Armored Division was further north of their position near Tillola.

Turning to look behind them, Childers almost felt a chill run down his back as he saw columns of German Leopard II tanks with their black Iron Crosses painted on them, advancing toward the Russians. They started to change their formation from a single-file column to a full-abreast attack line. While the first line formed, a second line of German tanks formed up and was quickly followed by a third line, this time a Finnish unit. The three armored lines were quickly being followed up by column after column of infantry fighting vehicles and armored personnel carriers.

"This is going to be an epic battle," Sergeant Major Childers thought with glee.

He snapped a couple of pictures from his miniature camera. When he could, he had been sneaking pictures with his digital camera, documenting his participation in the war. Aside from a few mementos for himself, he thought they might hold some historical value someday.

****

Explosions reverberated through the air as Oberstleutnant Hermann Wulf's 25th Panzergrenadier Battalion of forty-four Puma infantry fighting vehicles raced to keep up with the Panzers that were charging right into the Russian lines. Sitting behind the gunner, Wulf was looking at the video monitor display of what was happening in front of them. He could see red-hot tank rounds crisscrossing back and forth between the two opposing forces.

Bam! Boom!

Their vehicle was rocked by a near-miss, forcing Wulf to grab for something to hold on to. The driver of the vehicle somehow managed to keep them from rolling over. The soldier manning the vehicle's 30mm autocannon fired at an unseen target. Then a slew of bullets hit their armored shell, reminding them that the enemy also got a vote in the fighting. This was by no means going to be a one-sided fight.

Wulf's radio crackled. "Oberstleutnant, the Panzers are breaking to the right. It looks like they found a hole in the enemy lines. Should we follow them or dismount and fight here?" asked one of his company commanders.

"No, stay with the Panzers," Wulf answered. "Our mission is to support their advance and keep the Russian infantry off their backs. We'll let the Finns deal with this group of Russians." Their driver did his best to follow the group of tanks that were now rushing through a hole in the enemy lines.

Wulf looked at the video image being relayed to his screen from the small aerial drone a thousand meters above them. The drone was giving him a wide top-down view of the battle happening around them. He could see several of his vehicles had been destroyed, while many others were heavily engaged with an unseen enemy at the edges of their flanks. Seeing them fighting off to the side meant they were doing their job, keeping the Russian infantry from getting too close to the tanks and firing off their RPGs and other antitank weapons.

Scanning further ahead of where the Panzers were headed, he saw several strong points that might prove challenging for the tanks to overcome. He signaled to the Air

Force LNO traveling with him to see if they could get some air support to hit those units.

"Move the drone higher, I want to get us a better overview of the battle," he said to the young soldier manning the battalion's eye in the sky.

Boom!

Another explosion rocked their vehicle, slapping it with shrapnel as they continued to keep up with the tanks. The gunner let loose a series of short bursts from their main gun at a target Wulf couldn't see.

When the drone reached one thousand meters, he saw a cluster of Russian tanks forming up on the opposite side of a small village they were approaching. Spotting the unit, Wulf looked up the frequency to the Panzer unit closest to them, then sent them a quick message, alerting to what he had found. The Panzer unit adjusted their approach to the village while an artillery strike was ordered in.

Looking at the scene unfolding around them was almost like watching a video game or movie; yet this was very real. Groups of tanks and soldiers on the ground were moving into positions to attack and kill each other, and here he sat, in his armored vehicle, observing it. In minutes, he saw a series of elongated tubes slam into the ground, hitting some of the buildings in the small village, blowing them apart as the rocket artillery pummeled the combatants. Minutes turned to hours, and the day turned to night before the battle was finally over, leaving behind a trail of burnt-out wrecks of armored vehicles and torn and twisted bodies.

The tank battle between the German 21st Panzer Brigade and the Russian 3rd Motor Rifle Division and 1st Separate Guards Tank Brigade raged on for nearly six hours as both sides fought viciously before the Russians were forced to withdraw. Once the US 1st Armored Division punched through the Russian lines at Tillola, the Russians had to pull their armor group back to the Russian border and the positions their engineers had been busy building the past several months.

****

Operation Nordic Thunder would continue for another two months as the Allies fought hard in northern Finland and Norway to push the Russians' northern operation back to the Russian border. While the fighting had been fierce, it had accomplished its goal of removing the Russians from the Nordic countries and forcing the Russians to divert forces from Western Europe to strengthen their northern border or face the likelihood of a possible threat to St. Petersburg. While the number of troops involved in

Nordic Thunder paled in comparison to the armies being assembled on the Continent, it kept the Russians from being able to commit to a large summer offensive as they had to divert significant numbers of reinforcements to keep the Allies from pressing into Russia proper and potentially threatening their second-most-important city.

Russian Resolve

Moscow, Russia

President Petrov was fuming after the defeat of the Russian forces in Finland and Norway. He was furious that, despite months of reprieve and additional reinforcements, General Yury Bukreyev, the commander in charge of Russian forces on the northern front, had failed to hold his ground. His forces should have held for longer than a couple of days.

A short but fiery debate erupted amongst Petrov's top leadership over what to do about this "problem." Alexei Semenov, the Minister of Defense, had argued that Bukreyev should be publicly executed, to make an example of him. Colonel General Boris Egorkin explained that he felt this would erode confidence among the leadership with the army, that they might fear that if they retreated, even if it were for a tactical advantage, they would be executed too. Of course, there was also the legal aspect; capital punishment was technically outlawed in Russia. The last public execution was in 1996.

Ultimately, Petrov's ire overruled any objections by General Egorkin. The law banning executions was speedily overturned after a little arm-twisting from the president, and within a few days, Petrov and his senior cabinet members were seated to watch General Bukreyev's execution by firing squad.

Before the official presentation began and the cameras were turned on, Minister of Defense Semenov dared to protest one last time. "Mr. President, I must caution you that I feel this is a very bad precedent for us to set. The Soviet Army did this during World War II, and we lost far too many officers at a time when every competent leader was needed to defeat the Nazis."

"You've made your point, General, and I have made mine," said Petrov, half-surprised that Semenov had spoken at all. "We're not going to win this war if we don't hold our military leaders accountable for their failures. We have achieved an enormous success in getting the British to withdraw from the war. We won't squander that victory by having generals squander their time and resources. I don't want to discuss this matter any further, is that understood?"

"Yes, Mr. President," answered Semenov dutifully.

"Good, now smile for the cameras," said Petrov. "We will have our briefing after this."

****

A few hours later, Petrov was seated in a room with the same senior leadership members. He turned to his General of the Army first. "What I want is an update from you. First off—when is our summer offensive is going to start?" he asked, not quite yelling, but clearly irritated. "We're more than halfway through the summer, and it still hasn't started."

"If he doesn't deliver, Bukreyev won't be the only officer I make an example of," Petrov thought.

"I know we've had a longer delay than we'd like," conceded General Egorkin, "and I'm afraid we're going to have to delay the start of our offensive by at least two more months, but please allow me to finish my brief so I can let you know why this delay is imperative."

Seeing that he wasn't immediately removed from the room, Egorkin continued. "At the start of the war, we had roughly 3,000 T-80 tanks and roughly 6,400 T-72 tanks in cold storage across the country. When the conflict started, we immediately brought these tanks out of storage and began a rapid modernization program. While the T-14 Armatas have been a game changer for us, we're still only able to produce roughly 100 of these tanks a month. The T-80s and older T-72s may not be nearly as capable, but their sheer numbers will overwhelm the Allies, especially now that the British armored forces have been ordered home."

"In two months, I will have the necessary number of tanks and new soldiers to launch Operation Armored Fist. Our offensive will start with a massive cruise and ballistic missile attack of the Allied front lines, and then a Spetsnaz attack of several dozen military airfields in Poland, Germany, and the Czech Republic. The Indian manufacturers are now delivering us thousands of missiles a month, and we intend to hit the Allies with such force that it will throw them off balance for our ground offensive."

He pulled up a visual on the screen in the room, which showed the plan of attack and the timeline for achieving each objective. "General Chayko's army group will hit the Allies at Ternopil with an armored fist of nearly 10,000 tanks and over 40,000 armored vehicles. Once his force breaks a hole in the Allies' line, they will drive on Lviv, the provisional capital of Ukraine, and then head straight for Krakow. As his forces advance toward Krakow, two prongs are going to branch off. One will head toward Warsaw and threaten to cut the entire Allied lines off in Belarus and Lithuania. The other arm will drive down to Kosice, Slovenia."

Before the general could continue, Foreign Minister Dmitry Kozlov interjected. "If General Chayko is able to break through and capture Prague, and even threaten Dresden, Nuremberg or Munich, we may be able to pursue a ceasefire with the Allies and secure a better peace deal than we would if we are only able to hold on to our current gains. I'm fairly confident we can get the Allies to agree to more favorable terms if we're holding a large portion of Poland, Slovakia, the Czech Republic and parts of Germany," he proclaimed with a sense of excitement in his voice.

Petrov wanted to bring an end to the war with the Allies as soon as possible. The longer this war dragged on, the more likely it was that his country would lose. Getting the British to withdraw from the war had been a real coup, but that could quickly change if it were ever discovered how PM Chattem had come to power. Plus, that flamboyant demigod in America had somehow managed to rally the majority of the country against the Eastern Alliance. Gates was no longer interested in winning a battle with Russia—he wanted to destroy Russia and China once and for all.

"*Well, as long as I have nuclear weapons, it'll never get that far,*" Petrov thought.

"That is the goal, Minister Kozlov," Egorkin said to the group, "to put ourselves in as good a position as possible for peace talks. This is why I'm not starting the offensive until September. When we launch this offensive, we need to hit the Allies with everything we have. If this attack does not work, then there's a high likelihood that our forces will have to withdraw back to our own borders, and even then, I'm not sure we could stop a concerted Allied push."

Sighing, Petrov surveyed the men around the table before settling back on Egorkin. "What about our Indian allies? Their troops have been arriving in strong numbers. Are they going to be of use, or not?"

"They will help," Egorkin answered. "Right now, I have them working feverishly on developing a series of defensive lines near our borders, should the offensive fail. While I don't believe we will be unsuccessful, since the Americans have shifted their military focus to the Pacific for the time being, I'm not going to risk leaving our borders defenseless. I plan on holding the Indian Army in reserve. Should our offensive collapse, we won't be left having to rely on third-tier reserve divisions to defend our borders."

Satisfied with the military part of his briefing, Petrov dismissed his generals and Minister of Defense. He needed to speak privately with Minister Kozlov and Ivan Vasilek, the FSB Director.

With the room now empty, Petrov leaned in and looked Ivan in the eyes. "We've known each other a long time, Ivan," he said, speaking softly. "I need to know how much of a danger this Alexei Kasyanov is to our regime."

Ivanov was prepared for this question. "He is a grave danger, Mr. President. I would like to say otherwise, but he's now being supported by the American CIA, the German BND, and the British MI6. They are backing him with money, technology, and social media support to spread his message. He is steadily giving speeches across Russian radio waves and on internet platforms. I have every available resource looking for him as we speak, but he's gaining traction with the youth and those who are weary of the war. The casualty lists on his website are the biggest draw. People go there to see if their family member has been killed or captured, and from there, they're given a steady dose of Western propaganda. These poisonous lies are then spread and, eventually, believed," he replied.

"We have to do what we can to squash them and find this traitorous swine," Petrov asserted, venom in his voice.

"Yes, Sir," said Kozlov. He sighed. "It would appear the West is doing to us what we have been doing to them for years."

Petrov turned to his foreign minister. "Alexei, how strong is our alliance? Are the members holding strong?" he inquired, hoping this grassroots traitor was the only major concern they were having to deal with.

Minister Kozlov had been working hard to make sure the alliance stayed together. The Eastern Alliance was still a bit shaky, especially as the Americans rallied the rest of the world to stand against them. The quick dissolvement of NATO was met by the creation of the American-led Global Defense Force. While many of the GDF nations could not contribute much to the war in terms of soldiers and weaponry, they were contributing immense amounts of resources and manufacturing capacity to the war effort. Brazil had increased its ammunition production of 5.56mm NATO rounds from roughly 300 million rounds annually to more than four billion rounds—that added capacity in rifle ammunition alone was making a huge impact at the front line.

"The Asian alliance members are shakier than our Eurasian allies," Kozlov admitted. "Indonesia is my big concern. While they've practically given their military over to the PLA, they are slow in growing their military and getting them properly equipped. Malaysia is even worse. They only joined under threat from the PLA, so they're sluggish rolling everything out. The Chinese Army may be large, but it can't be everywhere at once, and the Americans are getting ready to invade the Philippines. Once they secure the Island of Luzon, they'll prepare to liberate Taiwan."

Shaking his head disapprovingly, Petrov inquired, "And what of our Eurasian allies? Are they training their military to our standards and ready to assist?"

"Yes and no, Mr. President," replied Kozlov. "They are training and growing in size. But they're largely underequipped. They're using very outdated equipment. Right now, most of these troops are moving to Iran, where they'll join with their Muslim brothers for the fight against the Israeli-Saudi-led alliance. They're not going to be of much help in our campaign."

"You know, I don't even care if the Iranians are successful in their conquest of the Middle East," said Petrov with a snort. "Their campaign will draw further resources from the GDF and the Americans, which, in the end, will help us as we prepare for Operation Armored Fist."

The president turned his attention to Ivanov. "I want this rebellion in our country crushed. Use our new pawn in Britain and find out what you can about this MI6 operation that is cultivating this rebellion. Let's see if we can put

Chattem to use in ferreting out these traitors within our country," Petrov ordered.

The men then turned to discuss other matters of state, after which the meeting became more of a social visit among old friends. They stayed there late into the evening, drinking vodka and sharing laughs. The world was not worth defeating if there couldn't be some enjoyment in life in the meantime.

Operation Strawman

Pushkino, Russia

Alexei Kasyanov added a few bullet points to his upcoming broadcast. True to his word, the *Der Spiegel* reporter, Gunther Brinkbaumer, had introduced him to a couple of men from the CIA, who had taken him in and become responsible for his personal security and housing. Now he was moved from one safe house to another after every broadcast to keep them one step ahead of the Russian FSB, which was dedicating more and more resources to finding him.

Once Alexei had agreed to work with the Allies, they'd collaborated on a social media campaign that would be designed to sow discord and distrust between the population and the Petrov administration. All the while, they continued raising the prospect of an alternative government to the corrupt Petrov regime that the country had been enslaved by for the past eighteen months. The CIA arranged a steady stream of news about the war to be provided to Alexei, who then compared that information to the official stories being shown to the people by RT and the other Russian news agencies.

The initial goal of the podcasts and radio broadcasts was to provide the people of Russia with a reliable alternative source of news to what the government was putting out. This caused the number of followers and listeners Alexei Kasyanov had garnered up to that point to swell from the tens of thousands to nearly a million people within a month and a half. People were starved for information and more importantly, the truth about the war. While there had been many victories by the Russian forces, there were also a number of major defeats, and these facts were being kept hidden from the Russian people.

The CIA had also provided Alexei with a list of Russian prisoners of war that had been captured up to that point—as soon as he'd published this list on his website, the number of followers on his site had ballooned to nearly six million people. The government had been withholding the names of POWs and openly downplaying the number of casualties, causing many family members to wonder what had happened to their sons during the major battles, so they were starving for any explanation of what had really happened to their loved ones.

After several months of this, along with subtle questioning of the government's motives, an underbelly of frustration and anxiety with the government was growing.

Now that Alexei's list of followers had grown substantially, he was prepared for a new phase in his broadcasts—one of more direct challenges to the Petrov regime.

Gordon Welsh, the MI6 agent who was helping to craft the speech for the evening, walked up to Alexei to try and pump him up for the night's event. "This speech is really going to get people riled up," he said with a smile.

Alexei was deep in thought and just nodded. He hated working with these foreign intelligence agents, but he knew that without them, he had no hope of saving his country from the destruction Petrov was bringing upon their homeland.

"*The enemy of my enemy is my friend*," he reminded himself.

"As long as we get the people to come to our side and we can rid Russia of Petrov, then that is all I care about," Alexei responded.

The British agent got the camera ready and made sure everything was recording correctly on the computer before he signaled that they were ready.

After looking down at his notes one last time, Alexei looked at the camera and signaled he was ready to begin. The small red light next to the camera flashed on. They were recording.

"My fellow Russians, welcome to today's Broadcast of the Truth, where we bring you the stories Petrov does not want you to know about," he began. "As many of you are already aware, President Petrov has signed a no-longer-secret agreement with the countries of China, India, and Iran to form a new alliance called the Eastern Alliance. His never-ending conquest for war will surely lead to the ruin of Russia."

"In response to Petrov's new alliance, the Allies, led by the United States, have formed their own global alliance to defeat us. Just this past week, our forces were defeated in Finland, and even now, the Allies are less than two hundred miles from St. Petersburg. It won't be long until we have foreign invaders marching in our streets."

"We must demand an end to this war," he continued, his voice becoming more forceful and passionate. "If you haven't seen the list of casualties on our website, I highly encourage you to scroll through them. We've updated our lists with the most recent casualties from the battles in Finland. It's time that we as Russians wake up to what the Petrov regime is doing to our great nation. We're systematically being destroyed by Alliance bombing attacks, lied to about our young men and women dying in combat, and deceived about the causes of this war and its continuation. While I've called on the people of our great nation to protest peacefully, there's going to come a time when peaceful protests won't be enough."

Gordon Welsh gave him a signal from the sidelines to say it was time to really push it home. Alexei nodded slightly, then went on. "We must be the masters of our future, not Petrov. Our nation has a wealth of oil, natural gas, and minerals, yet all that prosperity has been squandered for the last twenty years by the rich few who rule us like kings, and the military that protects their power. The time is coming when we must say enough is enough. I call on each of you to talk with your family members, to talk with your friends. When do we take control of our futures and end this war? Until next time, stay tuned for more information and instructions on what to do next."

With that, Alexei ended his short speech. Immediately, he wanted to watch it and see if he needed to make any changes before they published the video. Once ready, the short speech would be transmitted multiple times a day across numerous radio frequencies on the AM and FM bands and promulgated across dozens of Russian-language websites and streaming services.

After a few minor edits, Alexei was satisfied with the speech. They uploaded it to the various servers that would spread the message across the internet inside of Russia.

Once the file was safely online, Mitch Lowe, the CIA agent in charge of Alexei's security, announced, "It's time to go."

"*Another day, another safe* house," thought Alexei in annoyance. All of the constant moving was getting tiring, and there was always the worry that someone might follow them. Constant vigilance was exhausting.

Still, Alexei had a certain respect for his handler. Prior to the war, Mitch had been a deep-cover CIA agent working for a Russian tech firm. When the war had started, he'd conveniently arranged for his official death to occur from one of the many American bombing strikes that had hit Moscow during the opening days of the war. This allowed Mitch to roam free within the city without him suddenly being missed by his employer. When Operation Strawman had become a reality, it had been determined that the CIA would run the security and financial arm of the underground resistance, while the British would focus more on the social engineering of the speeches and the stirring up of civil unrest in the major Russian cities. They did this by providing a lot of young people with money to protest and generally encouraging a lot of mischief between the youth and the government.

When played out over many months, Operation Strawman was having the desired effect. Popular Russian support for Petrov and the war had plummeted, and while he didn't need the popular support to wage his war, their apathy to it was having a negative effect on the production of war materials and other essential tools needed to fight in the various conflicts. The popularity of the People's Freedom Party, or PARNAS, and Alexei Kasyanov as an alternative to the Petrov regime continued to grow. Posters and pictures of Alexei and PARNAS symbols popped up all over Russia, and so did calls to end the war—especially once the people were able to get their hands on unfiltered casualty reports from the battles.

The next phase in the operation would call for direct recruitment of military commanders to switch sides and to openly rebel against the Petrov government.

Pacific Prep

Tinian Island
North Field

Looking over the Marines of Echo Company, Captain Long felt a great sense of pride in his men as they sat in a semicircle in front of him. He had worked hard drilling them during SOI and getting them ready for war. Thousands of Marines from the 6th Marine Division had filtered into the South Pacific as US forces continued to build up for the eventual invasion of the Philippines and Taiwan. While the Navy continued to clear them a path to the enemy, the Marines were ramping up their training and preparation for the coming battle.

Captain Long's Marines were nearly ready for battle, and it was time to fine-tune some of their individual skills that would help to keep them alive. "Listen up, Marines," he said. "Whether we hit the beaches or fight our way through the jungles of the Philippines or the mountains of Taiwan, you're going to need to know how to shoot accurately under pressure and not freak out. Today, we find ourselves on the North Field of Tinian Island. This field was used to house the 313th Bombardment Wing, the same bomb wing that carried out the atomic bombing of Japan. It was from this island that the war in the Pacific was won, and it will be from this island that our generation will end this terrible war with the Eastern Alliance."

Long could tell by looking at the crowd before him that he had them fired up, so he pressed in. "Today's training will focus on a couple of critically important skills, which I can attest from my own combat experiences are vital to your survival and our success. We're going to run through a series of firing drills. In the first drill, you will have to hit targets from five meters, fifteen meters, thirty meters, fifty meters, and one hundred meters while one of the Ranger officers fires a M240 and an M2 several feet over your heads. I want you to hear it and know what it's like to have to shoot your weapons while under fire, to feel that pressure to hit the target. You'll also go through a series of magazine-changing drills while under fire. When the crap hits the fan, it's going to get crazy, and you need to know how to react under immense pressure. With that said, I'm going to hand you over to the range control officers, and I'll continue to monitor everyone's progress."

The rest of the day was spent running his company through a series of challenging shooting exercises and identifying those soldiers who would need extra training and those who were going to thrive on the pressure. This type of exercise was designed to get them truly ready for what they would ultimately have to face when it came time to evict the PLA from the Philippines and Taiwan.

****

Two weeks went by as the Marines continued to train their units relentlessly in preparation for the final assault. Then, the word finally came down that it was time to retake the Pacific.

Captain Long walked through row after row of tents until he came to the tent that was being used as the brigade's headquarters and operations center. He walked up to the entrance and made his way in to find Colonel Micah Tilman's office. He quickly noticed a lot of the other company and battalion commanders in the tent as well.

"*Maybe this was changed to more of a group presentation*," thought Long.

A couple of minutes went by before they were led further back into the tent to a small group of chairs and a map board with a lot of Post-it notes and other markings. The board was quickly flipped over to present a blank whiteboard, which Long assumed would be used as the backdrop for a PowerPoint presentation.

Walking to the front of the group, Colonel Tilman cleared his throat. "OK, men, it's finally happening. We've been given our orders to attack. While many of you knew we'd invade soon, most of you had no idea where we would be attacking. The 6th Marine Division has been given the task of liberating the main Philippine Island of Luzon, and as such, our brigade will be assaulting the beach area around Dingalan, roughly twenty kilometers from the Philippine base at Fort Mag, where we've previously trained at in the past with the Filipino Army."

Turning to his aide, he signaled for the PowerPoint presentation to start. "As you can see, we will be hitting the beaches along this section." Tilman pointed to a series of beach resorts and a tourist town that led along Dingalan-Gabaldon Road, which snaked its way through several miles of the Minalungao National Park.

"I'm not going to sugarcoat it," he said bluntly. "This is some tough and rugged terrain we'll have to truck through to get to our objective. By road, we're looking at 71 kilometers. If we go through the national park, we cut that down by two-thirds, but it's tough going—lots of jungle and no roads—which also means no support vehicles."

Someone in the crowd let out a grunt. Colonel Tilman ignored it and continued. "We're going to approach this a couple of ways. 1st Battalion will go ashore with their amtracks and will lead the way up through the road with armor support. 2nd Battalion is going to be flown indirectly via our Ospreys and other helicopters to assault Fort Mag directly and capture the airstrips there. 3rd Battalion is going to be held in reserve and will be sent in one company at a time to reinforce whichever battalion appears to be hitting the most resistance."

"Now, we could also get lucky and have an unopposed landing. The enemy may, for whatever reason, determine that they would rather fight us further inland—in which case we'll be able to secure our objective quickly and capture Fort Mag without much fanfare. Keep in mind, once we do land, our orders may change quickly, and we may need to adjust accordingly," Tilman explained. "If you have further questions, please stay behind and ask them. Otherwise, get your commands ready to move and I'll see you guys at Fort Mag. We board the ships in twelve hours, and we launch the attack in two days."

With that, the meeting was dismissed.

****

Three days later, Captain Tim Long was packed into a V-22 Osprey with several of his men and all their body armor, gear and weapons. The air was oppressively hot and humid as it rushed through the various openings of the helicopter. Within minutes of the tiltrotor aircraft being loaded, the pilots gave the engines more power and the aircraft lifted off from the USS *America*, joined by dozens of other Ospreys and attack helicopters as they turned toward the shores of Luzon and the enemy that was waiting for them.

Long caught a glance outside through the tail ramp and was impressed with what he saw. Arrayed below them were dozens of US warships disembarking thousands of Marines to head toward the shores and establish the all-important beachhead. There were also rows of V-22 Ospreys and many other helicopters moving toward land and their various objectives. He hadn't spotted any sign of opposition just yet, but that wasn't to say the Chinese weren't lying in wait for them once they set down.

One of the crew chiefs leaned toward Captain Long. He spoke loudly to be heard over the noise of the chopper. "We're ten minutes out, Sir. The base should be off to our right when we approach it," he said.

Long hoped that the Air Force had cleared the area of any possible air-defense vehicles. "*This landing could get rough,*" he thought.

Just then, a string of green tracers flew past their Osprey, and the pilots banked hard to one side to avoid flying into the next stream of them. Tim turned and saw a concerned look on the tail gunner as he readied his weapon to engage the enemy.

The Osprey jinked hard to the left, just in time for Captain Long to see another string of green tracers fly past them so close that he felt like he could reach out and touch them with his hand. Looking past the tail gunner, he saw one of the Ospreys move away from one string of enemy fire, only to fly right into the path of another. It was a horrific crash; the front section of the tilt-wing aircraft was shredded, causing it to fall quickly to the ground and explode.

No sooner had that happened than he saw two missiles streak in toward a pair of Super Cobra attack helicopters, which were now speeding ahead to engage the enemy anti-air-defenses. One of the helicopters pulled up hard, spitting out a shower of bright red flares to throw off the enemy missiles while the second helicopter turned hard to the right and attempted to dive away from the threat. The one that dove to the ground was obliterated by the enemy missiles in an enormous fiery blast, while the one that pulled up hard and dispensed flares lived to fight on.

"We're coming into a hot LZ! Everyone out as fast as you can!" yelled the crew chief. At this point, everyone was just praying they would live long enough to get off the flying death trap. At least on the ground, they had a chance of killing the person shooting at them.

Less than a minute after the crew chief's warning, the Osprey flared, pulling its nose up and dropping its tail to bleed off speed and position themselves to land. Then they landed with a thud, and the crew chief shouted, "Get off this bird now!"

Long quickly lifted himself off the cargo net seat and followed the rest of his men out the back of the aircraft. Once outside, he witnessed pure chaos happening all around them.

While maybe a dozen Ospreys had managed to land on the airfield of Fort Mag, two of them were now burning wrecks. Long looked to the left toward the few hangars at the base and quickly found the source of their problems. A Type 95 self-propelled antiaircraft artillery vehicle was nestled just slightly behind the hangar, firing dozens of 25mm projectiles at the troop transports flying in to secure the airfield.

Turning to find the senior NCO near him, he pointed at the enemy gun, yelling, "Gunny, get your men together and take that gun out ASAP!"

The gunnery sergeant saw what Long had pointed at and nodded. Then he signaled for the Marines near him to follow him forward. Once they started running in that direction, several enemy machine-gun positions spotted them and laid down suppressive fire to help protect the vehicle. The Marines dropped down in the drainage ditch between the runway and the taxiway to use the slight indentation in the ground as cover.

A couple of the M240 gunners returned fire, sending hundreds of rounds at the enemy so they would have to keep their heads down. In the short reprieve, a small group of Marines jumped up and headed for the next position they could use for cover. While the heavy gunners were giving covering fire, one of the Marines, who had been lugging an antitank rocket, dropped down below the lip of the ditch and unstrapped the rocket from the side of his pack. After checking it over briefly to make sure it was ready, he got up on one knee, placed the rocket on his right shoulder and took aim at the vehicle. He turned briefly to check his back blast to make sure no one was directly behind him, and then he flicked the safety off and depressed the trigger. In a split second, the rocket raced out of the tube and headed right for the Type 95 antiair gun. The rocket flew true and slammed into the side of the vehicle, causing it to explode.

The Marines who had been charging the enemy position now turned their attention to the Chinese soldiers who had set up multiple machine-gun positions just inside the woods, overlooking the airfield.

"*They were smart,*" thought Long as he realized the Chinese had allowed the first wave of helicopters to land only to open fire on them as they were vulnerable and trying to leave.

Red and green tracer fire flew back and forth across the runway and taxi strip as the two sides fought it out. Captain Long knew if the Marines didn't clear the airstrip of these enemy positions, it would be difficult to get more reinforcements, let alone a resupply; the helicopters wouldn't be able get close enough to deliver them. Looking toward the now-burning antiaircraft vehicle, Long saw two fire teams closing in on a machine-gun bunker.

Lifting his own rifle to his shoulder, he closed his left eye and sighted in on a soldier who was feeding ammunition to the gunner. Long gently applied pressure to the trigger until he felt and heard the rifle bark. He was rewarded by the sight of the enemy soldier clutching at his chest and collapsing next to his comrades.

"*One down, now to take out the next guy,*" he thought.

Suddenly Long felt the irresistible need to duck and dropped down just as a string of enemy rounds tore into the dirt right above him while the buzzing sound of hot lead flew right over his head. One of the Marines a couple of feet to his right hadn't ducked—Long saw his body thrown back into the ditch as a single enemy round impacted the soldier's face, pulverizing it. The young man was dead before he even knew what hit him.

"Captain Long!" a lance corporal shouted as he crawled over next to him and handed him the radio handset. "It's Dog Pound Six on the radio." Since their battalion was called the "Dog Pound," all the companies had been given attack dog names.

Reaching over, Tim grabbed the handset, depressing the talk button. "This is Pit Bull Six, go ahead, Dog Pound Six," he said, speaking loudly to be heard over the roar of gunfire going on around him.

"Pit Bull Six, what is the status of the airfield? Is it secured yet?" asked his battalion commander.

"Dog Pound Six, not yet. We encountered a couple of Type 95 antiaircraft vehicles hidden in the jungle near the airstrip. We're taking heavy enemy fire but moving to neutralize the threats. Two of them have been destroyed. An unknown number of them are still present in the immediate area. How copy?"

"Good copy, Pit Bull. We have some fast movers inbound to your location now. Pass along the coordinates to them and secure the airfield. Dog Pound element is inbound to your positions. ETA twenty mikes. How copy?"

Long nodded, more to himself than for anyone else's benefit. *"Twenty minutes should be enough time to beat the enemy back from the airfield, especially if he'll have access to a few fast movers,"* he thought.

"That's a good copy. Pit Bull out."

He handed the receiver back to his radioman. "We have fast movers inbound to our location. Raise them if you can, and hand the mic back to me when you have them. We're going to call in some air strikes."

Looking around briefly, Long spotted the man he was looking for. "Sergeant Mueller, come here!" he yelled as he waved to get his attention.

A second later, the sergeant was sitting next to him in the drainage ditch. "What do you need, Sir?" he asked.

Captain Long pulled his map of the airfield out and leaned in toward Sergeant Mueller to be heard over the gunfire. "We have fast movers inbound. I need you to help me identify where those enemy guns are." The sergeant nodded and pulled a small pair of field glasses out. He squinted as he looked through them. In a couple of minutes, he had identified where three of them were.

"Two of them are over near Second Platoon's positions. The other is over near Fourth Platoon's position here," Mueller said, pointing to the locations on the map. "Those appear to be the only ones left, Sir."

Long nodded as he looked over the map. He needed to call those platoon leaders and have them pulled back a bit so the aircraft could bomb the positions without killing his own men. "Corporal, send a message to those two platoons and tell them to pull back to these positions here. Make sure they know we have some fighters coming in that are going to bomb those gun positions," he directed his radio man.

Just as Captain Long finished plotting the enemy positions, his radioman handed him the mic. "The platoons acknowledged the order and are falling back," he said. "I also have the fast movers on the radio. Their call sign is Phoenix."

Long nodded and took the handset. "Phoenix flight, this is Pit Bull Six. How copy?"

The pilots of the F/A-18 high above the unfolding battle responded, "Pit Bull Six. This is Phoenix Two and Three. We copy loud and clear. What do you have for us?"

Captain Long smiled at the calmness in the pilot's voice. They sounded like they had done this a million times before. "Phoenix Two, we have three PLA Type 95 antiaircraft guns taking our helicopter support out. I need them cleared so the next wave of troops can land. How copy?" he asked.

Once the pilot acknowledged, Long relayed the number and type of enemy vehicles needing to be destroyed, along with their exact locations.

"Pit Bull Six, those are some serious threats. We copy. We'll be hitting them with 500 pounders, so make sure your troops are well enough away," the pilot explained. "Stand by for an attack run, three mikes out."

Captain Long briefly switched over to the company network to let everyone know the fast movers were three minutes out and would be dropping 500-pound munitions on the enemy guns. Looking around, Long saw that most of the Marines who had been in the drainage ditch with him had moved forward and were now taking up positions near the hangars they had just captured from the enemy. It was just him, his radioman and one of the other sergeants that had helped him plot the enemy positions.

"Let's relocate to a safer position once the fast movers take out the gun positions," he said. Just then, they heard the first thunderous explosion near the other end of the field. Seconds later, two more blasts sent reverberations through the air. The platoons nearby reported direct hits. They started moving forward to secure the positions and finish off any enemy soldiers in the area.

"Pit Bull Six, this is Phoenix flight. Did we get them?" asked the pilot.

"Phoenix Two, that's a good copy. A solid hit on all three enemy positions. How many more bombs do you have left? Can you hit a few additional strong points for us?" he asked, hoping they could help his unit take out a few more enemy positions.

"Pit Bull Six, we have five bombs remaining between us, and ten mikes of fuel. If you have more targets, send them, and we'll take 'em out for you," replied the Hornet pilot.

Long turned to his gunnery sergeant, "What other positions could we use the ordnance on?"

A couple minutes went by as they conferred with the other platoon leaders, and eventually five enemy locations were settled on. Another five minutes went by, and five more loud explosions rocked Fort Mag as Echo Company continued to push out beyond the airfield to secure the rest of the base.

As the fighters flew back to the carrier to rearm, Captain Long and a few of his other soldiers moved toward the flight operation building for the airstrip and set it up as their command post until the rest of the battalion arrived. While he was getting his various platoon positions marked on his map of the area, they heard the sounds of more helicopters nearing them. Looking out the window, he saw the next wave of Ospreys land and disgorge their human cargo.

As the troops of Delta Company fanned out, Captain Long could see them react to the sight of the wreckage of two Ospreys still burning on the runway, along with nearly a dozen Marines lying dead nearby. The black pillars of smoke and fire continued rising from the enemy vehicles just slightly back from the perimeter in the jungle, also adding to the carnage.

A small cluster of Marines made their way toward the flight operation building. A few minutes later, Lieutenant

Colonel Jackman walked in with a few of his other officers and staff members. He surveyed the room briefly and then walked toward Captain Long with a smile on his face.

"Bang-up job your men did in securing this airstrip, Captain. You should be proud of them. I've made sure Colonel Tilman knows how well you guys did in securing this objective," Jackman said, extending his hand for a congratulatory handshake.

Then Colonel Jackman looked past Captain Long toward the map he had set up. "Where's the enemy located now, and how soon until we can have the rest of the base secured?" he asked.

Long took a second to survey the map and then pointed to several positions. "I have platoons moving to these sections here, here, and here, which will allow us to make sure the airstrip is secured. Second Platoon is reporting heavy enemy fire near the base housing section just east of the airfield," he explained.

"Along with this section over here near the training buildings, we've taken a lot of machine-gun fire and even run into a few armored vehicles," Captain Long continued. "Fortunately, we had two pairs of Super Cobras that were able to help us take them out once those fast movers destroyed the enemy antiaircraft vehicles. I think there were two enemy light tanks and a handful of armored personnel carriers. Since they've been destroyed, we haven't come into contact with any additional armored vehicles."

Pausing for a second, Captain Long asked the next question. "Where do you want my company to focus on next?"

Nodding in approval, the colonel replied, "I'll have Delta Company focus on this section of the base. I want you to have your third platoon disengage once Delta shows up and reinforce your guys over here at the base housing section. Focus on clearing that out and setting up a new perimeter covering this entire side of the base. The rest of the battalion will continue to arrive over the next couple of hours to help us expand the perimeter."

Colonel Jackman then pointed on the map to where the two Ospreys were still burning. "We need to get these downed helicopters off the airstrip. The Air Force is going to send in a couple of C-130s, who are going to offload a mobile POL station, along with some munitions for the Cobras and the artillery guns that will start to arrive toward the end of the day. By tomorrow morning, we'll have a dozen Super Cobras operating out of the base, along with a battery of 105mm artillery guns. This base is going to get real busy quick, Captain."

Before Captain Long had a chance to leave, his boss pulled him aside for a second to talk privately. "Before I left the landing ships, I heard our sister battalion was taking a beating as they moved up the highway. I suspect they're taking a lot of casualties. Colonel Tilman wants to move the Corps area combat support hospital to our location instead of the beach area. He wants the CSH to be closer to the fighting. My concern, Captain, is that the Chinese soldiers they're fighting in that section are from the famed 43rd Paratrooper Division. If they fall back, they may try and fall back to Fort Mag, which frankly is not very far from them right now. There also may be other elements of that division nearby, which may cause us some problems," Jackman told Long.

Captain Long nodded. "Thank you for letting me know. I'll make sure to let my platoon leaders know about the presence of this unit as well. I'm not too versed in the Chinese unit patches, but it doesn't appear that any of the units we fought here were part of that unit. They did put up a heck of a fight. If those paratroopers fight even more skillfully, then we'll have our hands full for sure."

They talked for a few minutes more before the colonel sent him on his way and began to get his battalion headquarters set up and ready to receive the influx of troops that were heading his direction.

****

Philippines
San Vicente, Luzon
32 Kilometers West of the Beach

Captain Ma lifted the pocket binoculars to his eyes and scanned the road below them. The column of American armored vehicles had been snaking along for kilometers on the Dingalan-Gabaldon Road, heading west away from the beach. Their scouts had spotted the Americans roughly twenty minutes earlier as they continued to head toward the small village of San Vicente and the lone vehicle bridge that crossed the Pampanga River allowing vehicles to continue west further inland.

When it became clear the Americans were going to land forces on Luzon, there were only a handful of suitable beaches. One of them happened to be roughly thirty-five kilometers from his current position. Captain Ma and his commanders knew exactly what type of American vehicles would be leading the way and knew the type of weapons they would need to defeat them. They had spent a couple of weeks preparing a series of defensive positions and traps that would hopefully cause significant damage to the Americans.

Captain Ma glanced down at his map.

"*Good, they are about to enter my kill box,*" he thought.

He needed to make sure the Americans had crossed the bridge before they opened fire. His company had fifty Red Arrow 12 fire-and-forget infrared homing antitank missiles ready to hammer the Yankees. The engineers had also moved six 152mm artillery guns, which they had pointed directly at the road the enemy tanks would have to travel down. The 152mm guns would be used as antitank guns instead of traditional artillery, though he also had a battalion of artillery guns he could call upon if needed.

"When should we spring the trap?" asked one of the junior captains as he nervously fidgeted with something in his hand.

Captain Ma snorted before responding. "Patience, Yu. We want to wait until those American tanks get across the road first. Once they're trapped on our side of the river, we'll be able to slaughter them. When the Americans try to rush additional units over the bridge, then we'll blow the bridge, separating them." He was a bit perturbed that the junior captain was asking a question he had clearly been briefed on earlier.

Ten more minutes went by as the fourth M1A2 Abrams main battle tank crossed the bridge and continued to head west. Ma lifted the hand receiver to his face and depressed the talk button. "Fire on the tanks," he said to his gun crews.

Seconds later, the first 152mm cannon fired, quickly followed by three other guns. The 152mm rounds flew quickly across the ground, traveling the nearly four kilometers before they slammed into the side hulls of the tanks. As soon as the rounds hit the tanks, all four of them exploded, sending shrapnel, flames, and smoke in every direction. The rest of the antitank guns picked off other armored vehicles in the American column, lighting them up as well.

As the fighting on the ground heated up, a pair of American attack helicopters swooped in from the sky and fired antipersonnel rockets into the jungle area where his guns were dug in. Seconds after the helicopters flew in, a series of FN-6 MANPADS shot up quickly from the cover of the jungle and headed toward the American chopper. One of them was destroyed by the MANPAD, while the other helicopter fled the scene and didn't reappear.

At this point, dozens of American armored vehicles raced toward his positions. Rather than trying to cross the bridge as they had anticipated, the American tracked vehicles proved they could quickly and effortlessly ford the river and battle their way toward his position at the edge of the jungle, firing their own vehicle weapons at his soldiers. While the Americans raced toward them, a series of loud explosions rocked his bunker.

"*Those blasted Americans—they're already hitting us with high-altitude air strikes*," thought Ma.

Looking to his east, Captain Ma saw that three of his artillery guns had just been destroyed, and there was nothing he could do to stop it. Still, the three remaining guns continued to fire away on the now quickly approaching Americans. Once they got within two kilometers of his position, the RA-12 antitank missiles raced across the field and hammered the American vehicles. In seconds, nine American vehicles were now nothing more than burning wreckage.

Ma switched his radio frequency to the two Type 95 antiaircraft vehicles he had tucked away under a lot of jungle foliage. "Turn your radars on and take out those American aircraft," he ordered.

Less than a minute later, he heard the roar of their 25mm cannons intermixed with the swooshing noise of several of their missiles as they began to seek out and destroy the American helicopters and aircraft flying within a ten-kilometer radius.

Sadly, the two vehicles only lasted minutes before they were both destroyed by the Americans. Meanwhile, the US advance toward his position had been slowed down and then blunted altogether. There was nothing left but a burning wreck of what appeared to be an American company-level unit.

Thirty minutes later, another American unit of comparable size moved forward and advanced along the same road. Rather than continue forward or cross the river and run toward the jungle like their comrades had, they stayed back and called in a series of air strikes against Captain Ma's positions.

The jungle his forces had built their defensive forts in was subsequently pounded for nearly an hour. Each time the Americans would send in attack helicopters, his troops would pop out of their bunkers and fire off a series of MANPADS at them. A number of choppers had been shot down this way, and it was proving to be an effective tactic.

One hour turned to five as the Americans continued to try and fight their way past his position. Each time, they sustained heavy casualties and ultimately would fall back. During the five-hour running battle, Ma's company sustained close to fifty percent casualties, something he had never had to deal with in their previous battles. Under more normal circumstances, his forces had been relieved and not expected to fight on, let alone have to deal with having no air support or air cover.

Eventually, Captain Ma's commander ordered his company to withdraw to the next defensive position and prepare to repel the Americans at the next major junction.

****

Manila, Philippines
Luzon Island
Eastern Alliance Headquarters

Explosions could be heard off the instance, as well as the sound of jets soaring overhead. The few remaining fighters that had survived the American aerial bombardments were doing their best to provide cover for the handful of Nanchang Q-5 ground-attack aircraft that were going after the American beachheads. During the last two weeks, Major General Hu Wei's positions across the Philippines had been getting hammered by the Americans in preparation for the invasion.

Finally, the hour had come, and the Americans were hitting his forces all across the island. Reports were coming in from the various beachheads that the Americans had moved off the beaches and were now advancing inland.

"The question now," he thought to himself, *"is how long can we hold out with virtually no support from the Navy or the mainland?"*

"General," said one of the operations officers, "we received a communique from Major General Joko Subroto. The Indonesian 2nd Infantry Division has pulled back from Legazpi and is now taking up positions near Naga. It also appears that a large portion of his forces are falling back even further, to the Mount Banahaw area."

"Why is he having his forces fall that far back? He's giving up precious land that we could force the Americans to fight for. This makes no sense," General Hu countered as he looked at the map.

"If the Indonesians give up the entire southern half of the island, how am I supposed to defend Manila?" he pondered.

Another officer replied to the general's question before anyone else could respond. "He's falling back to the Banahaw area because he's afraid his division may get cut off by the Americans if they land forces behind him."

He shook his head. There was really not much he could do. The Indonesian commander had a point, but he also didn't appear like he wanted to fight the Americans very hard. "Send a message to General Subroto. Tell him he's to hold his positions and not withdraw any further. His forces need to stand and fight the Americans. We'll send him additional forces to help when we can," he ordered. He hoped with everything in him that his Indonesian partners would do their part.

Hu turned to his executive officer. "How are the rest of our forces holding up?" he asked.

"Our paratrooper element near the San Vicente area hit the American Marines hard. They nearly wiped out a whole battalion of Marines before they were ordered to withdraw. So far, the paratroopers in that region are holding the Marines from moving too far inland. However, the battalion of regular infantry we stationed at Fort Mag lost control of the base to an air assault by the Marines. They're trying to organize a counterattack, but it's going to be hard to dislodge the Americans. They're moving a lot of troops and equipment to the airfield," replied Brigadier General Wang, to the dismay of everyone present.

They had hoped to retain control of Fort Mag for a couple more weeks. If the Americans were able to establish a solid foothold there, they would be able to move on Clark International Airport and cut the top portion of the Island of Luzon in half. It would hasten their defeat if the Americans were allowed to hold Fort Mag for very long.

"Send a message to the airborne units in the area," ordered Hu. "They're to pull back and, if possible, retake Fort Mag from the Americans!"

Battle of Fort Mag

Palayan City
Two Kilometers Northeast of Fort Mag

Six hours after securing the initial airfield on Fort Mag, Captain Tim Long and his company had moved over to the small village of Palayan City, less than two kilometers from the airfield, to set up a defensive perimeter. Long hated the idea of using the local church as his headquarters, so he set up in a nearby building and opted to use the church as a field hospital, should they need it.

Throughout all the fighting, running, stopping, shooting, and the couple-kilometer trek through the heavy foliage to their current position, Captain Long hadn't had the opportunity to take a proper bio break. He hadn't eaten in nearly twelve hours or had nearly enough water to drink—both of which were probably the saving grace for how he had been able to hold out as long as he had—but now that they had a few minutes to think, he found the time to take care of some "proper" officer business. While seated on the lone toilet in the building, which surprisingly had running water, Long heard the sound of a vehicle approaching his headquarters.

"*God, I hope that's First Sergeant Madero and not a hostile vehicle,*" he thought.

Finishing his business, he reached into his cargo pocket, pulled out a small bottle of hand sanitizer, and liberally used it on his hands. If he were to survive the next few minutes, he didn't want to catch any unnecessary germs.

Walking out of his command building, Long saw the outline of the JLTV coming around the bend in the road toward them. In the front seat, he spotted his first sergeant and one of the privates who had gone down to the airfield on foot with him a few hours ago. Clearly, they had found transportation on the way back. Captain Long breathed a sigh of relief and then waved to them as they came to a halt in front of the small three-room building. The private got out and immediately went to the back of the truck to begin unloading its contents.

"I see you found a new set of wheels, First Sergeant?" Long asked jokingly.

"My dogs are killing me. If you thought me and this private were going to hump all that ammo back here, you're crazy, Sir," Madero replied in good humor.

"What did you guys manage to scrounge up?" asked Long.

"Aside from the list of ammo you gave us, I was able to pry away five 100-foot strands of concertina wire we can use to set up the roadblocks. I also grabbed us roughly thirty additional Claymore mines, about the same number of trip flares, and additional IV bags for the corpsmen," explained First Sergeant Madero with a smug smile of satisfaction written across his face.

Captain Long had to laugh at the man's resourcefulness. The guy had more connections within the brigade than he'd thought possible. Long was very fortunate that he had been given an experienced first sergeant when he had been promoted to captain. He hated to admit it, but he relied on the old guy far more than he probably should have.

"Good job, Top. I still can't believe you managed to snag a vehicle. See if you can make another supply run before it gets dark. I want to make sure we have everything we'll need before nightfall. I have a feeling it's going to be busy," Captain Long said, hoping he might be wrong and they might catch a break. Word had it their sister battalion that had hit the beach had run up against a brick wall and gotten mauled. He hoped they hadn't taken too many casualties.

"Yes, Sir," said Madero. He and a few other Marines nearby began unloading the supplies.

As Captain Long's men continued to fortify their various positions around this small village, he looked back in the direction of the airfield. He was happy with what he saw—several heavy-lift helicopters were sling-loading a battery worth of 105mm Howitzers.

"*Those may come in handy once they get set up,*" Long thought.

More Ospreys were flying in, dropping off what seemed like an endless supply of fresh Marines from the troop ships offshore. No one knew for certain when the Chinese attack would come, or what direction it would come from, but one thing was certain—the enemy wasn't going to leave them unfettered at this base for long.

****

Captain Ma Qiliang was exhausted. He hadn't worked this physically hard since he had gone through airborne training nearly six years ago. Following what was, by all accounts, a very successful ambush of the American Marines, his company had been ordered to fall back before they were pulverized by the American warplanes. Hiding those 152mm Howitzers in the hills to use as tank busters had been proven to be a brilliant move.

He felt immensely proud of how well his men had performed. They had shot down five enemy helicopters and three ground-attack aircraft, and mauling that battalion had been exhilarating. However, as great as he felt about how badly they had hurt the Americans coming ashore, the unit that had been assigned to defend Fort Mag had apparently been wiped out by heliborne troops. When his command had finally been able to get through to him, they'd ordered his company to withdraw from their current locations and move to attack the Americans at Fort Mag.

Pulling out his map, he looked at his current position in relation to the location of Fort Mag. *"Ugh, that's got to be close to thirty kilometers away, and it's through some fairly rough terrain,"* he thought.

Under normal conditions, his men could travel that distance in six hours. However, they had just spent the morning fighting the Americans, and now he was going to force them to march thirty kilometers and fight a much larger group of Americans.

"Well, at least this group at the airport won't have tanks," he thought.

****

"Captain Ma, it's 0200 hours. The men are exhausted. Can we let them rest for a few hours before we press any further?" pleaded his senior sergeant. "We should be approaching their perimeter, if they have expanded beyond the airfield." Ma usually deferred to his senior sergeant in these matters. After fifteen years in the 43rd Airborne, he tended to know just how far they could push the men before there would be problems, and he had earned Ma's respect.

Ma stopped walking and nodded in agreement. "Order the men to stop and set up camp. I want a 360-degree perimeter and one-third of the men on duty at all times. We'll roll out again at 0515. That gives everyone roughly three hours to catch some sleep before we move to contact with the Americans."

While his senior sergeant got the men spread out and issued the instructions for the evening, Captain Ma and his two lieutenants looked at the map under a poncho with a red light. "We have to be really close to the Americans," one of the officers said as he marked their exact location on the map. They were roughly four kilometers from the airfield at this point.

"I agree," said the other officer. "I'll bet they're no more than one or two kilometers away from our current position. It's a good thing you called a halt to the march, Sir. We could've walked right into one of their ambushes."

"*I'm so tired that I hadn't even thought about that,*" Ma thought. "*I have to get some sleep, or I'm going to get my men killed.*"

The only silver lining was that, as his company was leaving their initial ambush point, they had run into the remnants of two other companies that had been a part of the attack on the Americans at the beach. Both companies were down to half strength and were being led by lieutenants. Ma ordered them to fall in with his command and consolidated them for the attack at Fort Mag. Once they knew where he was headed and what his orders were, they gladly joined. That brought his 118-man reinforced company up to 331, a light battalion by many standards. How they hadn't been spotted by enemy helicopters, drones or aircraft up to that point was beyond him, but he was not about to look a gift horse in the mouth just yet.

"Before anyone goes to sleep, we have some work to do," announced Captain Ma. "Lieutenant Chu, I need you to make contact with headquarters. Let them know where we are, and ask if there is any fire support we'll be able to call on when we attack. See if you can find out what other units are in the area and if we are supposed to coordinate our attack. If so, at what time and with whom? OK?"

"I understand, Captain. I'll work on that right now," he replied. He ducked out from under the poncho to start making calls on the radio.

"Lieutenant Li, you have the most dangerous and most important mission," said Captain Ma. "I want you to pick two of the more senior sergeants or men who are most adept at sneaking up on someone. I need your team to scout what's in front of us and find the American positions without being detected. See if you can get their exact locations, strength, and the weapons they have. If we can get some fire support from headquarters, we'll relay that information to them and see if we can hurt the Americans before we launch our attack."

"Yes, Sir," said Lieutenant Li, who seemed excited about the mission.

"I want you to set out to do this around 0400, not right now," explained Ma. "I want you alert and rested when I send you out, so for the moment, go get some sleep. I'll wake you when it's time."

The following morning was going to be busy, and chances were, a lot of his men might not survive.

******

At 0445 hours, Captain Ma awoke from perhaps the deepest sleep he had had in weeks. Yawning, he stretched out his arms, then his legs, and finally his back and neck, noticing the creaks and cracks along the way.

"There's no way I can stay in the airborne for my entire career if I survive this war. My body just won't take it," he realized.

"Hey, you're awake, Sir. I was just about to come get you," remarked Lieutenant Chu, the officer he had tasked with identifying any other potential support.

Ma took a swig of water from his canteen, swished it around in his mouth and spat it out. He then took a couple of long drinks before returning his attention to his lieutenant. "Thanks for letting me sleep, Chu. I really needed it. So, tell me, what did you find out from headquarters?" he inquired.

Chu smiled. He had been the XO of a sister company that had met the American Marines at the beach the day before. After an hour of fighting, they had been ordered to fall back to their rally point, which was several kilometers inland, away from the beach and deep in the jungle. His company commander and the two other officers had been killed, and he found himself in charge. Having just joined the company a month ago, he'd didn't know a lot of the other officers in the battalion, so when the remnants of his company had made contact with Captain Ma, he was only too happy for him to take over command and let him lead them.

Chu pulled out the map and laid it on the ground next to them. "I've listed the location of the other units in the area. What the Americans don't know is that nearly the entire 128th Regiment moved to this position during the night and spread out across this entire zone," he said. He pointed to the village of General Tinio, roughly four kilometers from the airfield.

"The 14th Armored Brigade is located here," Chu continued, pointing to the city of Rizal. "General Toa said he wants us to begin our attack at approximately 0615 hours. At 0600 hours, they're going to launch a massive rocket artillery barrage on the base. When that happens, the 14th Armor is going to race toward the American positions and try to overwhelm them. I also made sure to give them the location of the American lines in front of us." A huge smile spread across his face.

Ma didn't know what to say. He wanted to hug Chu at that very moment. This was going to be a real attack, not some half-measure that would result in most of them being killed or captured.

"But how did the Americans not see that we are massing tanks, artillery, and all of these soldiers?" he wondered. *"How have they not already attacked us?"*

"Lieutenant Chu, if we live through today, I'm going to recommend that you be awarded the Order of the Heroic Exemplar. You may have just saved the lives of our entire company," Ma replied. He saw Chu just beam with pride, and he knew in that instant that Chu would follow him anywhere, under any circumstance, for giving him such glowing praise.

"What about the American lines in front of us? How far away are they?" Captain Ma asked. He turned to Lieutenant Li and saw that he was still asleep. Ma realized that Li must have gone out already and given his report to Chu.

"Lieutenant Li came back from his patrol about thirty minutes ago," Chu answered. "I've been updating the map with what he found and relaying those grid coordinates to our own artillery. Like he said last night, it's a good thing we stopped. The Americans are no more than one kilometer away from us. We would've walked right into them had we not stopped when we did. It was still dark, so he could not see their exact numbers, but using the night vision goggles, he was able to make out two roadblocks and a couple of locations where they had strung up some concertina wire. Judging by the way they placed the wires, it looks like they're trying to funnel us into certain areas. His best guess is they probably have antipersonnel mines set up in the areas they left 'undefended' and want us to run through. He marked them on his map, which I transposed to yours. We both suggest that we work our way around to this spot here and avoid hitting them head-on. If we hit their right flank, we can avoid the concertina wire they set up and probably get a good jump on them."

The two of them looked over the maps for a few more minutes before they woke up Lieutenant Li and then grabbed their senior sergeants. It was time to talk over their attack plan and figure out how they were going to nail this American unit without getting themselves wiped out in the process.

****

Palayan, Philippines
Fort Mag

Colonel Micah Tilman finished taking a morning bio break against the side of the building and then turned to head back into the makeshift headquarters Lieutenant Colonel

Chuck Jackman had set up the day before. It was now 0422 hours, and despite the sun having been down for nearly eight hours, it was still hot and muggy. As Tilman walked along the side of the building toward the side that faced the airstrip, he saw two V-22 Ospreys land and unload a small group of passengers, all carrying a lot of gear. As soon as they got everything unloaded from the aircraft, the Osprey was gone, headed back out to sea or wherever it had come from.

Walking toward the front entrance of the headquarters building, Colonel Tilman watched the group of soldiers throw a lot of their gear into a vehicle that drove out to meet them. Most of them hopped in, and the vehicle headed toward him. A couple of minutes later, the group got off the truck and stowed their gear near one of the burned-out hangars for the time being while three of the new arrivals walked toward him.

As they got closer, he smiled as he recognized one of the men.

"Lieutenant Commander Charlie Haversham, it's good to see you again!" Colonel Tilman said as he extended his hand to shake his old friend's hand.

Haversham returned the smile. "It's good to see you as well, Colonel. I see your brigade has gotten itself in a bit of a pickle here at lovely Fort Mag," he said jovially. He gestured for them to walk into the building and talk further.

Lieutenant Commander Charlie Haversham had worked with Colonel Tilman on a few other occasions in Iraq and Afghanistan, and more recently in Syria fighting ISIL. Of course, that was when Haversham had been a lowly lieutenant in charge of a SEAL platoon and not a troop commander.

When Tilman walked into the room with their newly arrived guest, he signaled for Lieutenant Colonel Jackman to come join them. "Chuck, I want you to meet Charlie. He's from SEAL Team Three. His troop has just been assigned to our brigade to help us out with some recon and special missions the division commander has coming down the pike," Tilman said.

The two men shook hands and did what all warriors do, sizing each other up.

"I'm glad the SEALs decided to join the fight," said Jackman, half-joking, half-serious. "Better late than never."

Haversham just shrugged. He didn't decide where they got sent—he just went where he was told. "Let's walk over to the map," he said. "I have some information we need to pass along to you guys. While you guys are playing patty-cake with the PLA here yesterday, I had my three platoons scattered across most of Luzon, feeding targeting data to the air wings and getting us eyes on the enemy. A couple of my teams have spotted some real trouble headed our way," he replied. He pointed out the location of the enemy armor brigade that had moved into position, along with what appeared to be an infantry regiment to their southeast and southern flanks.

"Commander, if your teams have spotted these enemy units, are they calling in air strikes, or are you waiting for our permission?" inquired Jackman, who was now very concerned. They had some antitank missiles with them, but they couldn't stand up to an armor battalion, let alone anything larger than that.

Haversham sighed. He had known that question would be asked, and he didn't really want to answer it. "Two problems with that," he said. "First, we needed to know where the friendly units were before we called in air strikes. I'm not going to be responsible for getting a Marine company smoked because I didn't know they were there. Second, and this is probably the bigger problem—the enemy air defense. Right now, that armor unit is staging in the city of Santa Rosa, using the civilians as shields. Despite the civilians, we were given the go-ahead to hit the tanks, so a couple of F/A-18s were vectored in to hammer them. As they got closer to the target, both aircraft were intercepted by Chinese stealth fighters and were shot down."

Jackman mumbled something under his breath.

Haversham continued. "After that incident, the carrier said they would send in a pair of F-35s. As soon as the F-35s dropped their weapons, both of them were shot down by a surface-to-air missile complex that's still operational near Clark International Airport. We took out maybe half a dozen or more enemy tanks but lost a total of four aircraft in the process. Needless to say, that is not a very good exchange," he concluded. This meant that their air support had virtually dried up over the evening.

Colonel Tilman jumped in before Jackman could ask any other questions. "What is the Navy doing to take those SAM sites out, so we can get our air support back?"

"That's our new assignment," Commander Haversham responded. "I'm setting up my headquarters here to run my teams. Our guys are now moving to get in position, so we can lase those SAM sites. Then the Air Force can hit them with some of their long-range guided glide bombs. They can launch those bad boys from nearly one hundred miles out and let them glide undetected toward their targets. Once they're down, we'll have our air support back up and running."

Jackman snorted. "Well, this is just great. We have a tank unit prepping to attack us and a heavy concentration of enemy infantry to our south. Colonel, we're going to need a lot more support if we are to hold this base."

Tilman nodded. "This information does change things for us. Commander, I want you to give the coordinates of those troop concentrations and tanks to our fire support guys. I have one battery of 105mm artillery on the east side of the base. It's been a cluster mess getting them set up and ready, but as of half an hour ago, they reported that they're ready to provide fire missions. I want to hit those enemy positions before the Chinese have a chance to hit us. Is that understood?"

They had a lot of things to do to get ready for a pending attack, and the action would most likely start within the next couple of hours. They spoke efficiently and stayed focused; hopefully their preparations would make a difference in the outcome.

****

Palayan City, Philippines

It was 0520 hours when Captain Tim Long awoke with a start as he heard the 105mm Howitzers fire off a volley at some unknown target. Sitting upright, he immediately got to his feet and grabbed his rifle. Then he walked over to his radio operator to find out what was happening.

First Sergeant John Madero and Gunnery Sergeant Mueller were already talking with his radio operator, giving him some instructions before he called back to headquarters. "What's going on, Top?" asked Long, hoping it wasn't anything serious.

"We're working on trying to get an update from battalion. All we know right now is they caught word of a possible tank unit getting ready to attack the airfield, so they're trying to disrupt the attack with the big guns," Madero replied.

"OK. Why don't you guys go ahead and get everyone awake and have them get ready?" Long asked. It wasn't really a question, but more of an order. "If they're going use an armor unit, then chances are, this could be a coordinated attack. In which case, they'll probably hit our positions as well. We're practically the only unit protecting those Howitzers right now." Captain Long suddenly felt a new sense of urgency. To add further emphasis to his concern, another volley of artillery fire exploded in the distance.

411

Nearly forty minutes went by as the company manned their fighting positions and got ready for whatever might be coming their way. The sound of the artillery fire picked up, and a few times, it sounded like they'd changed directions of where they were shooting. Then suddenly, while the Marines were sitting in their fighting positions, eating their MREs and waiting to see what would happen next, they all heard the unmistakable sound of incoming fire.

While many of the Marines were still green, they knew the loud racket was not friendly. Dozens and then hundreds of rockets hit Fort Mag, rocking the base. At first, it was just the airfield that was getting hit, nailing a few attack helicopters that had transferred to the shore, while other rockets hit some of the barracks and garrison buildings, rocking the defenders. A couple of minutes into the barrage, the men started to believe that maybe they were going to skate by without being attacked directly; then the first rocket hit the church, followed by dozens more that hit all across the small little village, smashing people's homes and the local school.

When it sounded like the barrage had lifted, the cries of wounded civilians and those in agonizing pain began in earnest. Just as Captain Long poked his head above the foxhole he had been hiding in, a slew of machine-gun fire overtook the screams of the wounded.

"The Chinese are attacking! Return fire!" yelled one of the sergeants maybe twenty meters in front of Long's foxhole. To his right, maybe a hundred meters away, one of the M240s opened fire, spraying the jungle to their front with streams of hot lead. A loud explosion shook the air as one of their Claymore mines tore into the attackers.

Boom! Boom! Explosions rocked the machine-gun position seconds later, and the M240 went silent, replaced by the roaring yell of hundreds of voices running right at Long's right flank.

"*Holy crap! They're going to overrun us!*" he thought as he heard the loud screams of the enemy charge.

"Shift fire to the right! Reinforce those positions now!" Long yelled over the company net. "The Chinese are trying to move around us!"

Another explosion rocked his right flank, and then he saw several RPGs fly past his soldiers' position and hit a few trees further behind them. One exploded right in front of three Marines who were moving forward to shore up their defenses, killing them outright before they even knew what had happened.

Turning to the group of five Marines near him, Captain Long ordered, "Fix bayonets and follow me."

The Marines collectively looked at each other, seeming to ask themselves if they'd really heard what they thought they had. Then their instincts and training took over, and they grabbed their bayonets, attaching the blades to the front of their M4 rifles.

Captain Long changed his magazine, placing a fresh thirty-round one in his rifle, and then lifted himself out of his fighting position. He dashed forward in the low ready position with his rifle aimed in front of him as he moved to reinforce his right flank, ready to shoot the first Chinese soldier he saw. Seconds after he left his position, the other five Marines got up and quickly followed him, lining up almost abreast of him as they advanced.

The chattering of both rifle fire and machine-gun fire was constant now as both sides threw more and more men at each other, trying to gain an advantage and fire supremacy. Another RPG flew over their heads, exploding somewhere behind them. The fighting zone in front of them was becoming hidden by the amount of smoke from grenades, RPGs, and Claymore mines going off. The smells of cordite, sulfur, and feces permeated the air.

Charging forward into the roar of gunfire and screaming men, a cloud of smoke wafted in front of Long's men, temporarily obscuring their view. As they ran forward through it, they tripped and stumbled over the dead bodies of fallen Marines intertwined with dead enemy soldiers. Several Marines were rolling on the ground in a desperate hand-to-hand fight to the death. One Marine swung his entrenching tool wildly as he hit a Chinese soldier in the face repeatedly, either not realizing the man was dead or simply overcome by his emotions.

Long rang toward one of the Marines, who was being straddled by a Chinese paratrooper who was desperately trying to drive his knife into the Marine's chest. In one smooth motion, Captain Long used the butt of his rifle to hit the enemy soldier under the chin, causing him to lose his balance and fall backward. As the man fell, Long lunged his bayonet into the man's abdomen. He pulled the bayonet out and thrust it into the soldier's gut again, twisting the blade before he pulled it out this time. The enemy soldier went limp.

The Marine who had been on the ground fighting for his life grabbed his M4 and fired several rounds into a Chinese soldier who had charged at Long, nearly running his own bayonet through him. Just as Long went to say,

"Thanks," the Marine was shot in the cheek and the bullet summarily exploded out the other side of the man's face.

"Look out, Sir!" one of his Marines yelled. Long ducked just in time to place his shoulder into the chest of the man who was charging right at him. In that instant, he felt the man's armor plate in his body armor and a twinge of pain in his own shoulder. He lifted up and backward with all of his might, throwing the enemy soldier over his shoulder to the ground below. Turning quickly to face him, Long fired several rounds into the man's upper body and face, killing him instantly.

"There's more of them coming!" another one of his sergeants yelled as even more of enemy paratroopers burst through the jungle in front of them.

"My God, that's a lot of Chinese soldiers," he thought as he saw yet another wave charging forward with their guns ablaze.

One of the five Marines that had charged forward with him jumped into the blown-out fighting position that had the M240 in it. He leveled the gun at the storming soldiers and opened fire. In seconds, he raked nearly a hundred rounds across the charging horde, wiping out the attacking force. As Long moved toward the Marine to help him keep the gun going, an RPG flew out of the jungle, blowing up right in front of the machine gunner. His body was ripped in half from the explosion, and the force of the blast knocked Long to the ground with a hard thud.

Captain Long struggled to catch his breath after having the air punched out of him from the fall. He felt a strong pair of hands grab the back of his IBA and pull him hard backward, toward the rest of his men. While he was being dragged, Long saw several enemy soldiers charging after him. He took aim with his M4 and fired as quickly as his rifle would let him, gunning them all down. Then he crawled behind a tree and took aim at the enemy soldiers, who were still trying to press home the attack.

"We need to fall back, Sir. We can't hold this position," said one of his sergeants.

"Someone, get on the radio and tell Fourth Platoon to double-time it to our position *now*! Also, see if you can raise battalion and find out if we can get some fire support from the gun battery or the mortar platoon!" Long screamed to be heard over the relentless sounds of men and machine.

Minutes after placing the call, another twenty-six Marines rushed forward to join them against a cluster of now fallen over trees and other odds and ends they were using for protection. The added firepower appeared to be enough to cause the enemy to pull back, and the two sides settled into still firing at each other without actively trying to overrun each other.

****

Palayan, Philippines
Fort Mag

Sergeant Gerald Phillips arrived at Fort Mag on one of the many CH-53 Super Stallions that had been delivering supplies to the base just prior to dark. His squadron of Super Cobras was going to rebase on Fort Mag so they would be closer to the actual fight, rather than having to waste fuel flying from the amphibious assault ships to support the ground pounders. The infantry was in near-constant contact and desperately needed the gunships.

When he arrived at the base, the first thing he noticed was how shot up the place was. There were several downed helicopters near the edge of the runway, along with numerous other enemy vehicles. A fair number of dead bodies were still strewn around the area, which further added to the macabre scene before him.

"Sergeant Phillips, get the tools and other equipment set up over near that section of the taxiway!" shouted his lieutenant.

Just then, a pair of Cobras settled onto the taxiway, shutting down their engines. Trudging toward the helicopters and the area where their platoon leader wanted them to set up as their repair section, Phillips saw the pilots climbing out of the helicopter.

"Sergeant!" exclaimed the pilot, waving him over. "I think my tail boom took a few hits on our last attack run. Can you guys check it over and make sure nothing major was hit while we get some food? We have to get back into the air as quickly as we can."

Phillips nodded. "We'll get right on it and have you guys airborne in no time," he said. The other pilot joined the first, and the two headed off toward one of the tents that had been set up as a field kitchen.

While Sergeant Phillips moved closer to the helicopter with his tool case, he saw one of the POL guys moving a small tanker near the helicopter as another guy hooked the fuel hose up to the helicopter to refuel. While that was happening, a couple of the munition guys reloaded the rocket pods, and another guy worked on reloading the nose gun. It was a true team effort as the various support personnel crawled over the helicopter, getting it fueled, rearmed and mechanically checked over while the pilots took a few minutes to get some food and water and take a bio break before they flew back into harm's way.

As the sun began to set, the air operations wound down, giving the mechanics the time they needed to fix a lot of the battle damage to the gunships: repairing bullet holes, fixing hydraulic hoses, and replacing electrical wiring and sensors. Come morning, those helicopters would be busy. In addition to the repairs the maintenance squad was responsible for, Sergeant Phillips also had to make sure his guys had dug a few fighting positions nearby. If the enemy managed to overrun the perimeter, then they might need to repel an attack on the airfield from these very same positions.

When the twilight of the new day peeled away the darkness of the evening, Phillips' crew had just finished repairing the Cobra they were responsible for. The crew of mechanics was just picking up their tools when the sound of incoming rockets and artillery fire rang out in the distance. Rounds landed at various positions around the base, shaking the ground violently and shattering the morning's serenity. Looking in the direction of where the pilots had been sacked out, Sergeant Phillips saw them grab their helmets and run quickly to get into their helicopters and get airborne before a lucky round landed near their gunships, disabling or destroying them.

Phillips jumped into one of the fighting positions they had just prepared a few hours ago and made sure his squad was readying themselves to deal with whatever happened next. One of the helicopters got airborne and headed off in one direction, while the second helicopter continued to climb and gain altitude. As the second helicopter banked to the north, it was suddenly hit by one of the many rockets flying toward the Marine positions. The gunship exploded from the large-caliber rocket, crumpling the frame of the helicopter as it fell to the ground below in a fiery mess.

"*Holy cow, that was close!*" thought Phillips. He hoped this artillery barrage would end soon.

Looking toward the other end of the airfield, he saw the 105mm Howitzers clearly fire back at the enemy. It was now incumbent on them to provide the counterbattery fire that would hopefully silence the enemy's guns. The dueling artillery fire went on for a handful of minutes before the enemy fire finally subsided. Then the Howitzers went back to firing in support of the ground forces, and so did the mortar platoon that was set up with them.

The next forty minutes was pure chaos. Light and heavy machine guns were firing all over the place. Wounded Marines were dragged back to the hospital tents near the artillery battery, while occasionally a medical helicopter would swoop in with its brightly painted red cross on the side to quickly load up the wounded and ferry them back to the higher-level trauma center on the amphibious assault ships offshore.

"Sergeant! Do you hear the sound of tanks?" asked one of the soldiers in the next foxhole.

"*We don't have any tanks with us yet, do we...?*" he thought in horror.

"Yeah, I hear it. I don't think it's friendly though. If we have to fall back, guys, we'll fall back to the artillery batteries' position, OK?" Phillips shouted.

The other Marines in his squad just nodded as they continued to point their weapons into the forest and trees around them, waiting to see if a horde of enemy tanks or soldiers would suddenly appear out of nowhere. Suddenly, half of the air operation building, which was acting as their brigade headquarters, exploded. They saw an enemy tank charge right at the building, but then a missile streaked in from one of the attack helicopters they had been working on the night before, blowing the tank apart like a firecracker on the Fourth of July. The enemy tank had been destroyed, but not before it caused the damage it had sought to inflict on the Americans.

Then, to their front, an armored personnel carrier came barreling out of the woods and headed straight toward them. In the turret, Phillips spotted a soldier in the turret manning a machine gun, firing at his men. Sergeant Phillips raised his M4 to his shoulder and took aim at the soldier who was spitting out death and destruction. He gently squeezed the trigger, sending a three-round burst at the soldier, who clutched at his chest and fell inside the vehicle. The machine gun had been silenced.

The vehicle suddenly hit one of the tank mines Phillips had seen some of the engineers placing around the perimeter the night before. The vehicle stopped moving and started to billow smoke. Half a dozen enemy soldiers emerged from the back of the vehicle and fanned out, shooting back at the Americans. Then, maybe a platoon's worth of enemy soldiers emerged from the woods and added to the volume of fire toward the Marines defending the airfield.

"Sergeant, what do you want us to do? It looks like the enemy is going to overrun the airfield!" shouted one of the soldiers in Phillips' squad.

Looking around, Sergeant Phillips saw his ten Marines were quickly being cut off from being able to fall back to the other side of the airfield near the gun battery. Their best bet now was to do their best to hold their current positions and hope the other Marines around them were going to do the same and the enemy would run out of steam.

"Everyone, listen up! We are dug in here," said Phillips. "We're going to stay put and make sure the enemy doesn't take our little section of the airfield. Is that understood? I want everyone to stay put. Conserve your ammo and only shoot when you're confident you'll hit something. We can do this, Marines!"

****

Chief Petty Officer Brian Conway, call sign "Punisher," sat on the roof of the air operations building at Fort Mag, wondering if this tour of duty was ever going to end. He had hit his six-month mark three months ago, with no end in sight. Then again, he hadn't heard of a single Special Forces unit that had rotated home for any amount of dwell time.

"*Well, I'm not getting shot to get some time off,*" he thought.

Conway had been a part of SEAL Team Three since he'd joined the Navy and completed BUD/S training twelve years ago. After surviving the world's most brutal training program, he specialized as a sniper. Having served multiple tours in both Iraq and, more recently, Afghanistan, he had built up quite a record among the teams as an exceptional sniper. When the war in Asia had broken out, his team had found themselves heavily involved in the opening of the Second Korean War, and then later in the Russian Far East. With the change in strategy and direction for the Marine ground war, his team had been pulled from Russia and sent to Guam to support the Marines in the Philippines.

He ran his hand across the flat black Stoner Rifle-25 semiautomatic sniper rifle he brought with him for this mission. Unless he was going to conducting long-range sniper operations, he preferred to use the SR-25 with its 20-round magazine. Conway had trained in the Philippines in the past—he'd even trained at Fort Mag before—so he knew he'd be faced with some dense foliage. That meant the majority of his shots would be under 500 meters. He was more concerned with being able to hit multiple targets in quick succession than he was about nailing an enemy soldier 2,000 meters away.

Intruding into his personal thoughts, his partner said, "Punisher, you think those Chinese paratroopers are going to attack our base?" He spat a stream of tobacco juice over the edge of the building they were lying prone on.

Punisher's spotter, Petty Officer First Class Leeroy Miley, call sign "Leeroy Jenkins," had the personality of a paranoid schizophrenic who would either charge into a situation without warning or hold back, depending on what mood he was in at that moment.

"You can bet your paycheck they're going to attack us. It's a matter of when, not if," Punisher told his country hillbilly of a partner. The two of them had worked together for close to three years. Conway loved Leeroy like a brother, but sometimes he was too brash to be a spotter. His true passion was being a breacher, the guy who blows the door of the building open and charges right in. That was why he had been given the call sign "Leeroy Jenkins," after the infamous World of Warcraft MMO gamer who would relentlessly charge forward into battle without taking the time to know the enemy and make sure he didn't just run to his glorious death.

"From everything I've heard, those Chinese paratroopers are vicious fighters," said Punisher. "They've led the invasion of every country China's invaded since the beginning of this war. If they attack, you can bet it'll be in force, and it'll be a real battle. I mean, look around us, there's what—maybe four companies' worth of Marines and an artillery battery and some helicopters here? We've been surrounded by close to 4,000 enemy paratroopers, maybe more."

Leeroy's face settled into a worried look as his paranoia took over. "You think we might not make it out of this one?" he asked.

Just as Punisher was about to respond, the enemy rocket attack began. All around them, rockets were hitting buildings, the runway, the hangars, and everything possible except the building they were sitting on top of. They could hear the whizzing of shrapnel flying through the air as the base around them was being blown apart. Men dove for cover. Others screamed out for a corpsman, begging for someone to help them.

"Scan the perimeter! They might rush us any moment," Conway urged his spotter.

What Leeroy saw as he searched beyond their own lines was horrifying. "Tanks! Holy crap, that's a lot of tanks!" he shouted. Twelve T-99 main battle tanks, covered in reactive armor, brush and tree branches, charged toward their lines at full speed. Immediately behind the tanks was a line of armored personnel carriers and other armored vehicles, ready to push through whatever hole in the American lines the tanks managed to punch through.

While the two of them watched the charging tanks, several antitank missiles streaked toward them from further behind the Marine lines, blowing several of the tanks apart with their shape charges. Seconds after the first four tanks were hit, another three more were blown up by the second wave of antitank missiles. However, before the Marines could get a third set of missiles off, the tanks charged right through their positions and continued to race forward, right toward the airfield.

"*I knew I should have brought the Barrett with me!*" Conway chided himself. He realized the SR-25 had no real antimateriel stopping power like the heavier-caliber .50 of the Barrett.

"Forget the tanks. Find me targets we can take out!" Punisher yelled. It was difficult for his spotter to hear him over the roar of diesel engines, explosions, and the rattle of machine-gun fire.

Leeroy began searching for targets for them to engage to their front. Suddenly, he caught a glimpse of something moving on the opposite side of the runway. As the smoke from the earlier rocket attack cleared, he saw dozens of enemy soldiers charging toward the battery of 105mm Howitzers. The gunners were desperately trying to lower their barrels to be flush with the ground, while anyone with a rifle was doing their best to shoot at the attackers.

"Turn around and stop those soldiers from overrunning our artillery battery!" Leeroy yelled.

Conway turned to look behind him and saw what his spotter had found. *"Crap! They're going to overrun our artillery support!"* he thought in horror.

Instantly, he jumped up with his rifle and ran toward the other end of the building, flopping hard on the ground. He brought his rifle to bear and quickly identified targets. Letting his breath out slowly, he squeezed the trigger and watched as the head of a Chinese soldier exploded in a bright red mist. His body fell to the ground, tumbling from his recent forward momentum.

He aimed for another soldier next to him and squeezed the trigger again, with the same result. In a matter of sixty seconds, he had shot sixteen enemy soldiers before they could overrun the gun battery. As more Chinese soldiers dove for cover, they continued to fire on the Marines manning the Howitzers, hitting many of them as they tried to hold their positions.

Conway swapped out his magazine, slapping a fresh one in place, and went back to systematically wiping out the attacking force that had nearly overrun their only artillery support.

"Switch back to the front of the building!" yelled his spotter. "Two armored personnel carriers just stopped less than a hundred meters in front of our building and are unloading their troops!"

If he didn't have a spotter with him, chances were Punisher would never see the guy that would ultimately kill him because he would be so focused on taking out the man on the other end of his sniper scope. Rolling over to his side and then quickly jumping back to his feet, Conway ran in a low crouched position to the opposite end of the roof and again got down and sighted in the next group of enemy soldiers.

Nearly a dozen enemy soldiers exited one of the armored personnel carriers, or APCs, and ran for cover, firing at the Marines near them. Seconds later, the armored vehicle they had just exited blew up from an antitank rocket. The other APC managed to get nearly half of their soldiers out before it also exploded from a direct hit by an antitank rocket.

Conway sighted in the first enemy soldier. The man appeared to be an officer, since he was yelling and then pointing at several Marines not far from them. Punisher gently squeezed the trigger, feeling the rifle kick slightly as the officer clutched at his chest, then collapsed next to the dead body of another one of his soldiers, who had just died from a bullet fired by another American nearby.

It was a complete melee breaking out in front of Conway. Several waves of Chinese soldiers bum-rushed the Marine positions and began fighting in hand-to-hand combat in the foxholes. Conway did his best to snipe at as many of the enemy soldiers as he could, trying to give the defenders as much covering fire as possible.

Suddenly, an explosion rocked Conway's building. Part of the roof they had been shooting from collapsed, and they fell into the building. Hitting the floor below them hard, Punisher and Leeroy spotted the tank that must have imploded this half of the building. Around them were several bodies of the men who had been manning many of the radios, keeping the base connected with the outside world. Their radios were largely destroyed by the explosion.

Before anyone had a chance to process what had just happened, bullets whipped past them, some of them hitting the building materials. One of them ripped through Leeroy's right hand, his shooting hand.

"I'm hit!" he yelled as he quickly switched firing hands and took aim at the enemy soldiers that were charging forward.

Punisher leveled his rifle at the first enemy soldier he saw and pulled the trigger, only to be met with a click.

"Ugh, I didn't change the magazine out!" he realized, still dazed from the fall. In seconds, he dropped the empty one and slapped another one in its place. He suddenly realized that his spotter had been shot in the hand and was bleeding profusely.

Two other SEAL members who had been with the radiomen ran toward them and helped to tear into the charging enemy. In less than a minute, the four of them had mowed down close to thirty charging enemy soldiers. The group collectively changed magazines and scanned for new targets as they worked to establish some sort of perimeter around the shattered command center.

As the SEALs reengaged another group of charging paratroopers, one of the wounded enemy soldiers threw a grenade in their direction. Punisher saw the object arc through the air right for them and yelled "Grenade!" as it bounced off an object that seemed to propel the grenade right toward them, instead of away.

It landed right in the center of the group, and without thinking, Punisher instantly jumped on the grenade just as it went off. While he didn't die outright, he couldn't move his body and just lay there as his body began to bleed out. In that instant, he saved his fellow SEAL members, though they would eventually be overrun before the day's fighting was done. Sadly, during the battle of Fort Mag, the entire SEAL platoon was eventually wiped out.

****

Colonel Tilman had been thrown to the ground when the command center took a direct hit. He didn't know what had hit them, only that the room above him was spinning. Tilman realized he needed to gain control of his mind and get back into the fight. He pressed his leg against something firm and did the same with his hand. In a fraction of a second, the spinning stopped and his mind stabilized itself. Rolling over to his side, he got up to his knees and saw the two SEALs who had been on the roof moments before, shooting it out with an unknown number of enemy soldiers that were clearly nearby.

Tilman saw Lieutenant Commander Haversham and one of the other SEAL team members rush to the gaping hole in the side of the building and add in their own firepower. "Colonel Tilman, are you OK?" asked one of the Marines, who had been talking on the radio to the offshore command ship before the explosion.

Getting back to his feet, Tilman nodded and reached for his M4 in case he needed to use it. Turning to look toward the SEALs who were still firing at the enemy, he saw an object fly into the room.

Someone yelled, "Grenade!" Before anyone else could react, one of the SEALs dove on top of the grenade as it went off.

"We need to fall back!" yelled one of the SEALs.

Boom! Bam! More explosions rocked the area, causing the structure to shake violently. The supports of the building had been thoroughly compromised.

Lieutenant Colonel Jackman turned toward the SEALs. "Fall back to the artillery batteries' position!" he yelled. He reached down and helped a wounded Marine get to his feet.

The Spec Ops guys nodded and said they would provide covering fire while they grabbed the wounded and fell back.

Colonel Tilman grabbed one of the lance corporals, signaling that they should run to the wreckage of one of the Ospreys from the previous day and set up a firing position to help cover their retreat. In seconds, the two of them were running at full speed toward the wreck, with bullets kicking up dirt and rocks all around them.

Bringing his rifle to his shoulder, Colonel Tilman sighted in on a cluster of enemy soldiers that were trying to come around the building. He fired a series of controlled three-round bursts into the soldiers, hitting several of them before they turned their fire in his direction. Bullets hit the destroyed wreck they were hiding behind, forcing Tilman and the lance corporal to seek cover. While they were keeping the enemy focused on them, one of the SEALs came around the corner and finished them off with a burst from his M240. He quickly waved for the Marines behind him to cross the taxiway and make their way back to the artillery batteries' position.

When the 105mm artillery guns arrived the previous day, they had the helicopters place the guns on the northeast side of the airstrip, near the firing range. It was a relatively large open field, which gave them more than enough room to set the Howitzers up on. They had also placed one of the two mortar platoons inside their perimeter. As the front half of the perimeter of the base began to fall apart, it made sense for them to try and fall back to the artillery position while they continued to call for help and reinforcements.

Had the Marines not gotten the Howitzers set up in the early hours of the morning, they wouldn't have been in a position to take out the enemy rocket artillery. As they ran toward them, Tilman thought, *"God only knows how long we would have held up if the enemy had been able to pound us relentlessly with rockets."* As it was, they had already caused a considerable amount of damage.

It took Colonel Tilman and the rest of what remained of his headquarters staff fifteen minutes to fight their way back to the artillery positions. When they crossed over into their lines, they were quickly met by a number of corpsmen, who helped get the wounded moved back to the ad hoc aid station they had set up. Looking back across the airstrip, Tilman saw small pockets of Marines fighting various clusters of enemy soldiers. Overhead, he heard jets high above them, engaging some unseen adversary.

"Man, we could really use some air support," he thought.

The artillery commander walked up to him with his radioman. "Colonel Tilman, thank God you're still alive. When your headquarters was taken out, we thought you'd been killed. I've got the division commander on the radio. He wants a status report. I was about to tell him you were killed, and the base was being overrun," the captain explained, obviously glad that he wouldn't have to be the one to relay that kind of information to the general.

"Thank you, Captain," said Tilman. "Let me see if I can try and get us some help before we all get wiped out."

Grabbing the mic from the radioman, he lifted the receiver to his mouth. "General, this is Colonel Tilman. Are you there?" he asked, too tired and rattled to remember what call sign he was supposed to be using that day.

The general responded, "You sound like hell, Micah. How bad is it?"

"My headquarters was blown up with me in it. Most of my staff was killed, and a lot of our radios were destroyed. I've got tanks inside the wire, along with God only knows how many other armored vehicles. These flipping paratroopers are all over this base right now. The north side of the base perimeter has held for the moment, but they're taking a beating. The east and south sides have held, despite the Chinese throwing what was probably an entire battalion at them. However, the entire west side of my lines has collapsed. For the moment, I'm hunkered down with the

Howitzer battalion. I need some freaking help here, or we're going to get wiped out," he replied.

"Colonel, I've lost nine surveillance drones over your position in the last four hours. We just got a new drone over your position, providing us with some real-time video of what's going on. You've got small pockets of soldiers holding various positions all over the base. I'm doing everything I can to get your reinforcements right now," the general explained.

The division commander let out a deep breath before he continued. "I told the strike group commander that we have to get you guys some air support, even if he has to lose a few planes in the process. He's sending six Hornets your way. Once they're on station, we'll let you know so you can coordinate their attack. As to reinforcements, I'm sending a company of Marines to you right now. They're roughly ten minutes out. See if they can retake the airstrip again. I'll see if we can get the better part of a battalion sent to you throughout the day," his boss replied.

Colonel Tilman was frustrated at the painfully slow pace of getting the Marines ashore. The enemy's air-defense systems had thus far proven to be a lot heavier and more sophisticated than they had been led to believe. His own aviation wing had lost nine Ospreys in the first four hours of the invasion, and another dozen CH-53 Super Stallions—not a good way to start an invasion.

He sighed before responding, "That's a good copy, General. We'll do our best to retake the airfield once those fast movers help us out. I'm not sure how fast you can get my reserve battalion ashore, but I sure would appreciate their help here at Fort Mag."

****

Sumay, Guam

After General Cutter took a quick shower and had a bowl of oatmeal and some orange juice, it was time to check in on the status of the various battles unfolding in the Philippines. Walking into his command center, he saw a number of officers animatedly talk amongst themselves over a map that was spread out on a table. Sensing something was up, he moved to investigate.

"What's going on?" Cutter inquired. The group of majors and captains suddenly grew quiet.

Seeing a possible moment to shine in front of the general, one of the young captains spoke up. "We're reviewing the latest positions of the Indonesian 1st Infantry Division. The bulk of their force has fallen back to the Mount

439

Banahaw area. They've essentially left the entire lower portion of Luzon open for the taking. We were discussing what our forces should do next in response," he explained.

A major, who had only recently joined his staff, chimed in to add, "We've managed to offload an entire brigade down near Legazpi, and they've moved inland. For some reason, the Indonesian general has left behind small units to harass us, but nothing serious. They clearly had a numbers advantage on us and time to prepare a layered defense; it just doesn't make a lot of sense that they would give that up without a fight," he concluded. A few of the other officers nodded in agreement.

General Cutter smiled. "It could be that this Indonesian general heard he'd be facing the United States Marines and decided it wasn't worth dying for, so he withdrew his army to a more defensible position," he said to the laughs of the men around him.

"No, on a serious note, they've probably fallen back because they fear us landing a blocking force behind them, trapping them down on a narrow part of the island. Nearly the entire island is in range of the Navy's 5-inch guns, which means they can provide a modicum of indirect fire support. Let's let him retreat for right now. We need to focus on offloading as much of our armor, artillery, and troops as possible for the time being. I want the entire 7th Marine Division offloaded before the end of the week."

Turning to a colonel who'd walked over to him, Cutter asked, "What's the status of the 6th Marine Division in the north? Last I heard, the battle of Fort Mag was still raging on into its second straight day. Have we finally secured that base and beaten back those Chinese paratroopers yet?"

Colonel Rob Porter nodded. "Colonel Tilman's brigade radioed in an hour ago that they had officially re-secured the airfield with the help of the new reinforcements. They're in the process of pushing the perimeter further out and going after the retreating paratroopers. I have his brigades' latest casualty report, along with the carrier strike groups'. You should know the admiral was furious at the aircraft losses his forces suffered in retaking that airfield."

General Cutter just nodded as he took a long drink of water from the bottle he had just opened. Looking over the casualty list, he just shook his head. "*So many Marines…*" he thought in despair.

"Did it really take one of his battalions two days to advance ten kilometers inland from the beach?" he inquired, not sure if what was just handed to him was correct.

"Yes, Sir," answered Colonel Porter. "That battalion also sustained 218 casualties securing the beachhead for the Navy. Apparently, those Chinese paratroopers were responsible for defending the roads and hills around the beach and had somehow maneuvered a number of 152mm Howitzers into the hills—the intelligence guys must have missed it. Those guns tore up our armor before they were destroyed by the carrier airwing."

"I take it the enemies' surface-to-air missile systems are to blame for the large number of losses we've sustained up to this point?" Cutter inquired. He wanted to know if it was the lack of air support that delayed them, or if it was poor leadership.

Porter pulled a different map from a stack on his desk and brought it over to the table the two of them were now standing next to. Placing the map on the table and putting a couple of objects down to hold the edges, he explained the problem. "The issue is much larger than one factor, Sir. The battalion commander was aggressive, just as we've instructed them to be, but we had poor intelligence of the area. The SEAL and recon teams were directed to find and eliminate the air-defense systems on the island, so the Navy and Air Force could provide us with air support. That led to us not having enough information to know what we were potentially walking into." As he spoke, he pointed to where the enemy air-defense systems had been located.

"The Air Force and Navy hit the SAM fields around these areas here," Colonel Porter continued as he pointed to two locations around Manila: one at Subic Bay and one near Clark International Airport. "When the Navy went in to support our guys at Fort Mag, the enemy turned on a new SAM nest we hadn't seen yet, and subsequently shot down a number of their aircraft. Destroying that nest took the Air Force another twelve hours, as the aircraft had to fly in from Guam with more standoff cruise missiles. It was during this delay that the Chinese launched that massive counterattack that nearly wiped our guys out at the base. By all accounts, Sir, it was one of the bloodiest battles of the war with China. Colonel Tilman was on the ground during the entire thing. He relayed a very hair-raising experience when I spoke with him."

"I'm glad you were able to talk with Tilman," said Cutter. "What's the status of the rest of the division? Are they ashore yet?"

"The 3rd Marine Amphibious Brigade just offloaded. They're now making their way to Fort Mag and will drive down to Manila. The 2nd Marine Amphibious Brigade will be ashore by evening. They'll head toward Clark

International Airport and then push on to Subic Bay. If I may, because of how badly mauled the 1st Marine Amphibious Brigade was during the last two days, I'd like to recommend that we leave them to garrison the surrounding area of Fort Mag and the beachheads. Most of the brigade is down to 50% manning. Until they're reinforced with additional replacements from the States, I'm not sure they would make an effective offensive force," Porter explained.

Cutter nodded at the suggestion. "OK. Send a message to Tilman and let him know his brigade is now responsible for the security of the area. Tell him he needs to focus on making sure the airstrip stays operational and securing the beachhead. When I talk with the Pentagon later today, I'll let them know I need the next batch of reinforcements to be flown directly to Guam. From there, we can throw them on C130s and have them flown to Fort Mag. I want Tilman's brigade back to full strength ASAP. He's my best forward commander, and I'm going to need him for the next invasion," the general said. Then he turned back to the larger map that showed the entire Chinese occupied territories—his eyes were fixed on Taiwan, the real prize to his plan.

Formosa Fortress

Yilan County, Taiwan

A soft mist of rain was drifting across the mountains that overlooked the lowlands of Luodong Township and the eastern shores of Formosa. Seagulls squawked off in the distance, and waves crashed against the shore in the early morning twilight.

Standing on top of a ridge overlooking the beaches several miles away, General Yang Yin took in a deep breath of the fresh saltwater air, slowly letting it out through his nostrils. *"This is a good position,"* he thought.

Turning to survey the rest of the ridgeline, he saw that even at the twilight hours, men and machines were hard at work preparing to meet the eventual American invasion force. He grunted in satisfaction at what he was seeing—these positions would be terribly hard for the enemy to capture.

Looking at the brigadier general in charge of the islands fortification systems, he realized how lucky he was to have such a competent man in charge of the island's engineers. Brigadier General Lee Jinping had developed an intricate layered defensive position across the most likely beach zones and ports the Americans would need to secure to liberate the island.

During dinner the previous night, Lee had told him that his inspiration for the defenses he'd built was rooted in the example of what the Japanese had done on Iwo Jima and Okinawa. In both cases, the Japanese had known they couldn't hold the islands forever but had been determined to bleed the Americans dry during the assault. Using that as his reference, General Lee had had dozens upon dozens of boring and tunneling machines brought in from the mainland within the first week of the invasion, before the PLA had even finished capturing the island. He had devised a series of interlocking fortresses that would be built at different positions around the beaches and lowlands, where the Americans would most likely land. He also built several of these forts near the major ports that would be used to offload the American heavy tanks and other equipment once they'd been captured and established a beachhead.

The fortresses were positioned so they could provide interlocking fields of fire with their short-, medium- and long-range artillery guns. They had also built hundreds of hidden machine-gun bunkers that would be revealed when the enemy got close enough to them. All of these positions had been built with the knowledge that they would be attacked mercilessly from the air by the American Air Force. They knew they would be hit with precision-guided missiles and bombs, so the fortresses were well designed, with cutback and blowout tunnels to allow overpressures and flames to escape without blowing into the larger tunnel system.

For the past eight months, nearly 60,000 soldiers and over 100,000 civilians had labored on the defenses. From filling sandbags to laying concertina wire to digging tank ditches, the civilians on the island were being put to use fortifying the island against their liberation—against their own free will, of course. Internal communications within the island had been shut down, to the point that no cell phone could get a signal. Even the Thuraya satellite phones had a hard time operating on Formosa. General Lee had been adamant that if they were to succeed in surprising the Americans, they needed to ensure none of the people either working on or observing the construction of the fortifications could transmit any form of knowledge or information about it to the Allies.

General Yang saw Brigadier General Lee catch his eye contact while he was surveying the scene and walked over to him. "I hope the fortifications meet your satisfaction," said General Lee. "We still have many more months of construction ahead of us, but we're largely ready for the Americans." He spoke confidently, like a proud father would talk to his friends about his son's athletic or academic achievements.

Turning to look at General Lee, Yang smiled broadly. "I could not be happier with these defenses if I tried. You've done a marvelous job, Lee," he said. He paused for a moment, thinking through all the angles. "How many artillery pieces do we have overlooking Luodong Township?" he asked.

Pulling a small notebook out of his breast pocket, General Lee flipped through a few pages until he found the information he was looking for. "We have 310 artillery pieces hidden within the five fortresses here. All of the beach areas are within range of the guns as well as the fortresses. I cannot guarantee that they'll all survive under a sustained American bombardment though. Eventually, they'll identify where each gun is located and hit them with precision-guided munitions, but it will take them time, and they'll have to expend a lot of expensive weapons to take them out," he replied with a serious look on his face.

Letting out a short breath, Yang took in another deep breath of the saltwater air before responding. "They should last long enough for us to either destroy the American invasion force or at least bloody them worse than anything they have seen up to this point," he said. He secretly hoped the Americans' resolve would dwindle before the battle was done. "Have we been able to get most of the heavy machine-gun bunkers equipped with the Hua Qing miniguns I requested?" he inquired.

The Hua Qing minigun was a six-barrel, electronically operated minigun that fired 7.62×54mm rounds at a rate of 3,000 per minute. It was practically identical to the American M134 minigun used on many helicopters and vehicles that were operated by Special Forces. It had first been introduced in 2009 and had become an operational weapon within the PLA several years later.

Lee shook his head. "No, I'm afraid we have only been able to secure 110 of the weapons,' he answered, a bit disgusted. "I have tried to get more, but they're also being used in the Beizhen defensive line in our northern army group. I was told the factories are producing more of these weapons, but they're being prioritized for the Beijing defensive line. Perhaps you can speak with someone and get more of them shipped to us. We're short at least 800 of these weapons for the other fortresses as well."

"Thank you for bringing this to my attention," said General Yang, a bit surprised. "I'll speak with the logisticians who are denying us these weapons and get that situation corrected. If you'll excuse me now, I must speak with a few others about this festering insurgency that won't go away." Then he dismissed Lee and signaled for two other officers to come speak with him. A moment later, they were both standing next to him, slightly out of breath from running over.

"Generals, I'm going to be returning to the mainland tomorrow and will be headed to Beijing the day after," Yang began. "I need to know what the status of the rebellion is here, and what, if anything, you need to squash it." As usual, he was blunt and straight to the point.

"Sir, in the last two months, we've captured or killed over 4,000 enemy soldiers, who have continued to fight on despite the Taiwanese Army officially surrendering back in January. The insurgency still continues, but it's becoming less and less effective with each month. As we locate where they are operating, we cordon the area off and then search everything within that grid until either we locate the enemy, or they engage our forces. Per your instructions, we're using overwhelming force when we attack them. We are also taking hostages from the local area, and we inform the rebels that if they do not surrender, we'll execute the hostages.

Thus far, we have managed to get roughly 1,500 insurgents to surrender."

The major general cleared his throat. "Also, per your instructions, when they capitulate, we're providing them with food and allowing them to live—we make sure that the fellow insurgents know of our actions and encourage other insurgents to rejoin society. I was skeptical that this strategy would work, but after four months, we've seen more than 2,000 enemy soldiers surrender themselves."

Along with the Taiwanese forces that had moved themselves to the jungles to continue fighting the Chinese, some Japanese and American Special Forces had also infiltrated the island and joined the nasty rebellion that had sprung up. General Yang had known from the moment this began that he would have to devise a plan to end this guerilla war before it had time to firmly take root. So far, his tactic of fair treatment and survival as the carrot, and hostage taking and execution as the stick, had been working exactly as he planned.

"I'm glad to hear the insurgency is dying down," General Yang said. "I will report that to Beijing. How are your provinces for food and munitions for the coming battle?" he inquired.

"We have munitions for a sustained six months of heavy combat—more than enough to last us to the conclusion of the battle. Either we will all be dead, or all the enemy soldiers will be dead before we run out of munitions. As to food, we have six months of food, pending we were unable to live off the land. I'm confident we'll either inflict enough casualties on the Americans to convince them to leave the island, or die trying," the major general explained, speaking with a confidence that verged on cockiness.

General Yang almost wished he would be able to stay there at Formosa and oversea the island personally. However, Beijing would never let him be in a position where he might be captured.

"Excellent report, General," said Yang. "You've done a good job with the time and resources you've been given. Please continue to use the remaining time you have left until the Americans arrive. I'm not sure how much longer we may have to prepare now that Luzon has fallen, but you can be assured the Americans are going to have this place under heavy surveillance, identifying every possible stronghold. Do your best to incorporate our latest in camouflage technology. It's imperative that we surprise the enemy when they land. The Americans are soft. If we can inflict enough casualties, they will lose their stomach for war and seek a peace with China…on our terms and not theirs."

They discussed a number of other defensive strategies and ideas for a few more hours as the sun continued to climb into the sky. It was a beautiful view, and Yang wanted to enjoy it for as long as possible. In a few months, this area would be turned into a moonscape with the number of American bombs and missiles that would be launched at it. For the time being, he savored its serene beauty.

ANZACs

Dili, East Timor

The air was hot and sticky as Lieutenant General Rick Campbell of the 1st Brigade of the Australian Army looked at his senior commanders. He was about to order them to carry out a very risky invasion, one that might help cement Australia's relationship with the new Global Defense Force and give them a more prominent role in the postwar world that would be created in Asia.

General Campbell saw the men he needed to brief were all present and ready to get things going. "*Good,*" he thought. "*There's a lot to get done and not a lot of time to do it.*"

Clearing his throat to get their attention, he stood and walked over to a large map displayed on the wall and removed the sheet he had placed on it earlier. He wanted to keep what he was about to talk about a secret until this discussion. Once he'd pulled the sheet down, the others suddenly sat up a little straighter, seeing the magnitude of what the map showed. They were going to invade the Island of Java directly and bypass a lot of the other Indonesian island garrisons.

"Two days ago, the Indonesian Army on Luzon surrendered to the American Marines. It is expected that the PLA ground forces will also surrender within the next couple of days. I spoke with General Roy Cutter, the American Marine Commander for the Pacific. He told me that his intention is to bypass the bulk of the Chinese and Indonesian forces on the remaining Philippine Islands. The Americans will turn their focus on Taiwan once Luzon has been fully liberated," General Campbell explained.

"The surrender of so many Indonesian forces on Luzon, and the fact that many more of them are now going to be essentially trapped on the remaining islands, has given us a unique opportunity to deal a death blow to the Indonesian government and perhaps end their participation in the war. General Cutter told me that he will detail off one American carrier strike group and additional ground forces and landing ships to assist us in our invasion of Java. Our goal—" he said, pausing for effect, "—is to threaten Jakarta and force the government to surrender."

Brigadier General Alan Morrison, the senior ground commander for the ANZAC force, interrupted to ask what they all wanted to know. "How in the heck are we going to invade Java? We don't have the sealift capability to move our equipment and forces to assault a hostile landing like the Americans have been doing."

The others in the room nodded their heads in agreement and mumbled a few words to that effect as well.

General Campbell held up his hand. "In addition to our two Canberra-class amphibious assault ships, and the HMAS *Choules*, the Americans are going to send twelve of their own amphibious assault ships with the carrier strike group. They'll also be sending one Stryker brigade combat team to support our ground operation. With the Americans having substantially increasing the size of their brigade combat teams, we'll have a total of 6,000 additional infantrymen for the invasion. With the American troops, it'll bring our invasion force up to 31,000 soldiers, and the latest intelligence reports estimate the Indonesian Army has, at best, 9,000 soldiers spread across Java. Our forces will be landing with tanks, infantry fighting vehicles, and self-propelled Howitzers—more than enough of a force to deal with the remaining enemy troops on the island."

For the next two hours, the group went over the plan and ironed out a lot of the details of which units would land first and secure the port city of Cirebon. Once the port was captured, the heavy roll-on, roll-off ships would be able to dock and offload the rest of their armored vehicles and the supplies needed to keep the army moving. The port city of Cirebon had been chosen for a few reasons. It was only 218 kilometers from the Indonesian capital, and it was a relatively small city of just a few hundred thousand people, unlike the other port cities, which had populations in excess of one million. A small population meant fewer potential problems. Together, they decided that this course of action would isolate the capital from the remaining forces the Chinese had on the island, giving them the best chance of a quick victory.

****

Karimunjawa Island, Indonesia

The coral reefs around the island of Karimunjawa were absolutely stunning. Had Major Jason Warden of the New Zealand Special Air Force not been toting all of his combat gear with him, he certainly would have enjoyed the rich reds, pinks, and other colors of the living reef and the sight of the colorful fish that darted in and out of their underwater village.

He and his men had been transported to a place a couple of miles away from the island by an American ballistic missile submarine that had been converted to fire cruise missiles and carry the American Navy's elite SEALs. When the mission had been put together, Major Warden had inquired why this assignment wasn't being carried out by one of the American SEAL teams. The captain of the USS *Georgia* had told him a large contingent of the SEALs in the Philippines, who normally would have carried out this mission, had been killed, so the mission had fallen to his squadron to complete. Fortunately, they did have a couple of SEAL members to help them use the equipment and guide them through the process of leaving the underwater boat. He had to admit—the submarine was a beast. It was enormous and could carry a plethora of underwater vehicles and special operators.

Major Jason Warden looked over his shoulder. Now that they'd arrived at their destination, the rest of his team was unpacking the SEAL delivery vehicle. They'd parked the underwater vehicles on the opposite side of a reef; they'd swim through the break in it to the shore, where they would conduct their mission.

After what felt like a long time but was really only five or so minutes, the New Zealand Special Air Service, or NZSAS, was ready to move. The sixteen members of his team and the three US Navy SEALs accompanying them were about to pull off one of the most dangerous missions of the war for the Australian and New Zealand Army Corps, or ANZACs.

In preparation for the ground invasion of Java, the NZSAS had been tasked with neutralizing a series of Chinese anti-ship missiles batteries and surface-to-air missiles in and around the Karimunjawa Airport. It was the last major threat to the invasion force that needed to be destroyed before the fleet could sail any closer. Because of the close proximity of so many civilians to the military targets, it had been determined that this mission should be conducted by Special Forces rather than left to cruise missiles or high-altitude bombing. Enough civilians were being killed in the war as it was; if they could minimize the casualties while still accomplishing the mission, then it was a risk worth taking.

Fifteen minutes went by as the underwater special operators made their way to the beach, then slowly left the cover of the water and waded ashore.

****

Sergeant Shang Ha was doing his best to stay awake when one of the motion sensors on the southeastern side of the island suddenly detected movement and an alarm sounded, startling him.

"Probably just another animal," he thought, *"or maybe, if I'm lucky, a young couple looking to get busy on a deserted beach."* He remembered back a month ago, when the beach sensor had picked up a young couple making love on the shoreline.

Turning the monitor over to inspect the source of alarm, Shang spotted something. Unfortunately, it wasn't a bird or a romantic date—a small cluster of soldiers was emerging from the water. They appeared to be carrying a number of heavy bags with them as well.

"I better get the lieutenant in here ASAP," he said under his breath as he lifted the telephone receiver on his desk.

It rang three times before he heard the very sleepy voice of his lieutenant on the other end. "This had better be good. You woke me out of a wonderful dream," he said.

"Sir," said Sergeant Shang. "One of the ocean sensors picked up some movement a few minutes ago. When I checked it out, it showed images of soldiers emerging from the water and heading up the beach on the southeastern side of the island. I believe we're under attack!"

The lieutenant, who had sounded nearly drunk from tiredness just a moment before, must have sat up in his bed, because his voice now sounded like he had been hit with a quick jolt of adrenaline. "Alert the base commander, but do not sound the alarm. Let's see if maybe we can lay an ambush for these guys," he ordered. "I'll be right there. I just need to get dressed."

****

As the SAS teams split up and headed toward their targets, Major Warden couldn't shake the feeling that something was wrong. The hairs on the back of his neck were standing straight up. It felt like they were walking into a trap.

Everything inside of him screamed to get away, but he also knew they had to accomplish this task. The invasion force was set to sail through this area in the next few hours, and if his team didn't take out the anti-ship missile launchers, hundreds, maybe even thousands of soldiers' and sailors' lives would be at risk.

"*No, we need to press on and deal with whatever danger may be lurking ahead,*" he told himself.

Ahead of him, his point man raised his right hand in a balled fist and then lowered it slowly, indicating they needed to stop and get down. The seven-man team immediately took up a defensive position as they waited for

Major Warden to move forward and find out what the point man had found.

"What do you see?" he asked. His point man had his rifle aimed at something ahead of them.

"I found the first launcher site. It's right past that cluster of foliage in front of us, maybe thirty meters. Do you see it?" he inquired.

Looking more closely, Warden saw through the camouflage and found the hidden structure. "I see it," he said.

"There's a guard just to the right of the entrance. I think we should fan out and advance forward. I can take the guy out with my knife, and then we can move into the area where the launchers are set up," the point man offered, not taking his eyes off the guard.

"Copy that, let's do it," said Major Warden. He turned and signaled with his hands what he wanted everyone to do.

Slowly and methodically, the SAS men and the lone SEAL crept up on the sentry that was guarding the launchers. The guard appeared to be half-asleep. The point man looked at Warden one last time for the go-ahead, and then lowered his weapon and reached for his knife. Creeping slowly forward, he moved to within a couple of feet to the right of the guard, who still seemed unaware that he was about to die. In one swift move, the SAS man darted with lightning speed and had his hand tightly around the man's mouth as he thrust his knife into the guard's throat, severing his arteries and windpipe in one violent move.

As the sentry was dragged to the ground and bled out, the rest of the SAS team moved in. Approaching the entrance, one of them pulled out a small electronic camera that was on a snake cord. He turned it on and moved the head of the cord around the corner to see what was on the other side. Major Warden walked up and looked at the small video display as well. With the night vision scope on, they saw one additional guard sitting on the opposite side of the wall from them.

Slowly, his teammate pulled the cord back and put it back in his pack. Warden moved his rifle to behind his back and retrieved his silenced pistol from his leg holster. Motioning for the others to follow him, he stacked up on the wall with the rest of the team falling in line behind him. Raising his hand with three fingers extended, he slowly counted down from three to one and then moved quickly around the wall.

Major Warden leveled his pistol at the guard, who nearly jumped out of his seat. Before he could yell or alert anyone else, Warden had already fired two quick shots into the guard's chest and one to his forehead, dropping the man where he stood. In a flash, the rest of the team pushed forward with their rifles at the ready as they fanned out into the structure. When they came out of the hallway, they saw rows of rail launchers with anti-ship missiles on them aimed out to sea. Taking these missiles out was their primary objective.

As the team fanned out into the room, they spotted twelve soldiers and moved quickly to take them out. Ten of them were asleep in their cots near the back wall of the missile room, while two more were looking at what appeared to be a radar screen, probably watching to make sure no surface contacts came within range of their missiles.

Within seconds, the six SAS men and the lone SEAL had opened fire with their silenced pistols, killing everyone before they had a chance to activate the alarm or go for their weapons.

With the hostiles neutralized, Major Warden got the attention of his demolition expert. "Rig the area to blow," he ordered.

Looking at his watch, Warden realized the others should have reached their positions by then and wondered how things were going on their end.

With the explosive charges set, the SAS team exited the facility and made their way back to the rendezvous point, where they would wait for the others and then slip back into the water and head back to the waiting submarine. Thirty minutes went by as the men stealthily made their way through the jungle, doing their best to leave no tracks and make as little noise as possible. Suddenly, there was a series of loud noises nearby.

Bang, bang, bang, boom!

A sequence of rifles and machine guns opened fire, maybe a quarter kilometer away from them in the direction of the airstrip. Then they heard what sounded like a grenade, or maybe an RPG round going off. Seconds later, the loud sound of an air raid siren, which must have been the base alarm, blared into the midnight air, rousing everyone on the island and alerting to them danger.

"*Crap! What happened?*" thought Major Warden. Everyone in the team now quickly moved to the beach where they'd stowed their gear.

Just as they were about to bust through the jungle cover in a final dash, a single gunshot rang out, and their point man's head exploded. His body dropped to the ground. Everyone instantly hit the dirt as a fusillade of bullets ripped through the air where they had just been. Several of the SAS men immediately returned fire, matching the barrage of hot lead that the enemy soldiers were spewing at them.

The Navy SEAL with the team realized that they couldn't let themselves get pinned down and threw a fragmentation grenade at the enemy. Then he jumped up and charged right at the Chinese forces, firing his Fostech Origin 12 semiautomatic 12-gauge shotgun. As he screamed and rushed toward the enemy, one of the SAS troops jumped up and followed him forward, only to be cut down in a hail of bullets.

Major Warden saw the SEAL take several hits, but he continued charging. In seconds, he had jumped into whatever the enemy was using for cover and had summarily gunned them all down before collapsing lifeless in a heap, surrounded by other dead bodies. The rest of the SAS men ran as quickly as they could to get to the rendezvous point where they met up with one of the other teams. As the remaining team members grabbed their underwater gear, mortar rounds landed not far from their position.

The shouts of Chinese soldiers and more gunfire rang out all around them as the enemy closed in on them and boxed them in. At that moment, Major Warden knew what he needed to do. "We need a diversion to lead the enemy away from the beach so you all can get away," he said. "I'm going to run a few hundred meters to the south, and then I'll head into the water. I'll swim over to the reef, and you guys can pick me up from there."

The others in the team nodded, not wanting to challenge him on his logic, even though they all knew the likelihood of him meeting them at the reef was low. If nothing happened, they realized they would all probably die there.

"Let me blow the charges now, Major," said the demolition expert. "That will at least cause them to turn away from us so you can have a chance to make a run for it." He pulled the remote detonator from his pocket.

Warden nodded as he changed out his magazine, placing a fresh one in its place. A second later, the small island was rocked by two large explosions, which caused a massive fireball to appear in the night sky.

Major Warden made his break. He took off at breakneck speed, firing at the enemy as he ran, making a lot of noise. He also shouted in English and made it sound like his team was trying to coordinate an escape.

The loud ruckus had the desired effect, and the enemy shifted their fire toward Major Warden and began following him in hot pursuit. As the enemy ran after their squadron commander, the remaining members of the team moved quickly into the water and swam out to the break in the reef, where they'd stowed their underwater vehicle.

One of the team members stayed near the reef on the surface of the water, waiting with his scuba gear on to see if Major Warden was going to make it. As he listened to the activity on shore, he heard Warden's rifle firing for a while; then a couple of explosions went off, and he no longer heard the major's rifle fire. At that point, the SAS man knew their squadron commander had either been captured or killed, and it was time to make their way back to the sub. Major Warden had given his life so his team could get away and fight on another day.

****

It was still dark outside as the amphibious assault ships moved through the murky waters of the Java Sea, past Karimunjawa Island. In the distance, some fires were burning on the island. In the sky above them, Navy fighter jets whooshed by as they conducted their aerial dance of death with Chinese and Indonesia warplanes. On the flight decks of the troop transports, the roar of helicopters spinning up overshadowed the sounds of aerial combat.

The soldiers of Fourth Platoon, Alpha Company, Third Battalion, 81st Infantry Brigade lifted the eighty-six-pound packs onto their shoulders as they lined up to head to the flight deck. From there, they would board one of the waiting helicopters, which would whisk them away to the unknown, and hopefully not certain death.

Snapping his magazine pouch closed and then grabbing his pack, Lieutenant Slater placed the heavy load on and picked up his rifle. He found himself wondering how he landed in this situation again. He wasn't supposed to go back to a line unit. Somehow, he had survived battle in Korea and capture by the Chinese, and now, here he was, doing it all over again in the Pacific.

Several months into Ian's new training gig at Fort Lewis-McCord, Captain Wilkes had informed him that the battalion they'd been training was being sent to the South Pacific; the NCOs and officers that had been carrying out the training would be deploying with them as their permanent leadership. Before Ian could voice his objection, Wilkes handed him a pair of silver bars, telling him he was being promoted to first lieutenant and would be taking over command of Fourth Platoon, Alpha Company. Three weeks later, the entire battalion found themselves boarding a troop ship in Australia headed to the Java Sea.

"Lieutenant, you ready for this?" asked Captain Wilkes. He walked up to Ian with that naïve excitement a soldier has before he's seen combat.

Slater shook his head. "I don't think I have much of a choice," he replied glumly. The two of them waited for the word to head out to the flight deck to board the helicopters.

Leaning in closer so only the two of them could be heard, Captain Wilkes said, "Look, Slater, I know you're not pleased about being sent back into combat. I'd be fuming if I were in your shoes, too. You know I went to bat for you with the colonel to try and get you out of this deployment, right? Unfortunately, right now I need you to suck it up and do the best you can to keep your platoon alive. Can you do that for me?" Wilkes asked with a bit of concern and fear showing in his eyes.

Letting a deep breath out, Slater looked up and placed his hand on the captain's shoulder. "Sir, I may complain softly to myself or to you, but you have always been able to count on me. My platoon will do what's necessary to accomplish our mission. That may mean a lot of them have to die—that's a risk we all have to accept when we go into combat. Just make sure you're ready yourself, to lead us. Don't freeze up when the bullets fly, because trust me, every plan we've put together is going to get thrown out the window once the fighting starts," he said.

Wilkes nodded, knowing Slater was right. When Ian had first shown up to his command, he hadn't known what to make of the sergeant with a bad attitude. As he had gotten to know him, he had seen the attitude was more of an act, something that helped him deal with his fear and pain. Lieutenant Slater had taught him and the other officers and NCOs a lot about what it was like to be in combat, and how quickly things could get thoroughly bungled. The greatest asset they had in a battle was to be fearless and aggressive and remember that the other guy didn't want to be there any more than they did.

"Thanks, Lieutenant. You help me guide the company through this crap storm we're about to wade through, and I'll get you through being an officer…deal?" Wilkes asked with a smile on his face as he stuck his hand out.

Laughing at the comment, Slater shook his hand. "Sure thing, Sir. Besides, your wife said she'd kill me if I didn't make sure you returned home," he replied. The two chuckled briefly before one of the other sergeants walked up to them and told them the rest of the platoons were ready to move.

Twenty minutes went by before one of the crewmen from the ship said it was time for them to file up the ladder that would take them to the flight deck. The 260 soldiers of Alpha Company made their way up three levels through the ladder well until they emerged through a side door on the superstructure that opened up to the flight deck. Once there, they were greeted with the smells of jet fuel and seawater, and the roaring engines of dozens of helicopters.

The sun had just crested over the horizon, bringing the new day to life. When Lieutenant Slater walked out onto the flight deck, the morning twilight revealed nearly a dozen V-22 Ospreys and CH-47 Chinooks, along with lines of infantrymen feeding into the flying chariots of war. Slater stood to the side of the door once he exited and encouraged each of the soldiers in his platoon to move forward to the helicopter they were being directed to. One by one, the soldiers exited the stairwell and made their way to one of the Ospreys. When the last soldier of his platoon exited, Slater got back in line and followed them.

His platoon was being filtered into two of the tiltrotor aircraft. This was the first time Slater had ever flown in one of these new types of helicopters, and he had to admit, he was pretty excited. He had flown in Blackhawks and Chinooks, but never an Osprey. Ducking his head out of instinct as he approached the loading ramp, he walked into the cargo bay and found the last seat, next to the landing ramp and the rear door gunner/crew chief.

Within seconds of getting settled into his seat, the Osprey lifted off the deck along with the other helicopters and turned toward land. Slater looked out the ramp; he was amazed at the sight of the warships below them. He had never seen so many different types of ships. Looking back at the soldiers in his platoon, he saw that many of them were as impressed with the display of naval might as he was. A few of his men were whispering prayers or playing with their rosary beads, and otherwise engaging in any other ritual they felt might help keep them alive.

While the Ospreys picked up speed, Ian saw dozens upon dozens of other helicopters fall into formation. He also spotted a number of Super Cobra gunships at the fringes of the formation, probably their escorts. Twenty minutes went by, and then the helicopters dropped down low, flying just above the water.

The sun had finally risen above the water, revealing more of the world around them, as well as the danger they were now about to fly in to. When their armada of helicopters approached the coasts of Java, small black puffs of smoke appeared in their midst, shaking nearby aircraft and throwing shrapnel in every direction. This was quickly followed by bursts of green tracer fire crisscrossing back and forth across the sky. The attack helicopters that had been escorting them broke off and engaged the enemy guns.

The crew chief and tail gunner closest to Lieutenant Slater turned to him and signaled they were now two minutes away from landing. Slater turned to his soldiers and gave them the same message. Most of the soldiers either gave him a thumbs-up or nodded in acknowledgment.

The Osprey turned hard to the left as they flew over the beach, which gave Slater an exceptional view of the city, intermixed with enemy tracer fire and black pillars of smoke on the ground. Before Slater knew what was happening, the Osprey flared its nose up hard and then landed with a thud on the ground. The door gunner signaled for everyone to get off the aircraft quickly.

Lieutenant Slater ran off the aircraft and quickly darted toward a cluster of trees near the junction of Highway 1 and Highway 5, which ran from the port city of Cirebon to Jakarta, 197 kilometers away. Looking behind him, Slater saw the rest of his platoon was quickly following him to the tree line. Once they were all off the Osprey, it took off and headed back to the ship they had just left.

Once they had all fanned out inside the trees, Slater directed the squad leaders to get a perimeter set up. They needed to move quickly and get their roadblock established and dig in a defensive position. His platoon had been charged with setting up a roadblock on Highway 5 and making sure no one was able to get toward Cirebon. The other platoons were setting up positions on Highway 1 and the town around the road junction.

One of the sergeants began to string a roll of concertina wire across the two lanes of traffic that headed toward the coast. They left the other two lanes open for the moment—if people wanted to leave the area, they were more than willing to let them. Their orders were to not let anyone head to the port city, but they were not about to stop anyone from leaving it.

A couple of his soldiers found some vehicles and drove them to the coiled wire, using the vehicles to help act as a barrier. A few vehicles that saw their roadblock approached them cautiously, apparently not aware at first that they were American soldiers and not Indonesian units, and asked what the roadblock was being set up for.

When Slater looked over and saw two of his soldiers having a very animated conversation with one of the drivers, he signaled for their lone translator to come with him to investigate what was going on. As they approached the vehicle, where the argument was growing louder, Lieutenant Slater saw more and more vehicles were approaching the checkpoint.

"*This isn't good*," he thought.

"What's the problem, Specialist Tailor?" Slater asked. "Just tell them to turn around and go back where they came from."

Tailor sighed audibly. "I tried that, Sir. He doesn't want to listen, and I can't speak whatever language it is they speak here," the soldier said, clearly frustrated with what was going on.

Shaking his head, Lieutenant Slater walked up to the vehicle with the translator. At this point, the driver looked like he suddenly had an epiphany and said in broken English. "You American soldiers?"

Slater snorted and pointed at the American flag patch on his uniform. He turned to his translator. "Tell this guy that, yes, we are American soldiers. He needs to turn around and go back to wherever he came from. He cannot travel down this road."

The translator and the driver conversed rapidly in their native tongue. The driver was clearly furious that he could not continue down the road, but eventually, he turned around and left. This scenario played out a few more times before the rest of the drivers figured out they could not drive down this road and turned their vehicles around.

Four hours later, after they'd turned away a lot of angry drivers, a column of Australian tanks and other armored vehicles traveled down the road toward them. They slowed briefly, and then passed through their checkpoint, continuing down the road that would eventually lead them to the capital city of Jakarta. It was hoped that if the ANZACs and Americans could land forces quickly on Java, they could make a mad dash for the capital and potentially capture the government during the ensuing confusion.

An hour after the first column of armored vehicles passed their positions, a second armored column followed the first, and then a long supply convoy followed them. Ten hours into the landings, the vehicles for Alpha Company, Third Battalion, 81st Infantry Brigade finally arrived, and they were able to hand over their roadblock position to a military police unit while they did their best to try and catch up to the ANZAC forces that should by now be encircling the capital. It was hoped they could convince the government to surrender the city, rather than forcing them to have to fight it out. By surrounding the city quickly, they could prevent

any local military units from reinforcing it or coming to the aide of the government. The key to this operation was speed.
****

Lieutenant Slater was sitting in the back of the Stryker vehicle as they raced down Highway-1 to Jakarta. "Lieutenant, you think we're going to see any action when we get to Jakarta?" asked one of the young privates. He fiddled with one of the ammo cans, grabbing an extra hundred-round belt for his M249 machine gun. The kid was young, but he was built like an ox—a true corn-fed farm boy from Kansas.

"Private Anderson, if everything goes well, we won't have to fire a shot, and the enemy will surrender," he replied to the obvious dismay of the young soldiers surrounding him.

Slater had to remember that these young guys had just graduated from basic training, and they hadn't experienced the horrors of combat yet. *"To be young and naïve like that again..."* he thought glumly.

His radio crackled. "Alpha Four Six, this is Alpha Six," said Captain Wilkes. "The Aussies ran into some enemy units near the outskirts of Jakarta. They're moving now to encircle the city. We've been directed to head straight into the city. I'm sending you the grid. You're the lead platoon for the company, and we're guiding the battalion into the city. Stay frosty and lead the way."

"Copy that Alpha Six," Slater responded. "We'll keep you apprised as we enter the city."

"So, where are we heading, Sergeant?" Lieutenant Slater asked Staff Sergeant Nassem, his platoon sergeant, who was busy entering the coordinates into their navigation system. They were only an hour away from the outskirts of the city at this point.

Nassem let out a soft whistle. "You aren't going to believe this, LT. We're going straight for the president. The coordinates they sent take us right to Istana Merdeka, adjacent to Merdeka Square. It's basically the Indonesian version of the White House," he replied. The men in the back of the vehicle went through a series of emotions from excited to terrified and everything in between.

Slater knew they'd be driving into a firestorm. He immediately switched his radio frequency over to the platoon net to let everyone know what was going on.

"Listen up, Bulldogs," he announced. "The captain just sent us the coordinates for our next objective. Our battalion has been given the task of securing the presidential palace and capturing as much of the government as possible.

That means we're going to be driving right into the heart of the city and will most likely meet resistance from the security forces assigned to protect the president and other members of the government."

He paused for a second, wanting to let some of that information sink in. "All drivers, you need to stay frosty on this. Speed is the key to our success. I need you to do whatever you have to in order to keep us moving. We're going to hit a lot of traffic and a lot of panicked civilians. Drive on the sidewalks, medians, opposite lanes of traffic if you have to, but do *not* stop. We cannot allow ourselves to get stuck and not be able to move, or worse, get trapped. If you have to run over a few cars to keep us moving or push them out of the way, then do it."

A few of the men in his Stryker started to look a bit nervous as they overheard these instructions. It was going to be a bumpy ride.

"When we get close to the residence, I want the lead vehicle to breach the gate or walls or whatever you have to, but drive straight up to the entrance of the building," Slater continued. "Once we're there, whichever squad it is that makes it there, you need to secure the area. The next two squads to show up are going to breach the building, and we'll move as quickly as possible to find the president and round up prisoners. We can do this. Out."

"*Thank God for frequency-hopping radios,*" thought Lieutenant Slater. That would have made a very long transmission. Slater laughed to himself about how he'd just broken every radio protocol he'd ever been taught. Brushing that thought aside, he knew it was imperative his men knew what to do, and if breaking the norms saved a few of his guys from getting killed, then forget protocol. "*I'm the guy in charge of this platoon, and I'll run it as I see fit,*" he thought, standing up straighter.

Ten minutes later as they neared the outer ring road of the city, they caught their first glimpses of combat. Several Indonesian armored personnel carriers were burning wrecks on the side of the highway. There were also a number of dead enemy soldiers strewn about the area, as well as at least one Australian armored vehicles burning along the road. When their platoon got closer to the first major ring road, they saw a couple of Australian tanks and infantrymen fighting it out with a small contingent of enemy soldiers.

Seeing the blockage forming, Sergeant Nassem got Lieutenant Slater's attention. "Sir, we're about to hit a major bottleneck, and it looks like the Australians haven't fully cleared it of enemy soldiers yet. I have an idea that might work to get us around it. Before I joined the Army, I spent a year here in Jakarta as part of a study abroad program. There's another road we can take that's a bit more off the beaten path, but it'll get us to Merdeka Square a lot quicker than trying to fight it out on the major roads, which will surely be roadblocked," he informed him.

The two talked for a couple of moments and looked at a couple of maps of the city and their Blue Force Tracker before deciding on what to do. Once they had outlined the new route they would take, they entered the path into the navigation computer and sent the proposal to Captain Wilkes and the battalion CO. Meanwhile, the rest of the battalion at this point had all caught up to them as they waited on the highway for the Australian tanks to clear them a path. The enemy had apparently set up a number of antitank missiles and other vehicles to slow the Australians down. Two Aussie tanks had been destroyed along with a few other armored vehicles while they tried to clear a path.

Fifteen minutes after proposing their plan, the battalion CO came over the radio. "Lead the way," he ordered. "We'll follow you."

Smiling, Slater slapped his sergeant on the shoulder. "Good job, Nassem. Now if you just spoke the language better…," he said jokingly. Despite having spent a year there, his skills in Indonesian and Javanese were quite rudimentary. Nassem had told him that he had spent too much time during his study abroad program chasing skirts and partying with classmates. Slater had wondered how much fun those parties really could have been, given the country's strict rules about alcohol consumption.

In minutes, their column had found an off-ramp. They snaked their way through a number of now-empty city streets. A lot of the locals had either decided to hunker down in whatever building they were already in or were moving on foot. Any military-looking vehicles moving around on the streets were being engaged by Allied attack helicopters or drones.

When they turned down Menteng Raya Street, they hit the first major obstacle of traffic. The road heading toward Merdeka Square was packed with cars, buses and other vehicles overloaded with people trying to flee the fighting. When Slater's six eight-wheeled Strykers turned onto the road, mass panic by the civilians began to ensue. Most of these people had never seen an American infantry fighting vehicle.

Seeing the traffic problem, Sergeant Nassem told the driver, "Veer over into the opposite lane of traffic. It's practically empty. People are trying to flee the Allied troops, not drive into them."

As Slater's platoon veered over to the opposite side of the road, the rest of the company and battalion followed them. They continued moving along unhindered until they got within eyesight of Merdeka Square. Once there, an enemy armored vehicle suddenly appeared and fired a slew of machine-gun rounds at them. A couple dozen enemy soldiers also emerged and fired at them as well.

The gunner manning the 30mm autocannon didn't need to wait to be told to fire back, and immediately sent a dozen depleted uranium rounds into the enemy armored vehicle, which summarily blew it up. The rest of the soldiers in Slater's Stryker, who were already standing up through the troop hatches, opened fire on the enemy soldiers as their vehicle continued to race toward them. Not stopping, their vehicle zipped right past the now-burning enemy vehicle and the enemy soldiers still firing away at them and their comrades.

Busting out onto Merdeka Square ring road, they gunned the engines and raced across the square toward the presidential building and the other government buildings. Slater stood up and held a set of field glasses to his eyes to try and get a better look; of course, that was challenging to do considering how fast they were racing across the square, but he spotted a couple of very expensive-looking vehicles near the entrance, with a lot of people running all over the place. Sensing that this might be the president trying to make a break for it, he ordered the gunner, "Send a few dozen rounds at those vehicles at the entrance. I want you to destroy them."

"You're not getting away if I can help it," thought Slater.

In a matter of minutes, they were at the gates of the building, next to the vehicles that were probably meant to whisk the president and his staff away. They weren't going anywhere—they had all been engulfed by flames. Bulldozing their way through the front gate, Slater's group of six Strykers drove right up to the front of the building before they finally stopped. They all jumped out of their vehicles. Slater's first squad engaged the remaining security personnel outside the building, while the other three squads busted their way through the front door of the government edifice. As they ran into the entrance, two of his men were gunned down by a slew of gunfire from the security guards inside.

"Hold up, guys!" yelled Lieutenant Slater. "Toss some grenades in the room, and then we'll charge in."

Sergeant Nassem grabbed two grenades from his chest rig and handed one to the soldier standing next to him. They both pulled the pins on the grenades, counted two seconds and then threw them in.

Boom! Boom!

"Now!" yelled Slater as Sergeant Nassem led his squad into the room. Confusion reigned as many machine guns started firing and voices in both English and Indonesian were shouting to be heard above the din of battle. Seconds after Nassem's squad entered the room, the next squad went in to support them. In less than two minutes, they had cleared the first room and fanned out inside this massive building.

Lieutenant Slater told Nassem and his squad, "Follow me to the roof. We might by chance catch the president trying to escape using a helicopter."

Before they moved, he ordered the other two squads to begin clearing the rooms and rounding up prisoners. As Slater started to head to the stairwell, he spotted Captain Wilkes entering the building from the corner of his eye.

"Good, the rest of the company is here," he thought. *"That's a lot more soldiers to add to the mix."*

Huffing and puffing by the time they got to the top landing of the stairwell that would open up to the roof, they paused to catch their breath and then tossed a couple of grenades through the door. Seconds after the explosions, they ran through the opening onto the roof, expecting to be surrounded by security guards. Instead, there was no one up there at all. They had just blown up the air conditioning units.

Once he realized there was no danger, Lieutenant Slater plopped down on the ground. "Hmm…I guess they either got out another way, or the president had been evacuated before we got here," he said to the soldiers around him, who likewise had sat down on the ground to rest for a second and catch their breath. Lugging eighty pounds of body armor and weapons and a CamelBak up four flights of stairs while fighting your way through an enormous government building was extremely physically exhausting.

After a moment of rest, Slater recovered enough to come up with a new plan. "OK, guys, let's head back down and help the rest of the platoon and company clear the building and round up prisoners."

Before walking down though, Slater took a quick look across the city from the top of the building. He could see black pillars of smoke rising from many areas of the metropolis. He could also hear tons of machine-gun fire and see dozens of red and green tracers bouncing off buildings and armored vehicles, adding to the chaotic scene unfolding all around them. He glanced to the side and saw that most of the other men were likewise transfixed by the scene.

"As much as I want to stand here and look at everything going on, we all need to get back downstairs," Slater said, breaking his own trance. "We still have a job to do, guys."

It took them another hour to round up all the people from within the building. They herded them all into a couple of large rooms and then slowly identified who was who and moved the high-value individuals to a few separate rooms the battalion intelligence folks had set up to question them.

Many of the new prisoners were clearly stunned to see American and Australian soldiers standing in the presidential building. They couldn't fathom how this could have happened so quickly, or how their military had so epically failed them.

****

During the mad dash to capture Jakarta, the US, Australian and New Zealand forces managed to catch the bulk of the government by surprise with the swiftness of their landing at Cirebon. From the time they landed and secured the port and beachhead to the time they advanced on Jakarta, only roughly nineteen hours had elapsed. The

Indonesian Army had been confident the Allies would wait to advance on the city until they had offloaded all their armored units and other forces, and they had figured they would have at least two full days to get the city prepared to meet the invaders. They were caught completely by surprise by how fast the Allies just rushed units straight from the port to the capital.

The lightning dash netted the Allies the Vice President of Indonesia, the Indonesian Minister of Defense, the Minister of Foreign Affairs and the majority of the cabinet. The president had been able to escape and had made it to Malaysia before being flown away to China, where he'd attempt to set up a government in exile. With the capture of the majority of the government officials, the Vice President, who was considered the leader of the country by the majority of the people, ordered the Minister of Defense to order the surrender of Indonesian forces to the Allies. There was no reason to lose any more civilians or soldiers to a war that, for them, was already lost.

Eastern Alliance Reckoning

Beijing, China

President Xi wasn't in a panic just yet, but he was having some serious doubts about the outcome of the war. Just one year ago, it had looked like Operation Red Storm was truly going to prevail. While defeat was not certain, victory was not nearly as guaranteed as it had been just a few months ago. The loss of their navy meant they could not keep control of the Philippines. It also meant holding on to Formosa was going to be incredibly difficult. His generals had told him the Americans would probably launch an invasion of Formosa before the beginning of the typhoon season, which meant they didn't have a lot of time to prepare. As it was, they were using nearly every vessel they could to ferry munitions, food and other supplies to the island before the Americans completely cut it off.

Sensing his generals staring at him, President Xi stared back at Vice Admiral Ning Sheng, the head of the PLA Navy, and then General Xu Ding, the head of the PLA Air Force.

"I've got half a mind to have these men shot," he thought, *"but I need their expertise if we are to try and salvage this war."*

He took a deep breath and tried a more constructive approach. "Admiral, what more can the Navy do to prevent, or at least contest, the inevitable American invasion of Formosa?" he inquired, not taking his eyes off his top navy man.

Shifting uncomfortably in his seat, Admiral Shen obviously knew he'd have to account for his defeat in the Philippine Sea. Even though his forces had sunk a second American carrier and severely damaged two more, they had been unable to defeat the Americans, and as a consequence had lost nearly eighty percent of his entire surface navy—the navy they had spent the last twenty years building.

"I have ordered our forces to defend the coasts," Admiral Ning responded. "The few remaining submarines I have will operate near our waters and will focus on attacking the American invasion force. We've also moved the remaining Dongfeng-21 anti-ship ballistic missiles to protect Formosa. I've commandeered nearly every ship I could to transport as much supplies as we can to our ground forces there as well. I can't guarantee that the Americans won't severe our supply lines once they begin their invasion, so we're doing our best to make sure the army has as large a supply store built up as possible."

Xi took the information in and briefly made eye contact with Chairman Zhang, who was taking notes, before he turned to look at his Air Force general. "The Americans are gearing up for a major offensive in the Russian Far East and look to make a second attempt to break out of the Korean Peninsula. What is the status of your forces, and what are you doing to slow or stop this from happening?"

General Xu puffed his chest out a bit. "Mr. President, while we haven't secured air supremacy over the Korean Peninsula, we've achieved near parity with the Americans, South Koreans, and Japanese Air Force through working in concert with our surface-to-air missile systems. We've built a multilayered air-defense system that has made it nearly impossible for the Allied air forces to attack further than ten miles from the front lines."

President Xi's face soured. "General, if that were true, then why are American stealth bombers and their B-1 Lancers still hitting our factories and other critical aspects of our economy? The continued destruction of key rail tunnels, roads, and bridges is making it incredibly difficult to transport goods and materials around the country, let alone to support our military fronts. What are you doing to stop this?" he demanded.

"We're working on that, Mr. President," said Xu, a bit more conciliatory. "We know the location the Americans are launching their stealth bombers out of now, and plan on hitting those bases with our new H-20 bombers. We just took delivery of six more a month ago, and now have them ready for combat. We've been hesitant to use them up to this point because we didn't have enough of them to really carry out an effective raid on their bases. My intent was to wait until we had enough H-20s to deliver a devastating blow to the American stealth bombers. Now that I am confident we can do that, I am establishing the plans for a raid that will take place within the month."

"Fine," said Xi in a passive-aggressive tone. "Whatever you have to do to eliminate this problem, do it. We have to stop these incursions by their stealth bombers. Their attacks were pinpricks the first few months of the war—now they're turning into the death by a thousand cuts. It needs to stop."

General Xu simply nodded.

Xi then turned his attention to the PLA ground force commander, General Wei Liu, fixing his steely gaze on him. Without saying a word, he had conveyed the message that he wanted to—if General Wei didn't have any good news to report, it might be his last meeting. "General," said Xi after an awkward pause, "has our northern army recovered from your failed attempt at retaking the Korean Peninsula?"

Like Admiral Shen, General Wei shifted uncomfortably in his chair at the reminder of his enormous failure. His "trap" he had laid for the Americans had nearly succeeded, and probably would have, if so many resources hadn't been tied down with the invasion of Taiwan and the Philippines. As it was, his offensive had cost the PLA northern army group nearly 140,000 casualties—something that was impossible to hide from the public eye and had resulted in a lot of angry protests across the country.

"We have, Mr. President," answered General Wei, trying to save face. "Thanks to the reinforcements from the PLA Militia, the northern army group has now swelled to over 600,000 soldiers. We've also pulled nearly 3,000 T-62 tanks out of our reserve force and performed the necessary modifications to get them combat ready. I know the Americans have been building up their forces for a multipronged attack, and so have I. If you will allow me, I'd like to discuss our strategy to deal with their coming offensive." He was looking for permission to use a version of PowerPoint to visually walk everyone through the plan.

Xi softened his face a bit and nodded for General Wei to begin. "*Perhaps the fool has learned his lesson and may still have a use,*" he thought, although he made mental plans to speak with General Yang who was commanding the southern forces, in case he needed a replacement.

Turning the presentation on, General Wei brought up the first map. "The Americans have broken their forces down into three main army groups. Army Group Two is currently in Korea, and they're planning to launch a massive 100-kilometer-wide attack within the next six weeks," he explained.

Chairman Zhang interrupted to ask, "—How do you know it will begin within six weeks? My sources tell me the Americans will try to coincide their northern offensive with the invasion of Formosa."

Everyone's eyes shifted back and forth from Chairman Zhang, the deputy head of State Security, and the PLA ground force commander, not sure who might be telling the truth.

"Mr. Chairman, your source may be correct, and I'm not disputing what your intelligence has discovered. The PLA has several sources within the South Korean Army and the Japanese Defense Force that have given us a rough timeline of when their forces will be attacking China. They told us the timeline could shift, but it would happen plus or minus two weeks of the dates they gave us. That may very well coincide with the timeline for the invasion of Formosa," he said, doing his best to play both sides of the fence.

When no one else said anything, General Wei continued. "Prior to the American breakout of Korea, the Americans' First Army Group, which is currently in the Russian Far East, plans to launch an offensive to capture the Russian city of Irkutsk. If they're able to do this, it'll place a very large contingent of American soldiers dangerously deep behind our lines. When the Americans start their offensive in Russia, then we can anticipate them also launching their breakout of the Korean Peninsula within the following couple of weeks," he said and then brought up another slide that talked in greater detail about how they planned on dealing with the Americans once they did invade again.

The discussion lasted for another thirty minutes before Xi asked another question. "Your plan appears to be sound, at least on paper, but right now, you're relying on the Americans overstretching their supply lines. If there is one thing the Americans are masters at in war, it's logistics. How do you believe your strategy will account for that?"

"We've pondered that question a lot, Mr. President," said General Wei. "You're correct—the Americans are masters at logistics. It's perhaps their greatest strength. The only things that we have in great abundance are time and distance. Our supply lines from the factory to the front lines are short, so we can keep our men supplied faster and easier. That is not the case for the Americans."

Wei took a swig of water before he went on. "We're going to let them advance until they hit the Beizhen Line. As I've briefed before, we've built a defensive line from the outskirts of Panjin to Hure. This line is 220 kilometers in length and has been built and fortified for the past seven months with around-the-clock work crews and engineers. We have underground tunnels, bunkers, artillery positions, antiaircraft guns, missiles, and everything we need to prevent the Americans from getting through and threatening Beijing. We decided on this line after the Americans destroyed Shenyang with a nuclear bomb, destroying all but only a handful of routes the American ground forces could travel to threaten Beijing. In addition, a large swath of that area is still radioactive, which means they won't be able to have their forces stay there. We've focused the bulk of our defenses on the most likely avenues of attack, and I am confident that our men have been extremely thorough."

"Hmm...," said President Xi, deep in thought.

"More importantly, this frees up our armored forces to cover the northern passes between Changchun and Harbin, which is far better tank country," General Wei asserted. "Again, my biggest concern is not so much with the forces in front of us—it's with that American army group in Siberia. If they're able to break through the Russian lines and decide to push down into Mongolia, then that could be disastrous. Our armored and mechanized infantry divisions are going to be protecting Harbin and Changchun; they won't be able to turn and meet an American army group in our rear area without collapsing my northern front."

Chairman Zhang spoke up at this point to add, "I've been assured by the Russians and our Indian allies that they will be able to stop the Americans. The Indians have moved a substantial part of their army to Siberia over the last five months. They should be able to defeat the Americans," he said convincingly. The others seemed pleased with this information, and the threat of this army group wasn't discussed any further.

Satisfied with the brief, President Xi dismissed everyone except Zhang. He wanted to talk further with him about some personnel changes that may need to happen. The two men deliberated over potential successors to the current heads of the navy, air force and army, should these commanders fail them again. Xi was particularly interested in finding new, younger, more talented generals that had proven themselves in the war thus far, and more importantly, would be loyal to Xi and Zhang. These recent defeats had weakened both of their standings, and this wasn't something either of them could allow to go on.

Cowboys and Indians

Russian Far East
Mukhorshibir, Russian Steppe

General Tony Wilde had been put in charge of the US First Army Group, which had formed around the original I Corps, or "Eye Corps." Once the Marines had been ordered to the South Pacific, he had moved his soldiers from the Korean front to the Russian Far East. It had been a real challenge in the spring to get the entire Corps and Army Group formed up and ready for combat. I Corps, like the other army commands, had essentially doubled in size with all of the draftees arriving by the thousands per day. When his army group surpassed 180,000 troops, General Wilde felt ready to take the Indian Army head-on and defeat them. Now he was poring over maps, reviewing the battle plans.

All that stood between him and the Russian city of Irkutsk was the newly formed Indian Fifth Army. While the Russians had been fighting a delaying action against his forces, the Indians had consolidated their army near Irkutsk. Once his forces had pushed the Russians to within a few hundred miles of Irkutsk, the Indian Army finally moved forward to meet the Americans.

Intelligence indicated the strength of the combined Russian-Indian Army to be somewhere around 240,000 soldiers, a solid 60,000 soldiers more than the Americans they were gearing up to battle. However, the American soldiers were battle-hardened, not just from the recent fighting in Korea, but the decades of fighting in Iraq and Afghanistan. What General Wilde lacked was a sufficient number of vehicles to allow the majority of his forces to be mobile. He had to rely heavily on helicopters to transport troops near their objectives, and then they had to move in on foot. This lack of necessary equipment was the one area that concerned General Wilde the most, but it was also the one area he had no control over until the factories back home were able to produce the needed tools to support such a massive army fighting in both Europe and Asia.

Brigadier General Sam Sykes got his attention as he pointed to sections on the digital map. "Sir, the latest reports from the field show the Indians are deploying their armor units here, here and here," he explained.

Wilde nodded. "Those are good positions. It gives them a lot of maneuver room," he replied and then ran his hand across the map along the road that led to this particular plateau.

"*This is good tank country,*" he concluded privately.

"Deploy our tanks here but do not engage," General Wilde suggested. "The Indians are using T-72s. Those tanks do not have nearly the reach ours do. Let's draw them in to us and then snipe at them from a distance." He looked around the room to see if there were any objections from the group or any possible considerations he might have missed.

Brigadier General Todd Jackson spoke up. "If we deploy the tanks there, then we should move some of our antitank vehicles and troops to these locations here," he explained, pointing. "This will protect our flanks. My concern with luring the enemy armor closer to us is that they outnumber us a good six to one. By placing our antitank units *here*, we not only protect our flanks, but we'll be able to hammer them when their reserve units charge forward in a pincer move."

General Wilde smiled. "I knew there was a reason why we invited you tankers to these strategy meetings," he said to a few laughs and head nods.

"Well, someone needs to make sure headquarters knows what's going on out there," General Jackson replied with a wry smile.

General Wilde put a lot of stock in anything Jackson said—he was a brilliant tanker. He commanded the newly reconstituted 4th Armored Division, which had famously spearheaded General Patton's charge at the Battle of the Bulge during World War II. General Jackson had commanded a tank brigade during the early days of the Second Korean War and had fought with great distinction. His reward had been taking command of this newly constituted and largely inexperienced division in the Russian Far East.

"If I could, General, I'd also like to recommend that we place a battalion of self-propelled 155mm Howitzers, our Paladin unit, in this area here," Jackson said, pointing to an area a few kilometers back from where the battle would take place. "This gives the guns space to maneuver when they take counterbattery fire and still keeps them close enough to hit the enemy's rear area."

General Wilde nodded. "No objection here," he said.

Since General Jackson had received one ask, he decided to push for two. "I was also made aware that the 57th Field Artillery Brigade had recently been equipped with the new M142 high-mobility artillery rocket system or HIMARs," he said. "When the enemy moves their armored force ten kilometers into the bulge, I'd like your permission to have the entire brigade's worth of HIMARs launch their antitank rockets. Saturating the enemy advance with hundreds of 227mm rockets will hammer them right before I unleash my ambush."

Looking at the map, and at the units he had available for this coming battle, General Wilde nodded in agreement again. "I think that's a good plan. Once the enemy armor has spent themselves, we'll need to go on the offensive, and this still keeps that battalion close enough to the front, so they can catch up when we advance and still provide good artillery coverage."

General Wilde signaled for his Air Force liaison officer, or LNO, and his Army aviation LNO to come join them at the table. He addressed the Air Force LNO first. "Colonel, it's going to be imperative that you flyboys keep the Indian fighters and ground-attack aircraft off our backs during this battle. I've heard nothing but good things about those Jaguar aircraft, and that is the last thing we need hitting our tanks. Plus, if you can't keep the skies clear, I can't make heavy use of our own Apache helicopters and the handful of A-10s. Do you foresee a problem with being able to keep the skies open?"

When the US Seventh Fleet had moved to the South Pacific along with the Marines, it had placed a much larger burden on the Air Force to provide air cover for the Allied forces. Fortunately, a Japanese squadron of F-15s had joined

504

them in Russia, but what they really needed was a couple of squadrons of F-22s or F-35s—two aircraft that were in hot demand all across Europe and Asia.

"We're going to do our best, General. We've got the Japanese tasked with high-altitude combat air patrols while a squadron of F-16s will handle the Jaguars. The best news I can give you is that the two squadrons of aircraft we have assigned for this battle are at 100% strength and have combat experience against the Russians," the Air Force colonel offered, trying to reassure everyone present that they would do their part.

Sighing, Wilde reached down, grabbed his mug of coffee and took a couple of gulps. "This is going to be a tough battle, gentlemen, but it's one we can win. The enemy may outnumber us, but let's not forget, they're largely using older-model Russian equipment—equipment we know we can defeat. Our soldiers are better trained, better equipped and highly motivated to go kick some butt. Take some time and go over the plans with your own staffs. This offensive will get underway in a couple of days," Wilde concluded.

Once they all left the room, the planning officers and division commanders went about implementing the plan they had just discussed. Wilde was hopeful, but he was also hedging his optimism with a heavy dose of realism.

****

Tarbagatay, Eastern Siberia

Brigadier General Todd Jackson was taking a few minutes to be alone in his tent before the day went into full gear. It was his twelve-year-old son's birthday in ten days, and he wanted to make sure he took some time out of his day to write a personal letter, just in case something did happen and he didn't make it back home. Pulling his pen out of his breast pocket, he wrote:

Son,

You are growing into a wonderful and strong young man. I know the past few years have been tough on you with our recent move, but I need you to be strong for your mother and your sister.

There's so much I want to tell you, and I promise when I return home from this war, we'll take a few days for just you and me to talk. We'll go to Grandpa's cottage and do some fishing. No phones, no emails, no work, just the two of us.

I hope you enjoy your birthday party with your friends. I wish I could be there for it. Turning thirteen is a big milestone. You're now a teenager, and I couldn't be prouder of how well you've turned out. I brag about you as often as I can to my friends here and tell them all about that huge fish you caught last summer at Grandpa's place. I can't wait to see pictures of your party when Mom posts them on Facebook.

Stay safe, and go easy on your mom and sister. This has been hard on them as well. I love you, more than you will ever know.

Love, Dad

Placing his pen down, he gently folded the piece of paper and placed it in an envelope he had addressed earlier. After he peeled the self-adhesive strip and sealed it up, the letter was ready to send back home.

It was now 0530, time to get some breakfast before the division pulled up stakes and headed toward the first major battle of US and Indian forces in the two nations' history. Walking into the field kitchen, he got in line with the others for some morning grub. "*Ah, the smell of fresh bacon, biscuits n'gravy, and black coffee...this is the best part of being a soldier in the field*," he thought. Well, that and shooting tanks at the range.

Prior to the beginning of hostilities, he had planned to retire in December after twenty-eight years of military service. He had risen to O-6 colonel and commanded an armor brigade. When the war had started, his retirement papers had been withdrawn, and he'd been told he would be given his first star. He was to command a large armored force in Korea, as part of I Corps, moved to the Korean Peninsula in preparation for the Second Korean War.

That was eight months ago. Now his division had moved from Korea to the Russian Far East. Never in a million years had he thought he'd be leading an armor division into Russia-Siberia, but here he was, preparing for a massive tank battle that would take place near a small Russian village he hadn't known existed just a few weeks ago. The battle, of course, had been brewing for some time as the three factions maneuvered their forces, angling to find the right ground from which to do battle.

Walking into the back of his command vehicle, General Jackson looked for his operations officer, a charismatic young lieutenant colonel who had risen quickly through the ranks of the Minnesota Army National Guard. In the private sector, the man worked for Amazon as an operations manager. Thus far, he had proven himself to be an adept operations staff officer.

"General, here's the latest intelligence report on the enemy troop movement," said the colonel. "They've moved their armor and supporting units to the exact location you said they would. The enemy has deployed their formations and should be advancing to meet ours within the hour."

Jackson smiled. He had used one of his battalions as bait the day before, and now the enemy was advancing right into his well-laid trap. "*I knew they would go for it*," he thought.

"Excellent, Paul," Jackson responded. "Send the order to the rest of the division. The enemy has taken the bait. Prepare for contact." It was now a matter of letting things play out and adjusting to the enemy's movements and countermoves.

****

Captain Bennie McRae, captain of Charlie Company, yawned. He had just finished brushing his teeth, so he quickly spat the toothpaste residue out onto the ground in front of him. He reached over, grabbing his canteen. He took in some water, sloshing it around in his mouth before spitting it out as well on the ground as well. That task complete, it was time to do a quick shave before they moved out. McRae grabbed the portable electric shaver from his little toiletry bag and ran the vibrating blades across the stubble that had grown in during the last thirty hours. *"This might be the last time I shave for the next couple of days,"* he thought as he ran over the day's plan of action in his head.

His battalion was going to be advancing to contact with the enemy. Once they ran into the opposing force, his battalion would conduct a fighting retreat, hopefully luring the enemy to the well-placed trap the division had set up.

"You ready to get moving, Sir?" inquired Captain McRae's gunner, Sergeant Justin Spence.

Placing the last few items back in his bag, McRae looked up with a grin on his face. "Yup. Face is as soft as a baby's butt," he replied as he ran his hand across the now-stubble-free skin on his face.

Sergeant Spence shook his head, sporting a half smile. Then he placed his foot in the cable stirrup hanging from the bottom of the front ballistic skirt, reached for the metal handle welded to the top of the fender and pulled himself upon the hull of the tank. He climbed onto the turret, dropped down the loader's hatch, and moved to his gunner seat, which was positioned in front of the commander's position.

McRae did likewise, and less than a minute later had plopped down in the commander's position in the tank. Reaching over, he grabbed his CVC helmet, placing it firmly on his head. He attached the communications cord to the vehicle's communications system and then did a quick crew report check with his crew before reaching out to the other vehicles in his company.

"OK, guys. Let's get this bad boy ready to go," McRae announced. "It's nearly time to roll out. Crew report!"

A few minutes went by as the individual crewmen ran through their various checks to make sure the targeting computer was up and running, the radios were set on the right frequencies for the day, and they had entered in the various navigational waypoints they'd be working off of for the next couple of days. Having completed their checks, all three crewmen reported ready, and it was time to get moving.

Changing to the company net, Captain McRae called out to his company, "This is Black Six to all Guidon elements. We're moving out in three mikes. I want a wedge formation with Blue Platoon in the middle, Red Platoon on the right and White Platoon on the left in echelon formation. Acknowledge and send Redcon status." he inquired of his platoon leaders.

"This is White One. Roger, Second Platoon is Redcon One," said Sergeant First Class Mark Moore, who commanded Second Platoon.

"This is Blue One. Acknowledged, and we're at Redcon One," said Sergeant First Class Bobby Rickets, the sergeant in charge of Third Platoon, which consisted of the attached infantry platoon in the Bradleys. The Third Platoon also had the company artillery LNO, riding in his own fire support team vehicle, a Bradley Fist, which was why Captain McRae wanted them placed in the center of their formation.

"This is Red One. Red is Redcon One and ready to get some," answered the young second lieutenant in command of First Platoon.

"Black Six, this is Black Five. We are Redcon One," reported his executive officer, First Lieutenant Charley Smith.

"Roger, Guidons, begin your movement," said Captain McRae.

In short order, his company team of tanks and Bradleys quickly formed a wedge and moved forward down the side of the P-258 highway toward the enemy. Intelligence said they were roughly sixty kilometers away, so they had a few minutes before they would run into each other. As his company of tanks and Bradleys continued to move toward the enemy, Captain McRae couldn't help but think back to just five months ago.

His Minnesota Army National Guard unit, the 1st Combined Arms Battalion, 194th Armor had just completed an intense armor refresher course at Fort Benning, Georgia. One of their instructors, Major Joe Dukes, or "JD" as he preferred to be called, had been awarded the Medal of Honor. He often regaled them of tales of tank battles he had taken part of against the Russians; McRae couldn't help but marvel at what this guy must have seen and lived through. What he'd said always carried a lot more weight than any of the other instructors, so at this moment, McRae had his words burned into his mind: "When in doubt, attack without mercy."

As their tank rumbled down the field next to the two-lane road, his gunner keyed the intercom on his CVC helmet. "Captain McRae, you think your finance job at the dealership will still be there for you when we get back from the war?" he asked, trying to take their minds off the inevitable battle.

The mention of the car dealership immediately brought McRae back home. While in college, he'd worked part-time selling cars for a Chevy dealership in town. Once he'd finished his degree in finance, a position for assistant finance manager at the dealership had opened up. He had talked to the general manager about it and had been hired for the position. Three years later, he had been promoted to finance manager for the entire dealership and had personally been doing extremely well financially. He loved helping families and individuals acquire the financing to purchase the vehicle they either needed or dreamed of having. Of course, being gone and fighting in this war might have placed that position in jeopardy. Someone needed to fill in for him while he was gone, and the longer he was gone, the more the current managers might take a liking to that person over him. It concerned him, especially since he had four little kids to think about.

"I think they will, Spence. At least I hope they will," said McRae. "I've worked with the general manager for eleven years and know the owner well. I send them a short note every now and then to remind them that I'm still alive and kicking. What about you? Is your boss still holding your job for you?"

"Yeah, I'm pretty sure they will. If they don't, I'll sue," the gunner shot back, which brought some laughter from the others in the tank. Sergeant Justin Spence worked as a pharmaceutical rep for a large drug company. Judging by the Maserati he drove to drill weekends, he must have been pretty good at his job. He always picked up the tab when they'd go to a bar after training in Georgia.

Forty minutes went by as their tank rumbled through the prairie when they heard the first sounds of war. A jet engine roared overhead. "Whoa, what was that?" asked Specialist Gary Kostic, the loader.

"Probably just a jet on his way to attack the Indians," replied Spence, trying to calm the young kid's nerves. Specialist Gary Kostic was the newest member to their company, having arrived as a replacement roughly five weeks ago. The team wasn't exactly coddling him, but they were trying to help ease the transition a bit.

Captain McRae opted to poke his head out of the tank to see if he could catch a glimpse at the aircraft that had just buzzed over them. He heard several jets: some were close, others far off in the distance. Looking to his right, he saw one aircraft explode in the air. That was the first time he had witnessed a fighter plane die, and while it was spectacular to look at, it suddenly sent a shiver down his back. "The enemy must be close," he said under his breath.

A voice came over the battalion net. "All units, enemy planes in the vicinity. Expect enemy contact at anytime."

Returning his gaze to the front, Captain McRae caught sight of the silhouette of an aircraft swooping up and over him and several objects falling from beneath its wings, right toward his company of tanks. Reaching for the talk button on his headset, he yelled, "Guidons! Incoming bombs from enemy warplanes!"

He ducked into the tank, and the ground around his tank suddenly rocked hard from one explosion after another. McRae grabbed for anything that would help him stabilize himself as he prayed none of the bombs landed on him or any of his tankers or infantry.

Seconds later, Sergeant Spence yelled out, "Tanks to our front, 3,500 meters!"

Turning to look at the commander's sight extension, Captain McRae at once spotted a line of tanks deploying from a single-file line to a full battle line, just as they had been told a lot of the Russian-equipped militaries did with their T-72s. "Holy crap, that's a lot of tanks!" he exclaimed.

He switched to the company net. "Guidons, enemy tanks to our front, 3,500 meters. I want all tanks to change formation and move to a line formation. We're going to snipe at them while they advance. Engage when you see my tank fire!"

He turned his attention next to his FIST team. "Black Eight, this is Black Six. I need a fire mission. Get us some arty immediately!"

Captain McRae then switched back to the battalion net, sending a quick message to his commander letting him know what they were seeing and asking if it would be possible to get some air support.

"Captain those tanks are charging!" alerted Sergeant Spence. "They're crossing 3,200 meters." The turret turned slightly to the right as it tracked their first target.

Looking into the commander's sight, McRae saw the cluster of T-72s his gunner was tracking, and he picked out the one with the most antennas on it—it was probably the company or battalion commander's tank. "Gunner Sabot Tank!" he ordered.

"Identified!" exclaimed Sergeant Spence.

Specialist Kostic yelled, "Sabot up!"

"Fire!" screamed McRae.

"On the way!" shouted Sergeant Spence.

Boom!

The cannon fired, recoiling back inside the turret as the vehicle rocked back on the tank's tracks. The spent aft cap of the sabot round clanged on the turret floor as the turret filled with sulfuric fumes after the round was fired.

McRae watched the round fly out from his tank, the flat trajectory crossing the distance in a couple of seconds, only to see the round sail right over the tank and hit the dirt harmlessly, right behind the tank.

"Crap! We missed," he yelled. "Load Sabot. Spence, manually adjust for the speed of the enemy tank and lead it a bit."

Now that he had led the way and fired the first shot, Captain McRae watched the rest of his company fire on the enemy. A couple of his fellow tankers also missed their targets, but many more found their marks. The turrets of some of the T-72s blew clean off from the sheer force of the

Sabot rounds, slicing through their armor and setting off their own ammunition. He made a mental note to ensure that all his tanks do a complete boresight when time permitted, to avoid further misses in any future engagements.

"Sabot up!" shouted the loader as he pulled up the arming handle.

"Fire!" ordered McRae.

"On the way!" yelled Spence as he depressed the firing button again.

This time the round found its mark, and the tank they had originally aimed at took a direct hit. The enemy tank slowly came to a halt. Seconds later, the top hatch opened up, and as McRae watched the enemy soldier try to get out of the vehicle, it blew up. A flaming jet of fire shot through the enemy soldier and blasted past the turret, blazing at least ten feet in the air before the entire structure of the tank was ripped apart by another explosion.

"Good hit, Spence! New target identified. Load Sabot," he bellowed.

While Captain McRae's company was steadily picking off the attackers, their tanks received a series of enemy artillery rounds, indicating they had stayed still in one place for too long.

"Guidons, pop smoke and fall back two hundred meters," he directed over the company net. They needed to obscure the enemy artillery observers and back out of their crosshairs.

Crump! Crump! Crump! Crump! Explosions continued to rock their area as pieces of shrapnel pinged off their armor shell.

"Doppler, back us out of this artillery," McRae said to his own driver as he toggled his own tank's smoke grenade launchers.

"Those tanks are now 3,100 meters. We'll be in their range momentarily," Spence yelled to be heard over the roar of enemy artillery going off around them.

"This is all happening too fast," muttered McRae.

Looking through the commander's sight extension, Captain McRae found the next target just as he observed a series of their own artillery rounds landing amongst the enemy tanks. Some of the rounds scored hits, while others did not. Taking his eyes away from the commander's sight, he looked at Spence. "I need you to take over calling targets and engaging them. I have to start managing the company," he said. Then he turned his attention his computer tracking system, which let him see an electronic overview of where his tanks were.

He needed to get a status on his platoons and find out how many of his tanks had been hit. In all the confusion, he had neglected his duty to make sure the other platoons were doing what they were supposed to do. As he made contact with his platoon leaders, he learned they had lost two tanks to that enemy air attack. One other tank was destroyed during the enemy artillery bombardment and one more damaged. He quickly got on the radio relaying the information back to battalion headquarters, once again requesting an air strike to hit the enemy force advancing on him. He also ordered his medics and first sergeant to evacuate as many of the wounded as they could. The dead would have to wait.

When Captain McRae was just about finished relaying the information to his battalion commander, his tank was jarred hard. He knocked his head against the commander's extension, causing him to momentarily see stars.

"It bounced off our armor," someone yelled as McRae tried to regain his composure and continue to relay his report. It took a second for his mind to register what had just happened.

His battalion commander interrupted his fuzzy thoughts. "Charlie Six, I'm ordering your unit to withdraw to rally point Bravo now. You guys are about to be overrun. Fall back now!" he yelled.

Realizing his commander was right, McRae snapped out of his head fog and sent a message out to the rest of his company to fall back to rally point Bravo.

Their driver plugged in the coordinates, and they began a fighting retreat rearward. As they fought their way back, they would eventually cross the next line of American tanks as they continued to make their way further back in the intentional bulge in their lines they were letting the enemy carve out. Once the Indian forces had pushed their way deep into the bulge, the division would close the trap, and if the Americans were lucky, they'd destroy a large chunk of the Indian Army in Russia.

****

Russian Far East
Mukhorshibir, Russian Steppe

General Jackson looked on in amazement as the tank battle continued to unfold on the digital monitor they had set up in his makeshift 4th Armored Division headquarters. His forward tank elements did a phenomenal job luring the enemy in. The Indian Army seemed to sense hesitation on the Americans' part; once they saw a battalion of American tanks retreat, they must have assumed they had broken the Americans will to fight and now wanted to press their attack. They ordered one brigade after another into the ever-growing bulge in the American lines.

Five hours into the attack, it looked like the entire center of the American lines was in the process of falling apart. The division's PSYOPS and signals intelligence group were sending out frantic calls for reinforcements, saying that the tanks were running out of ammunition and fuel. They did their best to spread general hysteria over the open net and frequencies they knew the Indian Army could intercept. This must have caused the enemy commanders to believe they were on the verge of an American collapse if they could just press the Americans a little further.

Six hours into their offensive, the Indians sent in their third brigade of enemy tanks into the bulge, which had now expanded to fifteen miles deep.

Jackson turned to his air operations LNO. "I think it's time we send you flyboys into the soup," he said.

The LNO smiled. The Air Force had a couple squadrons of new tank busters they wanted to test on the Indian Army. He made a call to the airfield to release the hounds.

The Air Force had been terribly short on ground-attack aircraft since the commencement of the war, and there weren't enough A-10 Warthogs to go around. The A-10s had also been taking some terrible losses in Europe and Asia, which were taking a long time to replace as older airframes were still being pulled out of mothball and made ready for combat. Searching for a stopgap, the Air Force had ordered 1,000 Beechcraft AT-6 Wolverine turboprop ground-attack planes.

The Wolverine was unique in that it was the first turboprop aircraft the Air Force would be using in combat since the Vietnam war. It had a large glass bubble canopy, which provided exceptional visibility for both the pilot and the weapons officer. Because it was a turboprop as opposed to a jet engine, it could land and take off on a much shorter runway. It could also operate on some pretty rugged airstrips, which made it highly suitable to the hostile environment of Siberia. Although the Wolverine was incredibly inexpensive in comparison to its jet counterparts, it still packed a lethal punch.

Once the Air Force had torn into the enemy tanks, it would then be time for the four battalions of tanks that General Jackson had lying in wait on the outer edges of his flank to move into position and prepare to close the trap.

For the next forty-five minutes, the brigade he had at the center of his line continued to fall back, giving ground to keep drawing the enemy in. Then the two squadrons of Wolverines swept in and began to hit the enemy positions. Each of the Wolverines had been armed with four Hellfire antitank missiles and antimateriel rocket pods. The 32 turboprop planes flew in fast, just above treetops, hitting the enemy's frontal attack units with their Hellfires and then hammering the rear-echelon units with their rockets.

As the AT-6s turned for home, several Indian MiGs swooped in and managed to down four of the Wolverines before a pair of Japanese F-15Js shot them down and covered the withdrawal of the remaining ground-attack planes.

Once the Air Force had hit the Indians, General Jackson sent a message to his hidden tank battalions that it was time to swing the gate shut on their pincer movement and finish the enemy off. It was time to stop retreating and stand and fight.

The following three hours were complete chaos as nearly 320 American tanks and three times that many Indian tanks fought it out on the fields of Siberia in what was probably the largest tank battle of the war in Asia. The American AT-6s returned several more times, adding their own carnage and so did several dozen Indian Jaguars and

MiGs. As the day turned to evening, the battle continued, only it turned decisively in the favor of the Americans whose tanks were better equipped to fight in the dark and had trained extensively in this type of environment. The lone squadron of Apache helicopters General Jackson had also torn into the remaining enemy vehicles, using their specially equipped night and thermal targeting equipment.

By the time the sun came up the following morning, the Indian armored force that had been the tip of the spear the previous day now lay as a burning graveyard strewn across the nearly 400 square-mile battlefield. It was the single greatest combat loss the Indian Army had ever experienced up to that point. More than a thousand tanks and another two thousand armored vehicles had been destroyed. Over five thousand Indian soldiers had been killed, while another seven thousand had been captured.

With the defeat of five Indian armor divisions at the hands of the US 4th AD, General Wilde's First Army Group was quickly able to encircle the remaining Indian Army group and tighten his noose on the enemy force.

****

Captain McRae rubbed his hand across the front armor of the turret, noticing the dents and gashes from hits they'd taken the day before. By all accounts, he and his crew should be dead. Their tank had been hit no less than three times, but their armor had held. Unfortunately, not all of the other tankers in his company had fared as well, and many of his fellow comrades in arms had died.

"*Why did I live when so many of my soldiers did not?*" he asked himself. He wiped away a tear. Suddenly overtaken by emotion, he sank to his knees on top of the turret.

Sergeant Justin Spence walked around to the front of the tank, and they locked eyes for a brief moment. When Captain McRae realized that someone had seen him cry, he wiped away his tears and pulled himself up.

"It's OK, Sir," said Spence. "We've all thought the same thing. Why were we so lucky to live when so many died?" It was as if he was reading his captain's mind.

McRae nodded. "We were hit three times. How did we survive? I lost seven of my ten tanks and one of my five Bradleys yesterday—men we've known in many cases for years. How do I explain to their families that we lived, and they died, Spence?"

"Sir, I know it's tough, but Charlie is still here, and Charlie don't surf!" said Sergeant Spence.

Captain McRae smiled slightly when Sergeant Spence mentioned the unofficial company's motto.

"Yeah, Charlie don't surf, but Charlie can fight and die...," McRae mumbled to himself.

A second later, the radio inside the turret crackled to life. "Charlie Six, this is Cowboy-Six." Shaking off the moment of sadness, Captain McRae reached down inside the commander's hatch for his CVC.

"This is Charlie Six. Go ahead Cowboy Six," he said in reply to his battalion commander's call.

"I need your tanks to return to the rear area and resupply. Come see me when you get here. Out."

Captain McRae put down the radio with a bit of a grunt. "Great, that's all I need," he said, muttering to himself. "Go see the battalion commander—he's probably going to chew my butt off over the loss of more than half of my command."

Looking at the rest of his crew, McRae announced, "Saddle up, boys. We're headed to the rear with the gear."

The others nodded and climbed back in. His driver, Private Edgar Doppler, started the tank up and moved toward the rear of the American positions. The remaining three tanks and four Bradleys of his company followed as they made their way back. While driving down the road, they drove past hundreds of Allied vehicles that had not participated in the battle yet. Many of the crewmen who were standing in their turrets looked at them in amazement, seeing the battle scars on their tanks. Several of the officers and NCOs rendered salutes out of respect. A column of Type 90 Japanese tanks passed them on their way to the front; the officer standing in his turret even bowed as they passed.

It was strange seeing so many of their own countrymen and allies rendering them respect like this, with the rumblings of war still audible in the distance. These men were heading into the battle, while Captain McRae and his men were leaving it.

Nearly an hour later, their ragtag group of tanks made it back to the marshaling area their battalion had set up in. When Charlie Company pulled in, they saw that Alpha and Bravo Companies had taken some losses as well, though not quite as bad as McRae's unit. When the tank was finally parked, and he checked to ensure what was left of Charlie Company was set in their portion of the battalion's assembly area, Captain McRae made his way to find the battalion CO. It took him a few minutes to find the CO's tank and command vehicles. Once he did, he saw the other company commanders were present as well.

"Ah, there you are, Captain McRae," said Lieutenant Colonel Lewis. "I was hoping you hadn't gotten lost on the way back here. I was about to debrief you all on the battle and what brigade has planned for us next." He walked up to McRae, placing a hand on his shoulder and guiding him toward the map board he had hanging by some five-fifty cord from the tent walls.

Once he had ushered McRae further into the room, Lewis cleared his throat to get everyone's attention. "First off, I want to acknowledge the horrible losses most of you guys suffered yesterday—especially you, Captain McRae. I know Charlie Company took the brunt of the battalion losses and saw the most combat. Your tanks were the tip of the spear for the entire division, and you guys performed marvelously. Your crews performed so well, in fact, that General Jackson wants to meet your men personally and award your crews some valor medals…but we'll discuss that more later," Colonel Lewis said, trying to acknowledge the men's losses but also making sure they knew the battle was not over just yet.

Before anyone else could ask any questions or get sidetracked on anything, Colonel Lewis continued. "When the battle began yesterday, we had no idea how hard or how well the Indians would fight. America's never faced off against the Indian Army, so they were a complete wild card. They showed themselves to be incredibly aggressive and proficient in their weapon systems, even if they are outdated. That said, General Wilde has stated the Indians aren't ready to give up the fight just yet. While the 4th AD continues to encircle the Indian 4th Army Group, the enemy is moving two divisions to our south in an attempt to try and force us to break our encirclement of their army group."

Captain McRae raised his hand. "Sir, I lost 60% of my command, and nearly half of my remaining tanks and Bradleys have extensive battle damage. Shoot, my own tank took three hits, which tore large chunks out of our armor. What are they planning to do with our battalion after we took these heavy losses?" he asked, hoping he hadn't just sunk his career. He felt that he had to ask for the sake of his remaining soldiers.

Lieutenant Colonel Lewis' face fell. He seemed to be overcome with immense sadness. In a calm and reassuring voice, he replied, "I said as much to Brigade. They can't take us off the line entirely, but they're going to hold our battalion in reserve. What I need to know from you guys is how many of your tanks are combat effective, and how many have too much battle damage to continue to fight? I'm going to form a small task force of tanks combining those that are still combat effective to form our reserve force. The rest of you will serve in support functions until your vehicles are ready."

Everyone nodded. Once they had tallied up the tanks that could still fight, they had roughly twelve tanks out of the original thirty-six that were still battle-ready.

The battle in Siberia raged on for another five days before the remnants of the Indian Army withdrew back to Irkutsk to lick their wounds, and to figure out what to do next. With the battle of Siberia largely over, the US First Army Group now turned its attention to Mongolia and the liberation of Ulaanbaatar, the capital of the country. With little in the way of Chinese forces in the area, the capture of Ulaanbaatar wouldn't take long, and the liberation of Mongolia would have the immediate effect of cutting off access to the mineral-rich mines the Chinese factories desperately needed.

The Resistance

South Kingstown, Rhode Island
Peace Dale Shooting Preserve

"Slowly let your breath out and then hold it. Then gently squeeze the trigger," the shooting instructor said calmly as George Philips applied pressure to the trigger.

Bang!

The round hit center mass. "Excellent shot, George!" his instructor said.

Smiling, George felt good about the hit. "Finally," said George with a sigh of relief. "Now I just need to consistently hit the target like that."

The instructor laughed at the comment. "You know, George, when you came here several months ago, you couldn't hit the broad side of a barn. Now you're hitting targets 600 yards away. I think you're more than ready for that corporate hunting trip this fall. No one is going to laugh at you because you can't shoot," he replied.

"Yeah, I guess you're right," George said as he ejected the spent casing out of the chamber and left the bolt open to show that the rifle was unloaded. Then he placed the

Winchester Model 70 rifle on the ground and proceeded to get up.

"It helps that you have an excellent optical sight on that rifle," George's instructor commented. "That Trijicon Accupoint makes all the difference when shooting a target at the distances you guys will be shooting at. I personally love hunting elk out in South Dakota, but man, are they long shots."

"This is going to be my first hunt," George admitted. "Who knows if I'll even see an elk? But at least if I do, I know I'll be able to hit it. Thanks again for all your help; I'll let you know how things go when I get back." George extended his hand and shook his instructor's hand before he finished packing his rifle and other belongings and headed to his car.

Secretly, George hated guns. Like many of his fellow Antifa activists, he was all for taking away people's right to "bear arms." However, he didn't see any other course to stopping this fascist regime from waging their global war than to try and cut the head of the snake off. When George's younger brother shipped off to the Pacific with the Marines, he suddenly felt a sense of urgency to do something.

Once George had decided on his course of action, he researched hunting and the types of rifles used by hunters when they were going to shoot something beyond 400 yards. His investigation led him to elk hunting. Then he looked into the types of rifles and optics used by those types of hunters. Next, George created a cover story for why he had developed a sudden interest in hunting. When he bought his rifle, he found a range that offered training on how to shoot a rifle and used this tall tale about a corporate hunting trip to make it all seem normal.

Every Saturday for the past three months, George had spent between two and four hours at the rifle range with his instructor. With each outing, George became better and more comfortable with the rifle. He even had to admit to himself that he was actually starting to understand why people enjoyed sport shooting. It was fun to hold an object that could reach out and kill something from so far away.

After placing his rifle back into its case, George closed the trunk, got into his vehicle and headed back to his apartment in Providence. Once home, he looked over the map of where the GOP rally was going to be held and felt confident that the Airbnb room he had rented would give him the best vantage point for what he was going to do. Now it was a matter of waiting until the appointed time.

"Hang in there, little brother," he thought as he looked at a picture of his kid brother. *"This war will end soon enough."*

****

Aboard Air Force One

"Someone, please tell me what the heck is going on in Great Britain?" demanded the President.

Secretary of State Travis Johnson looked exhausted and haggard as he stared back at the President. He shook his head before responding, "I honestly don't know, Sir. I think something is seriously wrong inside Prime Minister Chattem's office. It was one thing for them to withdraw from the war and sue for a separate peace, but to try and intern our forces operating on the bases we're leasing from them is going too far," he replied.

Jim Castle, who was speaking to them through a secure video conference from the Pentagon, broke in to add, "This is ludicrous, Mr. President, *and* illegal. We have base rights to use those bases as we see fit. Furthermore, the United Kingdom had agreed to allow us to use those bases in defense of Europe. They cannot simply renege on the agreements!" he added angrily.

"They've already reneged on their treaty obligations with the Global Defense Force. Why should we expect them to honor our basing rights?" said the National Security Advisor in a snarky voice.

"I'm with Secretary Johnson on this one," said Jedediah Perth, the Director of the CIA. He was also joining via teleconference. "I think there is more going on behind the scenes in 10 Downing Street than we are aware of. I have no proof, but a friend of mine who works for MI5 believes something is amiss with the PM. They're currently looking into the situation, but right now, they say it's completely out of character that he would be issuing this threat."

Gates nodded. "JP, continue to look into this further," he ordered. "Find out what's going on. Maybe the Russians somehow got to Chattem and have him over a barrel. Something just isn't right with what's going on over there."

"I've had more than a few generals reach out to me, Mr. President, saying the mood within the Ministry of Defense is rather foul," Castle added. "While they wouldn't openly talk about removing Chattem from power, there's a lot of grumbles about what he's doing. One of the generals—I won't say his name—did say that if the PM was to order the MOD to intern our forces, they would not obey that order. He said they may have to cease fighting the Russians, but they won't lift a finger to help the Russians defeat us or Europe."

Leaning forward, the President put his head in his hands for a moment. "Gentlemen, we will have to come back to this…what is the status of our operations in Europe?"

Clearing his throat before beginning, Secretary Castle answered, "We've launched Operation Nordic Thunder. General Cotton's forces are now pushing the Russians out of the Nordic countries. They've encountered resistance, but by and large, the Russians are giving ground without much of a fight. We anticipate that changing as we get closer to the actual Russian border."

The President nodded.

Castle continued. "As to the Continent—the French, German and Polish armies are set to launch Operation Eisenadler, which means Iron Eagle. The name was agreed upon by the three countries, so we're letting them run with it. While General Cotton is overseeing the operation, it's largely being led by the Bundeswehr. The offensive will start in a week and will begin the liberation of Ukraine. We're still hoping that Operation Strawman will ultimately succeed, and we won't need to invade Russia directly."

Sensing that he should provide some sort of update on the covert action to remove Petrov, JP jumped into the conversation. "We're still moving forward in that direction. As you know, we've encountered a couple of recent problems, mainly with the withdrawal of the British from the war. Part of the operation was being run by MI6, who have been ordered home. The direct handling of Strawman is still being carried out by the Germans, while the digital arm and funding are being carried out by us. It's hard to gain outside coverage of what's going on inside Russia, but what's managed to leak or get out has shown a lot of civil unrest among the population."

"Do tell," said the President.

"The majority of the civilians are still in support of the war, but they're mad at how long it's dragged out and how it's negatively affecting their daily lives," JP answered. "The shortages in fuel and food are having the desired effect, so we should keep that pressure on. What has caused a mixed reaction in the country right now is the arrival of the Indian troops. While India and Russia have always had a good working relationship politically and economically, this is the first time the average Russian has seen large numbers of Indian people inside Russia."

JP took a swig of coffee before he continued. "Right now, the Indian Army is largely being deployed along the actual Russian border, as opposed to inside Ukraine or the Nordic States. They appear to be fortifying the border and building a series of defense-in-depth positions to force our troops to have to travel down specific routes they want us to. Secretary Castle can probably talk more about this angle than I can."

Castle nodded. "If we can, Mr. President, I'd like to go over this with you during our next war update. My people are still putting together a detailed assessment of what they're doing, and I think it would be prudent if I had that information present when I talk about it."

The President grunted. "OK, then let's talk about Asia. Bring me up to speed on what's happening there," he said.

Castle nodded. "General Cutter has officially secured the Island of Luzon from the Chinese Army. His forces and the Navy are largely going to bypass the remaining PLA soldiers on the other Philippine Islands and either force them to surrender or starve them out. Now his Marines are staging and preparing to invade Taiwan. General Cutter says he'll need at least 45 days to get his forces ready to retake Taiwan. The Navy also needs some time to rearm with missiles before they move closer to the Chinese mainland, and Admiral Richards wants to get a few of his ships repaired so they can be available for the invasion."

Castle paused for a second, then resumed. "Invading Taiwan is going to be like Iwo Jima or Okinawa was during World War II. The PLA is going to throw everything they have at us, and it's going to get real dicey. I'd expect a lot of casualties when this operation kicks off, so we need to be prepared for that when the time comes."

He turned a couple of papers over. "Now on to the good news. The ANZAC force that landed on the Indonesian Island of Java caught the enemy with their pants down. They were able to capture the Indonesian capital of Jakarta and many of the military and political leaders. While the president of Indonesia did manage to escape, the rest of his government did not, and they opted to surrender rather than fight it out in the capital. We're in negotiations with them now to get them to drop out of the Eastern Alliance and surrender the rest of their military forces on the Philippine Islands."

The President smiled. He needed some good news.

Castle continued. "This was, by all accounts, a resounding victory in the Pacific, Mr. President, and will greatly reduce the threat to Australia. We can now look to liberate Malaysia and the rest of Southeast Asia with the Australians in the lead." Castle spoke with genuine satisfaction written across his face. It had been a huge gamble to have the ANZACs and a single American brigade combat team conduct a surprise landing on Java and then race to the capital, but it had succeeded beyond their wildest dreams.

"Jim, that is good news indeed," said the President. "Send my congratulations to the commanders and the soldiers involved. They've moved us one step closer to victory."

An aide walked in and handed a note to the Commander-in-Chief.

"All right, gentlemen," Gates announced, "I'm being given the signal that we're less than twenty minutes away from landing. I need to let you all go, but we'll continue our discussion tomorrow when I'm back in Washington. Apparently, elections still have to happen during a world war, and I'm still required to do some campaigning."

****

Township, Michigan
Selfridge Air National Guard Base

When the President's plane landed at the military base, the Secret Service was ready with their convoy of vehicles to escort him to his speaking engagement. Due to the heightened risk of Russian and Chinese saboteurs, the Secretary of Defense had insisted that the military also have a Special Forces team involved in the security.

Gates descended the stairs and was greeted by a member of his campaign staff, and businessman Andrew Turner, the man he'd be stumping for in a few hours. Extending his hand, the President shook Turner's. "It's good to see you again, Andrew. I'm glad we were able to work this out."

Andrew Turner smiled. "Likewise. I'm glad you were able to fit this into your schedule. It's a tight race here, and we could really use your help."

Turner was an Iraq War veteran and local businessman and was running against the Democrat Senate incumbent. It was a close election according to the polls, although by all accounts, it should have been a slam dunk for the incumbent. The sitting senator had recently made a few gaffes that had been caught by the media when he'd made comments about how the new British Prime Minister had found a way to deal with the Russian President Petrov, leading Britain to secure a separate peace with the Eastern

Alliance. This had created a bit of a media firestorm as conservative radio pundits reminded the public that it was the Eastern Alliance that was responsible the nuclear destruction of Northern California.

Since then, the race that had been written off by the GOP was suddenly within reach. Despite Gates' unpopularity and combative relationship with the media and the polls prior to the war, the nation had largely rallied behind him during the country's struggle, just as America had done for previous wartime presidents. So now the GOP was eager to use his new popularity to potentially influence this election.

"Before we head into town, let's sit down in the conference room in the hangar here and talk," said Gates. "I want to know from you, Andrew, what are the meat-and-potato issues for your constituents? What are they concerned with? What are they optimistic about, and what can I specifically do to help Michigan, etc."

This was something the President did whenever he spoke somewhere. He preferred to find out from local leaders, not pollsters, what the situation on the ground was like. In his experience, the people who lived in a district were by far the ones who knew the issues the best.

The two of them talked for roughly twenty minutes before settling on a couple of main talking points Gates would focus on and projects that could really use government assistance. Following the discussion, the President signaled it was time to bring in the security folks and discuss the potential threats and what they would do should a threat materialize.

Taking the lead in this discussion, the FBI agent in charge for Detroit explained, "We do not have any credible threats from any foreign actors. There is no chatter on any of the cyber rooms we monitor and nothing from our sources on the ground. That isn't to say the Russians or Chinese may not try something, which is why we have Major Natal and his team with us on loan from Joint Special Operations Command or JSOC."

The military man, wearing 511 clothes and decked out in full combat gear, just nodded.

"We do anticipate a large number of protesters in the area—mostly Antifa and antiwar protesters and student groups," the FBI agent continued. "We have a number of agents wearing civilian clothes intermixed with them to help keep an eye on the protests and make sure they don't turn violent. We've also limited where they can protest, so they shouldn't clash with any of your supporters or those just coming to hear you speak. We're trying as best we can to minimize our security presence per your request, but please keep in mind, it's incredibly difficult for us to secure an outdoor venue for you during a war."

The head of the President's Secret Service detail nodded in agreement. "I still wish you'd hold this event indoors, Mr. President. We have an alternate site secured and set up. It wouldn't be difficult for us to shift the event to that location," he offered, once more hoping the President might agree to a more protected venue.

Looking at Andrew, Gates saw in the man's eyes that he was really looking forward to this outdoor event. The park could hold a few thousand people or more, and word had it the park was already solidly packed. If they changed venues now, it would be to a much smaller indoor location that could probably only accommodate maybe three or four thousand people at best.

Gates shook his head. "No, we'll keep the outdoor venue. I don't want to have to exclude people when we don't even have any credible threats. People need to see that their political leaders aren't afraid to see them, and we need to project confidence in our law enforcement and military to protect us," the President said, ending the debate.

A half hour later, the presidential motorcade left the Air Force base for the first of many 2018 campaign stops.

****

Detroit, Michigan
The Jeffersonian Apartments

As he waded through the throngs of people who were coming to hear the President speak, George thought to himself how much he loved Michigan, and how he would really be enjoying this trip if he weren't so wrapped up in his purpose for being there. *"What's not to love?"* he thought. *"Beautiful parks, the Upper Peninsula, and of course, Canada right across the border."*

Walking up to the Jeffersonian, George entered the electronic code his Airbnb host had given him, unlocking the outer door to the lobby. He smiled warmly at the young woman manning the reception desk as he made his way to the elevator bank. A bell dinged as he approached the elevator. A second later, a young couple wearing obnoxiously gaudy Gates T-shirts emerged, laughing at something as they walked past him and headed out the door to join the mass of humanity that was gathering in the park to hear President Gates speak.

George pressed the button for the eighteenth floor and waited for the doors to close. Once he got off, he headed toward apartment 1818 and entered the second electronic code that unlocked the door. Walking in, George immediately headed over to the kitchen and grabbed a bottle of water. He opened it and took a long drink, rehydrating himself.

Next, he walked over to the family room and plopped himself down on the La-Z-Boy recliner and grabbed the remote control for the 65-inch flat-screen TV. He turned it on and clicked through the channels until he found MSNBC, his favorite channel, and listened in on the coverage of the President's motorcade as it continued to make its journey from the Air National Guard base in Townships to Detroit, where it would eventually stop in Erma Henderson Park. The talking heads on MSNBC were in a bewildered state as they discussed a new Gallup poll that showed the race in Michigan to be toss-up at this point. George shuddered. The President was doing his best to help elect more of his own party to the Senate, and George and many of his fellow Antifa activists feared this would only enable the fascist Gates to pursue more of his radical agenda.

George watched intently as the local news helicopter showed an aerial picture of the President's motorcade driving down I-94 before it would turn south to head toward the park where that night's speaking event would occur. Twenty minutes went by with various pundits talking about what the President might say, or what they believed he should say. Slowly, the motorcade eventually made its way to the park. As it entered the perimeter, George could hear the roar of the crowd.

Getting up from the chair, he walked over to the sliding glass doors and looked through them out at Erma Henderson Park next door. He found himself amazed that so many thousands of people had gathered to hear one man speak. *"How can so many people be deceived by this fascist?"* he thought. It blew his mind to think that all of those masses before him were blind to how the dictator Gates was destroying the country. *"How many people have to die in this fascist war?"*

He was still struggling with what he was about to do—it went against everything he had ever been taught, but deep down, he knew he couldn't sit by and let his little brother die in a senseless war, not if he could do something to stop it.

Turning away from the sliding glass doors, George examined his setup one last time. He had moved the kitchen table further back into the kitchen, placing additional distance between it and the sliding glass doors. Then he'd placed a few pillows on the table and propped up his Winchester Model 70. He had a pillow plush against the tripod to help provide more stability for him. When George had arrived at the Airbnb condo three days ago, he'd checked the park out and calculated where the President was likely to speak from to make sure he had placed the table and the rifle in a position that would allow him to shift his aim as needed. He knew he was likely only going to get one solid shot off, or else another sniper would probably find him and shoot him.

Being a novice shooter and having never shot anything living before, he was nervous he might miss, or that his hands might be shaky. He looked down at his fingers. They were still, but definitely sweaty.

The crowd outside broke his circling thoughts as they roared and then chanted, "USA, USA, USA!"

George couldn't really hear exactly what the President was saying over all the noise. Then again, he really wasn't focused on the speech, despite the audio of the President's speech being relayed over MSNBC. Placing his head against the stock of the rifle, he leaned his right eye into the scope. He closed his left eye as he tried to zero in on Gates.

George shifted the rifle a couple of times before finding a comfortable position that still allowed him to place the red dot on the man's chest.

"Aim small...miss small," he said quietly as he recited the phrase his shooting instructor had taught him. That retired Marine sniper had spent every Saturday at the range with him for nearly three months, teaching him everything he knew about marksmanship.

As the President raised his right hand with the Senate candidate's hand up in the air, that was the moment when George decided to make history. "*This is for you, little brother*," he thought, hopeful that his actions would speed the war's end and bring his brother home.

He took a deep breath, then applied pressure on the trigger, just like he had been taught, until he heard the rifle bark, recoiling hard into his shoulder. The glass sliding door in front of him shattered instantly as the .300 magnum round flew out the barrel at 3,000 feet per second, crossing the 500 meters between George and the President in less than a second.

Through the scope, he saw the round hit the President. Before he could comprehend what he had just done, he immediately pulled the bolt back, ejecting the spent casing and loading another round into the chamber. George took aim at the stage, which was suddenly being swarmed by Secret Service agents who were attempting to cover the President. The businessman who had just been holding the President's hand ducked for cover, just as George squeezed the trigger again, sending a second round at the stage. His next round slammed center mass into the upper body of the Secretary of State, who was being led off the stage by the Secret Service.

Once his second shot was fired, George immediately worked the bolt, loading the third round into the chamber, and scanned the stage. A cluster of Secret Service agents was carrying the President off the stage, and now the Secretary of State. George was scanning quickly for another high-value fascist to take out as precious seconds were ticking by.

"There you are," he said aloud, speaking to no one in particular. The President's vehicle, "The Beast," pulled up and an agent was yanking the door open as several agents tried to throw the President inside. George fired his third round, hitting one of the agents as he attempted to move the President into the vehicle. The agent fell, and it looked like the President fell with him. Then the two of them were shoved into the vehicle together, and it sped away faster than a vehicle that size and weight should be able to move.

Just as George scooted off the table away from his rifle, the optical sight on his Winchester exploded, scaring him half to death. George fell to the floor and began to backpedal toward the wall when a second round flew into the room and hit the floor where his foot had just been. George quickly jumped to his feet, grabbing his backpack, and was out the door of the apartment seconds later. He quickly made his way down the emergency exit stairs, practically leaping from one landing to the next as he desperately tried to get out of the building.

When he entered the lobby, he immediately made a beeline for the front door. Outside the apartment complex, hundreds if not thousands of people were running down the street, screaming and yelling, trying desperately to get away from the danger. No one knew if another attack was going to happen or not. Then they heard a loud *Boom!*

About a block away, a small charge in a dumpster blew up right on time.

"*'Bout time my Antifa brothers did their part,*" George thought as he joined the throng of people trying to run away.

There was chaos all around him. George could hear helicopters flying overhead and police sirens traveling in multiple directions. Several clusters of police were trying to stop the mass of humanity from running past them as they attempted to set up a perimeter.

"*Crap!*" thought George. "*I need to make it past that perimeter before they get it set or I'm screwed.*"

Several dozen police cars suddenly descended on the crowd maybe a block ahead of him. Looking up in the sky, he saw a police helicopter and several of those new tiltrotor helicopters he had seen on the news circling above them. George darted to the left down a side alley when he spotted several teenagers veer off that direction. He sprinted with all his might, trying to keep up with them as they did their best to find another way past the police. Huffing and puffing to keep up with them, he called, "Wait up, guys! I'll pay you each a hundred dollars if you can help me get past the police."

As they stopped to catch their own breath, the teenagers looked at him suspiciously as he pulled out five one-hundred-dollar bills. "Look, I'm on probation," he said, "and the last thing I need is to get stopped by the police. My probation officer will have my ass. Can you guys help me?" he asked, hoping his cover story might be enough.

The kid with red hair just nodded as he reached over and took the money from George's hand. "My brother has a PO who's a real piece of work. I understand. Follow us this way. Bill here works for a pizza joint, and we can walk through it to get to the other side of the police roadblock, but only if we hurry." They took off down the side street toward the road the police were cordoning off.

    A half hour later, George had made it past the police roadblock and was waiting at the bus stop for the next available bus. When it arrived, he paid cash for three stops and then got off. Activating the new smartphone he'd purchased the day before, he opened up the Lyft app and called for a ride. When the driver showed up, he ducked inside and was on his way out of the city to a friend's house, where he'd be able to hide and lie low for a while until he figured out what to do next.

****

Erma Henderson Park

    "Shots fired!" shouted Major Natal. He immediately lifted his binoculars to his eyes and scanned the building just beyond the park. His eyes quickly settled on the most likely position of an enemy shooter, a thirty-story building nearly opposite of the stage where the President had been speaking. While Secret Service agents were swarming the stage, Major

Natal scanned the building, making his way up each floor. Then a second shot rang out, followed by more screams.

Someone yelled, "Secretary Johnson has just been hit!"

A new sense of urgency took over as Natal desperately looked for the sniper. *"There you are, you old goat!"* he thought.

Natal clicked the talk button on his mic. "White apartment complex directly across from the stage, eighteenth floor. Enemy sniper. Take him out!" he shouted to his own sniper. The FBI and Secret Service snipers would surely also shift to get a shot on the shooter.

Bam! A third shot rang out.

Boom! The report on the Barrett M82 .50 sniper rifle barked as a JSOC sniper fired into the enemy sniper nest. Seconds later, another sniper fired, and then he heard his JSOC team yell out, "We're moving to the location of the shooter. Requesting primacy!"

Then the combat-equipped men took off at a full sprint toward the apartment complex.

****

Special Agent Terry Lightman could barely breathe as he coughed up more blood. "Hang in there, Mr.

President," he said. He climbed off the President and tried to help turn him over, so he could inspect the President's wound. He needed to relay as much information as possible to the hospital, which would be standing by to receive the President. When Lightman turned the president over, all he saw was blood, but he wasn't sure if it was the President's or his own. Looking down, Terry saw he had been shot clean through his back, and the bullet had exited his chest.

"Dear God—did the bullet go through me and hit the President?" he thought in horror.

"How's he doing?" shouted the driver. The Beast took a hard turn and then accelerated again.

"I don't know. He's covered in blood, but I'm hit as well. I can't tell if he's covered in my blood or if the bullet went through me and hit him," he yelled back. Then he started coughing. His coughing increased in intensity until he felt lightheaded and suddenly passed out on top of the President.

"Terry, stay with me!" yelled the driver. Hearing no reply, the driver just pressed his foot harder on the gas pedal, racing down the street, his speedometer blowing past 100mph as the engine just roared and other vehicles did their best to keep up with him.

A couple of cars were on the same road as the hospital, most of them steered themselves off to the shoulder out of the way of the armored limousine that was racing down the road. One unlucky driver thought they could dart across the road, but completely underestimated the speed at which the Beast was traveling. The tail end of the car was hit and sent into a hard tailspin as they barreled on through toward the hospital.

Approaching the emergency entrance to the hospital, the driver of the Beast saw the police had already cleared away any traffic that had previously been there. A small cluster of doctors, nurses and Secret Service agents were also standing under the overhang waiting for him to arrive. Nearby were close to two dozen military soldiers in full combat gear. As they pulled up, two more military helicopters landed, unloading more soldiers.

Racing up the road leading to the emergency room, the agent hit the brakes, causing the wheels to squeal as the Beast lurched forward from the sudden change in velocity. As soon as the vehicle came to a halt, the rear passenger door with the presidential seal was opened, and a pair of hands reached in and grabbed the now-unconscious agent lying on top of the President. They placed him on a gurney and got him out of the way, so they could get to Gates.

Seconds later, they had pulled the President from the back of the Beast and placed his body on the gurney. The cluster of nurses and doctors rushed the leader of the free world into the ER and headed straight to an operating room.

"He's covered in blood!" yelled one of the doctors. "Somebody, get me a set of vitals!"

Nurses and paramedics had already cut the President's shirt open. Once person was wiping up blood as they looked for the source of the bleeding. Another was starting an IV line, a third was attaching a BP cuff. It was like a beehive, chaotic but very well-orchestrated.

"His BP is low, 82/50," said one of the nurses.

"His pulse is weak and thready," said another. After a slight pause, she announced, "I just lost his pulse!"

Then they entered the elevator that would take them to the operating floor.

****

As soon as the door closed, Tom McMillan grabbed his smartphone and hit the speed dial to the SecDef.

"This is Castle," replied the gruff voice on the first ring.

"Jim, it's Tom. The President's been hit. I have no idea how bad or what his condition is. Travis was also hit.

The last word I heard from the Secret Service is he's dead. I'm not sure what more to really tell you, but I needed to make sure you knew what happened," he told his friend, who was silent on the other end, probably digesting what he had just been told.

"Tom, what the heck is going on?" Jim Castle finally asked. "Call me back as soon as you hear anything more about the President. You should probably call the Vice President," he replied, and then the call was ended.

Looking through his contacts, Tom found the Vice President's number and hit dial. It rang twice before he picked up. "How bad is the President, Tom?"

"I don't know yet. All I know is he was covered in blood, and one of the doctors said they couldn't feel a pulse and then the elevator doors closed. I honestly don't know, but I'm going to stay here until I do," he replied.

"OK, keep me informed. The Secret Service has just taken me down to the bunker. The Chief Justice is also on his way. They are going to invoke the 25th Amendment for the time being, until we know what the President's status is," he replied, his voice a bit shaken and unsure.

"You'll do fine, Sir," Tom McMillan said reassuringly. "We have a good team in place, and we'll get through this. I'll call you as soon as I know more."

They quickly concluded their call. Both men had a lot of things to take care of.

****

"Doc, he's got jugular venous distension," said one of the nurses as they continued wheeling toward the OR.

"Crap," said the surgeon. "He's probably got pericardial tamponade." He turned to one of the other nurses. "Did you get the pulse back?"

"I can't feel it any more, Sir. We'll find out more once the EKG is completely hooked up," she answered. Most of the stickers and leads had already been placed—only a couple more to go.

Everyone continued with their duties as they moved along, until the green line started to dance across the screen. A string of expletives filled the room. "He's got low QRS voltage," the surgeon finally said. "He's definitely in tamponade. We've got to get him open and drain the bleeding that's pushing on his heart, or we're going to lose him."

The President's breathing was becoming more shallow and rapid. His face started to look pale.

The surgeon consulted with the anesthesiologist. Meds were pushed and just like that the President was intubated. A nurse kept a steady rhythm going on the Ambu bag, one breath every six seconds.

Just as the surgeon was about to make a cut so he could get a scope in there and see what was going on, he noticed blood oozing out around the President's IV site. He stopped.

"*No, please no,*" he thought.

Blood started to spill out of every orifice of the Commander-in-Chief's body, including his eyes and ears. He didn't need a blood test to tell him what was happening.

"Get me some platelets, frozen plasma, and Factor 7 STAT!" he yelled. "He's going into DIC." Two people ran out of the room. The President's clotting factors had been disrupted by the violent trauma of the gunshot wound, and if didn't get these treatments quickly, he would bleed out.

A few painful moments went by as they waited for the bags to arrive. They ran normal saline wide open, trying to preserve what little blood pressure he had left. Finally, the two heroes of the moment returned, and they began to run the vitally needed infusions.

It was too late. The President's skin was already turning yellow from damage to his liver.

"He's flatlining!" yelled one of the nurses.

"Give compressions and let's see if we can get a rhythm," said the surgeon.

After five cycles of chest compressions, there was no change. His heart had stopped. The surgeon couldn't open him up because he would bleed out while in DIC, and without a functioning heart, the platelets and clotting factors wouldn't circulate throughout the body. There was nothing they could do.

"He's gone," announced the surgeon.

They all took a step back. One man saluted the President, and then the others followed suit. President Patrick Gates was dead.

From the Authors

Fear not—the battle is not over. We are already working on the next book in the series, *Battlefield Russia*, which is available for pre-order. We are on track to release it in September of 2018. So the adventure is not finished, just to be continued.

The two biggest ways that you can help us to succeed as authors are:

1. Leave us a positive review on Amazon and Goodreads for each of our books you liked reading. These reviews really make a tremendous difference for other prospective readers, and we sincerely appreciate each person that takes the time to write one.
2. Sign up for our mailing list at http://www.author-james-rosone.com and receive updates when we have new books coming out or promotional pricing deals.

We have really appreciated connecting with our readers via social media. Sometimes we ask for help from our readers as we write future books—we love to draw upon all your different areas of expertise. We also have a group of beta readers who get to look at the books before they are officially published and help us fine-tune last-minute adjustments. If you would like to be a part of this team, please go to our author website: http://www.author-james-rosone.com, and send us a message through the "Contact" tab. You can also follow us on Twitter: @jamesrosone and @AuthorMirandaW. We look forward to hearing from you.

You may also enjoy some of our other works. A full list can be found below:

Non-Fiction:
Iraq Memoir 2006–2007 Troop Surge
    Interview with a Terrorist

Fiction:
World War III Series
    Prelude to World War III: The Rise of the Islamic Republic and the Rebirth of America (also available in audio format)
    Operation Red Dragon and the Unthinkable (also available in audio format)
    Operation Red Dawn and the Invasion of America
    Cyber Warfare and the New World Order

Michael Stone Series

Traitors Within

The Red Storm Series

Battlefield Ukraine

Battlefield Korea

Battlefield Taiwan

Battlefield Pacific

Battlefield Russia (to be released September 2018)

Battlefield China TBD

For the Veterans

I have been pretty open with our fans about the fact that PTSD has had a tremendous direct impact on our lives; it affected my relationship with my wife, job opportunities, finances, parenting—everything. It is also no secret that for me, the help from the VA was not the most ideal form of treatment. Although I am still on this journey, I did find one organization that did assist the healing process for me, and I would like to share that information.

Welcome Home Initiative is a ministry of By His Wounds Ministry, and they run seminars for veterans and their spouses for free. The weekends are a combination of prayer and more traditional counseling and left us with resources to aid in moving forward. The entire cost of the retreat—hotel costs, food, and sessions, are completely free from the moment the veteran and their spouse arrive at the location.

If you feel that you or someone you love might benefit from one of Welcome Home Initiative's sessions, please visit their website to learn more: https://welcomehomeinitiative.org/

We have decided to donate a portion of our profits to this organization, because it made such an impact in our lives and we believe in what they are doing. If you would also like to donate to Welcome Home Initiative and help to keep these weekend retreats going, you can do so by visiting the following link:

https://welcomehomeinitiative.org/donate/

Acronym Key

ANZAC	Australian and New Zealand Army Corps
APC	Armored Personnel Carrier
ASBM	Anti-Ship Ballistic Missiles
BAE	Battlefield Area Evaluation
BDA	Blast Damage Area
BND	Bundesnachrichtendiens (German intelligence agency)
BUD/S	Basic Underwater Demolition/SEAL
CAC	Common Access Card (universal ID card for American military)
CAG	Commander, Air Group
CCTV	Closed-circuit television
CG	Commanding General
CIA	Central Intelligence Agency
CIC	Combat Information Center
CIWS	Close-In Weapons Systems
CO	Commanding Officer
CSH	Combat Support Hospital
CVC	Combat Vehicle Crewman
DARPA	Defense Advanced Research Projects Agency
DDG	Guided Missile Destroyer

DIA	Defense Intelligence Agency
EOD	Explosive Ordnance Disposal
FIST	Fire Support Team
FSB	Federalnaya Sluzhba Bezopasnosti (Russian intelligence agency that came after the KGB)
GDF	Global Defense Force
GRU	Glavnoye Razvedyvatel'noye Upravleniye (Russian intelligence directorate)
HE	High-Explosive
HF	High-Frequency
HIMAR	High-mobility Artillery Rocket System
HQ	Headquarters
JSOC	Joint Special Operations Command
KSO	Russian Special Operation Command
LNO	Liaison Officer
LRASM	Long-Range Anti-Ship Missiles
LT	Lieutenant
LZ	Landing Zone
MANPAD	Man-Portable Air-Defense System
MiG	Soviet military fighter aircraft
MI6	Military Intelligence 6 (British Intelligence)
MOD	Ministry of Defense
MP	Member of Parliament

MRE	Meal-Ready-to-Eat
NATO	North Atlantic Treaty Organization
NCO	Non-Commissioned Officer
NORAD	North American Aerospace Defense Command
NZSAS	New Zealand Special Air Service
PARNAS	People's Freedom Party (Alexei's resistance party in Russia)
PLA	People's Liberation Army (Chinese Army)
PM	Prime Minister
POL	Petroleum, Oil, and Lubricants (military acronym to refer to gasoline, diesel and other types of fuel)
POW	Prisoner of War
PRC	People's Republic of China
PSYOPS	Psychological Operations
R & R	Rest and Relaxation
RAF	Royal Air Force (British Air Force)
RAAF	Royal Australian Air Force
RAM	Rolling Airframe Missile
ROK	Republic of Korea (South Korea)
RPG	Rocket Propelled Grenade
RT	Russian Television Network, formerly known as Russia Today

RTO	Radio Transmission Officer
SAM	Surface-to-Air Missile
SAS	Special Air Service
SecDef	Secretary of Defense
SINCGAR	Single-Channel Ground and Airborne Radio
SOI	School of Infantry
SWAT	Special Weapons and Tactics
TDY	Temporary Duty
UHF	Ultra-High-Frequency
VIP	Very Important Person
VLS	Vertical Launch System
XO	Commanding Officer